HOLY SHROUD

ORDER OF THADDEUS • BOOK 1

J. A. BOUMA

EmmausWay
P R E S S

PROLOGUE

I t was the spicy scent of something burning that first needled Jacque de Molay's consciousness to awaken. Crackling pine logs and burning hay connected the synapses in his brain to the impression of a distant childhood memory, when times were simpler, happier, less threatened.

It was the putrid smell of burning flesh that snapped him back to reality.

Jacques' eyes flittered open, a darkened picture fading in and out of focus. The right side of his head made him regret his decision.

What...Where am I?

A wave of nausea crashed against his stomach, forcing his eyes shut. He caught his breath, suppressing the urge to retch. It wasn't working. He tried to sit as his mouth watered and the gag reflex began working overtime, but he was bound. Both arms, both legs. He strained weakly against the cords, the tide rising within. There was nothing he could do. He strained again, trying to pivot his body and head as much as he could, but it was no use. His mouth exploded in sour bile, and half-digested potatoes, carrots, and venison awash in fermentation.

Jacques gulped for air and spat to clear his mouth, then

weakly sank back against the table, the memory of the events from so long ago beginning to surface in his aching head—reminding him of what had led to this fateful day.

The Brotherhood had been celebrating the birthday of one of their members the night before. Ian, the youngest of the brothers and his godson, had turned twenty-five. Which meant he was now a full member of the religious order. Smoked venison from the day's hunt, and tart mead brewed from the early spring, were plentiful. As was enough song, dance, and laughter to last a lifetime of memories.

Jacques was in high spirits and beaming with pride. He raised his glass, brimming full with the finest wine from the choicest grapes from Burgundy, ready to toast the young man's milestone, when it happened. So suddenly, so unexpectedly.

A series of *thumping* sounds beating rhythmically, like a war drum from the outer wall, first caught his attention. At first, he mistook them for the sounds of celebration. But shouts of disturbance rising from the outer courtyard of the mighty fortress of the Brotherhood quickly dispelled those impressions, twisting his gut with fear. A large crashing sound was immediately followed by more shouts and then screaming. The unmistakable sounds of thousand-pound horses and a raging fire removed any confusion.

They were under attack.

Jacques hurried to a large window in the gathering hall of the second floor. Flames were consuming the gatehouse. Mounted horse units and infantry bearing the seal of King Phillip IV of France were flooding the courtyard, their navy-blue banners bearing gold fleur-de-lis, demanding entrance into the main compound. He caught sight of women and children running, seeking shelter from the onslaught, before he rallied his men for the fight ahead.

Rumors had swirled for months among the fellow Brotherhood chapters across Europe and the Holy Lands that the king was moving against them, having become panicked over their outsized wealth, power, and influence. Reports told of mounted units of fury and fire raiding secret compounds in outer regions. Arrests were made. Brothers were tortured. "Confessions" were extracted, though for what reason was beginning to come to light.

An ancient holy relic bearing the power of faith and life was being sought.

They knew the day would come. They had prepared for it. Signed up for it, even. The holy relic had been entrusted to their care, and they would die protecting it. Some did that day almost seven years ago. Many more through the years undergoing "ecclesial procedures." Also known as the Inquisitorial hearings.

Now it appeared his day had come at last.

A face emerged from the soft light and hard shadows sending a jolt of adrenaline to Jacques's stomach, threatening another round of retching.

It was the face of an ancient threat, the dreaded ibis Bird-Man. Thoth, the Egyptian god of knowledge. The man who wore the ancient face was bare-chested and tanned to a burnished bronze, his upper shoulders ringed by an intricate weave of gold and turquoise beads at the base of his neck. A long beak of onyx black, silent and probing, peered down at Jacques from behind a mask of gold, flanked by ribbons of indigo.

It can't be true...

Jacques swallowed hard, his head throbbing in protest. He strained forward against the thick cords of rope holding his well-muscled body, tilting his head for a better look at his surroundings. He was in the center of a large rectangular barn made of stone and vaulted by solid oak beams, punctuated with the sour smell of manure. Stacks of hay were shoved to the periphery. The stalls had been emptied of their four-legged creatures, and in their place were his brothers, strapped to tables like his own. Shadows danced around the vast interior, mirroring the ghastly beings hovering over his brothers.

Like the one staring him in the face.

A bloodcurdling cry sent his skin crawling with static shock, snapping Jacques's head toward the large entrance drenched in dancing yellows and oranges and reds. The view through the maw of darkness sent his stomach to the dirty ground beneath. Within minutes the screams faded, and Jacques's brother was resting in the arms of his Savior.

"That," said Bird-Man, "was a trial run for the main attraction." He leaned in, a large grin of white gleaming behind the gold mask. "The lad who I've been told is your godson, Ian."

Jacques went pale, and bowels went weak, at the mention of his precious son. He eased himself upright, straining to see into the nightmare of darkness beyond, seeking a glimpse of the young man.

He could make out a tall, slender figure tied to a pole, hands bound behind him. He was older than the last time Jacques had seen him. Straw-colored hair hung to the man's broad shoulders. His face was unmistakable with its high, angular cheekbones. A gift from his late mother.

"Noooo!" Jacques screamed, spittle flying out of his mouth. Another wave of vomit threatened to arise as he strained uselessly against the thick cords bound to his wrists and ankles. He screamed until his lungs gave out, his voice fading into hoarse nothingness, face darkening crimson as he raged and strained forward. He paused and heaved large breaths, then screamed and strained again, mind swimming with delirium.

"Molay," Bird-Man intoned silkily. "I had no idea you were such a sentimental man."

The figure masked in gold and indigo pressed a glove-encased hand on Jacques's chest, shoving him back against the table with purpose, stilling him. He turned back and stared into Bird-Man's beady, little eyes. Then launched a well-aimed glob of spittle into Evil Incarnate.

Bird-Man recoiled. Pale goop dripped off the golden mask

onto the dirt floor. A smile curled coolly upward as he slowly wiped what remained of the insult away. Then he leaned down over Jacques's face, holding his gaze.

"What a beautiful lad," he said. "A real shame he has to die. Unless, that is, you co-operate."

"What is the meaning of this?" Jacques roared uselessly.

The masked figure leaned in closer, his beak nearly touching Jacques's chest. "I think you know exactly the meaning of this."

He did. Jacques sank back against the wooden table, then turned his head, panic welling within as he stared at a shadow on a distant wall.

His Brotherhood had been commissioned to keep the holy relic safe stretching back a hundred years. Since the sacking of Constantinople, they had pledged their treasure and lives to keep it from falling into the hands of the wicked once again. Given their unique position within the political and religious climate, the Brotherhood was strategically positioned to act as the relic's guardians. Their heavily guarded fortresses would ensure the secrecy and safety of the Church's most important object of veneration.

For decades rumors had swirled that the Brotherhood was in possession of an object of great religious prestige and power, capable of turning the hardest of hearts and doubters into true believers. During their initiation ceremony, members were given a momentary glimpse of this most sacred object: the supreme vision of God attainable on earth. The Image of Christ himself.

Even more, rumors circulated throughout Europe of an idol before which they prostrated themselves at their headquarters at the Villeneuve du Temple, a massive fortress complex of stone and iron in Paris. The holy object was said to be like an old piece of skin, as though embalmed, and like polished cloth, pale and discolored with a divine image etched in its fibers.

Several groups and individuals had attempted to seize its likeness over the centuries. One, in particular, had attempted for generations to destroy it, with ancient roots stretching back to the early Church. At times they had sought a syncretic version of the faith, resulting in aberrant variations deemed heretical by the Church. Ultimately, it sought the Church's extinction.

And the face representing that ancient evil was now hovering over Jacques de Molay, Grand Master of the Poor Fellow-Soldiers of Christ and of the Temple of Solomon. Also known as the Order of Solomon's Temple.

The Knights Templar.

Suddenly Jacques's face exploded leftward in pain. A geyser of blood burst from his nose.

"Where is it?" Bird-Man roared.

Jacques sputtered and coughed as blood poured down the front of his face, the metallic taste of copper threatening another retching episode.

"My patience is thinning, Molay," Bird-Man said silkily. "We know the Order assumed guardianship of the Church's most prized relic a century ago. We've been tracking its movement for decades, biding our time until we had full confirmation, until the moment presented itself. Fortunately, one of your own was willing to offer us the necessary information."

Shock pinged Jacques's gut. The right side of Bird-Man's mouth curled upward.

"Oh, yes. Squawked like a chicken, telling us quite a tale about a long span of cloth with the faint image of a man in death's pose."

Jacques strained toward Bird-Man with all his might, coming within an inch of his face. He roared and snapped his jaw at the abomination, but it was useless. He collapsed onto the table, weakened and breathing heavily.

So the secret is out. The one the Church has been guarding for nearly thirteen centuries.

"And you'll be as cooperative, won't you? Because if you aren't—"

Bird-Man took Jacques's head in both hands and shoved it up off the table so that he was looking once more at his helpless godson outside. Bird-Man nodded, as if signaling to someone far off into the dark of night.

A few seconds later, a faint light flickered to life in the distance beyond the open barn door. It bobbed and weaved in the blackness, growing with each second. Then the tiny flame roared to life near the ground beneath someone else's bound, erect body just beyond Ian. Long, undulating, breathy cries of agony joined the snapping flames as the fire started at the base of the pole and worked its way upward, crescendoing into a dirge of death.

"Do you see that, Jacques?" Bird-Man whispered, steadying the Grand Master's head and eyelids. "There are eleven more left, just like him. Including your precious godson. All waiting to die for your secret. Is it worth sacrificing these lives to protect your pathetic relic?" Bird-Man shoved him against the rough wooden surface, the cries of agony dying down to nothing as the victim passed on from this life to the next. "Now tell me. Where is the Holy Shroud?"

I cannot. I will not. The Shroud must be protected at all cost.

"I will spare the young man's life and yours and the rest of your brothers if you tell me the location of the Holy Image. Last I knew, it was safely tucked inside the parish within your compound. Now it's missing!" Bird-Man slammed Jacques's head against the table, the sounds of agony outside drowning out Jacques's own pain.

Lord, Jesus Christ, I will not abandon you. I will not forsake your Image.

"What was that?" Bird-Man asked in irritation. "Do you have something to say?"

Jacques swallowed, trying to clear his dry, raw throat. But it was no use. He winced instead, and whispered, "I have nothing to say."

Bird-Man stood next to Jacques's table, head cocked. "Nothing to say? Really?" Then he paused, nodding off to the side again. "So be it."

Suddenly, a burst of flames illuminated the darkness. Jacques leaned forward.

Ian!

"Noooo!" he screamed.

He strained against his bindings, twisting them this way and that, fighting like hell to rescue the young man he'd vowed to protect.

Flames licked Ian's feet before moving up his legs. He arched his body as the flames rose higher, as if to escape the maw of fiery death awaiting him. As the inferno began stretching higher, his long, blond hair flittered away, like dandelion seeds carried along by a mid-summer afternoon breeze.

Punctuating the screams of pain and agony was a final cry in Latin: "In nomine Patris et Filii et Spiritus Sancti."

In the name of the Father, the Son, the Holy Spirit.

Then it ceased. No more screams. No more cries.

Jacques sank into the wooden boards, his body spent of all energy and emotion, delirious from the agony of losing the one person who was like family.

The next hour was something out of a nightmare. Bird-Man grabbed the same scythe he used against the young captive and thrust it probingly, deliberately underneath Jacques's right bottom rib. He moved it to and fro, as if the secret to his question about the Shroud's whereabouts were hidden deep within Jacques' chest cavity.

But nothing fell out. No secret. No confession.

Jacques gasped for breath, but he was undeterred. As Grand Master, it was his sworn duty to maintain the secret in order to preserve the memory of the central element of the faith: the resurrection of his Lord and Savior, Jesus Christ.

Even at the expense of his brothers.

And his own godson.

This went on for another hour. Blood was seeping through the cracks of the table, pooling beneath. Bird-Man had another of his brothers lit on fire, and then another to wear down Jacques's resolve. It didn't work.

Exhausted mentally, emotionally, and physically, the Grand Master finally offered: "You could burn the countryside down, but I will never betray the memory of our Lord's resurrection. Neither will the other brothers. And they'd torch me themselves if they discovered I'd told you the secrets of the Shroud's location."

Bird-Man stopped. Splattered blood shone crimson on the golden mask. He threw the scythe to the ground and smeared his hands clean on his bare chest.

"So be it, Jacques. I have to admit, I admire you for your strength and resolve. But it's fruitless. Eventually, we'll find it. Eventually, we'll destroy it. It may take a decade. Centuries, even. But Jacques..." His beak slid over Jacques' face as he whispered his final growl: "When we do, we will blot out the memory of your faith's central belief forever. It will wilt under the weight of our might—our *resolve*—until there is nothing left of it."

He stood and motioned to another of his associates. "Take him to meet his godson and the rest of his Brotherhood. And his dead god."

Jacques's head was swimming with pain and confusion. "What...where are you taking me? Ian...Ian!"

A burly man began dragging the table holding Jacques through the barn doors and into the deathly dark night still lit by the waning embers of his brothers. The man lifted Jacques's table on end, propping him up with two strong beams from behind, next to Ian's charred remains.

"One last chance, Molay. Just say the word. The location where you've hidden away the Holy Shroud."

Jacques, barely conscious, raised his head. He took three deep, wheezing breaths before replying: "Abba, I pray for their forgiveness. For they know not what they are doing." He slumped forward against his bindings, his life slipping away as blood oozed out from the wound in his chest.

Bird-Man's eyes narrowed. He nodded and walked away.

The fire quickly consumed the hay and branches before hungrily moving up the wooden table. The pain was more than Jacques could have imagined, but he had neither the energy nor the breath to protest. The flames ate away his feet and legs before quickly moving upward toward his outstretched arms *in crucifixio*.

Lord Jesus Christ, Son of God, receive my spirit, he silently prayed to the risen God to whom he was bearing witness, in order to protect the memory that sat at the heart of his faith for over fifty generations.

CHAPTER 1

Silas Grey was going to be late for class, again. But for good reason. He was waiting for the results of a scientific test that would rock the religious and non-religious worlds to their core.

Why teach class when he held the fate of faith and doubt in his hands?

He stood and grabbed his favorite cream-colored ceramic mug stained brown from a decade of use, emblazoned with a crimson Harvard University logo, his rival alma mater. He shuffled over to Mr. Coffee for a refill, took a swig, and grimaced as he swallowed the leftover brew gone stale, tasting of burnt toast. It would have to do.

He paced the inside of his Princeton University office, one once held by the venerable Protestant Fundamentalist J. Gresham Machen. Which was ironic, because Silas was a former Catholic turned Protestant. At another level it wasn't: like Machen, Silas relished the opportunity to inspire a new generation to rediscover religious faith in the face of a modern world that rejected it as a delusion, the ravings of madmen, an opiate for the naive masses. And he did it in a way that would make ol' Machen turn over in his grave: through relics.

His "History of Religious Relics" class was the most popular elective in the Department of Religion. Indiana Jones probably had something to do with that. As did Dan Brown, having popularized relics after wrapping them in the garb of religious conspiracies. Silas also guessed the experiential nature of religious objects of veneration also made the topic inviting.

Gone were the days when any of the religious faiths could justify themselves purely on tradition alone. Personal experiences, not dogmatic beliefs, ruled the day. And the relics from every religion offered interested students—from the committed Christian to the spiritual-but-not-religious type—the chance to explore their spiritual questions through objects rooted in historical experience.

As an academic, Silas had spent the majority of his research probing these objects and plumbing the depths of their history. As a Christian, he was interested in connecting historical objects of Christianity to his faith in a way that enhanced and propelled it forward.

Which was remarkable, considering Protestants dismissed such things as fanciful spiritualism at best and gross idolatry at worst. Perhaps it was the inner Catholic convert rearing its head. Or maybe it was an extension of his own longing for more tangible ways to experience the God he had been searching for his whole life. Maybe still, it came from his interest in helping his students find faith.

Regardless, his research had led him down interesting paths, including becoming one of the foremost experts on the single greatest, most well-known of Christian relics: The Shroud of Turin.

Which was the topic of the day's lecture. The one he was running late for.

Silas flopped back down in his well-worn burgundy leather chair, one of the few things he took from his late father's estate. He checked his watch, then huffed. *Where are those blasted results?*

He went to drain his mug when a football-sized furball bounded up onto his lap, nearly sending the remaining brew onto his checkered dress shirt.

"Barnabas!"

He swung the mug upward just as his feline friend nuzzled against his chest and curled up in his lap.

"Make yourself at home, why don't you?" he mumbled. But then he set the mug down, took a breath, and smiled. He scratched his faithful friend's ears, thankful for the interruption to his worrying. "There you go. That's a good boy."

Silas had picked up the beautiful slate-gray Persian while serving with the Rangers during the early days of Operation Iraqi Freedom. The skin-and-bones feline had wandered into camp looking for a handout. He had always been a dog lover, but the pathetic sight and the cat's single clipped ear, which told all the story he needed, tugged on his heart. He knew he was breaking protocol, the U.S. Central Command having created an order called GO-1A just before 9/11, which outlawed companion animals. But he was nearly done with his tour, and it seemed like the right thing to do. And when things went south that fateful day on the road to Mosul, Barnabas lived up to his name: son of comfort. Now he was fat and happy, offering continued comfort when times got stressful.

Like today.

Silas drained his mug as Barnabas stood and stretched. Barnabas bounded off Silas's lap and trotted out of his office. He glanced at his watch again, then his hand instinctively moved toward his middle desk drawer, where a bottle of little, blue pills nested. Just one of his friends and a glass of water would make the anxiety go away.

No. Not yet.

Instead, he called out, "Anything?"

"They'll get here when they get here," Miles called back, Silas's teaching assistant for the past three years.

Silas sighed and leaned back in his chair, bringing a hand up to a knot that was needling his right temple. "Well, did you call him to check on the sample?"

"Three times!"

Silas grimaced with a mixture of pain and pleasure as he worked on the knot with his knuckle. "And you're sure he said he actually ran the sample? That he'd get word today?"

Miles appeared in the doorway, folded his arms, and leaned against the wooden door frame. "These things take time—"

"I know, I know, I know," Silas said cutting him off. He closed his eyes as he continued to massage his temple. "But today is D-Day. I can't wait any longer! I've got deadlines for that journal paper. And I need time to sift through the data beforehand—"

"Professor!" Miles said, cutting him off in return. "Dr. Avery is your friend. He won't let you down. If he said you'd get the results today, you'll get the results today."

Silas leaned back and took a breath. He nodded, then ran his hands across his crew-cut black hair, a hold-over from his days with the Army Rangers. "Fine." He took another deep calming breath and startled. "Gosh, I'm gonna be late!"

He grabbed his coffee mug and walked over to Mr. Coffee for another refill. He poured himself the rest of the brew and took a swig. He grimaced again but took it back to his desk. It was going to be one of those days. Mr. Coffee portended it.

"By the way," Miles said loudly from his outer office adjacent to Silas's. "This came for you." He came back in and handed Silas an expensive-looking, cream-colored envelope. "Dr. Silas Grey" was scrawled in black ink across its face, written by a black fountain pen by the looks of it.

Silas smiled. He knew that handwriting well, having received plenty of notes on that paper stock and written by that well-used nib.

"It came by courier this morning," Miles said walking back out.

"Courier? From Henry?"

"Don't know," Miles shouted. "I'm not in the habit of opening your mail."

Dr. Henry Gregory was a long-time family friend. A friend of his father from West Point. After serving in Vietnam together, the two had become war buddies, but the relationship was deeper than that. They were like brothers, inseparable even though they pursued different paths: one military, one academic. When Thomas Grey died in 2001, Henry had driven down from Boston to DC to comfort Silas during his junior year of college at Georgetown University. He became something of a second father, eventually taking on the role of an academic mentor when Silas studied under him during his doctoral work at Harvard, studying historical theology and church history.

Henry had taken an early interest in Silas's academic career, bringing him in as his teaching aide and research assistant. Like Silas, he was also a Catholic-turned-Protestant. And as one of the foremost experts on the emerging field of relicology, the study and research of historical religious relics, he taught Silas everything he knew about early Christian religious artifacts and their significance for the Church. Which led Silas to his own relic passion project, the Shroud of Turin, the cloth believed to be the burial garment of Jesus Christ of Nazareth—and the most significant Christian religious artifact.

Silas caressed the thick envelope, then began tracing over the black curves of his name with his index finger. He frowned, wondering how his dear friend was getting along. A year ago, Henry had suffered a stroke. He had survived, thank God, and the damage was minimal. But he'd had a harder time getting around physically. Thankfully, his mind was still sharp; his wit was even sharper.

Miles walked back in and set another stack of mail on Silas's desk. "How is he?"

"I don't know. Last I heard he was wheeling around campus

on one of those motorized carts. Poor guy. He was preparing a paper on a recent discovery surrounding the history of the Shroud between AD 1200 and 1300. He was thrilled where the research was going. Couldn't wait to share the details. That was a few weeks ago."

"Well, what did he say in his note?"

"I haven't gotten to it yet."

"You better get to it," Miles said, walking out again. "You've got class in five."

Silas looked at his watch, then tore open the back of the envelope, the scent of musk drifting out. Inside was a single sheet of cream parchment, folded in half with the letters HAG stamped on the front in gold foil cursive lettering. Henry Alfred Gregory.

He opened it and saw two short lines of cursive text, scrawled in black. Silas furrowed his brow. He could feel his pulse quicken, his breathing picking up pace as he read:

We need to talk. ASAP.
It's about our faithful friend. He's in ill health.
-HAG

That was it. Silas turned over the paper. Nothing else. He laid it flat on his desk, then re-read his friend's note.

What on earth?

He fixated on "faithful friend" and "ill health." Faithful friend was a nickname the two had given the Shroud years ago, a sort of code name they had developed for the Holy Image when they were working closely on developing more of the history of the relic. After all, that's who Jesus Christ had been to each of them. It seemed fitting.

But in ill health? What did that mean? The cloak-and-dagger routine was unusual for Henry. Silas surmised it was more code, like "friend." Danger, perhaps. But why? How could the Shroud be in "ill health," in danger? It was under strict Vatican protection. Seemed overly melodramatic for Henry.

Silas folded his arms and leaned back in his chair. Then he picked up his cell phone to dial his mentor. It rang. He got nothing but his voicemail. He smiled. It was good to hear his voice. He hung up without leaving a message.

"He's probably teaching," Silas mumbled.

He checked his watch. Probably right.

He looked at his phone again, then picked it up and dialed his friend once more. It rang again. He looked at his watch again, remembering that Henry only had morning classes. So he should be free. And should be answering his phone.

It went to voicemail again. Silas sighed before leaving a message telling him he had received his note and to call as soon as he could. He was worried about their "friend" and wanted to get the news on his health.

He tossed the cell on a stack of papers and sat back in his chair. He sighed and stared outside, growing increasingly worried about the health of his actual friend.

The door to his room was thrown open, thudding heavily against a bookcase. It was Miles. His eyes were wide. His nose was flared. He looked grim.

Silas widened his eyes and cocked his head. "What's wrong?"

"It's Father Arnold. Line one. You need to take this. It's about Henry."

CHAPTER 2

Silas snatched the headset from his desk phone. "Hello?"

"Yes, Silas, it's Father Arnold. How are you?"

"I'm fine, Father. But Miles said something has happened to Henry. What's the matter? Did he fall again?"

Ever since that blasted stroke, Henry hadn't been the same. At the start of the school year, he had fallen and broken his hip in the shower after slipping and falling out of the tub. He needed surgery, and with no one to care for him afterward, Silas had volunteered. Henry's wife had passed away a few years ago, so managing his care was up to him. He had rejected a nursing home, insisting he was "fit as a fiddle!" His mind sure was, still able to run laps around Silas. His body was not. But Silas had relished the few weeks he took over Christmas break to care for his mentor. It gave him the chance to repay the debt he owed the man who had been a second father to him after his first one had died.

"No, it wasn't a fall..." Father Arnold trailed off.

Silas waited for a few beats, willing him to continue. Finally, he said, "Father, what's going on?"

The man sighed, then said softly: "He's dead, Silas."

All the air left his lungs at once, like he was sucker-punched in the gut. "Dead?" he whispered.

"I'm afraid so."

His mind swam in a cauldron of questions that assaulted and paralyzed his mind in rapid succession: How? Why? What? He couldn't manage to get them out. His mouth literally hung open in disbelief. Emotion tried to climb its way to the surface, but his past wouldn't let it.

"There's more," Arnold said, emotion choking in his own throat.

Again, more silence. This wasn't like Father Arnold. He was usually straightforward, very to-the-point. These short, clipped responses were telling Silas more than what Father himself was.

"Father, what's going on?" Silas asked again.

Father Arnold hesitated. "Henry died...mysteriously."

Mysteriously? Silas squinted his eyes and shook his head, staring at his desk, his right hand raising involuntarily to his forehead. He leaned forward resting his elbow on his desk to consider this massive turn of events.

"What does that mean? Mysteriously?"

"It means his death may not have been an accident." Father Arnold paused again. "By all accounts, it was a natural death. Died in his sleep from a heart attack. Which doesn't make sense, because nothing about the man would have suggested such a health problem was looming over the horizon. After his stroke, he had been fine last I heard."

Arnold was right. Aside from some nerve damage from the stroke, Henry was indeed fit as a fiddle, as Silas' old friend had said.

"OK..." Silas said, not understanding.

"And yet, dead of a heart attack. Pronounced at the scene."

"So what's the problem, then?"

"The problem, Silas, is that three other STURP members

have also passed away from heart attacks in the last twenty hours."

Silas felt his mouth open again. His hand involuntarily moved from his forehead to his temple. Four members of the Shroud of Turin Research Project, the premier research group of the Holy Image, were dead? Of heart attacks? Within twenty hours of each other?

How could that be a coincidence?

"Who, Father?"

"Carson from England. Selvaggi and Boselli from Italy."

"Not Carson," Silas said, stunned. He was one of the few sindonologists who had appreciated Silas's contributions to the international cohort of Shroud experts. "And Sevaggi and Bosseli?"

"I'm afraid so. And you know the latter was from the Vatican." Arnold paused, then whispered, "Which has caused quite the stir, to say the least."

Four international deaths under the same circumstances, with people among the same association. Definitely not a coincidence.

"So what's being done about this? Is the Vatican involved, the gendarmerie perhaps investigating the links?"

"Nothing's being done. Too soon. I've only learned about the deaths a few hours myself. I'm sure there will be an investigation, but on what grounds? The link is circumstantial, at best."

"Circumstantial?" Silas said, voice slightly raised. "Four STURP members die under suspicious circumstances, and nobody cares?"

Father Arnold sighed. "I know you and Henry were close. Like a second father to you, caring for you and your brother Sebastian after 9/11. I didn't mean to rile you up. And I could be wrong. All four were getting on in age so it could be a coincidence. Regardless, it's a shame. Tragic. And yes, mysterious, and I assure you we'll get to the bottom of all of it."

"Because four men dedicated to uncovering and unveiling the secrets of the Shroud..." Silas trailed off, sitting straighter.

He looked at his desk, eyeing the cryptic note Miles had given him. He picked it up and reread it. Then set it back down and turned around in his chair to look out the window. The note seemed to grow in significance in light of this revelation about Henry. These were the last words his friend wrote before he died. And they were addressed to him. Wanting to meet and discuss the health of their faithful friend?

What was going on, old chap?

"Silas? Are you still there?"

Silas closed his eyes and breathed deeply.

"Yes. I'm still here."

"I thought the line went dead. Are you alright? I know this is a lot to take in. Henry dying and all. I know how much he meant to you."

"No. It's not that," Silas said softly. He turned back toward his desk, then picked up the note again. "Well, it is. But it's more than that."

"OK..." Father Arnold said, trailing off. "Silas, do you know something?"

Silas took a breath. "Before you called, my assistant Miles handed me a note. It was from Henry. Sent by courier, which I thought was odd. He wanted me to get his message quickly because he overnighted it yesterday."

"Yesterday?" Arnold interrupting.

"Yesterday."

"But that doesn't make sense. He died yesterday. Well, in the evening, according to the coroner's report. The last of the four, actually."

"Which means he wrote the note in the morning or early afternoon, then hired the messenger to deliver it today."

Silence fell between the two.

Silas continued. "Did he know this was coming? That his life was in danger?" He stopped. "That the others were in danger?"

Father Arnold himself took a beat. "Well, what did the note say?"

Silas unfolded the note again and scanned his friend's last words. "He wanted to meet. Here, listen: 'We need to talk ASAP. It's about our faithful friend. He's in ill health.'"

Father Arnold said nothing.

"Cryptic, right?"

"Indeed. Who do you suppose *our faithful friend* is? Do you have any ideas what he meant by this? And why he would send this to you?"

"I wondered that myself. We did often refer to the Shroud as our faithful friend."

"The Shroud?" Father Arnold said in alarm. "The Holy Shroud of Turin?"

"Right. Though maybe it was a slip of the tongue, and he meant one of our colleagues." Silas paused. "Perhaps talking about another STURP member? Maybe one of those who died in the last day, overseas?"

"Maybe," Father Arnold said softly, as if in thought.

Silas added: "But how could he have known about those other deaths? Or the threat of their deaths?"

"Mysterious, indeed."

"Has any protection been given to the other members?"

"It's in the works. I have been in touch with Vatican officials, as well as coordinating with a friend at the FBI. He hadn't heard about the other deaths overseas. But it made him concerned, for sure."

More silence fell between the two as they considered this added layer to the death of their friend.

"Can you email me a copy of the note. Make a scan of it and forward it along? Maybe my friend at the FBI can help."

"Sure thing, Father."

"I know you're busy and probably have a class to teach soon, so I won't keep you."

Silas looked at his watch. Ten minutes had already eaten into his lecture.

Father Arnold continued, "But I have a favor to ask of you. I need your help. This seems almost pointless now in light of the circumstances. And I hesitate even to ask...but Henry was supposed to give the keynote address to our annual sindonology conference tomorrow." Father Arnold paused, took a breath, and sighed. "Obviously, that's not going to happen."

Silas had forgotten about the annual gathering of the sindonologists, a band of researchers and scientists dedicated to studying the Shroud of Turin. There was usually fascinating tidbits of information and gossip passed around between the researchers, but nothing groundbreaking. Hadn't been for some time. He wasn't going to attend because of his own research and the impending results.

"Sorry, Father, but I wasn't planning on it this year," Silas simply said.

"Can I change your mind? I desperately need you to fill Henry's shoes and give the opening remarks this year."

Silas sat up straighter in his chair. "You want me to give the keynote? At the annual gathering of sindonologists?"

"Now, I know you haven't exactly seen eye-to-eye with many of the members."

"No, I haven't," Silas said. He was the youngest scholar among a cohort of aged, mostly Catholic men, who had given their lives to the Shroud. To them, Silas was a young buck who was trampling on their turf. It didn't help he had gone directly to the Vatican for samples of the Shroud for his latest research project, without their knowledge or blessing. But Silas wasn't going to let a bunch of old fuddy-duddies stand in the way of his research goals. And the recognition that came with them.

"But think of this as an opportunity to show those old farts a thing or two. And I've heard your research has been going swimmingly, so you should have material. Have you gotten your results back yet? Something about the Shroud and nuclear radiation?"

"Right. Not yet." Silas looked at the door, thinking he had heard someone outside. Another courier with his results, perhaps? "Should be here soon. But you know Avery. Said I'd get word when I get word, that I was as impatient as his six-year-old."

Father Arnold chuckled. "Yes, I do. And yes, you are!"

Silas laughed. He also liked the idea of sharing his results with his colleagues. Maybe they would take him more seriously if he had a thing or two to show them.

"Would it be OK if I share some of my latest research? If I get them in time, that is?"

"That would be splendid! A real show, I reckon, for the annual conference."

A knock at his door caught Silas's attention. His heart skipped a beat. The results?

"Come in."

It was Miles. Silas smiled and tilted his head, begging for some news. Miles shook his head, then tapped his watch. It was almost a quarter past two.

Silas nodded. "Sorry, Father, but I really should be going. I'm late for my lecture. On the Shroud, actually."

"Go. Go. And inspire those young minds of the memory of the resurrection contained in the Holy Image. Who knows, maybe you'll even convert one or two."

Silas smiled. "Lord willing."

Father Arnold offered condolences for the death of Silas's friend and mentor, vowing to get to the bottom of his death. He said he would email Silas the details of the conference, then said goodbye.

Silas sat still. He blinked, then sat back.

He closed his eyes and breathed deeply. He tried to feel something for Henry's death. Sorrow. Loss. Even shame for not visiting him more often. But nothing came. No emotion. Nothing. The walls he had built after his father died wouldn't let him.

Dead? He looked back at the note from Henry again. His mouth had gone dry, so he licked his lips and swallowed.

What a bittersweet day. The day I receive word my mentor and second father died is the day I'm getting results to an experiment that could change the course of my career.

Silas stopped, chiding himself. *That could change the course of the Church, proving the resurrection of Jesus Christ was scientifically and historically real.*

"You better get going, Professor," Miles said softly. He offered a weak smile, handing Silas his book bag and laptop.

Silas smiled back and nodded. He stood and grabbed both, stuffing the laptop in his bag.

"By the way, looks like I'm heading to Washington, DC, later."

"DC? Why?"

"Father Arnold needs me to stand in for..." He trailed off, still not able to believe his mentor was dead. He cleared his throat. "For Henry Gregory. He was supposed to headline the annual sindonologist conference there. Obviously, that's not going to happen."

Miles nodded. "I see..."

"But Barnabas—"

Miles waved a hand and cut him off. "Say no more. I'll feed him again while you're away. Two scoops a day, right?"

He smiled. "Right. Thanks, you're a lifesaver."

"However I can help. But you'd best get going! Run along."

"Alright, alright. Get me the minute you get those blasted results," he called back as he jetted off to his awaiting lecture.

CHAPTER 3

A bitter wind and biting rain threatened Silas's face as he hustled across campus. He pulled the collar of his charcoal wool coat tighter against his neck for relief. It was barely working.

"Good afternoon, Dr. Grey. Late again, are we?"

Silas stopped short, nearly colliding with Mathias McIntyre, his department dean.

"Not according to my watch. One minute to spare." Silas held up his wrist and nodded as he continued on toward the burnt-colored stone building wrapped in ivy that housed his lecture hall. While not a lie, it was less-than-honest; the cheap gift hadn't kept the time well in years.

He glanced down at the faded fake gold-plated Seiko watch clinging to his wrist, a high school graduation gift from Dad pockmarked from ten years and three tours of duty with the Rangers across the Middle East. He picked up his pace, the rain having the same idea.

It was days like this he missed his father. Come bitter rain or crisp sunshine, the two ran eight miles well before the rest of the world was ready for their feet to hit the floor. The training kept his military father in tip-top shape. Same for him, both as a quarterback for the Falls Church Jaguars and in preparation for his future life as a grunt. Though the latter didn't happen until later, much to the disappointment of his father.

Silas pushed aside the memory as he hustled into the hundred-seat lecture hall, a time capsule of decades gone by. If those walnut walls could talk, they would tell tales of fascinating lectures on Proust and Freud, logarithms and algorithms, thermodynamics and microeconomics that had shaped the minds of nearly three hundred graduating classes of America's brightest.

Today's lecture was of a different sort entirely.

"Good afternoon, class," Silas bellowed as he hustled down the aisle to the front of the lecture hall. Pockets of students huddled in conversation began to break up and return to their seats. Others quickly finished sending a text and checking Facebook before putting away their digital devices. He had a strict policy against using such things in class; it was a paper-and-pen-only zone.

"Professor Grey!"

He stopped short, nearly running into a clean-cut junior wearing torn blue jeans, a faded red and blue flannel, and Converse shoes. Jordan Peeler, quarterback for the Hoyas, and one of his brighter, more engaged students.

"Yes, Jordan," Silas said taking off his coat.

The young man handed him a well-worn paperback. "Finished it last night."

It took Silas a moment to register, but then he smiled as he took the book and looked at the cover. His copy of C. S. Lewis's *Mere Christianity*, still bearing the dust of Iraq and Afghanistan where he first discovered the Oxford professor.

He stuffed the book in his satchel. "So, what did you think? Especially his argument about Jesus being a liar, lunatic, or Lord?"

"See, I had this idea," Jordan said excitedly, "that there could be another 'L' word." The junior leaned in like he was about to drop a knowledge bomb on his professor. "Legend," he whispered, then smiled.

Silas loved it when his students were eager to best him. Showed they were using their brains and trying. But that argument wasn't new. Pop theologians and genre novelists with a Christian ax to grind had recycled it from dead Germans for years.

"Interesting," he smiled knowingly. "Go on."

Jordan's eyes widened slightly with delight. "The way I see it, maybe Jesus' disciples had created all of these stories to sort of keep his memory alive after he died. You know, like the Roman hero narratives. Jesus' disciples *made* him legendary."

Silas nodded and brought his eyebrows together as if he was contemplating Jordan's fresh insight.

Jordan crossed his arms in satisfaction. "So, what do you think?"

"I think you'll be very interested in today's lecture. But I like your thinking." He slapped Jordan's back and continued on toward the front. "Let's talk more after class, maybe grab coffee or something."

Jordan nodded, then took his seat.

Silas kept smiling as he reached the front. He lived for those kinds of moments, the chance to engage his students with religious ideas and help shape their spiritual journey. Whether they committed to Christianity or not, at least they were forging a path. Unfortunately, such conversations were few and far between. He hoped today's lecture would change that.

"Sorry for the delay," he said as he hoisted his bag onto the A/V cart and brought out his laptop. He opened it and hooked it into the room's projector system, then he brought up his PowerPoint lecture. The class settled down and settled in for the next three hours.

After arranging his notes, he began. "If you were to name the central element to the Christian faith, what would you say that is?"

The multi-faith and non-faith group of students were silent. Some of them shifted in their seats. Others looked around for guidance. One student shot his hand in the air. It was Jordan.

Silas nodded toward him. "Go for it."

"Jesus."

A few classmates giggled.

"Thank you, Captain Obvious! I'd say that's pretty much a given."

More classmates giggled.

"The Bible," a co-ed from the front offered.

"Nope, but good guesses. Think about the central belief of Christianity."

Silas received nothing more. So he brought out a well-worn black-covered book, its sides stained crimson red. He opened it and began searching its pages, turning them gently, reverently.

"Try this on for size. It's from the first letter a man named Paul wrote to a town called Corinth." He cleared his throat, then read:

> *Now if Christ is proclaimed as raised from the dead,*
> *how can some of you say there is no resurrection of*
> *the dead? If there is no resurrection of the dead,*
> *then Christ has not been raised; and if Christ has*
> *not been raised, then our proclamation has been in*
> *vain and your faith has been in vain.*

He closed his Bible and set it on the lectern. He walked out in front of it and stood before the students, arms crossed.

"Anyone?" Silas questioned, leaning back against the lectern.

Jordan raised his hand again. Silas nodded toward him to answer.

"The...what do the Christians call it. The resurrection?"

"Is that a question?"

"No. The guy in your reading said it. If Jesus didn't come back from the dead, then the Christian faith is bunk."

Silas chuckled. "Bunk. That's probably a good twenty-first-century translation of *your faith has been in vain*. And *the guy*, as you say, was the apostle Paul. A Jew who became a follower of Jesus and a missionary to non-Jews. And you're right."

He returned back behind the lectern and changed slides. "The entire Christian religion hinges on the claim that a dead guy came back to life."

"Like, a zombie?" Jordan blurted out.

The room laughed. So did Silas.

"Good one. No, not like a zombie. Early followers of Jesus didn't claim he was undead. They claimed he was alive. And, as Paul said, if Jesus hasn't been resurrected, then the faith of billions of Christians is empty, completely worthless. And they are to be pitied above all other people."

Jordan's hand shot up in the back again.

Silas saw it and nodded. "Go ahead."

"I don't mean to be rude, but I didn't sign up for no catechism course, Mr. Grey."

Silas smiled. "And I don't mean to be preachy. Obviously, this isn't Christianity 101. And today's lecture isn't about the Christian faith, but a *relic* of the faith that has preserved the memory of this most significant event in Christianity for two millennia."

Silas paused, scanning the room. "Anyone care to guess which relic I'm talking about?"

A few shifted in their seats. Mostly, there was silence, and several quizzical, interested looks.

Silas sighed with disappointment. Apparently, his life-work had done little for the generation behind him. Which made tomorrow's revelations all the more critical.

"I'm speaking of the Holy Image. Or, as it has been commonly known, the Shroud of Turin. Anyone familiar with the Shroud, or at least has heard of it?" A few hands rose in recognition.

That's a start.

"There is a long and sordid history surrounding this most fascinating fourteen-by-four-foot piece of burial linen. It's been known by many names: the Holy Image, the Image of Edessa, the Mandylion, and more commonly the Shroud of Turin, where it keeps its home in Italy."

Silas brought up his first slide. On it was a ghostly, ghastly black-and-white image of a man many have puzzled over for centuries, his front and back sitting side-by-side: underneath his closed eyes was a mustache and beard, and long hair fell beyond his shoulders to the center of his back; his arms were crossed, one hand over the other, and engraved with several white markings; hundreds more of the same white etchings shone brightly on the man's back and chest, crisscrossing each other at jagged right angles; similar white zig-zags marked the crown of his head and seemed to be dripping down his forehead; the same white lacerations marked both sides of his legs.

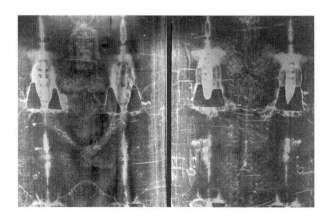

The story this image told was clear: whoever it was, the man had suffered the worst kind of death imaginable.

Several students gasped from seeing the image for the first time. Several others whispered to one another, marveling at the sight. Not a one were dozing off or sloughing. All were at respectful attention, as if the ground on which they were sitting had suddenly become sacred, holy.

Silas let the image hang in the air for a while, marveling at it. He never tired of looking into those eyes, never tired of looking at him. Some insisted it was a medieval forgery, but he believed without a shadow of a doubt that it was the genuine burial cloth of Jesus of Nazareth—who died, was buried, rose again, and was witnessed in bodily form.

Now, if only he could prove that beyond a shadow of a *scientific* doubt.

Silas looked to the back of the room, willing Miles to come bursting through the back doors triumphantly with news of the results.

Suddenly, one door opened. Silas's pulse quickened. Just a student, probably coming back from using the restroom.

He frowned, then stepped back to the lectern, having realized several minutes had ticked by.

"What are your thoughts?"

In unison, the students stared back at the faint image of the man thought to be the resurrected Savior of the world. Jordan was the first to raise his hand.

"Honestly? Sorta creepy. No offense."

Creepy?! The back of Silas's neck started turning red, his ears warmed at the disrespect. "Interesting," was all he could manage. "Anyone else?"

"I can kind of see it," said a woman said near the middle.

"See what?"

"Jesus. What I would imagine him, anyway."

"Speaking of which," Silas said, clicking forward a slide in his PowerPoint, "why don't we get into the main historical, scientific evidence for the Shroud's authenticity?"

Silas looked down at his notes, then back at the class.

"Are you ready?" he asked before launching into the heart of his lecture. In response, the class brought out notebooks to take notes.

Silas smiled. *Good.* "Let's start with the most compelling evidence. The faint imprint you see there is that of a real corpse in rigor mortis. In fact, the image is of a crucified victim!" Silas's voice rang high and loud with this revelation. He couldn't help himself.

"This was the conclusion of multiple criminal pathologists during one of the most pivotal periods of dissecting and testing the Shroud in the '70s. One of those pathologists, a Dr. Vignon, said the anatomical realism was so precise that separation of serum and cellular mass was evident in many of the blood stains. This is an important characteristic of dried blood."

Silas stopped for effect, looking out at his audience. "Did you catch that? That means there is real, actual dried human blood embedded in the cloth."

Many of the students whispered to each other. Just as Silas wanted.

"Not only that, but those same pathologists detected swelling around the eyes, the natural reaction to bruising from a beating. The New Testament claims Jesus was severely beaten before his crucifixion. Rigor mortis is also evident with the enlarged chest and distended feet, classic marks of an actual crucifixion."

He let that revelation settle before continuing. He turned around and looked at the screen of the ghostly-looking figure.

"The man in that burial linen," Silas continued whispering, his lecture hall mic barely picking up his revelations, "was mutilated in exactly the same manner that the New Testament says Jesus of Nazareth was beaten, whipped, and executed by means of crucifixion."

Silas brought up on the screen an enhanced version of the Shroud in blue and white.

"This positive image taken from the negative one left on the

Shroud shows in detail many of the historical markers that connect to the Gospel accounts of Jesus' death. You have the scourging marks from a Roman flagrum on the arms, legs, and back. Lacerations around the head from the crown of thorns. His shoulder appears to be dislocated, probably from carrying his cross beam and falling. According to scientists who examined the Shroud, all of these wounds were inflicted while he was alive. Then, of course, there is the stab wound in the chest and the nail marks in the wrists and feet. All consistent with the eyewitness accounts recorded in the Gospels."

"That's crazy," Jordan said aloud.

Silas grinned. "Dude, I'm just getting started! The image of the man, with all of his facial features and hair and wounds, is absolutely unique. Nothing like it in all the world. Totally inexplicable. And given there are no stains indicating decomposition on the linen itself, we know that whatever body was in the Shroud left before the decomposition process began. Just as the Gospel writers testify."

He stopped again and turned around to marvel at the thing of beauty staring out into his lecture hall.

"But how? How did this happen? How did a dead man come back to life? Not as a zombie, thank you very much." The class laughed. "But as a real, live human being. Fully restored back to life. New life. How did this happen?"

He let the question hang in the air before launching into his closing argument.

Just then, the door to the lecture hall creaked open and thudded heavily against the back wall. A few heads turned. As did Silas's. In stepped Miles.

From what Silas could tell, Miles was breathing heavily, as if he had just run a 5k. His eyes were wide, his mouth open and nostrils flaring as he heaved heavy breaths.

A few more of the seventy heads turned back to see the commotion. Silas's adrenaline spiked, quickening his pulse and breathing. He cocked his head as if to ask a question: *Are the results in? Good news or bad?*

Miles leaned against the door, trying to catch his breath. His mouth narrowed flat and he shook his head. He motioned for Silas to follow him. It didn't look good.

Silas took in a breath and heaved it out. He furrowed his brow and looked out at his class of students before looking down at his lecture notes again.

What happened?

Silas looked back up. Miles had left into the hallway, the door closing with a thud behind him. He still had forty minutes left in his class period. He looked back at the Shroud, the ghostly eyes staring back at him. He had done enough damage for one day. There would be time for more tomorrow. But his presentation awaited. So did those blasted test results.

And from Miles's indication, the tests were not good. Something had happened.

Silas closed his laptop. "Class dismissed."

CHAPTER 4

"What's the matter?" Silas asked, meeting Miles in the hallway. "Did the results not come in? Or did they, and they're not what we expected?"

Miles said nothing. He was leaning against the wall bent over, resting on his knees.

Silas stood staring. "Miles," he said loudly. He snapped his fingers. "What's going—"

"There's been a bombing."

Silas stood straighter, then looked outside. "What? Where?"

Miles looked up. "Not here! At the MIT Physics Department."

It took a few seconds to register. "Stephen Avery!"

Miles frowned and nodded.

"Walk with me."

The two hurried out of the hall and back to Silas's office. Miles recounted what he had seen on CNN. There had been an explosion of some kind at one of the main science buildings housing offices and lecture halls. Early reports claimed a man had walked into an in-session class and detonated a bomb. Massive destruction, lots of mayhem. Students and professors were dead.

This can't be happening.

Stephen and Silas had been introduced through Father Arnold a few years back at a get-together he was hosting. Though Harvard and MIT were cross-river rivals, Arnold liked to entertain faculty at his home in Boston. One evening, Silas was in town for a lecture on early Christian symbolism when the introduction was made. Though they differed in age by twenty years, the two hit it off initially because both were military brats. They kept in touch, and when Silas's research into the Shroud needed the touch of a physicist, he called on Stephen.

Avery was intrigued when Silas shared his research the first time they met at Arnold's home: "The original team of scientists that tested the Shroud back in the '70s," Silas explained to Avery, "verified with scientific certainty that the image imprinted on the Shroud was absolutely not painted or stained. Which rules out a medieval forgery, the story concocted and perpetuated by Shroud detractors for generations."

"So the image is—"

"Not of this world," Silas interrupted. "Not of ordinary means. It is, by definition, extra-ordinary."

Avery took a sip of his brandy, then folded his arms. "Now I'm intrigued. Go on, go on!"

"Several sindonologists and even skeptics of the scientific community have offered various explanations for the resulting image. The most common one is that of a radiological event within the Shroud."

"Radiological event? As in a nuclear explosion?" Avery smiled wryly.

"As in the result of the resurrection. If a body did dematerialize in such a fashion as the Gospels purport, then it would have given off trace amounts of radiation. Neutrons to be exact."

Avery saw where he was going, considering the implications. His eyes widened, and he unfolded his arms. "I think I have just the thing for you..."

Little did Silas know when he showed up at Father Arnold's

home, he would happen to meet the foremost expert on emerging nuclear physics in the country. He had even developed an advanced detector of so-called neutron flux events, the very events Silas needed to test in order to verify whether a resurrection-style nuclear event occurred inside the Shroud, as well as Jesus' tomb, two thousand years ago.

Silas appreciated the providential hand of God in putting the two together.

Within a year, Silas had secured a sample of the cloth from the Vatican for Avery to test. The one he was awaiting.

As the two hustled across campus, Silas couldn't help but think about those awaiting tests. "You didn't happen to get an envelope from Avery, did you?"

Miles shook his head.

Are you kidding me?

He cursed himself for thinking about his blasted tests at a time like this. For all he knew Avery was dead. In all likelihood he was. But his own reputation was on the line. So was the future of Christianity.

As he flung open the door to the Department of Religion building, his mind leaped to his brother. If he could just prove that the resurrection scientifically and historically happened, then perhaps his brother would finally believe.

Miles opened the office door, and Silas went through.

"Good afternoon, Professor," Millie said as the two raced inside. She was holding a tissue, clearly wet with tears from mourning. "Awful. Just awful what happened."

Silas breathed in sharply. "What are they saying? What happened?"

Millie sniffled and waved her tissue. "Go to CNN. It's all over the news."

Silas went to his office and sat in his chair, swiveling around to face his desk. He took his laptop out of his bag, then opened it up, clicking on to his web browser and going to CNN.com.

At the top was a bright red banner, which read: "Breaking News: MIT Suffers a Suspected Terrorist Attack."

A clear picture of the wounded newly-remodeled science building dominated the screen. Silas sat back, heart thumping harder than when he got news of Henry's death. For just last week he had been in that very building that was now a maw of belching smoke and spitting red flames.

Stephen Avery. The neutron flux detector.

My research!

Miles and Millie stepped closer as Silas scrolled through the report. It signaled possible terrorism. The school was on lockdown. FBI and Homeland Security counterterrorism forces were deployed. A mass-casualty unit was visible in a rolling video fixated on the burning building. Dozens were suspected killed. Including a prominent physicist. Stephen Avery.

"No!"

"My God..." Millie moaned. "Not Stephen!" She put her hand gently on Silas's shoulder.

Silas sat back, his military training worming a thought to the surface: Two colleagues who worked closely on the Shroud were dead within twelve hours of each other. Then add to that the three other STURP deaths-by-heart-attack.

Coincidence? Or planned? It seemed crazy to think the two were linked. But with his years in the military, and experience in the Middle East, he had learned not to underestimate the crazy. Especially the crazy coincidental.

Silas tried to regulate his breathing. His mouth watered for a shot of whiskey. His hand moved impulsively for the middle desk drawer in search of his small pillbox.

No. You need your wits about you. Now more than ever. Especially for tomorrow.

The computer refreshed with more information: One-hundred-and-eight students were reported dead or missing. Eight faculty dead or missing. While no known terrorist organization had yet claimed responsibility, the FBI and Homeland Security were referring to it as an "act of terror," the worst since the Orlando nightclub and Las Vegas country music festival attacks.

"What does this mean for tomorrow?" Miles broke in.

"What do you mean?" Silas asked.

"Well, with Dr. Gregory dead, and now Dr. Avery, the primary architect of the heart of what you were going to present..."

Silas sat back in his chair. "Doesn't change a thing. I should have the results soon. And I can at least share the project Avery and I were working on, that we had a working theory the Shroud possesses scientific proof of a neutron flux event, validating the Gospel accounts of the resurrection. That would surely honor Stephen." He shook his head. "This hasn't changed any of that. We need to let the world know about what I've discovered—" He stopped short. "What *we*, Stephen and I, are revealing about the Shroud. About the resurrection."

"But the possible terrorism...Don't you think DC will be on high alert? And your academic colleagues, what with their deaths. And...you, sir. Two of your friends just died."

"No," Silas said definitively, getting out of his chair and picking up his bag and coat. "I've worked too hard for this. *We've* worked too hard for this, compiling this research. It's going to change everything."

"I understand that, sir, but your colleagues are dead!"

"I don't—" Silas began before stopping himself. Miles and Millie stepped backward. Silas took a breath and bowed his head and said softly, "Of course I care. I was going to say I didn't care, but of course, I do." He looked up at his assistants. "My friends are dead. Two men who helped shape one of the most monumental discoveries of the Church. They would want that information out there. They would want us to show the world that the Shroud is real. And more than that: Jesus Christ really is alive, and we've got scientific proof."

Silas looked at the computer screen again. It refreshed to show a sliding display of images streaming in from the disaster.

"I will go to Washington to honor their work, as much as to honor our Lord and Savior."

Miles nodded and abruptly left. Millie nodded as well, then bowed her head.

"You know I never told him how much he meant to me."

"Sir?" Millie asked, raising her head.

"Henry. He was like a second father to me. And I never told him that. Never told him how much he had gotten me through Dad's death and all. How he had helped me grow and find myself. Like Dad would have."

Miles returned holding a brown manila envelope and Silas's coat. He handed the envelope to Silas.

"What's this?" Silas asked as he took the envelope.

"Your ammo, Dr. Grey. The results of Avery's tests, I presume. They just arrived by courier. Now you've got everything you need to make the case."

"What do they show? What did he say?" Silas questioned Miles greedily as he snatched the envelope from his assistant, forgetting the recent tragedy.

"Slow down, Professor," Miles chided. "I didn't open a thing. Didn't want to ruin the fun."

Avery had insisted on sending the results through old-school snail mail, given the sensitivities of the project and a personal paranoia against sending things through cyberspace. Inside was a single slip of paper, cream stationery from MIT. Silas pulled it out and frowned, expecting more to the package than that. On it was scrawled a note in barely-legible blue ink:

Grey,

I have completed my initial assessment of the linen material, and preliminary findings indicate particle radiation containing neutron flux. Remarkably, both forms of radiation radiate uniformly throughout the length, width, and depth of the cloth, signaling a unique extraordinary radiological event occurring, in which your religious relic was irradiated with a flux of neutrons.

There is still the matter of determining whether Ca-40 in the cloth had been converted to Ca-41, further confirming whether the cloth had been irradiated with neutrons. This means one more test, which I should complete in a day or two.

TL;DR: good news, but patience is a virtue.

Will be in touch,
Avery

Silas set down the sheet of paper and leaned back, then sighed heavily.

Miles shook his head slightly back and forth as if questioning him. "Well? Good, bad? What you expected? What you didn't?"

His questions woke Silas up from his thoughts. He smiled. "Here, take a look."

Silas handed Miles the results. He furrowed his brow as he read it, then gasped in surprise.

"My God. You have it," Miles whispered. He handed Silas back the sheet of paper. "Scientific proof that the Shroud is Jesus'. That he resurrected from the dead."

Silas stretched back in his chair, bringing his hands behind his head and smiling in satisfied victory. "Almost. Not quite there yet, but basically, yes." Then his face sunk and he got quiet. He whispered, "You did it, you old dog. Bravo."

Miles extended his hand. "Congratulations, Professor. May God use your discovery for his glory."

Silas smiled weakly, then stood and took it. "Soli Deo gloria."

"Spoken like a true Protestant."

They laughed. Silas was pleased. He was going to prove the resurrection. Prove to his brother it was real. If only he had the complete data from Stephen's experiments. His face fell at the thought, then he shook his head.

"You better get going, Professor," Miles said. "Or you'll miss your train."

Silas checked his watch, then nodded. "Yes, alright. And you'll remember to feed Barnabas?"

Miles tilted his head and frowned. "Don't worry, he's in good hands!" He handed Silas his satchel and coat. He took both, smiled and nodded. He put Avery's letter back into its manila envelope, then slipped it into his satchel and left for the train station to make the most important presentation of his life.

Perhaps in all of Christianity.

CHAPTER 5

WEWELSBURG, GERMANY.

The floor felt cold under his bare feet as Rudolf Borg slowly descended the stone stairway of his home in Wewelsburg, Germany. It wasn't so much a home as it was a castle. And a famous one at that.

Built in the seventeenth century, it later became the central headquarters of the German SS and central command for Heinrich Himmler. Though it had become a sort of museum and youth hostel post-WWII, Borg had acquired the estate from his hometown and transformed it into his own needs: a fortress and nerve center of spiritual enlightenment and war.

Borg coughed as he continued descending, LED lights along the base of the wall lighting his way to the chamber below. The wind howled outside as a mixture of rain and heavy, wet snow beat against the thick, interlocking stones of the ancient castle, a violent reflection of the nature of what was about to take place below. He flipped open his phone, checking for any missed calls. There were none. He slammed the phone closed.

He is late. He must not fail.

When he reached the bottom, it rang. Surprisingly, he got reception within the thick stone walls of the ancient structure. He brought his phone out and checked the small LCD notification screen: two bars, and it was him.

"You're late," Borg snapped.

Static and silence was the only response he received.

"Hello? Jacob." Borg turned around and climbed back into the stairwell, searching for a better signal.

"Yes. Sorry. We were...delayed."

"Delayed?" Borg asked, skepticism and irritation lacing his voice.

"Nothing to worry about, Rudolf," Jacob quickly added. "Boston has been swarming with feds. We needed to lay low and extract to safer ground before reconnecting."

"So you had success?"

"Perfect success."

Borg's eyes narrowed again, and a smile curled up on either end of his mouth. "Excellent. Tell me more."

"The bomb took out half the building, killing Avery. Decimated his research lab. Definitely destroyed the flux detector and any of the information it collected, including the Shroud specimen itself."

Borg descended to the lower chamber again, continuing toward his destination. "Excellent. And we're set for tomorrow?"

Static filled the phone again. He cursed and re-entered the stairwell. "Jacob? Are you there?"

"...set. Within twelve hours, phase one of the mission will be complete."

Borg smiled again. It was finally within his grasp.

"Good. Well done, my dear," he said silkily. "When all of this is over, I'll have something waiting for you."

"Really?" Jacob hummed on the other end, "And what's that?"

"Me." He closed the phone without waiting for a reply, smiling to himself at the thought of having Jacob back home.

He continued his descent, a red silk robe swishing with every step down the stairs. He kept on toward the chamber, but he stopped when he reached a statue. Bird-Man Thoth, the ancient Egyptian god of wisdom. Of revelation. Of *gnostikos*, the divine knowledge. It was a perfect replica of the colossal statue artifact discovered near the mortuary temple of Amenhotep III in Luxor a decade ago.

Measuring eleven-and-half feet tall and made of pure, red granite culled from ancient quarries in Egypt, the statue stood towering over Rudolf, reminding him of his ancient calling and setting his face like flint against the unfolding plans that would finally hand his ancient sect the victory it had been waiting for the last seven hundred years.

He focused his attention on the ancient face, the ibis head peering down at him with a mask of pure gold, with a black onyx beak, flanked by indigo ribbons, and the Atef crown of white and red feathers stretching upward. It was truly a testimony to the enduring legacy of the ancient cult.

Thoth's roles in Egyptian mythology were varied: he served as a mediating power between good and evil, as a scribe of the gods, and weighed the lives of the dead. The ancient Egyptians regarded Thoth as One, self-begotten and self-produced, like the Übermensch of his own ancient Germanic ancestors. He was the master of both natural and divine law, establishing the heavens and the earth and everything in them, directing the motions of the heavenly bodies and affairs of men. The Egyptians credited him as the author of all works of science and religion, philosophy and magic. His power was unlimited and unrivaled by all other gods. The ancients even declared him the inventor of astronomy and astrology; mathematics and geometry; medicine and botany; theology and civilized government; and the alphabet, reading and writing. He was the true author of every work of every branch of knowledge. Human and divine.

"You know all that is hidden under the heavenly vault," Borg whispered, bowing his head reverently before the stone effigy.

"Now, that which has been hidden shall be revealed. And it shall be mine."

Lightning flashed behind him through the windows up the stairwell, illuminating the god of knowledge in flickering white light. A few seconds later, thunder rumbled in the distance, bringing Borg out of his trance. He stiffened with purpose, then continued down the darkly lit hallway. As he walked forward toward the gathering chamber of his brothers, he considered the history of this sacred place.

Eighty years prior, Heinrich Himmler signed a 100-year lease for the seventeenth-century Wewelsburg Castle. It was a dilapidated, decaying structure at the time, but Himmler saw the potential for using it as a training facility for his beloved SS, as well as the cultic power it held for world domination. Desperately wanting a base to teach these values to SS soldiers, Himmler turned Wewelsburg into a non-military training grounds focused on the occult, pagan rituals, and making Wewelsburg the center of the world. Himmler nick-named his crown jewel of Nazi propaganda the Grail Castle. He believed that when the Nazis were the rulers of the entire world, artifacts from the castle would radiate magical power. Much work was put into acquiring such artifacts. One of which was the Spear of Destiny, which Hitler himself claimed had shown him his future.

Along with collecting these artifacts, Wewelsburg became the center of a number of pagan rituals led by Himmler himself. Chief among them was a baptism-like ritual. A former cistern in the castle was transformed into a crypt to facilitate the sacred ceremony. After the Allies took control of the castle, a round table with twelve chairs was also discovered, an obvious reference to the fabled King Arthur and his knights.

As the Nazis were losing the war, rather than let it fall into the hands of the Allies, Himmler ordered the castle set ablaze and demolished. Although most of the interior was destroyed, the exterior walls were preserved, and Wewelsburg was turned into a museum for reflecting on the horrors of the Nazi regime and Himmler's bizarre plan for world domination.

Until it was acquired by Rudolf Borg.

He coughed again, a violent, hacking cough that threatened to upend Borg on the floor. He braced himself against the cold, stone wall and recovered, swallowing hard before pressing forward. No cough would keep him from what was about to take place tonight.

A glowing light up ahead pulled him onward, orange and warm. Voices, low and incoherent, were chanting the ancient mantra he knew by heart. A screech sliced through the noise, and he quickened his pace. He reached the slightly ajar heavy, golden door, and pushed it open. The voices stopped as he entered. Facing him were seventeen Bird-Men, all wearing the face of Thoth. The god of knowledge.

"Brothers," Borg said.

The Bird-Men nodded in silent unison, welcoming their Grand Master. Borg stepped into the circular cavern, emboldened by the sight of his council and forgetting about his wretched cough.

High and domed-shaped, and made out of quarried stone, the room was illuminated by eight windows that flickered every so often with the storm's light. Thirteen torches displayed around the room offered a soft glow to provide the remaining light. They hung above thirteen small, stone seats upon which bare-chested Bird-Men sat with ornamented shoulder drapes of gold and indigo beadwork, all wearing masks of pure gold, flanked by ribbons of indigo, with beaks of black onyx.

Borg scanned the room, then lifted his head toward the high dome, smiling reverently at the symbol adorning its center: a Nazi swastika. Far from a modern symbol of fascist oppression, it was an ancient religious one, taking the form of the familiar equilateral cross with its four legs bent at ninety degrees. Considered to be a sacred symbol of such spiritualities as

Hinduism, Buddhism, and Jainism, it dated back to before the second century BC. Small terracotta pots and ancient coins from Crete were found to have borne the symbol. And it had been used as a decorative element in various cultures stretching back to at least the Neolithic period. For Borg, the symbol held all of the divine promises of these pre-modern cultures for such a time as this.

Directly beneath the dome, in the middle of the room, was the crown jewel of the crypt: the ceremonial basin. It acted as a baptismal pool for the rite of passage into the upper echelon of an ancient order of divine knowledge and power.

Tonight, it would be used for a very different purpose, a sacred purpose.

Borg entered farther into the chamber, the cool, dank air making the hairs on the back of his neck stand upright in delight. Seats were arrayed around the outer rim of the room for the Thirteen, the coterie of high-ranking associates representing the Wheel of the Year and the perfection of the earthly and heavenly alignment of seasons. Five more lined the front of the chamber, holding the Council of Five. The seats of the Pentacle, of Man.

Of God.

He breathed in and moved toward a throne-like chair in the middle of the Pentacle seats. His chair. He took his place among the Council at the center chair reserved for the Grand Master. To his right was the ceremonial ibis dress. It mirrored the statue of Thoth he had just passed, white and red plumes, gold mask and all. He smiled and placed the headdress upon his head, then affixed the gold mask to his face. He removed his outer red silk robe and draped it over his chair, revealing a hardened muscular chest hung at the shoulders by an intricately beaded gold and indigo sash.

As he sat down, a small muffled bleat was heard from the center of the ceremonial basin. He peered through his gold mask, over the onyx beak, to the four-legged victim tied and muzzled in the center of the floor. It strained at its bindings, jaw trying to nibble at the muzzle keeping its mouth tightly closed.

Baba, my dear. Your usefulness is nigh.

"Brothers," Borg intoned, "thank you for gathering at such short notice, but we must ensure the success of our mission. Phase one of our plans has commenced. I've just received word that our team in America has successfully destroyed the object that could have brought it all to light. They were also successful in eliminating the threat of the professor. But this is only the beginning. Soon enough, one by one, the pieces will begin to fall. And, soon enough, we will accomplish what our brothers in France failed to accomplish seven hundred years ago."

Around the room, the masked brethren nodded in approval. One of the members spoke: "What of the threat coming from Washington, DC, Grand Master? Surely the greatest concentration of sindonologists presents to us, and our mission, a problem of the highest order. Especially if the so-called 'evidence' my operatives say one Professor Silas Grey has amassed is allowed to come to light."

Borg dipped his head absentmindedly, before recognizing his weakness. He promptly stiffened and gritted his teeth before answering the senior member.

"I understand your concerns, but they are unwarranted. The threat from the West will soon be dealt a final, crippling blow. Greater than that of Boston. Pay the convention no mind. We have bigger things to worry about."

"And yet, the revelation could be catastrophic if—"

"I said pay it no heed!" Borg roared.

The member leaned back against the stone backing of his pillar. The snapping of the torch flames provided the only sound in the chamber as Borg settled into his chair himself.

"It will be handled," Borg said calmly. "Now we must proceed with the evening ritual, ensuring our success and preparing for what is to come. We all know the sacred vow given to mankind from Thoth before he departed. 'Now I depart from you,'" Borg intoned, closing his eyes and lifting his voice high into the darkened, cool chamber. The other members joined him in the ancient supplication. "'Know my commandments, keep them and be with them, and I will be with you, helping and guiding you into the Light.'"

A rustling in the center of the room caught Borg's attention. The goat. It was straining violently against its restraints, as if it anticipated what was impending. He eased himself off from his stone seat, put on his red silk robe, and strolled toward the center, his garment swishing in sync. He untied the animal and undid the muzzle. A bleating, mournful cry instantly escaped its lips.

Out from under his robe, Rudolf removed a jewel-encrusted athame knife passed down from Grand Master to Grand Master from each successive generation to use in ceremonies such as this one. In one swift swipe, he sliced the blade across the throat of the goat. The bleating stopped as blood spilled from its neck onto the cold, hard stone floor. The animal twitched in his tight grip, then went limp, its life-force draining into the baptismal pool.

The rest of the room silently looked on as their Grand Master performed the necessary sacrificial ceremony in anticipation of the greater good that was to come. For in short order, the central ceremonial altar would be used for a very different purpose.

One fueled by fire, now cleansed by blood.

CHAPTER 6

PRINCETON, NEW JERSEY.

S ilas reached the Princeton train station with room to spare. He needed it, as the terror threat assessment had changed that morning from cautious yellow to angry red in response to the events in Boston.

He settled into the maroon pleather seats on the Amtrak train bound for DC, leaning back and sighing. He stared out the window as the train engineers readied their departure, trying to steel his mind from the reality that his friend and research partner had been blown to bits. Along with the complete data set and only sure-fire way to prove the authenticity of the Shroud.

Silas applied pressure to his temple and began rubbing, trying to arrest a throbbing headache that threatened to derail his preparation for tomorrow's presentation. He couldn't shake the death of his friend and colleague. What about Martha, Stephen's wife, and the twins he had left behind? Stephen had been preparing a trip for his daughters once the semester had ended, a surprise jaunt to Paris to celebrate their final year of high school. What a shame.

A sudden blow of the train's horn startled him, jolting him back to his present trip. He shook his head, trying to bury the memory once more and suppress the day's events. Nothing would change what happened.

What's done is done. Move on and focus. Focus on redeeming Stephen's memory and work.

He tapped the window with the military ring that anchored his right middle finger in resolute defiance of the day's events. He turned to his satchel and drew out Avery's envelope with the findings he hoped would finally prove what he had worked the last five years for, to the detriment of his professional career.

The academic establishment doesn't take too kindly to professors who seek to prove the authenticity of religious artifacts deemed to be in the realm of fable. Particularly the Christian variety. Especially the kind that purport to prove a dead man lives.

Yet there it was in black and white, near-scientific proof. Now, his colleagues would take issue with the "scientific" part. They would demand peer review and replicability. That would come later. But the bombshell-finding would be enough to propel his project forward. And his career.

Silas smirked slightly at that last realization. Proving a first-century Jew, who died a terrorist death and launched the largest religious movement of the world, came back to life would send one's career into the stratosphere. Or at least enough to put one's career as an academic historical theologian on the fast-track to tenure.

He couldn't help but smile in satisfaction. *Take that, Princeton! And Sebastian.*

He re-read the letter and smiled at the findings, then set it down and looked back out the window. *Oh, Sebastian.* It wouldn't matter if the Son of God himself showed up with hard proof of his life, death, and resurrection, Sebastian still wouldn't believe. But how could he argue with science? After all, the man was a scientist! Yet Silas knew his resistance to anything Christian went beyond fact and evidence. It was existential. And just a little tinged with sibling rivalry.

As the train lurched forward, Silas shook his head slightly at the thought of what his brother would think, not to mention his faculty colleagues. But then his face fell slightly.

Is that what matters, Silas? he chided himself. *Approval from men? Proving your brother wrong?*

Of course not. Not entirely. The professional notoriety would be satisfying, no doubt. But it would be the icing on the cake of his personal ambition to prove the Shroud authentic. And, yes, to prove to Sebastian that Christianity was rooted in history, not merely faith. After all, Jesus' resurrection was why Christians believed, not merely what they believed.

Silas narrowed his eyes, resolving to continue the work he and his colleague began. If not for his brother and the Church, then to satisfy his own professional pursuits. He cursed himself for the thought, but it was true. Silas was a man of academic ambition.

The world blurred by as the train trundled onward toward Washington, DC. In the distance, he saw a church spire peeking up above the trees in the center of a small town, the remnants of days gone by when the Church was the center of public and private life.

How things had changed.

He understood why. Some of that change was inevitable as the world progressed and sought answers to life's ultimate questions outside of a framework of traditionalism. Much of that change was the Church's own fault, having decimated their trust and authority through scandal, the sexual and money kind, leaving countless lives crushed along the way. Then there were the less sordid, yet equally soul-crushing, aspects of the Church: the legalism and finger-wagging; the puritanical withdrawal from society; and the squashing of questions people were asking about faith, life, and everything in between.

Like his own brother.

Among the two, Silas's twin had been the one most destined for a life in service of the Church. Sebastian was much more in tune with his spiritual side during their childhood than Silas had ever been. While Silas was sleeping during the homily or busy making faces to the parishioners behind them, Sebastian was the one taking notes or cross-checking what the priest was saying with what he had memorized years earlier from his Bible. And while Silas was off playing baseball or soccer or running track, there was Sebastian serving in the parish soup kitchen and as an altar boy at St. James Catholic Church in the heart of Falls Church, Virginia.

But then from around fourteen or fifteen onward, he had noticed a shift in his brother. It was subtle, and one only a close twin might recognize. His mother probably would have, had she been alive. His father hadn't. Too focused on his military career saving the world.

The change started manifesting in small ways, a burst of anger here and combativeness there. Sebastian had always been the calm, quiet one of the two. It was Silas who had been born with the fiery temper, yet Sebastian had begun to mirror it in odd ways. Then he had started making excuses for not attending the church functions that had been so important to him. He stopped serving at the soup kitchen. He called in sick to the altar for several Sundays in a row until Dad forced him to go, even apologizing to Father Rafferty for shirking his responsibilities.

And then there were the conversations about the doubts that swirled in his brother's mind, challenging the core teachings of the Church that formed the heart of the catechism he and his brother had been dutifully taking. The problem was that Father Rafferty refused to engage his questions, refused to discuss the Church's teachings in any meaningful way that would help Sebastian work through his doubts. From issues of science and the origins of the universe to women's rights and human sexuality, "The Church says it, that settles it" was their priest's response. Which lost mileage on Sebastian pretty quickly, leading to frustration and a fraying faith.

It wasn't any surprise to Silas, because he himself had such doubts. But for Sebastian, who had been the stalwart believer of the family, even besting their own father at his Bible and catechism knowledge, it was a shift that seemed to have made his transformation complete from true believer to stalwart skeptic. Silas wouldn't have known about it until years later, but it was during this period, from about fourteen to seventeen that Sebastian's faith had been forged.

And yet his questions still lingered. So Sebastian launched into a dual major in philosophy and physics. Which led to a Ph.D. program in theoretical physics, leading to a tenure-track position at George Washington University in DC. Like Silas, he was the youngest in his department, and his scholarly pursuits informed much of his faith.

Or lack thereof.

In many ways, it was this disbelief that fueled Silas's own pursuit of the Shroud. Guilt over his brother's loss of faith as much as an interest in proving the faith true had been the impetus behind his endeavor.

As the train continued its journey southward, Silas continued staring out the window, cell phone in hand. He had thought about calling Sebastian and inviting him to the lecture. Perhaps the academic nature of the event, combined with supporting his brother, would spark his interest. Maybe it was a way to break through the barriers his brother had erected to ward off anything to do with faith, especially the Christian kind.

Sure, why not?

He slipped Avery's letter back into his satchel, then took out his phone, swiped it awake, and put in his password. Then he opened the phone app and selected his brother's number from his contacts. His thumb hovered over his brother's name, hesitating to make the call.

He sighed, then turned the phone off, and put it back in his pocket.

It had been months since they had talked. And the last time it hadn't gone so well. There had been a news item out of Harvard that had piqued Sebastian's interest. A small manuscript fragment had been discovered, researched, and presented by a Dr. Karen King, which supposedly suggested Jesus had a wife—a flat-out contradiction to the teachings of the Bible and the Church. Like Silas, she had an interest in early Christianity. But where his interests were in preserving the memory of the Christian faith, she was more interested in alternative versions and voices of Christianity that had been supposedly suppressed by the dominant powers of the Church.

Sebastian had dialed Silas the afternoon the story broke that Jesus had had a wife. The small parchment said it was so, being dubbed the Gospel of Jesus' Wife. He said he wanted Silas's take on it as a scholar in the field. What he really wanted was a fight, a chance to point out historical proof that Silas's faith was a fanciful myth tailor-made for the weak-willed. That it was a weapon of subjugation by those in power to suppress those outside of power.

And Silas played ball.

He tried to play fair, tried to gently point out the inconsistencies with the Coptic script and wording, problems with the chain of custody and mystery surrounding how the parchment ended up in Dr. King's hands, to begin with. All items other biblical scholars who specialized in such matters had already addressed. But Sebastian wasn't having anything of it. After Sebastian accused Silas of narrow-minded bigotry and blind ignorance, Silas drove the dagger of accusations into his brother's heart, tipped with the poisons of apostasy and damnation.

He regretted the way he had handled the conversation. Still

regretted it as he stared out the window recalling the memory. He had spent more nights and days than he could remember praying that his brother would come back to the faith, that God would use him as an instrument to gently guide Sebastian back to the fold of Christ's Church.

That conversation had been anything but gentle.

And yet, perhaps the good Lord had opened up a window with this opportunity at Georgetown. After all, the venue was only a few blocks over from where his brother taught. It wasn't like it would be a terrible inconvenience for Sebastian to pop over and hear his older brother give a lecture. Besides, it would be a way for him to support his professional pursuits. And it would be an opportunity to flex his intellectual openness he was so fond of trotting out in every conversation.

Silas took out his phone again and turned it on, this time tapping his brother's name. He brought the phone up to his ear and waited as the phone rang, another church steeple from an ill-forgotten era flashing by in a blur.

"Well, if it isn't his Holiness himself," a familiar voice blared on the other end.

"Hello, Sebastian."

CHAPTER 7

As kids, Silas and Sebastian were inseparable. Some of that inseparability probably stemmed from their family dynamic: after their mother passed away during childbirth, their military father did all he could to care for them and keep them in line, but his career took precedence. So Silas and Sebastian had to fend for themselves under the guidance of nannies and the military educational establishment.

Though twins, they were fraternal, looking nothing alike. Sebastian inherited their father's build and features: tall and lanky, with a fair complexion and slim build; blue eyes and blond hair; Silas inherited his mother's looks: average height and bulky, with a darker, ruddy complexion and solid, lean build; brown hair and hazel eyes.

Even though Silas and Sebastian were twins, Sebastian was technically Silas's younger brother, having been born twenty-three minutes after Silas when a complication arose: the umbilical cord was wrapped around his neck. Perhaps that was one reason why Silas felt so responsible for Sebastian's faith. It was as much nature as it was nurture.

Silas girded himself for what he knew would be an interesting conversation. He also said a quick prayer.

"So what brings the pleasure of this mobile call this evening?" Sebastian said. "Shall I gird my loins for yet another tongue lashing for my agnosticism and apostatizing ways?"

Silas inhaled deeply and closed his eyes, cursing himself for not throwing his phone out the window the first time he had the brilliant idea to phone his brother. He sighed, then smiled before continuing.

"I come in peace, baby brother."

"Thank the gods! I thought I needed to pull out the old rabbit's foot or necklace of garlic to ward off any curses you were about to rain down on me."

"Seba..." Silas groaned, regretting the call by the second. "Come on, bro. I said I was sorry about last time. And I'm not calling to fight this time, honest."

"Then why? I haven't heard from you since Christmas after our epic showdown when I refused to join you for your silly Christmas Eve service."

A worm of regret and shame wound itself around Silas's heart again.

Sebastian continued, "And now, out of the blue, you pop in to say howdy? Dodgy, bro. Dodgy."

Silas stared back outside, closing his mouth and gritting back any defensive reply he might have wanted to offer.

"You're right. It is dodgy. I'm sorry it's been so long. Honestly, I was ashamed of how I had left things."

"That is honest of you. And humble." Sebastian paused. "And entirely unlike you, Sy. What's going on? What do you want?"

Silas huffed. "Now, why do I have to want anything? Why can't I just call my brother to say, 'Hi'?"

"Because you never call your brother just to say, 'Hi'!"

He had him there. Silas was often far more wrapped up in his own work and life to worry about what was happening in his brother's life, or other people's lives.

"I don't want to fight. Actually, I'm on my way down to see you."

"See me?"

"Well, not you exactly. I'm on a train heading to DC as we speak. Got invited to make a presentation at an academic gathering at Georgetown University tomorrow morning."

Silas paused, waiting for a response. He got none. Closing his eyes, he took a breath and continued.

"And I wondered, if you weren't doing anything, if you'd like to come join me and support your bro."

"When have you ever been interested in my support? You've seemed to be far more interested in my agreement than—"

Sebastian stopped suddenly. Silas looked at his phone, wondering if the line had dropped.

"Sebastian? Did I lose you?" He looked at his phone again. Still connected.

"Is this some sort of trick?" Sebastian asked, his voice laced with skepticism. "Georgetown is run by a bunch of Romans. Is that what this is about? Some Christian meeting to serve as some excuse to indoctrinate your baby brother?"

He was referring to the Catholic roots of Georgetown, having been founded by the Jesuits in 1789. This wasn't going well. He was clearly resistant. Hostile even.

"No, no, no. This is not some super-secret ploy to indoctrinate you into Christianity. Yes, it is a gathering of mostly Christians. Not just Catholics, but scholars from across the denominational spectrum. Actual academics, and not all of them even Christian. Even you would be impressed by their credentials, Seba."

Silas heard a snort at the other end. He pressed on. "Anyway, I was asked last minute to give the keynote address, and since you were in town, I thought I would see if you wanted to tag along."

"Keynote," Sebastian said. "Impressive. So if this isn't some sort of attempt to convert me, what's the gathering about? What's the topic?"

Silas took another breath before answering, considering how silly his brother would find it.

"The Shroud of Turin?"

"What?! You're still riding that pony into the sunset? That thing has been discredited so many times as a Middle Ages forgery it'd give Dan Brown dreams of sugar plums dancing in his head for the rest of his life with all the material it would give him for conspiratorial books!"

"Sebastian, seriously? It hasn't been—"

"It has."

"Not true!" Silas's face was flushing, his breathing picking up speed with his growing frustration.

"Carbon dating, Silas. Listen, carbon dating by actual scientists three decades ago—not your Cracker Jack pack of miscreants—dated your bed sheet to the Middle Ages. Science, Silas. You should learn to spell it sometime. It would save you a world of heartache."

"So not true!"

Another snort at the other end.

"No, listen. That's what tomorrow is all about. Why I wanted to invite you. You're so keen to let science do all the talking and walking when it comes to questions and issues about faith and life. Well, tomorrow you'll get a head full of it!"

"Will I, now?" Sebastian sneered.

"Yes. Because tomorrow I'm going to prove to you, with science, that not only is the Shroud of Turin the burial cloth of Jesus. It contains scientific and historical evidence that Jesus rose from the dead. That the resurrection, which Matthew, Mark, Luke, and John all testify to, is real. Scientifically. Historically."

Silas realized he was breathing hard. And that he was talking louder and more animated than he intended.

He sat back in his seat and stared out the window. He had done it again. Not like last time. But close.

There was only silence.

"Seba?" Silas finally said. "Are you there?"

"I'm here," he said flatly.

Silas tipped his head back against his headrest. *Great. Once again, I alienate him.*

"So what about it? Why don't you come by, just for my opening? I really do think you'll find it interesting. As a scientist, I mean. A physicist who—"

"When are you going to stop?"

The question twisted his gut.

"Stop what?"

"Stop trying to convert me?"

"That's...that's not what this was about," Silas stuttered.

"Alright," Sebastian said.

"No, really. I don't want to convert you, Seba."

"Right."

"I mean, I'd love for you to come back to the Church. And I know I've said some things in the past. Hurtful things. But this time's different."

"Sure it is."

"No, it is. Listen. I just want you to hear the evidence. That's all. Come for my lecture, then leave. And if you want, we can grab dinner tomorrow evening before I head back."

His brother said nothing.

"How does that sound? No agenda. Other than intellectual curiosity."

Sebastian sighed. "I'll try and be there."

"You'll try and make it? You'll be there, then?"

"Yes, if nothing comes up in my morning. Because, you know, I am a successful professor at a highly prestigious university on a tenure track and all. I do have obligations."

Silas smiled. "Prestigious my ass." He thought he could detect a smile from the other end, too.

"Anyway, I should get going," Sebastian said. "These lab papers won't grade themselves."

"Right. That they won't."

Silence hung between the two brothers, a stretch of distance between them that seemed to grow with every phone call. Silas hoped tomorrow might change that.

"Thanks for the call. For letting me know you would be in town. Goodbye, big brother. And, hey, congrats on the keynote. I hope it does what you want it to do."

Me, too.

CHAPTER 8

WASHINGTON, DC.

S ilas was running late. Again. The hard spring rain didn't help, especially since he hadn't brought an umbrella. On top of the dismal morning, he slept not a wink, consumed with the fate of his research into the Shroud left behind in the wake of the bomb blast at MIT, and Stephen Avery's death. And he was already starting to get the jitters for his presentation at Georgetown.

A grande dark roast from Starbucks was just what the doctor ordered.

He tried using the blooming trees for cover as he made his way up the block to the coffee shop around the corner from his Georgetown hotel off M Street, but it was no use. Holding a newspaper he had snagged from the lobby above his head helped, but he was getting soaked.

He opened the door to the coffee chain and hit one of the patrons awaiting their own caffeinated relief. The man grunted and lurched forward.

"Gosh," Silas said. "Sorry about that."

The man was large, tall with a wide girth, and dressed in black with a black Kalansowa headdress embroidered with twelve gold crosses, resting on thick hair. He turned around to face Silas. When he did, Silas caught sight of a heavy gold chain with a gold crucifix attached hanging around the man's neck, peeking out from beneath a thick, wiry beard.

Not every day you see a Coptic priest standing in line at Starbucks. But he guessed even they needed their morning cup o' joe.

Silas smiled and mouthed "Sorry" again. The man smiled and nodded, but his face seemed to be trying to control annoyance and anger. He grunted again and faced the front, then stepped forward to the counter to place his order.

Silas unfolded his wet *Washington Post* and glanced at the front page while he waited. Economy was holding steady, as was the approval rating of the president. Which was no small feat considering his inexperience and penchant for the dramatic. He flipped to the international section and frowned when he saw a story about Syria and ISIS. He shook his head, feeling like the seven years he had lent Uncle Sam were a complete waste.

A commotion at the counter brought him out of his existential pity-party. Something to do with his new friend, the Coptic priest. For a man of the cloth, he was arguing rather heatedly with the Starbucks cashier. From what he gathered, the man's credit card had been declined, and he was telling the young woman to rerun it. She did, with the same result.

Time to help a brother out.

"Here, allow me," Silas said as he gently pushed past the man to lay a twenty-dollar bill on the counter.

The woman looked relieved. The man looked irritated.

He snatched the money and waved it in front of Silas. "No, I cannot accept," he said with a thick accent Silas placed in either Syria or Iraq. Not what he would have expected. And his skin was darker, too.

Silas smiled and took it. Then set it back on the counter. "It's the least I could do for plowing into you back there. After all, our Lord said it's better to give than to receive. Please, let me give you some coffee for your trouble."

The man held his scowl and checked his watch, then let his scowl fade and nodded. He grunted, then walked to the end of the coffee bar.

Silas watched him for a few seconds, then shook his head and mumbled, "You're welcome." He smiled at the woman, who thanked him and asked what he would like.

"Grande dark roast and multigrain bagel," he said.

"You've got it," she said grabbing a cup. "And this one's on the house."

He thanked her and told her to keep the change from the priest, then took his breakfast and walked back into the rain to hail a cab for Georgetown University.

Within a few minutes, he was sitting in the back of a yellow Ford Crown Victoria that smelled of pine trees and body odor. Between sips of the dark brew and bites of his buttered bagel, Silas looked over the notes he had finished preparing based on the research findings from the experiment he had run using the neutron flux detector. It was perfect, if he didn't say so himself. And massively controversial. It opened with an overview of current research and scientifically verified claims about the Shroud, before pivoting to the newest revelations that would send shock waves through the sindonology community. Not to mention the broader Church and world.

And he, Dr. Silas Grey, was the one breaking the news.

He suppressed a grin as his taxi bounded through the university's gated entrance and past the bronze statue of Bishop John Carroll, founder of the university, as it rounded the circular drive in front of Healy Hall, its façade weathered charcoal gray from age. He only wished his brother was there to witness the revealing. Maybe he would come in the end.

Silas handed the cabbie a twenty and climbed out of the vehicle. Thankfully, the rain had stopped.

He paused a moment to take in the sight of his old alma mater. He couldn't help but smile. It had been over a decade since he had set foot in the place. Bells from the hall's clock tower clanged loudly overhead, startling Silas and marking the nine o'clock hour. He frowned, but hustled up a set of stairs, across a mosaic of tiny, blue tiles marking its founding in 1789, then through sturdy wooden double doors that led into the hall, and out to the chapel in a center courtyard. The scent of cherry blossoms and the warm, misty morning air brought a flood of memories to the surface as he hustled through a canopy of cherry blossom trees and past a bubbling fountain to the modest red-bricked Dahlgren Chapel of the Sacred Heart for the most consequential lecture of his career.

It was six minutes past nine when he arrived. He had missed the glad-handing and the howdy-dos, which was fine. His gut tightened every time he had to make small talk at one of these events. The curse of an introvert.

The one-hundred-and-thirty-year-old chapel of cream-colored walls, vaulted by cherry wood beams and ceiling slats, and commanded by a massive, intricate stained-glass window of Jesus and the saints nestled between a bronze pipe organ behind the high altar was teeming with priests, all dressed in black cassocks and white frocks. Some sported scarlet piping and other shades, indicating their higher rank. Others were dressed in more modest suits and drab ties, betraying their Protestant heritage. Silas quickly scanned the hall, searching for Father Luke Arnold, chair of the American Council of Sindonology. He caught the man's glance from the front and quickly made his way to him before the morning was to commence.

"Silas," Father Arnold said smiling, grabbing his hand. "Good to see you, friend. Thanks again for filling in on such short notice. I had worried you wouldn't make it in light of yesterday's events in Boston."

"Me too. But I made it safe and sound last night. Did you hear about Steven Avery?"

Father Arnold bowed his head and shook it. "Yes, tragic. How are you doing with it all? First Henry and then Stephen? I know how much the two of them meant to you."

Silas nodded and breathed in deeply. "I'm OK." He paused. "Trying not to think about it, really."

Father Arnold nodded.

"Actually," Silas continued, "would you have some time this evening to talk about it?"

Father Arnold leaned in with concern, placing a hand on Silas's shoulder. "Sure. I'm here for you, Silas. Whatever you need."

Silas smiled slightly. "Thanks. How about wine tonight, after the final session?"

"Sounds good. Then we can chat about your presentation, too. Speaking of which..." Father Arnold looked past Silas and around the auditorium. "It looks like our friends are settling in for the morning. Are you ready?"

Silas smiled and patted his satchel. "Definitely."

"I saw your email this morning on the topic. Intriguing to be sure! *New Revelations of the Shroud: Leveraging Space-Age Technology to Uncover Ancient Truths.* You're not going to give this old man a heart attack, are you? Or unnecessary controversy?"

Silas laughed. "I can't promise either, Father."

Father Arnold smiled and patted him on the back. "Well, I look forward to hearing your remarks nonetheless. You're always one to provide thoughtful, thorough insights into the Shroud. Even for a Protestant!"

"Lapsed Catholic," Silas reminded Arnold.

"Even better!"

Silas laughed, adrenaline beginning to course through his veins in anticipation of the set of revelations he was about to unveil. He took his seat in the second row of polished wooden chairs as Father Arnold began his opening remarks. He rose to a walnut lectern on an elevated platform to the left of the altar and waited for the assembly to find their seats and wind down their conversations. "Greetings in the name of the Father, the Son, and the Holy Ghost. We gather together for this fiftieth annual gathering for the American Council of Sindonology during increasingly desperate times. Both inside and outside the Church."

Silas nodded along with several fellow believers seated around him. He pulled out his notes and began rehearsing his presentation, trying to pay attention to Father Arnold even as he finished his own preparations.

"Scandal has ruined the trust of the faithful in the authority and the institution of the Church. As a Catholic, I cannot deny this. But as Protestants, I must say you can't either. Financial and recent sexual scandals within all corners of the Church threaten our credibility."

Again, the room nodded in unison.

"Skepticism has lulled both believers and unbelievers into believing that the Church has nothing to offer their deep questions about faith and life. The New Atheists are leveraging the latest scientific advances and discoveries to bend toward their own agenda, insisting the Nietzschean Übermensch is finally emerging, and we can finally strip off the fanciful trappings of faith."

Father Arnold was sliding into a nice rhythm, riding the nods and verbal agreements like a Southern Baptist preacher.

"It is in the midst of this torrent of scandal and skepticism that we gather together as scholars and stewards of the Scriptures and the faith to explore and discover anew one of the most important relics of the Church that bore witness to the most important event of Christianity. The resurrection of Jesus, and his Holy Shroud. Perhaps the Shroud was preserved for such a time as this. To not only remind the faithful of the 'Why' behind our belief. But also draw the skeptics and seekers alike into the fold of Christ by scientifically and existentially testifying to the truth of his resurrection."

Again, more nods and verbal agreements. Silas made one

final pass of his notes, ensuring the pages were accounted for and in their correct order.

"Ladies, gentlemen, it is my privilege to open our gathering by presenting to you one of the younger members of our association. For most of us, he needs no introduction, a Catholic-in-Protestant clothing if there ever was one." The room laughed in agreement. So did Silas. "He has done more to advance our cause and the field of sindonology than most of us combined. And I trust that his opening remarks will further our understanding of the Shroud and its mission of drawing the world to Christ. So without further ado, I give you Dr. Silas Grey."

Silas stood and made his way up the platform to the lectern as the clapping crescendo died down. Father Arnold patted him reassuringly as he passed him before taking a seat a few rows from the front.

Silas arranged his notes on the lectern, then smiled and stared out at the crowd.

Time to make history.

CHAPTER 9

"Thank you, Father Arnold," Silas said, motioning to the man. "And thank you, members, for the privilege of sharing on this significant milestone in the history of sindonology. I came into this conversation in some ways through the back door. While I had grown up Catholic, I was far more interested in terrorizing my priest than confessing to him. It wasn't until my military service in Afghanistan, then later Iraq, that I had found interest in the Christian faith. Call it fox-hole syndrome. Living with what I had seen and heard and experienced in that war drove me to seek a deeper, greater meaning. It drove me into the arms of the resurrected Christ."

Silas paused to take a sip of water, his hand trembling slightly as he raised the short goblet of water to his mouth. He took a sip, then another, and set the glass down beneath the lectern.

"After my personal transformation experience at the hand of a Protestant military chaplain—much to the chagrin of Father Arnold." Silas smiled, the auditorium laughed. Father Arnold smiled and laughed, as well. "After that experience I set off on a pilgrimage, touring the famous holy sites. Church of the Holy Sepulcher. The Camino de Santiago. And Turin. It was there that I first met our faithful friend, the Holy Image of Christ.

"I'm sure we all have stories of our first encounters with the Shroud. Mine was the closest thing to a mystical encounter with Christ himself that I could imagine. That image pierced my soul. But it was even more than that. It was the reality that I was standing before tangible, existential proof of Jesus' resurrection that laid me flat.

"In the Gospel of John, the apostle Thomas was chided for requiring tangible proof that Jesus was really alive. Yet, Christ obliged. He showed Thomas his hands and feet. And he said future generations would be blessed for believing in him by faith, as countless Christians have since. And yet, I believe that Jesus still offers the memory of his nail-scarred hands and pierced side to countless people. The Shroud is that memory. And, just like Father Arnold, I believe it has been preserved for such a time as this. To be offered to men and women around the world as tangible, existential proof that Christ has died, Christ has risen, Christ will come again."

He stopped, scanning his crowd. Seeing they were with him, he turned over a page from his notes, readying for the big reveal.

"And today I come to offer new scientific evidence to show the Shroud is what all of us have been saying for decades is true. My hope is that it will be the proof the world needs not merely to believe in the Shroud. But believe in the One to whom the Shroud bears witness."

He stopped again, taking another sip of water. "But first. Let's remind ourselves of nine aspects of the Shroud that are already incontrovertible before I add two more that make it a slam-dunk case. Sound good?"

Several nodded and a few verbally agreed.

Silas smiled. "Good. First of all, the cloth is unique. Nowhere has any other cloth been found to have depicted the image of a dead man on its surface. Let me say that again: in the history of archaeology and the study of historical artifacts, nowhere have we come across a burial linen with a body imprint.

"Second, the imprinted cloth is old. The linen itself has existed for over 600 years as the so-called Shroud of Turin, and nearly 2,000 years as the Image of Edessa, named after a small town outside of ancient Antioch in modern Syria. While carbon dating in the '80s placed the Shroud's age in the middle ages, around AD 1300, new evidence has roundly discredited both the results and method of that dating. More modern evidence places the date comfortably within the timeframe that Jesus was said to have been crucified and buried in AD 33.

"Third, the linen used of this cloth is a herringbone twill most likely manufactured and distributed throughout the Mediterranean world at least two thousand years ago. This is crucial because it discredits the notion that the Shroud was a medieval forgery concocted by some confidence artist.

"Fourth, the imprints on the cloth are those of a real corpse in rigor mortis. This was the conclusion of multiple criminal pathologists during one of the most pivotal periods of dissecting and testing the Shroud in the '70s. One of those pathologists, a Dr. Vignon, said the anatomical realism was so precise that separation of serum and cellular mass was evident in many of the blood stains. This is an important characteristic of dried blood."

Silas stopped for effect, looking out at his audience.

"Moving on. Fifth, the man in the shroud was mutilated in exactly the same manner that the New Testament says Jesus of Nazareth was beaten, whipped, and executed by means of crucifixion."

"Not only is the blood significant pathological evidence of the Shroud's authenticity, but those same pathologists actually detected swelling around the eyes, the natural reaction of a live body to bruising from a beating. The New Testament claims Jesus was severely beaten before his crucifixion. Rigor mortis is also evident with the enlarged chest and distended feet, classic marks of an actual crucifixion."

Silas brought up on the screen an enhanced version of the Shroud in black and white. As the audience sat mesmerized by the image, Silas couldn't help but find it difficult to breathe, staring into the face he and others had come to believe was that of Jesus of Nazareth, the Christ. He took a moment, meditating upon the memory of his death and suffering for the sake of humanity. For the sake of Silas and his past. For Sebastian.

Silas swallowed before continuing. "This positive image taken from the negative one left on the Shroud shows in detail many of the historical markers that connect to the Gospel account of Jesus' death. The scourging marks, the lacerations around the head, his dislocated shoulder, the stab wound and nail marks. All inflicted while he was alive, according to scientists. And all consistent with the eyewitness accounts recorded in the Gospels.

"Sixth, the man was interred according to Jewish burial customs at the time, being laid in a sail-like linen shroud in the manner they required. Yet, he did not receive the ritual washing, as the New Testament indicates Jesus didn't, because of the Passover and Sabbath requirements for burying the dead."

"Seventh, the odds against this image being someone other than Jesus are astronomical. Anyone care to guess?"

There was silence.

Silas leaned in across his lectern for the kill. "225...billion to 1, according to Paul de Gail, a French Jesuit priest and engineer. And the newly discovered evidence I will offer today will finally put to rest the possibility that anyone other than Jesus of Nazareth is depicted in the Shroud. Not only that, it will scientifically prove a major doctrine of the Church and of Christ."

The audience murmured in anticipation. As Silas turned the page on his script, the door in the back creaked open, and a man entered. It was the Coptic priest he had helped out at Starbucks that morning. He waddled into the nave, searching for a place to sit. What a large man he was!

"Eighth," Silas continued, focusing his mind back to his presentation, "it is not unreasonable to conclude that the man in the Shroud is indeed the historical person we know of as Jesus of Nazareth, around whom—his life, death, and resurrection—the Christian faith was launched and built.

"But that leaves the ninth and final point unexplored. The most obvious question of them all that demands a response. The one I began this lecture with. The resurrection. That the man imprinted on the Shroud is that of Jesus of Nazareth doesn't in and of itself prove or disprove that Jesus came back to life and rose from the dead. But there are strong indications that, at the very least, something extraordinary and very unusual occurred in the cloth. And this morning I am pleased to share with you the results of an experiment that will definitively prove what happened inside the tomb, nay, inside the Shroud is what the Church has been claiming for two millennia and what the Gospels themselves testify to."

Silas stopped and blinked. The Coptic priest was still standing in the back, just behind the baptismal font of wood and marble. And for the first time that morning, Silas noticed something he hadn't noticed before. An important detail about the man's characteristics that an ex-Ranger should have caught the first time.

He wasn't that large after all.

Yes, the man was big. Appeared to be well over three hundred pounds. But where you would expect a jowly, flabby face, it was chiseled. Perhaps it was because of the distance and the angle at which Silas was now viewing the man, or maybe the lighting. But it was clear that the head attached to the roly-poly body was not the head of a roly-poly man.

Which, in that moment at the front of the chapel, begged the question: Who was this man?

And a second one: Why was he at the fiftieth annual gathering of the American Council of Sindonology?

Silas found his answer. Which was unfortunate. Because at that moment, his notes and Avery's letter revealing the scientific proof of Christ's resurrection were transforming into fireflies dancing in an updraft of fire and fury.

CHAPTER 10

The air was dense with heat and ash, a crematorium working overtime for a Tuesday morning. A series of residual blasts jolted Silas from unconsciousness.

He was crumpled a few yards away from where he had been presenting, thrown against the wood-panel wall underneath the massive stained-glass window. Mercifully, it hadn't shattered over him, for surely he would have been cut to ribbons. The rest of the chapel wasn't so lucky. Most other stained glass windows had been blown to kingdom come from the concussion blast, their shards strewn across the floor and piles of bodies like flavored ice. The entrance had been obliterated, slumping in a maw of death and destruction. A modest golden cross raised on a golden pole had been flung next to him, the crucifix of Jesus nowhere to be found, having been broken off in the blast. What a desecration! Surprisingly, the altar of solid oak still stood. Its lily-white runner and candles were nowhere to be found. But there it was, perhaps a testament to the presence of God even in the midst of such evil.

Silas attempted to right himself, but he found it painful to move. Both because his back was undulating in waves of pain—was it broken?—and because he was pinned down by something heavy and unwieldy.

The wooden lectern. That's what it was. It must have joined him in the morning blast after his lecture notes went up in flames.

Silas tried assessing the situation, his Ranger training trying to click into autopilot, but his mind was clouded by the sounds of confusion. It was as if a tuning fork were playing a high-pitched song on repeat, brought on by the blast no doubt, piercing the cries for help, adding to the chaos. He shook his head to try and reset his ears. It didn't work.

Silas could feel his heart slamming against his chest in waves of protest and fight-or-flight fear. His breathing became hard and labored. He clenched his eyes and gritted his teeth, trying to squelch the rising tide of anxiety transporting him back to that fateful day in Iraq. For years, sudden *bangs* and *booms* would similarly set him off, a car door or fireworks. Perhaps it was progress that he hadn't had an episode until he was at the center of a terrorist attack.

Silas tried to move again. A jolt of pain laid him flat on his back again. This time from his front left to his middle back. Cracked rib? He twisted left and felt his side. It was firm, but painful. Not cracked, bruised. Badly. He leaned back and tried to steady himself, a wave of nausea beginning to overtake him from the elevated blood pressure and ringing in his ear.

His mouth began to water, but he swallowed hard, finding a center of focus in his mind's eye to bring himself under control.

Focus, Grey. What the heck happened? How could you let this happen?

The picture began to draw into focus as he replayed the morning. It wasn't at all a Coptic priest he had been following. Obviously, that much was clear. The more he focused, the more he realized he wasn't Coptic. From the Middle East, perhaps, but not Arabic. The beard wasn't right. Persian. Had to be, the skin tone gave it away. Ashen and smooth.

The dress was right, though. The beard, long and bushy, a

pattern of wiry black and white hair. The heavy, chunky cross in the shape of the Copt's take on Jesus' boards of execution. Even the hat.

But again, the girth was all wrong. The nearly three-hundred-pound walrus was probably no more than two hundred pounds, tops. And of lean, hard muscle. Which meant underneath he was packing heat. Lots of powerful heat.

But why? A grouping of sindonologists made the most ridiculous of targets in a city full of high profile buildings and political conventions. That blowhard businessman from New York would have been a better spectacle for ISIS or al-Qaeda recruitment propaganda.

But a gathering of mostly octogenarian religious scholars blabbing about an obscure religious artifact? Did not compute.

How could he have missed it? Back in the service that sort of detail and mismatched appearance would have sounded the alarm. He would have doubled back and trailed him from a distance to get a read on the man, to discern his appearance and identity, his mission and motives. The man would never have gotten as far as the threshold of Georgetown University, much less the Dahlgren Chapel.

Epic fail, Grey.

Then it hit him: his satchel.

Avery's letter—containing the only scientific proof of Jesus' resurrection!

He leaned forward and frantically searched the surrounding area, but it was no use. He knew the letter was toast.

Silas laid back and cursed. His hearing began to return back to normal, even his breathing and heart rate were lowering. He strained against the heavy object of solid walnut pinning him to the ground. He finally managed to muscle it off himself, straining to sit upright in order to assess the damage.

The first thing he noticed was how wet it was. That was because a large hole had been punched through the roof and the morning rain had returned with force, filling the chapel like a cistern. It was met with hisses of protest and thick black smoke from the fires within the cauldron, the tentacles of its flames reaching along the walls and stretching into the heavens, trying to consume the chapel with fury.

The second thing he noticed was the body parts. Arms and legs were strewn about, as if a dog had shredded a toy chest full of stuffed animals. The back of the room was a black hole of nothingness, where no person was found that Silas could see. In the middle and off to the sides were people either screaming from the trauma or crawling and hobbling toward the front missing a leg or an arm or both. At least they were still alive. A few others near the front were like him, intact and fully-limbed because of the distance from the blast.

Father Arnold was one of them, lying motionless a few yards away in a pool of dark crimson. Probably flew ten or twenty feet in the air before landing in a pile of rumpled robes. Silas sat up to come to his aid but caught his breath at the feeling of yet more sharp pains. This time from his right side, and from something sticking out of his side.

A piece of the lectern had sliced into him like a dagger. Blood was oozing, not flowing. A good sign. Until he twisted sideways, then it gurgled up out of the wound. The shard was acting as a cork. Silas knew from his medical training that if he moved even a half inch one way or the other, blood would drain even more quickly, or he risked puncturing a vital organ if one hadn't been punctured already.

But Father Arnold.

Silas looked over to his old professor. He was still motionless. Probably dead. At that age, it was unlikely he survived being catapulted through the air, much less the blast from the bomb. Silas sighed with resignation, before noticing a third thing.

Shadowy figures were making their way through the maw of destruction where the entrance had stood and into the cauldron of rain and smoke and fire. Hope pulsed through Silas, and he sighed in relief. Help had arrived. Which seemed quick for first responders to such a chaotic disaster.

Too quick.

Silas squinted through the pain and rain, trying to focus on the visitors. Where he expected to see white shirts and medical bags, he instead saw images of blackness. And small, faint lights bobbing and emanating out from the darkness. The kind Silas would mount on his M4 carbine rifle back in Iraq while on mission for Uncle Sam.

Then, all at once, muted pops and short bursts of light began to fill the cavern of chaos.

Gunfire.

From a group of special forces.

Panic gripped Silas, sending him into action. He sat forward, bearing with the searing pain from both his bruised ribs and side wound, to shove off the anchor holding his legs to the ground.

Suddenly, a firm grip held him back. Actually, two strong grips, one on each arm. That's the last thing he remembered before feeling a slight pinprick in his neck and seeing the world go blacker than it already was.

CHAPTER 11

WEWELSBURG, GERMANY.

The blood was dark and thick, pooling at the bottom of the flask like mulled wine. Rudolf Borg watched it drip. *Drip. Drip.* Like the metronome from his childhood that kept him on pace at the piano keys in that old French orphanage.

Borg flexed his arm, quickening the pace of the red liquid through the yellow rubber tube. His mouth went dry at the memory of that wretched place. There were times he could still smell the stench of body odor and urine that caked the walls. Sometimes the screams and cries for help invaded his dreams, like a roach infestation that was always ready to come out to play as soon as the lights dimmed. And sometimes he would feel the touch of the priest who had pledged to care for him, protect him, nurture his soul. But he was thankful Jacob had shown him a way to extricate himself from the pain.

He flexed again, this time clenching his fist until it shook. His blood squirted into the flask stronger this time, rising to a steadier flow. He remembered the first time he had let his blood drain. It scared him, seeing his skin split open beneath the razor, his life's liquid rising to the surface along the tract, and then dribble down his forearm in a steady stream. And the pain was intense, like frozen winter air biting at his skin. It burned along the cut and beyond in both directions. At first, it was unbearable. But then it gave him a magical place to concentrate his shame and guilt, his humiliation and agony. The internal pain was able to escape through the external opening, draining away through his blood.

Borg squinted at the flask, measuring the amount of his life-blood that had drained into the vessel. It was enough for his purposes. Back then the cutting and draining were personal, visceral. It wasn't sacrifice as much as it was satisfaction. This time was different; it was his offering to the Universe, a tangible sign that he had fully divested himself for the cause. Before he gave out of weakness, now he gave out of strength. For he held the power of life and death over himself as much as the world.

Borg's phone vibrated as he slid the tube off from the needle sticking out from underneath his skin. It continued dancing along his well-worn desk as he squeezed down the tube the last remaining crimson liquid into the sacrificial vessel.

He licked his fingers, as the phone continued its waltz, the metallic, coppery taste of his own blood causing him to hunger for more.

In due time.

He sucked his fingers clean, then dried them on his pants and picked up the phone. He looked at the caller ID. Jacob Crowley. He smiled at the sight, but he was late.

He breathed in deeply while walking to a large window over-looking the courtyard, then slowly breathed it out.

"You're late. Again."

The only reply he received was the crackle of static. He pulled the phone from his ear and scowled at the piece.

"Hello?" Borg growled. "Jacob?"

"Yes. Sorry. Bad connection. We've had to make other arrangements given the city is now in lockdown after the morning's events."

"And what of those events?"

"Total and complete success."

A grin slowly reached upward. He began to breath more excitedly from a surge of adrenaline from victory.

"Sehr guter job, mein Lieber." *Excellent job, my dear.* "Then we've succeeded in wiping out every last one of those wretched Shroud experts keeping us from setting into motion our plan."

Silence again. But this time there was no static.

Borg sighed and looked at the face of his phone. Still connected.

"Hello? Jacob?"

"Yes, I'm here."

Then what's the problem?

"What aren't you telling me?" Borg demanded.

"We managed to eliminate most everyone."

"What do you mean *most*?"

There was another pause of silence, then more static.

"–escaped."

"Escaped? *Who* escaped? You were cut off by that blasted static."

"Silas Grey, sir."

Borg brought the phone to his side. He closed his eyes and clenched his teeth, willing his arms not to throw the device across the room. *Control yourself.*

"How did this happen? He was the one person whom I explicitly said had to be verifiably eliminated," Borg roared. "Verified, Crowley!" He cursed himself for using Jacob's last name, something so sterile, so less-than-intimate. Yet he had to reassert his control over the situation.

"I understand, Rudolf. It's all my fault." Jacob stopped, sounding like he was choking back emotion. "And I take full responsibility."

"Yes. You will." His affection for the man was outweighed at the moment by his commitment to the cause. Yet Borg knew he needed him to accomplish what he set out to execute. The man's muscle and experience with matters of security had proven invaluable. Up until now. But he was also his partner, in more ways than simply the cause. And if he was going to succeed, they needed to be on the same, intimate wavelength. Borg softened his tone in order to gird Jacob for the next phase of their mission.

"Explain, my dear," Borg said softly.

"The bomb went off as planned, in the middle of his presentation before Grey could make his revelations known. The radius was large enough to eliminate the vast majority of the people inside. The ones who survived the blast were eliminated by the team. But where we expected to find Grey, we only found blood."

"That makes no sense. Yes, the man had experience with such things, given his combat training. But how could he have survived such an explosion?"

"As far as we can figure it, sir, he was extracted. Had to have had help, given the loss of blood we saw."

"Extracted? But by who—" Borg stopped short. He breathed in deeply again, narrowing his eyes. "Ordo Thaddeum."

"That makes the most sense," Crowley agreed.

Borg cursed the added complication. No matter. He and his people had been fighting the Order for centuries. But they were no match for their might and resources. They would not succeed.

"You know what to do," Borg said.

"Yes, Grand Master. We've already set into motion some steps to mitigate any fallout."

"Good. Call the minute those...steps, are complete."

"Will do."

"And, Jacob," Borg added, "Fail me once, shame on you. Fail me twice, shame on me. I'm not in the mood for self-shame. Understand?"

Again, the silence and static.

"Do you understand?" Borg shouted into the device.

"Understand," Crowley replied, his voice quivering.

"Good. Because neither of us is greater than the cause. Failure is not an option."

CHAPTER 12

WASHINGTON, DC.

Where am I?

Silas tried blinking, but his eyelids felt heavy, stuck.

His stomach felt as if he were tumbling through space. Like a rollercoaster at his favorite Six Flags theme park. He slid back slightly as his world sped up, moving up and down at intervals that were not helping matters.

He breathed deeply, steadying himself before his world came into focus. He was shocked at what he saw.

He was in a small dingy in the middle of a vast body of water. A sea, perhaps, or even the ocean. Regardless, the expansive body of water was fierce and wavy, with a thick canopy of foreboding clouds that foretold of dangers to come.

Silas sat up, wincing at the sharp pain still radiating from both of his sides.

That's right. Bruised ribs and dagger of wood.

Yet when he felt his right side, the object that had pierced his lower abdomen was gone. He felt the flesh of his side, only to find smooth, hard muscled-skin. No wood, no scar, no nothing. Except the pain. He winced again, cursing himself for pressing in too hard, wondering what magic had overtaken him.

Another dip in the rollercoaster ride sent his stomach searching for stability. Seawater crashed over the sides, drenching him and filling his mouth with liquid salt. The wooden boat was threatening to capsize as the wind and the waves picked up steam. Silas sat straighter, steadying himself before noticing two oars resting at the belly of the boat. He grabbed them and positioned them in their fulcrums.

Might as well start rowing. Seize the situation, rather than be seized, his father always said.

He pushed the oars forward and pulled them back with force, willing the boat in any direction but there. When he did, he noticed something else had joined him on the open sea. Or perhaps it had always been there but was obscured by the wind and the waves.

Was it another boat? No, too small and narrow. It was bobbing in the water rather than floating. Almost like a—like a person...

Silas stood in the boat and squinted, his eyes straining for confirmation.

"Hey!" he screamed, waving his arms in the air. "Heeeyy!" he yelled louder.

The person pivoted toward him as a wave crested and smashed over their head. But before it did, Silas caught a glimpse of who it was. The face was unmistakable. Because it mirrored his own.

Sebastian?

The dense, dark water smothered any signs of remaining life on the open, raging sea.

"No!" Silas cried, struggling toward the stern of the small boat as more sea water crashed into him. He frantically searched for signs of his twin brother. "Sebastian!"

Silas jolted awake, snapping his eyes widely, furiously. He strained forward in the darkness, searching for his brother. Instead, he fell forward, face-first onto a cold, hard metal grating.

The floor of a tactical van, the kind his military unity had used in countless missions.

He strained to right himself, but his hands were tied, bound by the kinds of plastic restrainers he himself had used on suspects back in Basra. He strained again, pain blossoming on both sides of his body.

"Whoa, hey there," a voice called out calmingly. "Watch it!"

The pair of hands grabbed both arms to right Silas, but he refused. He thrashed wildly, struggling against the triple threat of the bindings, the pain, the human. He was unsuccessful at all three.

"Silas!" This time it was a woman. Middle-pitched, not sing-songy or high like you'd expect. But commanding, insistent. And unmistakably British. The force of her grip matched the tone and tenor of her voice. "Dr. Silas Grey, calm down. We're friends. We're not here to harm you."

Silas gave in to the dual grip, the ache in his sides forcing his hand. He was panting, trying to catch his breath. Probably the effects of coming out from whatever liquid they poked him with however-many-minutes ago.

"Friends? Are you kidding me?" he exclaimed. "You've got me drugged and bound in a dark-paneled van. Friends my ass!" Silas continued panting as he laid back against one of his assailants, trying to catch his breath and wrap his mind around the shift in circumstances.

The vehicle turned sharply, hitting a bump as it did, slamming both Silas and his new friend into the side wall.

"Gapinski! Slow down and watch it, would you?"

"Sorry," Silas heard from the front.

The woman righted Silas. He heard the switch of a blade and felt his arms move as it cut into the plastic binding his hands.

"There. Happy?" She asked, propping him up against the side wall. "Now, don't do anything stupid—not that you could anyway with the condition you're in."

Silas huffed. "Says you." He rubbed his wrists, then checked his right side. The shard had been removed. In its place were bandages tightly wrapped around his waist. He winced slightly as he pressed in, checking for damage.

"You were one lucky bloke, Dr. Grey," the woman said, settling in on Silas's other side. "The shard missed all major organs."

The British accent was now unmistakable. Silas quickly sized her up: tall for a woman, probably just over six foot; lean and muscled, it was clear she worked out; wearing tight-fitting combat clothes, the kind that a paramilitary unit would wear; armed with a handgun strapped to her side, a semi-automatic rifle was draped over her lap. This chick meant business.

"Did you do it? Fix me up?"

She nodded up front. "Gapinski did. After we extracted you from that bloody inferno at Georgetown."

Extracted? Sounded like a planned op, the kind he used to lead back in Iraq. In fact, that's how he and Colton became such good friends: the man had saved his ass from a firefight on the outskirts of Mosul after a hive of fighters had pinned him and his crew down in a market. Colton and his team of special forces had cleared the nest of Iraqi hornets, then saved him and his men. Extracted them, just like now.

A wave of nausea threatened to overcome Silas again as the van took a sharp turn. He bowed his head between his legs, this time his left side protested. The ribs.

"Jeez, Gapinski. Seriously!"

"Sorry!" bellowed a baritone up front. "Almost there. Ten minutes out."

"We've already given you some narcotics for the pain, but you'll get something stronger when we get to the command center. Poor thing."

He resented her pity. "I'll be fine," he grunted. "I've been worse." He turned toward the front, finding he was in familiar territory after all. In the distance, he saw the familiar pale Indiana limestone spires of the Washington National Cathedral glowing through the fog that had settled over the city.

Good. At least I'm still in DC! But who on earth are these people? Where on earth are they taking me? What on earth do they want? He decided he'd ask them himself.

"Who are you? Where are you taking me? What do you want?"

"Slow down pork-chop. We'll get to that. Just rest easy. You've got a lot of work to do?"

Pork-chop? Work?

He took a deep breath and leaned forward again, noticing the Cathedral was growing in size. He continued watching their journey, curious why it seemed like they were bee-lining it for America's church.

Then he realized they were bee-lining it for America's church.

"Hold on," Gapinski said from the front.

The man took a side street that brought them through a tree-lined neighborhood of red-brick and white-paneled houses stretching back to the nineteenth century. They sped past an elementary school with a weathered wooden swing set and soccer field. Blowing through a stop sign, the van took a sharp left into a drive entrance near the base of the north transept, the sacred structure looming large in the dead of night. Suddenly, the van disappeared through the black maw of a parking entrance and took a dip, moving swiftly underneath the national Christian architectural icon.

The edge of the narrow drivable passage was lined with LED lighting, showing the way downward and forward under the massive building. Old stonework shone in the faint light, before curving into a spiral that revealed newer masonry. Now they were turning ever downward, seemingly forever beneath the stately structure. Then they reached the bottom, which was vastly different than either the stone-lined passageway or the stone-built building above it.

The light had noticeably brightened into a dim white, shining off the large carpark of gray cement. Several cars, all black, were docked in parking spots, and a few more vans matching their own military-grade one. No doubt used for similar covert operations.

"Right, we're here," the woman said, the van coming to a halt.

"And where's that, exactly?" Silas asked as they exited through the back.

The air was cool and dehumidified, no doubt climate controlled for whatever activity was hidden away beneath the Cathedral.

Silas winced as he stepped out onto the concrete floor. He instinctively reached for the woman to steady himself, regretting his decision.

"You alright?" She held his outstretched arm with one hand and his back with the other.

Silas recoiled. "I'm fine," he grunted. He quickly walked from her help, breathing and willing himself through the pain, staggering as upright as he could manage.

"We'll get you morphine and get you to a bed after we debrief with Radcliffe."

"Who?" he moaned.

Before she could answer, glass doors up ahead *whooshed* open. A tall, portly man with graying, thinning hair wearing a black cassock, neck ringed by a white clerical collar, stepped out into the underground garage. He wore a tired, if not determined look, as if the future of the world rested on his shoulders. His long black cassock whispered as he walked to meet the arriving party, the carport light glinting off golden buttons.

Radcliffe, Silas presumed.

"Thank God you made it safe and sound." The man said in the same English-accented voice. He embraced the woman loosely, gently kissing her left cheek. She received it and kissed him back. Grandfather and granddaughter, perhaps?

"And Dr. Grey. I presume you've been given the utmost care during your extraction?"

Silas eyed the woman, Celeste. "Yes. It was...utmost."

"Splendid. And I assume you've met?"

Celeste stiffened and outstretched her hand.

"Celeste. Celeste Bourne."

Silas took it, the side of his mouth turning upward in a grin.

"Really?" he said, raising an eyebrow. "Bourne? Like Ludlum's confused fictional CIA covert action hero?"

Celeste narrowed her eyes and grinned weakly, letting her hand fall back to her side before stepping back slightly and folding her arms.

"I was a Bourne far before Bourne was a Bourne."

Silas put a hand up in surrender. "Nice to meet you. Celeste Bourne. And you must be Radcliffe Someone-or-other."

"Rowan Radcliffe, yes." Radcliffe stretched out his hand. Silas took it.

"Pleased to meet you, Rowan Radcliffe. Now, will someone tell me what the hell is going on? Why I've been—extracted? And where the hell you've taken me?"

"You're perfectly alright, Dr. Grey. We're friends."

"Yes, so I've been told. And Silas is fine."

Radcliffe smiled. "Alright, Silas. Let's take a walk." He stretched out his hand, motioning him to proceed forward.

Silas hesitated. He looked at Radcliffe, then at Celeste, before taking a step forward.

The glass doors gently swooshed open, the scent of sanitized air flooding his senses. They were in a hallway. It was slate gray and washed in the same dim, white light as the garage, and quiet. Which made sense since it was the middle of the night, though Silas half-expected the place to be swarming with men and women clad in either tight black-op gear or white lab coats. Something was going on here, that was for sure. But what?

Radcliffe stepped out in front. "This way, Silas. And we'll explain it all." He hurried forward, guiding their party to the right and down another hallway at a T-juncture. The hall was lined with windowless, nondescript doors, each armed with a keycard entry pad. It was as secure as any of the military installations Silas had worked in through his military career before joining Princeton. And below one of the most important religious buildings in America.

They arrived at a set of double doors at the end of yet another hallway. This one was armed with a palm-reading entry pad. Radcliffe placed his hand on the pad. It pulsed a light blue hue, before turning a solid green. Then the doors opened, revealing a very different room.

Instead of the sanitized slate gray, the room was entirely clad in dark wood. Cherry or mahogany. It was lined floor-to-ceiling with bookcases. At one end was a large stone fireplace, the kind a person could walk into if they desired. A fire was crackling away. At the other end was a large wooden desk, ornately designed with pillar legs and wooden sides. It reminded him of the time he stood before the Resolute desk in the Oval Office when a buddy of his gave him a tour of the White House after hours. Behind it was a series of monitors, all dark and hiding their purpose. The center of the room was commanded by a sizable Persian-style rug with two burgundy leather couches, complemented by four well-worn, overstuffed burgundy leather chairs. Radcliffe motioned for them to sit.

"You asked what was going on, where you were, and why you were brought here," Radcliffe began.

"Yes. Do fill me in, Father." He knew he was coming off as a jerk. But he didn't care. His sides ached, his head was pounding, and he wanted answers. And that morphine drip Celeste promised.

Rowan smiled, looking down at his robes. "Father, no longer. That was a long time ago. But I sympathize with your questions. I should think I'd be as freaked if the chapel in which I was lecturing was blown to smithereens, and then awoke to find myself in a van moving swiftly through the dead of night!"

He chuckled. Silas did not.

Radcliffe's face grew serious, he leaned forward. "Silas you've been the victim of a terrorist attack."

"No joke."

Rowan shook his head. "It's not what you think. This was not the work of some rogue cell of Muslims getting their jollies while showing off for ISIS."

"Got that much, Padre. Seeing that the man who blew himself to smithereens was a Coptic priest!"

"That was a ruse."

"No joke."

"We'd been tracking him and his crew the past week from Germany."

"Tracking?" Silas interrupted, leaning forward himself. He looked from Radcliffe to Celeste and back to Radcliffe again. "Who are you people?"

Radcliffe tilted his head and smiled warmly. "Why, we're the good guys, Silas."

CHAPTER 13

Silas sat back, trying to assess the situation, trying to work out what on earth he had stumbled into.

"It's hard for me to believe that you're the good guys, as you say," he said. "Given I was drugged and dragged against my will."

"Which was for your own protection," Celeste asserted.

"I'll be the judge of that," Silas asserted back.

Radcliffe interjected, "Had Celeste and her team not stepped in, things would be very different for you right now, Dr. Grey."

"Oh yeah? How so?"

"Because the same people responsible for that bomb blast are the same people who were responsible for the deaths of Dr. Gregory and Dr. Avery. And they were there to finish the job by taking you out."

Silas sat back and folded his arms. He had considered this himself on the drive over. But he wanted to hear it for himself.

"Explain."

Radcliffe sighed slightly. He crossed one leg over the other and settled into his chair, as if he had won a small victory.

"The perpetrators are an ancient adversary of the Church, called Nous."

"Nous?" Silas asked. "That's Greek for 'mind,' isn't it? Or 'reason.'"

"Divine reason, actually. It is Neoplatonic in origin stretching back to the early days of the Church. It has gone by many names over the ages. The 'mind's eye,' the 'inner consciousness' or 'inner knowledge.' It is considered to be the original divine principle, the eye of reason for comprehending the divine, leading to higher knowledge and salvation."

"Sounds like the kind of hippy, New Agey mumbo-jumbo some of my Princeton colleagues peddle."

Radcliffe chuckled. "This isn't Princeton variety, though they may recognize it, as the essence of its worldview is ancient Gnosticism."

"Sounds about right." He reached for his pocket to check on his stash of blue pills. His eyes widened slightly with satisfaction.

Thank God he still had his lifeline.

Radcliffe continued, "As you know, professor, this esoteric self-salvation through inner, divine knowledge has been something of a nemesis to the Church, stretching back to the earliest days of her existence."

Silas nodded. "Sure. The earliest heresies were gnostic in origin, teaching that salvation was reserved for a certain select few who could reach spiritual enlightenment and progress and push the human race forward."

"Exactly," Radcliffe agreed. "Nous and its various manifestations have all subscribed to *gnostikos*, the central kernel of gnostic teaching, beginning with the basic assumption of the divinity of the individual. The God-within, a God-consciousness that every person bears to greater or lesser degrees. Each person is a God-in-hiding, as they espouse. There is no sovereign deity, but lesser spirit-deities."

"Friedrich Nietzsche's Übermensch," Silas said, joining in the lecture. "Superman."

"Not Superman," Celeste corrected. "Overman."

Radcliffe smiled at Celeste's correction. Silas did not.

"Well, you're both right. The Übermensch of the German philosopher, or overman, is the essential aim of the Nousati. In fact, some of the highest-ranking Nazi officers were members of Nous. Joseph Goebbels, even Hitler himself were Nousati. Heinrich Himmler was a Grand Master. Which makes sense because Gnosticism and occultism are closely aligned. Pursuit of spiritual power through ritual magic is a constant theme throughout the history of Nous."

"Fascinating," Silas whispered, soaking up the deep-knowledge dive.

"If you've studied the occult at all, you know that the Shaman has a prominent place within the system of spiritual enlightenment. Gnostikos and Nousati are governed by such Guides, as they are known, the spiritual elite within the Nous caste system who steward human knowledge to help the masses climb out from the pit of ignorance and achieve spiritual enlightenment and salvation. Pantheistic to the core, Nousati believe God or the Divine invades all things, living and non-living. And they assume that pre-historical humans enjoyed uninhibited access to the kind of spiritual truth that would bring about a humanistic salvation."

"Hence the Shaman and the occultism," Silas added.

"Exactly. And Nous is the organizational manifestation of this ancient worldview. An organization that has laid hidden within the shadows of history, waging war against the Church. Oh, it has popped its head up here or there, to be sure. Beginning with Nicolaism in the book of Revelation, and Valentinus and Mani in the early centuries of the early Church. Joseph Smith reflected the Nousati in America with Mormonism, as did Carl Jung in Europe. The secret societies of the Illuminati and Masons were both tools of Nous. Even *Star Wars* and *The Matrix* subscribe to its essential teachings."

"As much as I love *Star Wars*, you're right. Gnostic to the core."

Silas paused to consider this. "Nous. That's the organization you're saying tried to blow me up?"

"Yes, Nous."

"Why haven't I heard about this group? After all, I am one of the foremost experts on Church history."

Radcliffe smiled. "Apparently not as foremost as one would think. Some of us have been following them for quite some time, trying to keep it at bay to preserve and contend for the faith. And stop Nous from destroying it."

"Destroying it? How do you mean?"

Radcliffe glanced at Celeste. "There is a...a militancy about Nous that has always threatened the Church and the faith. In the past, Nous struck at the heart of Christian ideas. Arianism for instance, and Arius and his followers' attacks on the deity of Jesus."

"Wait," Silas leaned forward. "Arius was Nousati?"

"Of course," Celeste answered matter-of-factly.

Silas rolled his eyes. "And we know that how?"

"We'll get to that, Silas," Radcliffe said. "So Nous through Arius attacked the very heart of the Christian faith by perpetuating an alternative version of Jesus. Speaking of alternatives, you're obviously familiar with the so-called Gnostic Gospels?"

"Obviously. Thank you, Dan Brown."

"All Nousati texts, crafted to undermine the essence of the authority of Scripture. So early on, Nous tried to undermine the essence of the Christian faith by destroying her teachings. And its power and influence has waxed and waned over the centuries and manifested in various ways."

"This is all fascinating, but you haven't answered my question."

Radcliffe sat back in his chair. "Which is?"

"Who are you? And what has any of this got to do with me?"

Again, Radcliffe glanced at Celeste. Then he leaned forward.

"Dr. Grey." He paused, as if considering his words. "We've brought you here not only for your own safety. Not merely to save your life."

"Thanks for that, by the way."

"Don't mention it," Celeste interrupted, the side of her mouth curling upward slightly.

Radcliffe continued, "We brought you here for something bigger. Something that Nous has been planning for some time to systematically destroy the Church."

Silas considered this language. Destroy the Church. "OK, we'll come back to that one, because...hello. Destroy the Church? I don't even know where to begin with that one. But you haven't answered my other question: who are you? Better yet: *what* are you?"

"Ordo Thaddeum," Radcliffe said.

Silas tilted his head and furrowed his brow in confusion. "Order of Thaddeus? Never heard of it."

"And you wouldn't," Radcliffe continued. "We've been working in the shadows as much as Nous has, protecting and preserving the memory of the Church from nearly the very beginning of her existence."

"Thaddeus..." Silas said, thinking out loud. "He was the disciple known as Jude. He wrote the letter to the churches in Asia Minor that bears his name."

"Exactly. And he was the founder of the order."

Silas scoffed. "Seriously? Orders, well, the ones we know of, weren't around then. The first one didn't even officially launch until the early Middle Ages. The Order of Saint Benedict, one of the earliest and most enduring, wasn't it?"

"Officially, you are right," Radcliffe acknowledged. "Unofficially, Thaddeus, or Saint Jude as he is also known, the patron saint of lost causes, was acutely aware of the forces already pressing in against the Church and the teachings of the faith. Just look at his letter! Jude told the Asia Minor Christians that he wanted to write to them about their wonderful salvation in Jesus, but there was a more urgent matter."

"*Contend for the faith that was once and for all entrusted to God's holy people,*" Silas mumbled. He had memorized the verse early in his Christian journey. He was drawn to its passion, to its conviction that there was an essence to the Christian faith that needed to be contended for. It's what launched him into his academic career in the first place. The one that brought him to Princeton to teach young people about the essence of Christianity. The one that brought him to tirelessly work to prove the Shroud. The one that drove him to speak with his brother about the faith.

"Exactly, Dr. Grey. Contend. Fight for. Preserve and protect. Not only the faith itself, but the shared, collective memory of the faith. Thaddeus had already seen evidence for the need to preserve and protect this memory. And, remember, this was within decades of the phenomenon of the Church launching from that Pentecost day. Within years of the Jesus movement launching and elements of the faith already being taught and memorized and recited—within years it was beginning to fray. There was the persecution on the outside from Rome and the Jewish authorities. That was bad enough, what with the beheadings and crucifixions and death-by-lion-mauling in the colosseums. But the more devious and dastardly and dangerous threat was on the inside from false teachers. People who wanted to pervert the message of God's grace into a license for immorality and to deny Jesus Christ our only Sovereign and Lord, as Jude wrote."

"Wait a minute. So Nous is an inside job?"

"Not exactly. But the Nousati have taken many forms. And Thaddeus knew this. He knew that even early on the Church needed to take proactive steps to preserve and protect, contend and fight for the memory of the faith. It is why we have the

Gospel accounts, after all. As well as all the letters from Paul, Peter, and John that were included in the canon of Scripture. And the others from Clement and Ignatius that weren't."

Silas folded his hands together, making a sort of tent, propping his elbows on his knees. His thinking posture. It was an interesting argument, and even more interesting revelation: the early apostles wrote their accounts of Jesus and their teachings about the Jesus Way to preserve the memory of the faith, and by nature allow the Church to contend for it. He liked that idea. That the Bible was both the Spirit's and Communion of Saint's memory-preservation effort.

"Of course, it didn't stop with the Bible..." Radcliffe trailed off, looking intently at Silas.

And then he knew. Radcliffe nodded.

"The Shroud," Silas whispered sitting forward, eyes widening, mouth going dry.

"The Shroud. And who was responsible for the Shroud's early debut?"

Again, lightbulbs. "Thaddeus! Of course."

"Yes, Thaddeus. And you know the story of good, old Abgar."

Silas did. He remembered being fascinated by the story of another Holy Image, the so-called Image of Edessa or Mandylion. The early Church historian Eusebius recalled the account about the ancient King of Edessa who had sent a letter to Jesus inviting him to visit. There was a more personal motivation to the invitation, though: he was suffering greatly from an incurable disease. And he had heard about the many miracles Jesus had performed south of his kingdom in Judea and Galilee. So he wanted in on the action. Who could blame him? Unfortunately, as the story goes, Jesus declined, but he promised the king that he would send along one of his disciples to cure him after his mission on earth was complete. And he did. Jesus' disciples sent Thaddeus, who had healed many while in Edessa. He also brought along with him something extraordinary: a linen cloth with a stunning likeness portrayed on its surface.

"And so, receiving the likeness from the apostle, immediately he felt his leprosy cleansed and gone," Radcliffe said, reciting the tenth-century account of the Shroud. "Having been instructed then by the apostle more clearly of the doctrine of truth, he asked about the likeness portrayed on the linen cloth. For when he had carefully inspected it, he saw that it did not consist of earthy colors, and he was astounded by its power."

"Impressive," Silas said. "You memorized the 'Story of the Image of Edessa.' So what? What's that got to do with me? And that terrorist attack at Georgetown. And some secret ninja society called Nous?"

Silas was getting irritated, exacerbated by the pain brought on by the weakening narcotics he had received earlier.

"Thaddeus established a church at Edessa early in the life of Christianity, now modern Syria. He brought with him the Shroud to preserve it. To preserve its memory, and the memory of Christ's resurrection contained within it. Which brings us to why you're here and what's going on."

Silas sat back and folded his arms, wishing he had his pills to make it all go away. "I'm listening."

"What happened at Georgetown University was no accident. It wasn't a fluke that the annual gathering of the foremost experts on the Shroud of Turin, who were all gathered together and sitting in one room like sitting ducks, just happened to be blown to bits. You do realize you were the only survivor, don't you?"

The news hit Silas in the face like a frying pan. His breath left him, his head swirled.

"Father Arnold..."

Celeste answered this time. "Another team extracted him and a few others who were—" She paused, searching for words. "Still intact. They didn't make it."

Silas's mouth fell. He heaved a breath, then huffed it out in disbelief.

Celeste continued. "And it was no accident that Stephen Avery and the others from across the globe were targeted, either."

"Nous?"

"Nous," Radcliffe confirmed.

Silas clenched his jaw and narrowed his eyes, regaining his composure after the momentary lapse. "What's going on, Radcliffe?"

"For the better part of nearly two millennia, the Nousati have been hell-bent on destroying the Holy Image, the essential object bearing the memory of the most essential event in Christianity."

"The resurrection of Jesus."

"Yes, the resurrection. It is, after all, the 'why' of the Christian faith. It is why the disciples early on were transformed from a bunch of petrified twenty-somethings into passionate men who died for a cause that challenged both the social and religious orders of the day. The Gospels obviously bear witness to this central event. For centuries this was enough. And they are, they should be. They are reliable records of eyewitness accounts that a man from Nazareth, a prophet, was crucified as an insurrectionist, a rebel against Empire Roman. As a terrorist, even. And then he came back to life and was witnessed by hundreds of people. Early manuscripts prove this account to be valid."

"But?" Silas asked, anticipating Radcliffe's argument.

"But things have changed. People want scientific, existential proof. They don't believe the eyewitness testimony of a religious text anymore. They certainly don't believe the historical, dogmatic teachings of an institution as storied as the Church."

Radcliffe paused, his eyes widening. He sat up straighter, moving to the edge of his chair. "The Shroud was preserved for such a time as this. I'm convinced of it. This relic...no, this *vessel* teaming with scientific, existential proof bears witness to the most important memory of the faith."

"And you believe, the Order believes that Nous or whatever is trying to destroy it?"

"Dr. Grey," Radcliffe said, staring into Silas's eyes. "Nous has set out to erase the memory of the resurrection of Jesus Christ. And we want you to stop them."

CHAPTER 14

CNN BREAKING NEWS REPORT

"This is a CNN Breaking News report," Anderson Cooper said, wearing a concerned-for-the-welfare-of-America furrowed face.

"We are still getting reports into the Breaking News studio this evening on the devastating blast that rocked southwest Washington, DC earlier in the day. The city is on a complete lockdown nearly twelve hours after the initial event. The Metro subway system has ceased operation within the district, and cars have been prevented from either entering or leaving the city, leaving commuters from the Maryland and Virginia suburbs stranded. Many have even taken the drastic step of walking across the George Washington Memorial Bridge to Northern Virginia to find alternative transportation home."

The camera changed angles, and Cooper followed.

"We now turn to CNN correspondent Mara Mitchell who is at ground zero on the campus of Georgetown University." Cooper swiveled in his chair to a large sixty-inch television monitor stage right as the camera pulled back. The television showed a well-made-up, blond reporter holding a CNN-emblazoned microphone standing next to a military Humvee, smoke billowing behind her from the face of the chapel.

"It has been an absolutely chaotic day, hasn't it, Mara? And I see you're standing next to a military vehicle of some sort. What's the latest from the events surrounding the act of terror in our nation's capital?"

"Yes, Anderson, it has been a chaotic day. And, yes," Mara gestured to the vehicle behind her, "this is a military Humvee. An army battalion out of Fort Belvoir in Northern Virginia was dispatched to the area within an hour of the attack. They quickly set up a secure perimeter around the blast site itself and took over search and rescue operations. I'm told that another military unit from the same division began quickly establishing checkpoints around the city, at the major highway entrances on I-95 and I-66 to latch down the city itself. Within that window, the President was taken to a secure location by helicopter, while the Vice President was taken to a separate location to ensure his security, as well. Because Congress was in session at the time, the Capitol Building was put on immediate lockdown, and Members of Congress secured within facilities deep underground the newest addition on the east promenade.

"Here is what we know so far," Mara continued, looking down to refer to a notepad. "Between 9:30 and 9:45 a.m., there was a massive explosion at the Dahlgren Chapel of the Sacred Heart on Georgetown University's main campus. The university is a liberal arts school affiliated with the Jesuits of the Catholic Church. They were hosting the fiftieth annual gathering of the American Council of Sindonologists, a group dedicated to the investigation and preservation of the Shroud of Turin, the purported burial cloth of Jesus Christ, which supposedly depicts an image of the man resulting from his resurrection."

Mara looked briefly down at her notes again before continuing. "We are told as of yet there have been no survivors of the horrific event. In total, nearly two hundred of the leading Protestant, Orthodox, and Catholic experts and other investigators of the Shroud perished in the blast. This comes on the heels of another similar, yet smaller terror event the previous day at MIT, where a hall of offices and lecture rooms was blown up by what was believed to be an IED, an improvised explosive device, probably in a backpack left in the building. Nearly two hundred students died in that blast, including professor Stephen Avery, a prominent physicist."

"So, Mara," Cooper interjected, "is the Administration labeling this domestic terrorism? Has anyone claimed responsibility?"

"So far, the Administration has only gone so far as to call it an act of terror, a bit of a nuance there. As of yet, no terrorist organization or individual has claimed responsibility. But Homeland Security, in coordination with several other intergovernmental agencies, is pursuing leads to determine whether what happened here at Georgetown is in any way connected to what happened at the MIT Physics Department and other terrorist activities by known terrorist organizations."

"Mara Mitchell bringing America a CNN Breaking News update from the site of the Georgetown University bombing. Thank you, Mara."

"Thank you, Anderson."

Cooper swiveled back to the camera, looking intently and resolutely into its lens. "Stay tuned to CNN and CNN.com to get all of the latest news and government updates on the act of terror at Georgetown University and the surrounding events unfolding in our nation's capital."

CHAPTER 15

Silas's sides continued aching for attention like a game of tug-of-war, waking him from a deep sleep. The pills were helping, as was the saline drip attached to his arm and the comfy recovery bed. Yet he hadn't felt this broken since the last time he was almost blown to smithereens.

He played with the tube coming out of his arm as he adjusted his bed. Radcliffe insisted that he lie down to let his body heal. Silas protested. And when Celeste demanded he get rest and recuperate, he complained even more loudly. In the end, his sides won the argument. The on-site doctors administered to him a cocktail of drugs, as well as injected steroid solution into each side to quicken the healing, but it would take a few days to come to full health.

Unfortunately, the Order didn't have a few days. Neither did the Church.

A soft purr emanated from the nightstand next to his bed. It was his phone. It had received a text.

Silas retrieved the device, bringing it to life.

"*R U ALIVE?!?!*" it read.

Silas smiled. It was Sebastian. In the chaos of the day's events and trying to grapple with the revelations of Nous and the Order, he had forgotten to phone home. Sebastian was prone to worry, and his penchant for theatrics made matters worse. Hence the all-caps, four-alarm text.

He texted back, "*Yes, baby brother. Made it out alive. I'm—*" He considered how he should put it in a way that maintained discretion. "*—recuperating. Will phone with details soon.*"

He sent it and leaned his head back, stretching right, then left. The tug-of-war continued.

His phone purred again. He looked down. "*GOOD!! YOU BETTER!!!*"

Silas chuckled. He went to set his phone back on the stand when another text came through: "*PROFESSOR??? ARE YOU ALIVE?!?!*"

It was Miles, freaking out as much as his brother. Probably more so.

Silas sent him a reply: "*Safe and sound! Was rescued by—*" How was he going to explain this one to his assistant? He typed, "*—a military unit.*" It was truth enough. He continued, "*Can't share more, too drained. Will be a while, so cancel my lectures for the week. How's Barnabas? Can you feed him a few more days?*"

He sent the message and waited. A few seconds later he saw the spinning, gray circle indicating Miles was typing a reply. "*Thank God!*" it read. "*We've been worried sick! CNN said terrorism! So you better spill the 411 pronto! Barnabas is fine. I've got him covered. Godspeed on your recovery!*"

"*Will do!*" Silas replied. He sighed and set the phone back on the stand. He sank into the bed and turned over to get some sleep. A knock on the door wouldn't let him.

Silas sat up. "Come in."

Radcliffe opened the door, followed by Celeste and Gapinski, the big guy who served as his chauffeur.

"Sorry to wake you," Radcliffe offered.

"No, it's fine. I was up anyway."

"How are you getting along? Is the pain being managed alright?"

Silas swung his legs around and onto the ground, wincing from both sides. "I've been in worse shape."

"Good. Because we need to talk about our offer."

"Ahh, yes. The offer of no uncertain danger and disaster by following the phantom you call Nous."

"It's no phantom, professor." It was Celeste. She stepped forward, crossing her arms.

"OK. Not a phantom. Got it. But this is your fight. Not mine."

"It is truly all our fight, Silas," Radcliffe corrected. "We've heard increased chatter from some known Nousati operatives. This isn't going away. And what happened at Georgetown is just the beginning. They are on a mission, we're certain of it."

"Oh, yeah? And what's that?"

"We're not entirely sure," Celeste said, stepping back in. "We know it has something to do with the Shroud. Hence the targeting of Gregory and the conference. And since you were the only survivor, I thought should think you would be ready to avenge."

Silas's eyes widened slightly and back stiffened. What do you say to that? So he said nothing.

"Targeting Gregory along with the other sindonologists suggests they are targeting the Shroud itself. And while it makes sense they might target a gathering of the American Council of Sindonologists, it seems they also targeted you."

Silas considered this. Then his gut tightened.

The data! If the threat against the Shroud was this real, and an organization called Nous was behind it, what lengths wouldn't they go to in order to suppress his findings? Especially the most significant of the results: proof of the neutron flux event embedded in the Shroud itself.

"Is something wrong, Silas?" Radcliffe asked.

Silas paused, then mumbled, "Stephen Avery..."

"Excuse me?" Celeste asked.

He cleared his throat. "Dr. Stephen Avery, a physics professor friend of mine, died the other day in a similar terrorist attack at MIT."

"Yes, we heard about that. Tragic. But what does that have to do with any of this?"

Silas glanced Radcliffe, then at Celeste. "Avery's death was no accident. We were working together on a project to authenticate the Shroud, a scientific experiment of sorts leveraging his expertise in nuclear physics. I had secured a piece of the relic through some channels at the Vatican to analyze it for trace indicators of a neutron flux event."

Radcliffe and Celeste both turned to each other, brows furrowed.

"I guess you didn't know that."

"No," Celeste answered, "we didn't."

"Perhaps you're paid overpaid, then."

Celeste smirked and folded her arms. "What, pray-tell, is a neutron flux event?"

"It's what results from a nuclear explosion," Radcliffe answered. "Or in the case of Jesus, a resurrection from the dead."

"Exactly," Silas continued. "We were verifying whether or not there was a scientifically verifiable trace of the resurrection event that could be measured and quantified within the Shroud fabric."

"And did you?" Radcliffe asked stepping forward slightly. "Verify a neutron flux even?"

Silas smiled. "I believe we did."

Radcliffe's eyes widened. He smiled in satisfaction and brought his arms up, shaking his fists with excitement. "Glory, this changes things, for sure!" He turned to Celeste, who also looked pleased.

Silas said, "Except the sample and the equipment were destroyed in the explosion at MIT."

Radcliffe frowned, slumping his shoulders. "Good God! But what about the data? Surely you had copies?"

Silas shook his head. "I hadn't received the data yet. It's what I was waiting on the day..." he trailed off, swallowing hard at the memory of Stephen's death. "Anyway, all Avery sent over was a single sheet of university stationery with a hand-scrawled note with his preliminary results. And that went up in smoke. But by all accounts, Avery discovered something significant. Said his analysis indicated particle radiation containing neutron flux."

Radcliffe staggered backward a step, as if he was blown back by the revelation, and its destruction.

Celeste looked at Silas. "Well, what about digital copies? If we can recover that, then we can broadcast it somehow and prove once and for all that the Shroud is authentic. That Jesus was resurrected. That he's alive."

"I'm guessing he had copies of the actual data from the experiment on the server at MIT."

"Then we need to get moving," Radcliffe said. "Follow us."

Silas stood up, his sides aching in protest. Not as painful as before, but still smarting. Before leaving his bed, Silas grabbed a bottle of pain meds the doctor had left him, as well as his own stash of little blue pills.

Radcliffe left the room, Celeste held the door open for Silas. He offered a weak smile of gratitude as he left. Radcliffe led him and the other two through a long hallway, around a series of bends, and into another room. This one was very different from the last room appointed with stately wood paneling and leather couches.

Instead, the room was gleaming with glass and brushed metal. It wasn't bright, but dimly white, lit from a series of lights running around the ceiling's periphery of the vast rectangular room. The rest of the light emanated from the array of computer screens that filled the room.

"What is this place?" Silas asked.

"Central command," Celeste answered.

"You could say that it is the nervous system of the Order of Thaddeus," Radcliffe added as they walked farther in toward the room's center. "At least one of the nodes in the system, anyway."

Celeste, Gapinski, and Silas continued following him toward a u-shaped desk, dominated by a series of screens in front and behind.

"Silas," Radcliffe said gesturing toward a young woman, "meet Zoe Corbino. She's our resident techie."

Zoe was petite with an olive complexion, sporting jet-black hair pulled back into a ponytail and wearing thick baby-blue plastic glasses and a wrinkled T-shirt and jeans. Straight out of a Palo Alto start-up. And Italian, if Silas were to place her. With a last name like Corbino, where else could she be from?

She took the hand Silas offered and shook it weakly. She pushed her glasses flush against her face, looked down, and then swiveled back around to the screens in front of her.

"Zoe, this is Dr. Silas Grey. He was the package from the GU extraction, and he has some mission-critical information we need your help with. Silas will explain."

Silas said, "You may have heard there was a similar bombing at MIT a few days ago."

"Sure did. All over the news."

"Well, it looks as though a friend of mine was targeted for his connection to me and his data."

At the word "data" Zoe's eyes seemed to light up. She flexed her fingers instinctively, eyes brightening with pleasure. Data was what she lived and breathed.

He continued, "We need that data. I had received preliminary findings indicating particle radiation with neutron fluxes were embedded in the Shroud linen, proving the resurrection." Silas stopped. "Until the only copy of those results was blown to high heaven!"

"I see," Zoe said turning to her computer. "MIT, you said?"

"Yes."

"Shouldn't be too difficult. Universities are known to have piss-poor data management and security. What was the name of the subject?"

"Steven Avery. He was from the applied sciences in the Physics Department."

"Roger that. Just give me a few minutes."

Zoe started typing, her fingers moving like a Rachmaninov protégé, her eyes fluttering around the screen in sync.

"We plucked Zoe out of a start-up in Palo Alto," Radcliffe said. *Called that one.*

"She's done wonders for the Order and for Project SEPIO."

Celeste turned abruptly and scowled at her boss. Radcliffe looked as surprised as Celeste, reddening slightly. Something he had just said clearly struck a nerve.

"Well, why not? If he's going to help us with the Shroud, he might as well know the entirety of our work?"

Celeste sighed, then folded her arms and nodded.

"Tell me what?" Silas said.

"About our little Vatican-endorsed project," Radcliffe said smirking.

Celeste huffed again, unfolding her arms and leaning against a metal desk.

"Don't mind her. She's a bit protective of her baby, SEPIO."

"SEPIO?" Silas asked.

"Project SEPIO. *Sepio, Erudio, Pugno, Inviglio, Observo.*"

Silas immediately homed in on the Latin, his mind quickly churning out an interpretation.

Celeste said, "It's Latin for—"

"Protect, instruct, fight for, watch over, heed," Silas interrupted.

Radcliffe raised his eyebrows in surprise, then turned to Celeste. "He's good."

Celeste rolled her eyes.

"So what is it? Some covert Vatican special-ops team?"

"You could say that. Around a decade ago, the Order realized it needed to take greater steps to preserve the memory of the faith. In the face of a number of threats from within and without, we realized the Church was quickly coming to a precipice from which it would never be able to walk back, unless we did something to deliberately preserve and protect the once-for-all faith and dogmatic tradition through faithfully passing it along and combating heresy. And Celeste here was recruited out of MI6 in London to lead the charge."

"So you're, what, Navy Seals for Jesus, then?"

Celeste smiled. "As you know, professor, *sepio* is Latin for 'surround with a hedge.' That's the mission of the project. To surround the memory of the faith with a hedge. To preserve and protect objects and relics of the faith, as well as the memory itself."

"Like the Shroud," Silas said.

"Like the Shroud and..." Celeste trailed off, as if not wanting to give away the secrets entirely to this unknown entity. "And other things," she said simply.

"We're mostly research-based," Radcliffe continued. "We also dabble in a bit of propaganda, you could say, seeking to broadcast the memory of the faith using new media, preservation mechanisms, and other exploits. But we also take seriously the 'P' in SEPIO."

Pugno. "Fight for," Silas said.

"That's where the special-ops part comes into play. Part of Celeste's duties is heading up the operations arm to fight for the memory. Technically, this more...kinetic aspect of the project falls under the Papal Gendarmerie Corps. The policing unit of the Vatican."

"So SEPIO is a Vatican-run initiative?" Silas asked.

"We're an ecumenical mission, with members from every

denomination. Protestant, Catholic, Orthodox. We even have some Southern Baptists on the force."

Makes sense.

Radcliffe stepped forward. "And this is why we've brought you here."

Silas's eyes narrowed as he considered this. "Because of my military background."

"That. And your academic one. You are the perfect marriage of what we look for in Sepioti. In agents of the Project and members of the Order." Radcliffe motioned toward Celeste. "You're almost a female doppelgänger of Celeste, here. As I mentioned, she was a former agent of MI6. But don't let those muscles fool you. She's got a Ph.D. from Oxford in comparative religion."

Oxford. Impressive.

"Your experience would go a long way in furthering our mission. Which I imagine you would be entirely on board with, given your own academic interests in the Shroud and the work you have done promoting and propagating the...what have you called it? The *vintage* Christian faith?"

Silas nodded, but said nothing. They had certainly done their homework on him.

"This matter of the Shroud is only the beginning. We've got agents following the activity of no less than eight Nousati cells."

"Doing what?"

"What Nousati do best," Celeste interjected. "Seeking the destruction of the Church."

Silas scoffed. "You keep saying that like the Church is some fragile entity that will just cease to exist with one puff of air. Like dandelion seeds puffed away into oblivion. The shared memory of the Christian faith is far too deep, runs far too long."

"But does it?" Radcliffe asked. "The amount of people in America self-identifying as Christian has dropped remarkably the last decade. And the rise of the so-called 'Nones,' those who don't identify with any sort of religion, is a phenomenon in-and-of itself."

"That doesn't prove the Church is in danger of collapse. Just our culture is."

"But you are forgetting the plummeting statistics on Bible reading and church attendance. And recent surveys show the beliefs Christians hold mirror heresies of the ancient Church. Which is no wonder, given how little regard we hold catechism and Christian education. A sermon on Sunday morning and a conversational Bible study during the week won't get the job done of informing and transforming people's minds in conformity with historic, orthodox Christian beliefs."

Silas nodded. "Look, you're preaching to the choir. So what's the solution?"

"Let it all burn," Celeste said, leaning back against Zoe's desk, looking over a monitor as she continued typing.

Radcliffe rolled his eyes and huffed. "You'll have to excuse her. She's a bit of a Negative Nancy when it comes to the Church. Some of us are more interested in renovating what we have, rather than tearing the thing down and building again from scratch, like Celeste."

Silas could sympathize with her sentiments. Having experienced the Christian faith from both the Catholic and Protestant sides of the aisle, he saw plenty that seemed to require a whole new structure.

"That's why the Order and SEPIO are so crucial," Radcliffe continued. "There are forces out to destroy the memory of the faith and the historic faith itself. Have been from the beginning. Dark, demonic forces, like Nous. This latest maneuver is just the latest in a long series of attempts to discredit and even destroy the Shroud over the centuries. Which is why your work is so crucial, Dr. Grey. Your data could be the final key that unlocks the powerful memory stored up within the Holy Image. Not only for the sake of those who don't believe in Jesus' resurrection. But also for those who do."

"Uhh, guys," Zoe interjected looking at her monitor, then at Celeste. "And lady."

Celeste smiled and winked.

Silas swung to the front of Zoe's desk to face her.

Radcliffe asked, "What do you have for us?"

"That's the problem. Nothing."

Silas looked wide-eyed at Radcliffe. He shrugged and shook his head. Silas looked back to Zoe. "Nothing?"

"Nothing. The folder is empty."

Silas breathed in sharply, his gut tightening with fear. "What does that mean?"

"It means you're out of luck, pal. The data's gone."

CHAPTER 16

"Gone?" Silas said, leaning forward. "What do you mean gone?"

"I sent out a bot to map the originating server, but all I got was error 500, probably because of the blast. Then I drilled into their redundancies and discovered Avery's user folder empty. Here, take a look." Zoe pointed to her screen.

Silas shuffled around behind her. "What am I looking at?"

"As I said, nothing. That's the problem."

"Alright, Spock. Spell it out."

She sighed with clear frustration at having to hand-hold the uninformed. "This is an FTP mapping program that reveals the files of an individual username on a local server, listing individual folders and files. In this case Stephen Avery's at MIT."

"It's blank."

Zoe snorted. "I'd say."

"Where are the files?" Silas asked, panicked.

"Hasta la vista, baby." Zoe cleared her throat. "Gone. Wiped clean, from the looks of it. And whoever managed to crack in there cleaned up any trace of their existence. There's no path in or out."

"So you can't say who or what did this?" Radcliffe asked.

Zoe looked up at Radcliffe and shook her head. "Nope."

"And there's no way we can retrieve the files?" Silas asked folding his arms.

"Nope. Sorry."

Silas cursed and pounded Zoe's desk. He turned away and raked his hand over his close-cropped hair and started pacing. The culmination of his academic work had just gone up in digital smoke. The one thing that could have convinced his brother of the authenticity of the Christian faith had vanished.

He stopped, remembering the words of Jesus from the Gospel of John. The ones he had for his disciple Thomas: "Thomas, because you have seen Me, you have believed. Blessed are those who have not seen and yet have believed."

For thousands of years, people had embraced Jesus as Lord and Savior—*resurrected* Lord and *resurrected* Savior—without the aid of the Shroud. They had believed without "seeing" the evidence that Jesus was alive, as Silas had been trying to prove. Why should it be any different now? Even for Sebastian?

Silas stopped pacing and sighed. And yet he couldn't shake the feeling that the Shroud had been preserved for such a time as this. By the Holy Spirit himself. Thomas had needed tangible proof, had needed to touch the nail holes and put his finger inside his Savior's wounded side to believe. And Jesus seemed to be OK with it. Why not today, with the photographic image left behind on a burial cloth when he burst forth from the tomb in full, resurrected glory?

Silas had a thought. A glimmer of hope.

"Zoe," he said, hustling back over to the tech genius's workstation. "These kinds of networks are often merely mainframe mirrors to professors' and students' desktop or laptop computers, correct? I mean that's the way it's set up at Princeton."

Zoe leaned back and put her hands behind her head. She nodded. "Probably right. Institutions of higher education aren't the brightest LED bulbs in the tech world, that's for sure."

"So Avery's results could very well have been stored locally, on his computer in his office. Isn't that possible?"

"It's possible," she said skeptically. "If it hadn't been incinerated when that bomb blew up—" She stopped short. Then looked at Silas. "Sorry. I know he was your friend."

"Thanks. He was." Silas turned to Radcliffe. "We need to assemble a team and get to that office ASAP to see if anything survived."

"Slow down. For what purpose?" Celeste asked.

Silas turned to her and furrowed his brow. "For what purpose? Did you not just hear her? The data from Avery's tests could very well be on his office computer!"

"And what if it is? What's the operational benefit?"

Silas made a face showing his confusion and cocked his head. "Tangible operational benefit?" He looked to Radcliffe for help.

"Yes," Celeste said, stepping closer. "If I'm going to risk my peoples' necks I need to know that it isn't for some personal snipe hunt."

Silas narrowed his eyes and folded his arms. "This isn't about me or my own personal agenda," he growled. "It's proof that the Shroud is genuine. The real burial cloth of Jesus. Scientific, historical proof that he rose from the dead."

He paused and stared at Celeste. She met his gaze. He turned to Radcliffe.

"You said you needed my help to stop Nous from undermining and destroying the Christian faith. Well, this is how I know how. This is it. Those files. If we can provide evidence the Shroud experienced a neutron flux event, the effects of a small nuclear blast, we can prove Jesus rose from the dead. If we can prove Jesus is alive, we prove not only the Gospel accounts are historically accurate, but that the heart of the Christian faith is real. That Christianity itself is real. Prove that and Nous is done for."

Radcliffe looked at Celeste, nodding in agreement. "He's right. Assemble a team. Silas will accompany you as co-lead."

Celeste opened her mouth slightly, as if she was about to protest. But then closed it tightly. She nodded, then turned to Silas.

"Alright, prof. Let's see if that Ranger training did you any good."

AFTER MAKING calls to three other SEPIO operatives, Celeste led Silas went back down the hallway toward the room they had gathered in when they had first arrived. They turned left down a separate hall, which dead-ended into another door with a security device.

Silas watched as Celeste placed her hand on the palm-reading device. It was larger than he had first noticed, attached to a well-muscled, tan arm. The black suit fit her well, accentuating her curves and highlighting her height. She was just about his height, which intimidated him slightly. Tall women were strong women, which had gotten Silas into trouble in the past. And she looked like trouble.

"Can I help you?"

Silas looked up, wide-eyed. The palm-reading device had finished its duty. The door was opening, and Celeste was looking at him, a smile curled on one side of her face, her amethyst eyes meeting his to inquire of his little exploration expedition.

"Uh, nothing."

"Good, then go inside."

He looked down, then back at those blue eyes. Celeste had motioned with her hand to go through the door, so he did. He pulled his collar up closer to his neck as he entered to hide its reddening.

The room was dim. In the middle was a polished steel rectangular table. Around the room was arrayed a collection of assault rifles and handguns. A case of detonation devices, too. Probably flash grenades and smoke bombs.

Silas whistled as he took in the Order's cache of weapons, appreciating their sophistication and strength. "God's armory for God's little army."

"Over the years SEPIO has found it wise to prepare for every possible contingency."

"True Navy SEALs for Jesus, aren't you?"

Celeste smiled, then walked over to a wall with a case of assault rifles. She opened it, then grabbed one. "Here."

Celeste tossed the weapon to Silas. He grabbed it with one hand. She smiled again. "Nice catch."

"What's this for?"

"Protection. Who knows what we'll find at the university when we arrive?"

Silas shook his head, then set the rifle down on the table. "Thanks for the party favor and all, but I laid down my weapons seven years ago when I left the Rangers."

"Yes, a decorated one at that."

"I can hold my own, if that's what you're implying."

Celeste smirked and leaned against the case. "You are what American's call a military brat. Father was Lieutenant General Grey, stationed at the Pentagon when a plane careened into the south-facing wall on that dreaded September 11, 2001, morning. You were finishing up at Georgetown University. A junior, but whip-smart. Finished in three years. Had a promising career ahead of you, then signed-up with the Army Rangers. As at Georgetown, you were first in your class at Camp Darby at Fort Benning. Led seven covert missions deep within the combat zones of Iraq and Afghanistan. Even the recipient of the coveted Purple Heart."

Silas narrowed his eyes, then rolled them at the credential run-down. "Sounds like you've got me all figured out, Bourne." He picked the weapon back up and held it out, closing one eye and sighting down the barrel. He flipped it over, inspecting the underside of the charcoal-black military standard issue.

"And then you traded that promising career," Celeste continued, "for the academy. Why?"

Silas looked up. "What is this, twenty questions?"

She folded her arms. "Just like to know who I'm dealing with. Now that we're partners and all."

He set the weapon back down. He pulled out a chair, sat down, then propped his feet on its surface.

"Alright. You wanna know who you're dealing with? A buddy of mine was blown up after our convoy ran into a series of carefully placed IEDs in the middle of Fallujah. The whole left side of our vehicle exploded, along with the left side of his body. The right side landed on top of me after our vehicle toppled over. That was right before the fire-fight broke out that killed four more of my buddies and I nearly died myself."

Silas paused, staring at Celeste before continuing. "Then I found Jesus, and Zoloft. And the rest is history."

Celeste unfolded her arms and stood straighter. "Sounds like you've had quite the journey."

"You could say that." He stood back up and picked up the rifle.

The door unlocked and opened, causing Celeste and Silas to look in its direction. The rest of the crew had arrived.

"Sounds like we've got a party on our hands," Gapinski said stepping into the room, followed by two more well-muscled men.

Celeste walked over to Gapinski and shook his hand. "You remember Gapinski from your ride over. The guy who saved your ass from Georgetown." She smiled and winked.

Silas smiled back. "I've been meaning to thank you for that."

"Don't mention it," Gapinski said, walking over to the case of assault rifles and picking one out for himself.

Celeste said, "This is Dax, that's Greer."

Silas rose from the chair and shook their hands. "Welcome to the party."

The five of them sat around the table. Celeste laid out the nature and objectives of their mission: locate Stephen Avery's computer; determine if any data survived the initial Nous assault; extract data and/or computer; return to SEPIO headquarters.

"Sounds easy enough," Gapinski said.

"Who's the new guy? He coming with us?" It was Dax. Looked like a farmhand from Iowa: lean, young, and sporting a blond crew-cut.

Silas looked at Celeste, then walked over to a case of handguns.

She replied, "Dr. Silas Grey. And, yes, he's with us."

"Doc Grey?" Dax replied, eyeing Silas as he slid out a drawer to choose a weapon. Beretta M6. His weapon of choice, even if the Army did replace it with the SIG Sauer P320.

"Let's lock and load," Silas said, turning around and sliding in a magazine.

"You sure you can handle that doc?" Dax asked.

He glanced at Celeste. "I can handle myself, kid. Can you, farm boy?"

Then he walked out the door. The rest followed.

CHAPTER 17

The newly-minted, five-person SEPIO operatives boarded a helicopter for Reagan National Airport. A private plane belonging to the Order was prepped and ready to ferry them to Boston.

The ride brought Silas back to one of his night-time missions in Iraq, and their objective: Ali Hassan al-Majid, aka Chemical Ali. The so-called King of Spades from the deck invented by the Pentagon listing the people connected to 9/11 or were high-value targets in the war on terror.

He led a team similar to the one he was co-leading with Celeste. It was small, the men dedicated and trained to take out threats to the United States and its way of life. The plan was to land a quarter mile north of a compound identified by a well-placed asset, then hoof it from there to maximize surprise. The landing went as planned, but when they arrived at the compound, it erupted in gunfire. It was supposed to have been sound asleep, but it was as if someone had poked a hornet's nest.

He and his men were forced back from the fight to the staging ground of the awaiting helicopters. Only one problem: his lieutenant was missing. And the hornets from the nest had begun converging on their location.

Embedded in the heart and soul of every Ranger is the creedal declaration: "I will never leave a fallen comrade to fall into the hands of the enemy." Silas lived by that creed. He left the small crew of four to search for, and then retrieve, the body of their fallen fellow soldier. Which earned him that Purple Star Celeste had reminded him.

As they boarded the awaiting jet on the tarmac of Regan National, he hoped there wouldn't be a replay of the night that still woke him in a cold-sweat panic from time to time.

The flight from DC to Boston was an hour and twenty minutes, putting them at MIT by 3:00 a.m. at the latest. Plenty of time to get in and get out without a soul knowing. At least that was the plan. Silas took advantage of the airtime by reclining his seat to catch a bit of shut-eye. He had forgotten how weak he still was from the bombing less than twenty hours prior. His sides still ached from the blast, though whatever it was the Order medical team did had worked wonders. Far better than any treatment he had received in the military. He drifted off quickly, shutting out the day's events.

He jolted awake after what seemed like minutes, instinctively grabbing the wrist that was shaking his shoulder. Ranger instincts. It was Celeste. They had arrived in Boston. Greer, Dax, and Gapinski were descending the stairs from the open door.

He winced when he sat up. Celeste noticed. Must have rested on it wrong.

"You up for this?" she asked, offering her hand to help him stand.

He looked at it but didn't take it. He stood himself. "I'll be fine." He leaned over and retrieved his dark nylon jacket and grabbed the weapon resting next to it, then walked out into the chilly pre-dawn air.

Celeste lowered her arm, then smiled and shook her head. "I better not have to save your ass again," she said following him.

A black Ford Expedition was waiting, fully fueled and heated.

Gapinski got into the driver's seat, assuming the position he had when he and Silas first met. Celeste followed him into the front passenger's seat. Dax and Greer climbed into the back-most seat, leaving Silas in the middle.

As they drove away from the airport and began making their way through the windy streets of Boston, adrenaline was beginning to shift Silas into higher gear. And that feeling of controlled nervousness, tempered by a moderate invincibility he had honed during his years with the Rangers, began to kick in. He closed his eyes and started counting backward from a thousand, a pre-engagement ritual he had developed in boot camp.

989, 988, 987, 986...

He was so close to getting what he had been working toward for so long. Proof of the authenticity of the Shroud, and of Jesus' resurrection. He would finally get the respect he deserved at Princeton. And that tenure he had been waiting for. How could the board overlook his monumental scholarly discovery?

943, 942, 941, 940, 939...

He chided himself. It wasn't just about the academic accolades. He knew it was more than that. Perhaps his brother would finally believe.

902, 901, 900, 899...

"So, prof," a voice said from behind Silas, interrupting his train of counting.

He opened his eyes and looked around to his left. He felt a tap on his right shoulder.

"Other side, prof."

It was Dax. Silas sighed and pivoted around to his right. He grunted, "Can I help you?"

"I'm not sure annoyance is needed right now."

"Neither am I sure talking is."

Dax held his hands up in surrender. "Didn't mean to offend. Just had a question for you to break the tension."

Silas pivoted back to the front. "I'm not sure how many

missions you've been on, lad, but where I come from, you don't interrupt a man's pre-mission ritual. You shut your mouth until the LZ."

"And where do you come from?" Gapinski asked from the front.

"The Middle East. Yourself?"

Gapinski took his eyes off the road and quickly looked back at Silas. "Spent some time in Europe."

Silas laughed. "That's what I thought. You think moonlighting on some comfy military base in Germany gives you the street cred to take on what we might be facing at MIT? A hundred bucks you did the NATO duty."

There was more silence from the front, and throat clearing in the back.

Silas dropped his head, shaking it. "Damn newbs. By the way, what was your question, Dax?"

It took Dax a beat to respond. "What's your stake in all of this?"

"Excuse me?" Silas said turning around.

"What's this computer hard drive or data or whatever mean to you? Why's it so important?"

Silas noticed Celeste turn around. She looked as curious, as if she had the same question.

"It's...professional." He skipped a beat before adding, "And personal."

"Professional, huh?" Dax said. "Well, I hope it's worth it."

Silas said nothing.

"Dax," Celeste said. "Cut it out. The history of the Church depends on it. So, yeah. I'd say it's worth it."

Dax sat straighter and nodded.

"We're here," Gapinski said.

Silas sat straighter too, scooting to the edge of his seat to get a better view out the front.

Gapinski turned the lights of their Expedition off as they

wheeled through the entrance to the campus. Up ahead Silas could see the charred husk of the Physics department. They parked a few blocks away and quickly emptied the vehicle.

So sorry, Stephen, Silas thought as he shoved his Beretta in the back of his pants. *But I pray to God you made a backup!*

Celeste nodded toward Silas, and said, "He and I will take point. The three of you fan out behind us. I doubt Nous would be so stupid as to have anyone sulking in the shadows after their stunt, but you never know. So stay sharp. Keep watch."

Greer, Dax, and Gapinski nodded in understanding.

Celeste took out the magazine to her SIG Sauer P226, eyed it, and then shoved it back in. "Right, let's do this."

The group walked quickly toward their destination, avoiding the street lamps that dotted the campus walkways. Fortunately for them, heavy clouds hung above them in the early morning sky, shielding their presence from the full moon above.

A misty fog clung to the ground as the group padded across the quad, making quick speed from their van to the chard husk of the former Physics department. Yellow "Caution: Do Not Enter" tape ringed the building, creating a healthy perimeter. Authorities had sealed the building post-blast, both for their pending investigation as well as for safety.

Greer trotted forward and lifted the yellow band. The other four quickly ducked beneath and continued making their way into the devastated building. Glass crunched beneath their feet, having been blown out of the windows from the concussion blast deeper inside.

"Over here," Celeste said, motioning toward one of the blown-out windows.

Dax and Gapinski made quick work clearing the large picture window of any remaining glass, moving their gloved hands over the mangled frame to clear the way for the team.

Silas climbed through the window first. The smell of burnt combustion, carpet, and bodies still clung to the inside air. He surveyed the damage as the others climbed in behind him, the memory of yesterday morning flooding to the surface.

He felt his chest tighten, his breathing became labored, his pulse quickened. The thought of what happened to Avery in this building overwhelmed him. As did the memory of Colton in the back of a military Humvee in Iraq.

"You OK?"

Silas was jolted from his trance. He turned to Celeste. He realized his eyes were slightly widened, and he was searching for air.

"You're not choking are you, doc?" Dax said, brushing past him farther into the darkened building.

Embarrassed, Silas clenched his jaw and nodded, then pushed forward himself, following Dax to a large stairwell up ahead stretching the height of the five-story building. Greer and Gapinski followed him, Celeste brought up the rear.

"Alright, doc," Dax said, turning to Silas. "Which floor was your buddy stationed?"

"Third," Silas said. "And I believe toward the back."

Celeste walked toward a framed directory on the wall adjacent to the stairs. She ran her index finger up toward the top, searching for AVERY.

"That's right. Third floor. Number 323."

"Lead the way." Dax held out his arm, motioning Silas to lead the ascent.

He looked at Celeste, then headed up the stairwell.

The quintuple echoed as they climbed, their nylon clothes swishing and boots tapping slightly as they ascended. Silas looked down, motioning with his hand to quiet, fearing they would give away their presence if a rent-a-cop decided to drop in on the place for a midnight security check.

Silas reached the third floor; the rest fell in behind. He reached for the door but held off opening it. He looked in through the small glass window.

"What are you waiting for?" Celeste whispered.

Silas rolled his eyes. "Just wait a second."

Red light from an exit sign at the end of the hallway bathed the large corridor. He counted down the row of doorways, seeking Stephen's office. He could tell from the two doors closest to him that the numbering scheme mirrored addresses on a street: evens on one side, odds on the other. He counted down eleven doorways...seventeen, nineteen, twenty-one.

That's when he saw it. The door to 323 was slightly ajar. The red light gave it way, casting a dark-wedge shadow inside the doorway where there should be a straight line.

Silas snapped his head toward Celeste and licked his lips. "His door's opened."

"Door's opened?" She replied.

"Avery's door. It's slightly ajar. Why would a dead man's office be opened at this hour?"

"Maybe it was left opened as part of the investigation," Dax wondered.

"Or he forgot to close it yesterday morning," Gapinski offered.

"Or someone's inside who shouldn't be there," Greer said.

Silas turned to him and nodded. He looked to Celeste, who nodded in agreement. He drew his Beretta from behind his waistband and raised it to his chest, fingers flexing around the grip in anticipation for what lay ahead. He held up two fingers, then pointed at Celeste and himself. He motioned toward the door, then motioned toward Gapinski and Dax to fall in behind with Greer at the door.

The four nodded and fell into place.

A loud shaking below caught their attention. Silas swore under his breath. Gapinski and Dax echoed in agreement.

They immediately fell to a crouching position and moved away from the edge that overlooked the common area below.

It was the main door to the building. A saber of light sliced through the darkened space, casting harsh, angular shadows on the wall above as it searched the interior space for intruders.

Rent-a-cop on midnight security duty.

Dax and Gapinski looked at each other. Greer kept watch at the stairs. Celeste peered over the edge. Silas shook his head, willing the man to move along.

The doors shook again, rattling Silas as much as the doors. Then the light shut off. And the man walked away. They could hear him whistling, utterly oblivious to what was happening inside.

Silas sighed. So did Celeste. Dax stood back up, helping Silas stand. As did Gapinski who grabbed Celeste's hand. Greer stood and positioned himself at the door, ready to open it for Silas and Celeste, then Gapinski and Dax.

It was go time.

CHAPTER 18

Silas looked at Greer, who had grabbed the door handle, readying himself to open it. He waited a beat, ducking slightly to ready himself to pad through the door toward Avery's office. Then he nodded to Greer to open the door.

Except it wouldn't budge.

Like a coiled spring, Silas had jolted slightly toward the door to move inside, before realizing it hadn't opened. He looked at Greer irritated, then down at the handle.

Greer was tugging at it. But it was locked.

Silas sighed, then put his hands on his hips and looked down.

Celeste pressed her hand against his right shoulder to move him out of the way. She slipped a small rectangular sleeve from her back pocket and crouched low at the doorknob. She chose her instruments, then brought two thin, metal pins up to the lock. She worked the pick carefully, turning her head toward Silas to concentrate. She leaned in as she worked the two metal pieces, then there was a soft click.

Celeste stood and quickly stowed away their little saviors in her back pocket, then motioned for Greer to start the falsely started operation over again.

This time the door swung open.

Silas slid inside, followed by Celeste.

The space was high and wide, with small trees commanding the center divide. They stretched upwards toward skylights, which were beginning to shine with the soft light of the moon peeking through the parting clouds above. Two exit signs filled the space with dull red light and a slight humming sound. Cool, filtered air blew against their skin from a sturdy HVAC unit.

Every one of Silas's muscles was taut as he padded carefully into the carpeted hallway, his rubber-soled boots making barely any sound. He leaned toward the left wall and tried the first office door, number 302.

Locked.

They needed protection as they confronted the open door at the end of the expansive hallway. He motioned toward Celeste to move ahead and do the same at office 304.

She complied, then shook her head. Locked as well.

Keeping his weapon aimed forward, he continued toward the next door, his body slightly bent as he padded through the corridor. 306 was locked, as was 308.

But then Celeste motioned up ahead. A small kitchenette midway stood doorless, giving the crew the protection and visibility they needed to approach Avery's old office.

Silas smiled and nodded. He looked back at Gapinski, Dax, and Greer, who had entered the broad corridor, motioning them to follow toward the open room up ahead.

They nodded and padded closer to Silas and Celeste, who were making their way toward the new staging area.

Then Silas saw it.

A soft glow, indiscernible from outside the hallway looking through the small window, was peeking out from the dark wedge created by the slightly ajar door. The kind of light that a computer monitor made when used in the dark.

Silas stopped short and held up his hand with a closed fist.

His mouth went dry as he sucked in a sharp breath, the taste of adrenaline weighing heavily on his tongue.

Celeste held her gun in both hands low to the ground and cocked her head, not being able to see what Silas saw up ahead.

He pointed two fingers at his eyes and motioned toward Avery's door at the end of the vast space.

Celeste eased her body rightward for a better look, then looked at Silas, nodding in agreement.

A soft noise up ahead, the kind that came from fast typing, confirmed it. Someone was definitely in Avery's old office.

Great.

Silas had wondered if someone might try to clean up their tracks. But when he signed up for this little mission, he hadn't actually thought he would be confronting anyone. The kind clad in black, weapon in hand. It sounded like an easy assignment.

He was wrong.

This was real. And it was about to get even more real.

He tried to regulate his breath, but his pounding heart was making that difficult. He recognized what was happening. It had happened after the roadside bombing in Iraq.

Panic attack.

After that mission had turned so horribly wrong, he hadn't had time to process and grieve the events. He had to push forward on to the next assignment. So he stuffed whatever it was he might have felt about his friend being blown to bits deep inside.

Until it came tumbling out in the middle of a hallway at MIT.

This isn't happening!

Silas padded forward, then stopped. He leaned against the wall and tipped his head back. He closed his eyes to focus on his breaths. Memories of Father Arnold's half-blown face crowded out his concentration, as did the thought of Avery being blown to pieces three stories below.

Celeste stepped over to Silas. She squeezed his arm, shaking him back to the moment. He turned toward her, eyes wide.

Then the wall exploded above her head.

They immediately fell to the ground as three more rounds were popped off. This time from behind.

It was Dax and Gapinski. Greer was guarding their rear at the door they had just come through.

Silas's mind snapped back into focus, years of military training and Ranger experience taking over and slipping him into autopilot.

"Make for the opening," Celeste yelled, shoving Silas forward.

More rounds came wildly out from Avery's office. Silas blindly returned fire as he pressed forward to their new staging ground.

He made it first, then Celeste tumbled inside. From the right side of the door, he could make out room 323. They were four doors away on the other side of the hallway, and it gave them the perfect view. Which gave those damned Nous operatives the perfect line of sight.

He briefly caught two faces in the dark. One top, one bottom.

A bullet ricocheted off from the metal frame, then another four splintered a set of cupboards from behind Silas, sending him stumbling backward. He caught his right side on a countertop. Pain shot outward. He winced but didn't make a sound. Probably tore the stitches again. The cost of doing business.

More gunfire erupted from where they had just come from.

"We've gotta get our boys in here," Celeste said, shuffling over to Silas as he righted himself from his tumble. She squeezed off four rounds, which drove the assailants across the hallway back inside the room.

The covering gunfire and then the enemy's retreat gave Dax, Gapinski, and Greer the chance to make a run for their new foxhole.

They did. Greer first, then Gapinski, then Dax. Celeste and

Silas both popped off another few rounds as their team made their way down the hall to the kitchenette. They paused as they dove in, giving the two Nous operatives the chance to return fire.

And they did.

Nine rounds between the two of them came buzzing back into their hideout. Two of them caught Dax as he brought up the rear and slipped through the entryway.

One bullet sliced through his calf, clean through. The other was not so lucky, or luckier depending on what side of the bullet you were. It drove deep into Dax's right side, bursting through his stomach and shattering the left side of his hip.

He screamed in pain, collapsing to the floor. Silas and Celeste returned fire as their comrade continued writhing in pain.

"Dax!" Gapinski cried, pulling his friend deeper into the room out of the line of fire. Having been trained as a medic, he quickly worked to find the bullet entrances and stop the blood loss. "Always something," he cursed as he continued his triage.

Celeste went to Dax to help Gapinski. In the confusion, Silas looked up to see the two assailants slip out of Avery's office and toward the exit closest to them at the end of the hallway. One of them was carrying a laptop.

"Forget it!" Silas said, crouching down and leaning into the hallway to try and stave off their escape.

One of the men turned and popped off two rounds to cover their escape, sending Silas back inside. They went wide and landed at their original entrance.

Silas leaned back out to return fire, popping off three rounds. But they didn't matter. Because the half-closing steel door ate them as the men fled down the stairwell to freedom.

He cursed. Dax gave out another agonizing cry, as if agreeing.

"What's wrong?" Silas asked kneeling next to Gapinski. "He's going to be alright, isn't he?"

"Hip is blown to hell, and his calf is shredded beef," Gapinski said as he worked to keep Dax alive. "He's losing a lot of blood."

Silas lowered his head and cursed again.

Dax reached up and grabbed Silas's arm. "Leave me," he said weakly. "Go get those bastards." He loosened his grip and settled into the floor.

"We're not leaving you," Gapinski said.

"No man left behind," Celeste agreed, kneeling next to Silas. "That's the rule."

Silas could tell Celeste was shaken by the turn and the condition of her man. He felt the same.

"No," Dax sputtered, trying to shove Gapinski off. "Go, go." He tried sitting up, then moaned in agony again and fell down.

"Stay still," Gapinski ordered with a firm hand.

Silas cringed, then looked back toward the door. He remembered the laptop. Those damned Nous operatives got his data! He sprang to his feet and made his way to the door, aiming his weapon forward.

"Where are you going?" Celeste asked.

"Those bastards got Avery's laptop. I saw them take it when they left."

"Silas, we're through! Mission's over."

"No! That's my data." He corrected himself. "That's our data. The one that will shut Nous and their Shroud-denying operation down! We need to go after it."

"Go!" Dax moaned as Gapinski continued working.

Greer had been silent, trying to keep Dax still. "He has a point. Both of them do. You gotta get that laptop back. That's why we came. Don't make Dax's injury meaningless. I can stay here while Gapinski fixes him up. You two go."

Celeste looked from Dax to Silas, then back again.

Silas could tell this was Celeste's first time dealing with a screw-up of this magnitude. She may have been MI6, but she wasn't a Ranger.

He walked over to Celeste and put his arm gently on her

shoulder. "He's right. You and I can take those Nous hostiles on. Let them handle Dax."

Celeste's brow was furrowed, eyes unblinking. She sighed, then stood. "OK, let's go. Greer, call Radcliffe when we leave and let him know what happened. We're going to need an extraction ASAP. Authorities will be swarming this place in no time after what happened here two days ago. You know that rent-a-cop downstairs has to be crapping his pants at the sound of a firefight at this early hour."

Then she looked at Silas, gun in hand. "Let's go."

Silas nodded toward Greer and Gapinski, then followed Celeste back into the hallway. She hesitated slightly, making sure the coast was clear before running toward the back stairwell. She opened the door carefully, then pushed herself through with gun drawn, training it on the descent. Silas followed close behind, training his own gun over the railing to the bottom beneath.

There wasn't a sound. They made their way deliberately down the stairs, keeping a wary eye trained ahead of them. A distant thwacking sound began to break the silence as they reached the bottom.

Celeste looked at Silas as they kept moving downward. The sound was growing. *Thwack, thwack, thwack.* Like the sound of a rotating lawn sprinkler.

Chopper.

Recognition seemed to hit Celeste and Silas at once. They glanced at each other and quickened their pace. They shoved through the doors, damning the consequences with arms outstretched ready to respond to anyone and anything in their way.

The sound was louder. And definitely a chopper, military grade. Thick clouds and a heavier fog had returned, masking their ability to see it for themselves. But the distinct sound down toward the center of campus gave them the direction they needed to take down the Nous agents and retrieve that laptop.

They ran toward the direction of the noise, but were stopped short by a large, dark figure standing in the sidewalk.

"Get out of our way," Silas shouted to their rent-a-cop friend.

He startled backward, nearly falling over. He grabbed his chest, as Silas and Celeste ran toward him. He quickly complied as the two ran by in chase. Silas could hear him screaming into his walkie-talkie for backup.

Up ahead, the whirl of blades sliced through the silent, still early morning air, flattening the grass and kicking up debris. As Silas pumped his legs in pursuit of the men ahead, he saw a rope ladder drop from the menacing black bird.

Oh no, you're not!

Silas pumped his legs harder in pursuit of his target. The loud sound of a mounted gun diverted his pursuit.

The covering fire caused Silas and Celeste to dive behind a group of bushes that buttressed the quad. They weren't going to do much for 30mm rounds of pure metallic hatred flying through the air. But at least they could regroup and shield the enemy from their vision.

The fog was clearing, and dawn started breaking. Silas peaked over the bushes and saw two men swinging from the lowered rope ladder. He squeezed off five rounds, paused to refocus his aim, then sent four more their way. Celeste joined him, popping off another five herself until her gun clicked empty.

She ducked down. "I'm out."

One of the men climbing the ladder nearly dropped. He cried out clutching his leg. The other one, the one clutching the laptop, quickened his pace, then started pulling up his accomplice.

The big gun sent Silas joining Celeste for cover. Round after round gave the injured man and the other assailant the necessary cover they needed to finish their ascent into the black vulture.

The firing stopped as it rose higher and turned west before disappearing.

Replacing the thwacking of the chopper blades and grinding

rounds was the sound of sirens. Lots of them. And heading their way.

Silas and Celeste ran back toward the emergency stairwell at the back of the Physics department. Greeting them was Greer and Gapinski, with Dax draped over Greer's shoulders.

The two stopped short. Silas was trying to catch his breath when he realized what had happened.

"No," he groaned.

Gapinski nodded. "He lost too much blood."

Celeste cursed and paced in a circle.

"Did you get those bastards?" he asked.

Silas looked at Celeste, then at Dax. "We will. Believe me. We will."

By Silas's score, it was Nous one, Order of Thaddeus negative a million.

Strike that, negative two million. They had lost the laptop and data, as well as one of their men.

He vowed to even the score one way or another.

CHAPTER 19

Jacob Crowley flipped open the lighter and held the small flickering yellow flame to the end of his cigarette, puffing it to life. The end glowed softly as he inhaled deeply. He let the nicotine-laced smoke linger in his lungs as he leaned against the earthen tunnel. Then tilted his head back, and slowly exhaled the smoke through his nostrils.

He had arrived in Paris in the early morning to oversee the final pieces of the operation moving into place. After the minor disaster the day before with losing Silas Grey to Ordo Thaddeum, Crowley couldn't afford any more missteps. A perfect Nous victory was a must.

Rudolf Borg wouldn't be as forgiving the second time. Especially given the stakes involved this time.

He took another long drag and smiled with pleasure. It was around this time, eight hundred years ago, that his distant ancestor, Nicolas Crowley, at the behest of King Philip IV of France, made a similar run on the Holy Image at this very location, which the Knights Templar had hidden away. Rumors had been circulating in Europe of an idol that the Templars worshiped at their massive headquarters at the Villeneuve du Temple. Philip seized on the public outcry as the impetus to assuage his worries about their amassing an oversized amount of power and influence.

Seeking to distance himself from a direct confrontation with the Knights Templar, Philip employed mercenaries to carry out his misdeeds. Nous was more than willing to oblige. Lead by Crowley, Philip, and his mercenaries made a surprising sweep against the Templars, arresting, torturing, and extracting "confessions" from its members. Under the guise of the political pogroms, Crowley, on behalf of the Nousati, meant to finally secure the Holy Image, later known as the Shroud of Turin. It was the perfect opportunity. Yet by the time he was able to confront their Grand Master, Jacque de Molay, the Shroud had been cut away from its frame in their great hall and ferried away for safe keeping. Even burning Molay's very own son at the stake couldn't extract from him the location of their prized pursuit. A dozen more Templars were burnt alive in Crowley's attempt to learn the secret location of Christ's cloth, including Molay himself.

Crowley paused mid-thought, trying to make out the relationship between him and his distant relative. How many generations back would that have been? How many great-grandfathers was he? He shook his head, abandoning the attempt, then inhaled again. *No matter.* He exhaled and smiled, because unlike his great-whatever-grandfather, he wasn't going to fail.

Stretching forward centuries from that fateful moment, the Crowleys had been at the forefront of Nous activity, seeking to wrench the pursuit of the inner divine man from the clutches of organized religion. Especially Christianity. Jacob's immediate grandfather, Aleister Crowley, had forged a particularly important legacy in raising man up to take his place among the gods. Remarkably, as Grand Master of Nous during the apex of the British Christian missionary movement in the late nineteenth and early twentieth centuries, Aleister had popularized, more than any other figure, the pursuit of the divine inner-man through ritualistic magic and the occult, giving Nous a foothold in the broader public consciousness like never before.

As a prophet of the New Aeon, which was destined to supplant the Christian era, Jacob's grandfather had sought to lead Nous in developing nothing short of a full-fledged successor religion to the Christian one in which the individual rational person would rise to become the gods we had merely worshiped in the forms of stone and wood stretching back to our primordial ancestors. Through his books *Magik* and *The Book of Lies*, Aleister sought to spread the kernel of ancient Nousati spirituality embedded within Easternism throughout the West. The Victorian occultist saw himself as representing a new stage in spiritual evolution, a soul in a heightened, advanced state of spiritual progress who regarded himself as the rightful teacher of humanity. He was a prophet without equal, a shaman of the New Religious Synthesis Nous had been prophesying and working toward for millennia.

It was this legacy that Jacob was continuing this day, bringing it to a triumphant climax. It was his destiny.

He took one more pleasurable drag, then threw the burnt stub of paper and tobacco to the ground, snuffing it out with his black military boot. A grinding sound once again echoed down toward him from the end of the dimly lit tunnel.

Shouldn't be long now.

Jacob followed the series of bulbs strung along the top of the dirt ceiling, crouching lower to accommodate his tall, bulky frame as the tunnel narrowed slightly the farther under the Paris streets he walked. He stepped to the side to avoid the train of dirt and rocks being carted away by the conveyor belt running down the center.

"How much longer?" he asked one of the workers standing behind the behemoth drilling machine eating away at the Parisian earth.

The worker startled, unaware Jacob had walked up behind

him in the cacophony of crunching earth. "We're nearing the end, sir. Right on schedule."

"Good. We will not have another misstep like in DC, understand?"

"Yes, sir," the man said, averting his eyes in understanding. "Just another hour and the chamber will be completely prepared for the extraction. Like the job we performed a few years ago in Venice. We left with the cash before the authorities knew what hit them. Don't worry, sir. It'll go without a hitch." He cleared his throat, then added: "This time."

Jacob stepped closer to the short, stocky man, his frame casting a menacing shadow over his face. "It better, for your sake. Because you and I both know Grey's extraction was your fault. And I'm not a man of third chances."

Over the next hour, the mining equipment finished preparing the chamber to receive their prize. The sun began rising over the city above, casting long, burnt-orange beams across the former Templar site across from the Louvre. Within the next few hours, the ceremony receiving the Shroud of Turin at its former resting place would commence.

And Jacob Crowley would end what his distant ancestor began, securing what Nous had sought for generations. And what he himself had been conditioned to loathe with a passion that burned bright and strong.

The Holy Image of Jesus Christ.

CHAPTER 20

The quiet hum of the plane was a soothing balm for Silas's wreaked psyche.

Not only had the loss of his data been totalizing, stolen by forces at work that were greater than he could comprehend. They had lost a fellow soldier in the field of battle.

He lost a fellow soldier in the field of battle.

His chest began to tighten as he continued marinating over the tragedy of Dax's death. And of Avery's and Gregory's and Arnold's, and all of his other colleagues who had given themselves to studying the Shroud and proving it to be authentic.

Silas closed his eyes, trying to stave back the well of emotion trying to force its way to the surface. Connected to those emotions was his own near-death experience and the death of his war buddy those years ago. Like a throbbing toothache, he couldn't ignore the memory of that fateful day.

And what a day that was.

It had started similarly to this one: sunny, warm, hopeful. They had been making progress trying to establish a U.S. presence in southern Iraq by befriending local village people. Community relations, the Army called it. The day before he had handed out soccer balls to the kids. Even played a few matches.

Those kids sure knew how to play! Resurrecting his college passion and position, he had played goalie, but had been bested for a five-to-two loss by a scrappy Iraqi boy half his age. Even if they didn't understand the war, the villagers seemed to have appreciated the gesture. The kids sure did.

The next day he and his unit loaded up another beige military truck full of items intended to further appease the locals, while the politicians and nation-builders worked toward putting the country back together again. Silas remembered the morning vividly while continuing to stare out into the endless sky outside his plane window.

It was hot and sticky like most days, temperatures already pushing into the 90s. A slight breeze blew across the flat Iraqi ground outside the military outpost, tinged with manure from the local pastures. He had slept like crap the night before, but the thought of getting a rematch from the scrappy Iraqi teenager and his friends gave him enough energy to finish loading up the shoes and medical supplies meant to win the hearts and minds of their parents.

The trip was another rough one, the massive wheels of the Humvee hitting every pothole left in the wake of the shock-and-awe siege that had ravaged the land. Twenty minutes out they came to what appeared to be a car accident. This wasn't unusual in the slightest. Vehicles would often break down in the middle of the highways that ran through the desert countryside, either because of ill-repair or from running out of fuel.

But this was different. He felt it the moment he saw how the cars were positioned. They were angled on both sides of the road, blocking passage. Almost like a barrier. Like they were meant to impede the flow of traffic.

Then he saw it. On the left side of the vehicle, nearly imperceptible for those who didn't have eyes to see. And then everyone saw it, for it exploded in a mushroom of fire and force, destruction and death.

The memory kept replaying itself in the darkened cabin, like a scratch in an old LP vinyl record skipping backward and replaying a set of notes. He couldn't shake the connection of the night's events—the firefight, the death of the young soldier—to those of a decade ago when Colton was blown to bits.

Like Avery and Gregory and Arnold.

And yet here he was: flying on a chartered Vatican jet by way of the Order of Thaddeus to Paris, France, when everything inside of him screamed, *Run away!*

Silas leaned forward and reached into his pocket to retrieve his stash of little blue pills. He unscrewed the top, shook the bottle until one dropped on his hand, then popped it into his mouth. Not having any water, he swallowed hard, then leaned back and waited for relief.

Thank God I decided to grab those before the mission.

He settled back in his seat, hoping for some shut-eye before the new leg of his mission began. After the team drove from MIT back to the airport, they had boarded a different plane for their return flight back to DC. Except it was an outgoing one. Once on the plane, Radcliffe explained that things had changed, and the Vatican was requesting their presence at a public showing of the Shroud in Paris, France. It was a special ceremony memorializing when the Poor Fellow-Soldiers of Christ and of the Temple of Solomon had taken possession of the Shroud of Turin.

Better known as the Knights Templar, Radcliffe had explained to the crew how the Catholic military order had laid possession of the Holy Image eight centuries ago after armies from the Fourth Crusade besieged and sacked Constantinople. It eventually made its way to their Paris Temple, a compound surrounded by thick walls with several buildings that included a church and living quarters for the brothers. Although no longer in existence, having been demolished under the orders of Napoleon, the rare memorial viewing was being held at the Notre Dame Cathedral, across the river Seine from where the original

Templar compound had resided. SEPIO was meant to help with security and intelligence.

Radcliffe informed Silas, Celeste, and Gapinski that they were to support the guard protecting the Shroud. SEPIO operatives had heard too much chatter for comfort from Nous cells operating throughout Western Europe, suggesting some sort of renewed activity against the Church. The Vatican feared a possible attack at the viewing and an attempt on the Shroud itself, which is why the Order was being asked to provide additional logistical security and intelligence support. Radcliffe had pledged the elite SEPIO unit to protect the public viewing of the Shroud, and defend the Holy Image itself, should it come to that.

Silas had been angered by Radcliffe volunteering his life for such a mission. After all, he was a professor of religious studies and Christian history at Princeton. He was not SEPIO. Had zero interest in their purpose.

But then he thought, what better way to fight for the Shroud and its scientific and historical significance than actually *fighting* for it? Protecting it. Watching over it. All to preserve it and its memory for the sake of the Church.

If the Holy Shroud was being opened for public viewing, and there was a threat against it, he wanted to be on the ground to make sure as many people could experience the memory of Christ's resurrection. If the Holy Image itself was being threatened, he wanted to be the one to save it.

He might not have been able to protect Colton or Avery, Gregory or Arnold, but perhaps he could redeem himself by protecting the Holy Image of Christ.

A sudden drop in altitude woke Silas from his contemplation. He opened his eyes, blinked, and sat up. They were descending. He opened the shade to a world waking up below. The early-morning Paris light was streaming through a few storm clouds left over from the night. Morning commuters snaked through the streets below, bringing the city back to life. As the plane approached Charles de Gaulle Airport from the south, he could see the unmistakable twin towers of the French Gothic cathedral known as Notre Dame, accented by the burnt orange light streaming down from above.

"Good morning, sunshine." Celeste was bearing a small Styrofoam cup of coffee. She offered it to him.

Silas took it and smiled. "Thanks."

She sat down in a seat across from him. "How are you feeling?"

He lifted the lid and blew across the steaming brew before taking a sip. *Heaven.* "I'm fine," he offered.

She paused. "Are you?"

"What do you mean, *am I*?"

"Come on, are you going to deny what happened back at MIT?"

Silas had hoped she would have left his episode alone. *Guess not.*

He closed the lid and looked back out the window. "Like I said, I'm fine."

"You didn't seem fine. PTSD, if I were to put my finger on it."

He turned to her and scowled. "I'm dealing with it."

"It sure didn't seem like it."

"What the hell do you want from me?" Silas instantly regretted his outburst. He huffed and looked back out his window.

Gapinski turned around from the front, then turned forward not wanting to get involved.

Celeste held her hands up in surrendering. "Look, I'm not trying to point any fingers, or open festering wounds. But after what happened with you freezing and all and..." Celeste trailed off, not finishing whatever she was about to say.

Silas's face fell. He turned back to her. "Go ahead. Say it."

"No, I didn't mean—"

"Sure you did. You think Dax is my fault."

Celeste's face was stern. "Not at all. No way. I shouldn't have said that. I'm sorry."

Silas waved her off, returning back to the window.

Silence fell between them.

"I lost a guy, you know," he said. "Back in Iraq."

Celeste leaned back in her chair. "No, I didn't know that."

"He was about Dax's age," he said gently. "Young, bright, cocky. One minute he was sitting next to me. The next..." Silas stopped, letting the memory relive itself. "The next, he was on top of me, half of him blown to bits by a roadside bomb."

"My God..."

Silas turned to her, his eyes burning hot with resolve.

"You asked if I'm alright. No, I guess I'm not. But I am ready."

Celeste nodded.

The pilot came on the loudspeaker and announced they would be landing soon. He advised his passengers to sit down, stow their gear, bring their chairs upright, and fasten their seatbelt.

"Right," Celeste said as she clicked her seatbelt tightly. "Let's kick some Nous ass."

CHAPTER 21

When it came to mission briefings, Celeste was direct and to-the-point. This briefing was no different, for its mission objective was simple, singular.

"Protect the Shroud. At all cost. Anything else is secondary."

She briefed Silas and Gapinski from the front seat of their SUV as the team of three raced through the streets of Paris from the airport toward the river Seine to assume guard duty at Notre Dame. While a light crew, they were a well-armed one. They had brought along two large weapons caches with plenty of ammunition. Each person got two sidearms and a high-powered, high-capacity automatic rifle. Gapinski, however, brought an extra one for himself. Just in case.

"What about the visitors?" Gapinski asked as he drove. "I don't want to be babysitting a bunch of nuns if the back burners get turned on."

Celeste answered, "Obviously, we need to minimize any collateral damage, should the heat get turned on, as you say. But we were brought here by the Vatican to protect the Shroud."

"About that," Silas said. "You honestly think Nous is going to make a play for it in such a public place? I mean, we're in the middle of Paris, and in one of the most recognized public religious places in the world, where there will be crowds of people shuffling through all day. How's that supposed to work?"

"All I know is what Radcliffe shared in our briefing. SEPIO has picked up chatter from multiple sources indicating high interest in a religious artifact that seems to coincide with the Shroud. All signs point to an attempt on its possession. When it comes to intel, nothing beats SEPIO. I trust it. So should you."

Silas threw a hand up in surrender. "Got it. So what's the plan when we get there?"

"We've been given cover identities that place us in the Vatican police unit."

"Swiss guards?" Silas asked.

"Does that mean we get to wear those sweet rainbow uniforms with MC Hammer pants?" Gapinski asked from the front.

Celeste smirked. "Yes, Swiss Guards. But no on the Hammer pants."

Gapinski frowned. "Well, can I at least get a black beret?"

She ignored him and continued. "The plan is to cover the great hall with special attention paid to the Shroud, while also giving room for the tourists venerating the sacred relic."

"Sounds like a tough balance," Silas said. "Cover the Shroud and be ready for any threat that might show itself, but don't get in the way of the Christian tourists and make sure no one gets hurt if something does happen."

"Basically," Celeste said.

Gapinski added, "What could go wrong?"

Within an hour the group had driven from the airport to the cathedral, even stopping for pastries and coffee on the way. Gapinski had started to complain that the breakfast bars and instant oatmeal served on the plane weren't enough to feed a mouse, let alone a moose like him. Celeste figured it was better to feed the guy than have a ravenous beast on their hands for the next several hours.

The Catholic cathedral glistened in the orange morning light after an earlier rainfall. From a distance, Silas could see the central spire stretching into the heavens, as if it were a conduit to Heaven itself. Constructed in the twelfth century and finally completed in the fourteenth, the iconic French Gothic church building had survived riotous Huguenots, the French Revolution, and both World Wars. Situated on a small island called the Ile de la Cite in the middle of the river Seine, its flying buttresses and massive, grand stained glass windows beckoned its visitors to taste and see and experience the grandeur and goodness of the Lord. Although one might say otherwise with the many gargoyles and chimeras dotting the building's architecture.

The early morning rain clouds were still hanging around when Gapinski pulled into the cathedral parking lot. A line had already formed to view the Holy Image, wrapping its way through a queue several times over. Silas watched several of them as they drove, wondering what brought each of the viewers to the cathedral that day. Was it belief or doubt? Out of reassurance, or perhaps out of skepticism?

He recalled what brought him to see the image for the first time in Turin: experience. Ever since his military-base conversion he had wanted to tangibly experience the memory of Christ's resurrection. Not so much to compel belief, but to confirm it. Perhaps some others standing in line were like Silas was a decade ago.

He said a quick prayer for those who would visit the Holy Image as Gapinski pulled up to a guard station, as well as for them and their mission.

Lord, be close to us this day. Be even closer to the Shroud.

Gapinski handed their credentials to the guard on duty. The man looked intently at their IDs, then at each of their faces, and then back to their IDs again. Satisfied, he handed them back to Gapinski and directed them to park along the north front where operations for the viewing were being staged. They pulled around and parked in an empty parking space, then exited the vehicle and walked over to a command tent filled with surveillance equipment, as well as a contingent of real-life Swiss Guards on loan from the Vatican for the viewing.

"Why do they get the rainbow Hammer pants," Gapinski complained as they walked, "and all we get are these black getups that make my thighs look like tree trunks?"

They entered the tent and scanned the large space, looking for someone who was in charge. Celeste nodded toward a tall, well-muscled man who was giving orders to a small group of guards. Radcliffe had given Celeste the name of the commander during the briefing as their point of contact. So she led the group to make introductions and offer their help.

"Excuse me, Commander Richter?"

The burly man turned around mid-sentence as he was handing out orders to a small group huddled around a panel of monitors. "May I help you?" the man said with an edge of annoyance.

"Actually, we're here to help you. I'm Celeste Bourne director of operations with SEPIO. You should have received notice of our arrival from the Order of Thaddeus. Rowan Radcliffe sent us."

The man squinted and eyed her from bottom to top, then glanced over at Silas and Gapinski. He sniffed, then turned back to the small group waiting for his next set of instructions. "I did hear something about a few...operatives being sent from the Order. Not sure why."

Celeste shifted from one leg to another, searching for how to proceed. "Yes, well, let's just say we've got some experience with the nature of the threat—"

"I'm sure you do," interrupted Richter. "But we've got things under control here."

He walked away to another group seeking his attention, leaving Celeste with Silas and Gapinski. She narrowed her eyes, sighed, and followed after him.

"I'm not sure how much you are aware of the threat that Nous poses here today, commander."

Richter stopped short and pivoted sharply around to face Celeste, nearly colliding with her as she followed. He folded his arms. "Do tell, director Bourne."

What's with this guy? Silas thought.

"Well, for starters they've already taken out four sindonologists, people who have dedicated their academic career to researching the Shroud. They destroyed an entire lecture hall and half an academic building to destroy research that would scientifically prove an event occurred inside the Shroud on par with the events of the Gospels. They then blew up a chapel of more than eighty researchers and conference-goers in order to silence one of the foremost experts from unveiling new research into its authenticity. Operatives broke into said academic building and stole a laptop of a deceased professor they targeted in their destruction, killing one of my men. And now there is strong intel suggesting they are planning something here today that will eclipse all four events combined. So let's drop the machoism, commander, and work together, so I don't have to summon any more body bags, and the Shroud can return to its home in Turin, safe and sound."

The commander smirked, then pivoted back around. "Alright. Follow me."

Celeste turned to Silas and Gapinski, furrowing her brow before following after Richter.

"What an idiot," Silas mumbled as he followed her.

"Why does he get a beret?" Gapinski mumbled following after the three.

CHAPTER 22

After finishing with another set of his own operatives, Richter took Celeste, Silas, and Gapinski through a security checkpoint, then guided them to the West Façade of the cathedral, dominated by arched portals with stone carvings and heavy wooden doors. At the center were three entrances: Portail de Sainte-Anne, Portail du Judgement Dernier, and the Portail de la Vierge. The portals of the Last Judgment, of Saint Anne, and of the Virgin. Passing through the Portal of Last Judgment, the crew was greeted by carvings of various saints, including the patron saints of Paris: St. Genevieve, St. Stephen, and St. Denis. Chimeras and gargoyles grimaced from above, as if to ward off evil spirits.

Silas hoped they did their job that day.

Out of habit, he crossed himself as they entered. Though a former Catholic, he still cherished and practiced some of the spiritual disciplines of his childhood. One of those being his practice of sacred rituals, like crossing and the divine prayer hours. The other being an appreciation for sacred architecture—soaring ceilings, enchanting stained-glass, flying buttresses and all. That's where Protestants missed the mark by a mile, by his estimation.

Gapinski whistled as they stepped into the nave. "Impressive. Though, not much of a looker."

Silas shot him a look. At some level he was right. Though the interior was cavernous and stretched heavenward for several stories, the stone masonry was plain, unassuming gray. But that was the point. Unlike other cathedrals like Sistine in Rome or La Sagrada Familia in Spain, the austere architecture directed the attention of the worshiper toward the most essential function of the sacred space: the high altar, where it was said the simple table elements of a loaf of bread and a cup of wine were literally transformed into the broken body and shed blood of the crucified Savior through the memory of Holy Communion, in order to nourish the faith of Christ's children.

In this case, the space functioned to direct the crowds of people forward to encounter the risen Savior through the memory of the Holy Shroud, in order to confirm the faith of Christ's children. And maybe even provoke it in some doubting Thomases.

"If you're so keen on protecting the Shroud from some... threat," Richter said with an edge of disbelief as he led the group toward the front, "then, by all means, protect." He led them through the nave past a line of people waiting for their glimpse of the Holy Image. He said they could have free reign of the interior, but added he preferred they stay near the front by the Shroud and absolutely out of his own team's way.

The cavernous space was silent, but for the shuffle of patrons moving forward, yet hummed with a holy presence and a sort of spiritual anticipation. The fourteen-foot beige cloth bearing the image of Jesus Christ was positioned beyond the rows of wooden choir pews in front of the high altar, a life-sized Christ-in-crucifixion of solid gold peering down upon the Shroud from behind.

Silas caught his breath as they walked past the crowd and approached the Shroud. It had been years since he had laid eyes on it, yet it was as familiar as his own shadow. The amber linen seemed to carry with it a special sacred glow, probably because of the contrast between the dark inner hall and the directional lighting positioned from above. Silas also believed it was because of the gravity of the mission, and an urgency to the memory it carried. The faint outlines of a man in side-ways repose stared out at them. Dried blood, dark and crimson, was obvious on the forehead and back of the head, at each of the wrists and feet, and all along the arms and back and legs from hundreds of thin laceration marks.

A verse from the prophet of Isaiah, chapter fifty-three, immediately sprang to Silas's mind:

> *Surely he has borne our infirmities*
>   *and carried our diseases;*
> *yet we accounted him stricken,*
>   *struck down by God, and afflicted.*
> *But he was wounded for our transgressions,*
>   *crushed for our iniquities;*
> *upon him was the punishment that made us whole,*
>   *and by his bruises we are healed.*

Like a lamb that is led to the slaughter.

"The thing looks like a really wicked Rorschach inkblot test!" Gapinski said loudly as they reached the front of the great hall, coming into full view of the Image.

Silas dropped his jaw and scowled in disgust.

"Sorry," Gapinski mumbled and lowered his head.

"Those marks you see there, the *really wicked Rorschach inkblot test*, as you put it," Silas said with irritation, gesturing at the twelve distinct patterns at the edges and spots on the linen. "Those are burn holes and scorched areas were caused by contact with molten silver during a fire in 1532 in the chapel in Chambery, France. Burned clear through the Shroud's linen while it was folded." Silas paused to catch his breath, staring at those marks.

"This, this, this tangible memory of Jesus' physical, bodily resurrection was nearly completely destroyed! And the sisters of Poor Clares convent repaired the linen by carefully sewing patches into the fabric to cover up the damage. And that *thing*, as you say, carries the blood and sacred image of our holy Savior!"

Silas turned to Gapinski. "So why don't you show the Shroud a little respect," he snapped before walking toward the center of the Holy Image, leaving his two companions behind.

Gapinski put his hands up in surrender. "Sorry, man," he called after Silas. "Didn't mean no disrespect."

"Alright," Celeste interjected. "We're all a little frayed from the past twenty-four hours, so let's simmer down, shall we?"

Richter cleared his throat. "Right, so I'll leave you to it. Ring me if anyone dressed in black bearing an Uzi shows up."

What an idiot, Silas thought again.

"So what's the plan, fearless leader?" Gapinski said to Celeste.

"I say we make our presence known by walking the interior grounds. Hopefully, our show of force will make plain to anyone that the Shroud is in safe hands." To emphasize her point, she chambered a round in her SIG Sauer, creating an uncomfortable echo and startling an older couple who had stepped up to the viewing area.

"I'll cover the Shroud, you and Silas cover either side of the nave."

Silas looked at Gapinski and nodded, then huffed and headed toward the right. Gapinski shrugged his shoulders and went off to the left, leaving Celeste at the front with the Shroud.

The rest of the morning saw several thousands of visitors. Student groups and nursing home groups. Young families and elderly couples. Even several lone teenagers came to experience one of the wonders of the Christian world. And all without a hitch.

At noon the crew regrouped after grabbing a quick ten-minute bite to eat from the command center. If the military taught them one thing, it was to eat quickly and eat whenever you could. Because you never knew when the next time you would get some grub.

The afternoon was as uneventful as the morning. Except when a middle-aged woman fainted in front of the Shroud. Luckily, Celeste had been there to come to her assistance. The woman blamed it on the heat, but it seemed like some sort of ecstatic experience had overtaken her after coming face-to-face with the man in the Shroud. Silas remembered feeling similarly light-headed during his first encounter. When it happened again to an older gentleman forty minutes later, and then again to a young woman ten minutes after that, he wondered if these rescues would make up the rest of their afternoon guard duty.

"So when are we eating?" Gapinski said when the team regrouped near the Shroud at a half past four. "My body blew through those jambon-beurres a few hours ago. I'm about to keel over."

Silas rolled his eyes. "Can you only think of your stomach at a time like this?"

"Hey, buddy, I've got needs."

Celeste said, "I'm sure there are some sandwiches or something back at the command post. Why don't we take a break? I'm sure we could use one."

"Not me," Silas said. "I'm staying."

Gapinski scoffed. "What a hero you are."

"Alright, stop." Celeste stepped in between the two men as they stepped toward each other. "Gapinski go feed yourself. Silas and I will stand guard."

"Fine," Gapinski said and sauntered off.

Silas said, "Try saving us a sandwich or two, would you?"

Gapinski kept walking.

"Was that really necessary?" Celeste asked.

Silas said nothing.

"We need our wits about us if we're going to guard the Shroud and keep these people safe. Who knows what Nous is planning? So how about you give it a rest, alright?"

"He started it. With the whole Shroud thing."

Celeste rolled her eyes and folded her arms. "You don't know Gapinski. That's just the way he his. Jokester and all. And why are you so uptight about the Shroud, anyway?"

Silas turned toward the amber cloth. "It's simple. The Shroud saved my life."

"What do you mean, saved your life?"

He brushed his hand over his head. "Nothing. Forget about it." He took several paces beyond the high altar, walking past the choir stalls and the crowd to the north rose window, stopping at the spectacular masterpiece of intricate glasswork. He paused to take in its beauty and center himself after his unwarranted explosion on Gapinski. Celeste came up beside him.

"Magnificent," she said.

Silas folded his arms and nodded. "Indeed."

She turned sideways to face him, then said softly, "So what was that back there? You and Gapinski?" She nodded toward the high altar. "You and the Shroud?"

He stood silently, staring through the rose window and beyond to a world that was right and good again after two days of chaos.

"It was after the war. Or rather, after I left the war. After what I had seen and experienced, I needed to center myself. Needed to reclaim my soul. So I set off on a sort of pilgrimage, visiting all of the holy sites I had heard about in my childhood. Of course, Turin was high on the list. Even though I had grown up in the Church, it hadn't meant anything to me. Not like it had to my brother. At least for a time..." He trailed off, silently revisiting yet another painful memory. "Anyway, it wasn't until I had gone to Iraq that I would say I had had my own personal transformation experience. That I really claimed my faith in Jesus and his death and resurrection as my own. Call it a foxhole conversion if you will, after all of the blood and chaos of the conflict. But it was real. Genuine. Personal."

Celeste listened intently, finding some of her own story in Silas's having similarly found faith during her time with MI6.

"But then after a series of...experiences with the war, my faith began to fray. A village massacre. Collateral damage from a stray bomb." Silas stopped, his throat growing thick with emotion. "My buddy Colton getting blown to smithereens next to me on that road." He cleared his throat and wiped his eyes on his sleeve. "So I went to visit these holy sites containing the memory of my faith. And when I met the Shroud, it was all made real again. Tangible. Like, experiencing the reality of Christ's resurrection through this fourteen-foot cloth reminded me why I believed what I believe."

"And why is that?" Celeste asked.

Silas turned to her and said plainly, "He lives. And that cloth proved it to me in that moment standing in the chapel of Turin. Knowing he was alive, sitting at the right hand of God, my fear just evaporated. Because I knew that he holds my future in his hands."

Celeste turned away, blinking away tears of her own, appearing to have been moved by Silas's experience.

"Wait a minute. Hold on." Silas pivoted toward the nave.

A disturbance arose from the West Façade. Silas thought he heard a scream. Then there was a shift in the crowd, the line widening at the back in a 'V' and pressing forward.

Then he saw them. Seven or eight figures in fatigues facing out from the Portal of the Last Judgment.

Adrenaline began to surge through Silas, steeling his muscles into action, sharpening his mind into fully-alert status.

He shot Celeste a look, who looked as equally primed for a fight.

"We've got company."

CHAPTER 23

Pop. Pop. Pop.

Pop. Pop. Pop.

Bullets from automatic rifles ricocheted off the masonry work near the main entrance, sending fragments of stone and dust to the ground, and bringing down a gold chandelier into shattering pieces.

Women screamed. Parents cried out the names of their children. The panicked crowd surged forward toward safer ground as the phantoms violated the sacredness of a space that had stewarded the spirituality of countless generations.

"Come on," Celeste said. "You take the right, I'll take them on the left. We need to open up a window to get these people out of the north and south portals."

"Commander Richter," Silas said into his wrist mic. "We've got a live confrontation in here with hostiles who are presumed to be Nous operatives."

Nothing but static.

"Commander Richter? Celeste and I are engaging ten or twelve hostiles in the nave at present. Do you copy?"

Again, nothing.

Silas cursed as he rushed forward to a position just beyond the transept. "Celeste, can you hear me?"

"Loud and clear."

"Then what the hell is going on outside? I'm getting nothing from Richter. And where is Gapinski?"

"Who knows, but we've got to push these hostiles back."

Gunfire erupted again toward the main entrance. Bodies went down for cover. Some when down after being hit.

Silas fired his Beretta, aiming for a hostile positioned near the baptistry on his right toward the entrance. With a single *pop*, his head snapped back.

Dang it. He was aiming for his shoulder, wanting to maim not kill. The Army had trained him well, hammering and honing him into a killing machine. Yet that was not the way of the Church, especially not the way of Jesus.

Silas leaned against the pillar and crossed himself.

Lord, forgive me.

He looked back toward the kill. The body slumped over the font, blood mingling with the holy water. What a desecration.

One down, ten to go.

Another spat of gunfire erupted angrily toward Silas in response. He twisted around the column as pieces of it exploded behind him and fell to the floor.

"Celeste..."

"I'm with you." She responded with her own set of rounds, using her SIG Sauer to disable another hostile, sending him to the ground and slinking out of sight.

A smattering of gunfire erupted from the rear of the cathedral, but it had changed in timbre and direction. It seemed lower in pitch than the hostile's gunfire, and it wasn't coming at Celeste and Silas, but was stampeding into the hostiles themselves.

Help was on the way!

A small group of the security apparatus stationed around Notre Dame had finally come to take control of the situation.

They caught the hostiles flatfooted, sending three down quickly. Silas gave Celeste a thumbs-up signal. She raised her fist in acknowledgment and delight, then laid down covering fire. He did the same.

It turned out the security force was made up of two separate groups, of four or five. They were making their way in behind the Nous operatives through the Portail de Saint-Anne and Portail de la Vierge.

Why weren't there more? Silas remembered counting at least six times that many. What was going on outside Notre Dame?

Nous quickly adjusted to the change in circumstances. A perfectly synced choreograph of bodies fanned out in V-formation, taking up positions against the north and south walls and using the columns and statues in the cathedral for cover. They may have been outmatched and outflanked, but they weren't outwitted.

Nous returned fire with precision, picking off half of each group in short order. The security forces stopped their advance, and Silas could see a few of the Nousati peeling off the leading groups on either end, using the break in the firefight to pad along the wall toward the entrances.

As if they could sense his peering eye, they shot toward him and then at Celeste, sending both twisting around their columns for protection.

Making another go at the hostiles, the security forces fired back into the cathedral with a vengeance, pushing their way back inside only to be met by the trap. They were picked off easily on both sides, ending their advance.

Bodies laid splayed on the stone floor, blood running dark and red.

More gunfire spat toward Celeste and Silas, the bullets doing damage only to their protective columns. However, two stray bullets hit an elderly couple behind Silas as they tried to escape, sending them to the ground in agony.

"Get them out of there," he commanded two teenage boys who were making for a set of heavy wooden doors. They obeyed at once.

Angry at the turn of events, Silas slung around from his back his own automatic rifle, an AR-15. Not as capable as his trusty M4 from Ranger days, but it would do.

He returned fire, sending another small group of tourists running for cover, not understanding Silas was on their side. Aiming for another hostile hiding behind a column trying to disable their advance, he only managed to chew the sides of the thirteenth-century masonry.

"Where the hell is Gapinski?" Silas complained to Celeste as he slammed his back behind his column for cover again.

"Right here."

As if to put an exclamation point on his arrival, a loud smattering of double-barrel gunfire erupted to Silas's left from where Celeste had been positioned, dropping another hostile and sending the rest for cover.

"About time!" Silas said. "At least you came bearing double-barreled gifts. Where've you been, and why haven't you been answering your com?"

"Trying to get here to save your ass after those bastards wiped out the camp."

"What do you mean?" Celeste asked.

"There I am, finishing up my second croque monsieur, and the tent starts erupting in gunfire. I immediately hit the ground and make for an open flap next to where I'm sitting. Totally unexpected. Took everyone by surprise. And everyone else is dropped by these guys."

"Commander Richter?" Silas asked. He could see Gapinski make a slicing motion with his finger across his neck from across the nave.

He shook his head.

"They immediately left for the Cathedral. Didn't take nothing, didn't search for nothing. Didn't even assess their damage inside. I tried to get here as fast as I could. It was only when I was hustling up the stairs that it dawned on me that I didn't have my earpiece turned on. Sorry."

Figures.

Celeste said, "That means we're all that's left between them and the Shroud."

Silas replied, "They will not get that far if I have anything to say about it."

"Me either," Gapinski said, nodding toward Silas.

Silas nodded back.

Pop. Pop. Pop.

Gapinski returned fire, both arms extended and blazing. So did Celeste and Silas from either side of the nave, sending the hostiles back for their own cover. Another check, another stalemate.

This wasn't working. They needed a plan, and fast.

By now most of the crowd had fled through the north and south doors. Several others were either dead or dying, blood pooling on the cold, hard stone floor. Silas pivoted slightly to his left, moving around the column to steal a glance at the remaining hostiles.

One, three, five. And a sixth moving forward toward Celeste, but stopping one column up. Mostly, they hadn't advanced forward, content to remain near their original attacking positions at the West Façade.

"I don't get it," Silas mumbled. "Why aren't they advancing?"

It made no sense. If they had come for the Shroud, then why weren't they making a push forward to clear the interior and move to take it? Did they merely mean to sow terror at the viewing? Scare people off?

No, that didn't make sense. They hadn't followed the crowd. They had stayed put. And yet, it was as if they were waiting for something. Hanging back for something to unfold, arrive.

But for what?

A rumble beneath Silas's feet caught his attention. It was tonally low. Like the thumping base of a concert, steady and rhythmic. And coming from the high altar.

It caught Celeste's and Gapinski's attention, as well. The three turned in unison as the base-pounding turned into an explosive growl.

The Shroud!

At once gunfire erupted from the six remaining operatives at the rear, drawing their attention away from the spectacle that was unfolding.

Geysers of ash and bits of masonry were shooting upward in an oval pattern, reminding Silas of the programmed fountains that had entranced him as a child at a local park in Arlington, Virginia. This wasn't a haphazard explosion designed to destroy. It was careful. Deliberate. Delicate, even. The kind of controlled explosion expertly crafted for high-stakes demolition projects.

Silas stood frozen. At once paralyzed, mesmerized, and horrified.

"No!" he screamed, the gravity of what was transpiring hitting him.

He pushed off from the protective column and began running through the choir pews. More bullets were sent his way, shattering wooden benches as he advanced forward. One exploded to his forward right, sending splinters and shredded wood in Silas's path. He stumbled, cursing loudly.

"Stay down!" Gapinski said, returning fire as he ran to his partner. Celeste was following close behind with the same covering fire, sending the Nous operatives for their own cover. The spectacular show of pluming ash and shattered masonry continued.

Gapinski sought cover under the wooden benches, and drug Silas under one of his own.

"Let me go!" Silas said, scrambling forward toward the Shroud but making no headway under Gapinski's tight grip.

"Dude, stay down! You're going to get us all killed."

"We need to save the Shroud!"

"Sorry, man. It's gone."

And in one instant it was. All of it. The explosive geyser, the hornet's nest of gunfire. Silence followed after the final slam of the heavy wooden door guarding the Portal of the Last Judgment.

Silas pushed off the ground, finding enough balance to stand by grabbing the arm of a wooden pew. He gazed at the front of the cavernous sacred space, ears ringing, dust and soot obstructing his view. He scrambled forward on uneven steps, but fell, twisting his ankle.

"Dammit!" He breathed heavily, kneeling on the cold floor to catch his breath, frantically looking around for his fellow comrades. "Celeste! Gapinski!"

"Silas!" It was Gapinski. He shuffled over, favoring his left leg. He lifted Silas up by the arm, setting him up upright.

"Have you seen Celeste?"

He shook his head. "Last I saw she had been running toward the front to protect—"

"The Shroud!"

They both looked toward the front, recognition settling in.

"Celeste!" They both cried, scrambling forward. The image of her materialized as they got closer to where the high altar stood, and the dust began to settle from the explosion.

The first thing Silas noticed was Jesus: he had fallen off the cross, having been jostled loose by the explosion. He landed upright, arms raised in supplication toward the heavens.

The second thing he noticed was Celeste. She was statue-still, staring downward. He followed her gaze toward where the Shroud had sat just minutes before.

At the center of the space was a void so black and dark and

totalizing that it seemed to suck into itself every religious affection of the great religious structure.

"No!" Silas yelled, running over to the maw of blackness, straddling its edge.

Celeste stood next to him holding her hand over her mouth. Gapinski stood behind them turning outward toward the room, both rifles ready to respond to anything that might come back toward them for more.

Staring into the black void of nothingness Silas realized Nous's real objective.

They didn't want to merely discredit the Shroud or prevent others from validating it.

Nous wanted the Holy Image of Christ destroyed. Vanquished from the face of the earth!

Along with the resurrection memory it contains.

CHAPTER 24

Totally and completely flawless.

That's what Jacob Crowley thought while taking a drag on his cigarette as the truck rental sped through the wet Parisian streets, pleased with himself at their success.

After the controlled blast, his men had moved quickly through the newly-carved crypt beneath Notre Dame to extract their precious cargo. Months of digging and even more months in planning had finally paid off. It wasn't the early bird who caught the worm, but the patient buzzard who caught the bird.

And boy did they make a catch today!

His men had made quick work to remove what masonry had fallen into the tunnel during the controlled demolition of the cathedral's floor. Then they hustled to load the fourteen-foot long encased Shroud onto the motorized mining equipment that would whisk it out of the tunnel. The plan had worked beautifully, just as he had practiced for the past year.

When the Vatican announced there would be a special viewing of the Shroud of Turin in Paris to commemorate the last time it had been kept by the Knights Templar, Crowley and Borg knew this was the Universe's appointed time to make their move.

They knew they wouldn't be able to storm the cathedral itself, given the very public nature of the event and the security the Vatican would provide to ensure the safety of one of the holiest artifacts of Jesus of Nazareth in Christendom. So they worked out a scheme to steal the sacred relic right from under the Church's nose. Literally. Crowley and a few of his men had embedded themselves with an onsite demolition and excavation crew in Nice to learn the art of controlled explosives and how to leverage the old sewer work beneath the cathedral to excavate the world underneath—all in order to extract the Shroud from the Church's possession.

This success would more than make up for bungling the mission to remove Silas Grey from the picture. No matter. Not only had they taken out the people who could have authenticated the Shroud and supposed historical event of Jesus' resurrection. They had taken the very object of their mutual affection.

All to destroy it.

Crowley stared out the window of the speeding truck as he took another long drag on his cigarette, hearing distant sirens racing toward the mayhem they had just created. The smell of burnt tobacco instantly transported Crowley to a childhood memory.

He was twelve, and it was after school had let out. His mother had picked him up and taken him to their English-countryside chapel to work her job as the church janitor. He complained loudly. Church was the last place he wanted to go. She drove silently, ignoring his complaints. After arriving, she told him to occupy himself for a few hours while she finished her remaining janitorial tasks, dutifully preparing God's home for God's people for the coming Sunday.

Occupy himself he did.

It took him awhile, but after rummaging through the kitchen basement, he found what he had been searching for. A lighter. He rubbed the small flint wheel against the metal, a sparking flickering flame to life. He smiled, the burnt orange glowing against his young, white face in the darkened basement, wicked shadows dancing upon the church kitchen.

He pressed his palm over the flame until it snuffed out, the sensation a curious mix of unimaginable pain and pleasure, heightened by the smell of burnt, young flesh. He squeezed his eyes shut to move through the pain, a small tear rolling down his cheek. Then he raced out of the kitchen and up the stairs to the sanctuary up above. His mother was still in the basement, vacuum roaring away.

Good.

The mustard-yellow carpet squeaked under young Jacob Crowley's feet as he walked up the aisle. A pale yellow was cast over the sacred space from the light streaming through muddy windows. It smelled of old wood and older people who had paid supplication for generations. A shiver of doubt wound up his spine as he approached the large wooden pulpit that dominated the platform, Christ hanging high and proud behind it on a large wooden crucifix.

He stood before that cross and sneered, then reached in his pocket for the lighter. He flicked it to life, still staring at those Roman boards of execution, eyes narrow and dark, breathing labored and heart thumping away in that small chest.

Then a smile curled upward on one side of his mouth. He approached the cross, lighter close to his chest. He could feel the heat, smell the afterburn of the fuel. The breath coming out of his nostrils made the flame flicker, almost puffing out. He held his breath and looked upward, straight up the emaciated body of the Lord he had chosen to deny. He hovered the small flame between him and the cross, but hesitated, still staring straight into the eyes of Christ.

Resolve flooded him, a forward-compelling sensation that

was both worldly and otherworldly, as if something—*someone*—outside of himself drove him to carry out the task.

So he did.

His small hands trembled as he held forth the lighter at the base of the cross. The small flame danced yellow against the old wood, at first merely singeing it black. But then a faint but steady stream of charcoal smoke began to twirl upward. The smell made the boy tingle with delight. He smiled as the smoke grew stronger.

And then it happened.

The crucifix caught fire. It was small, but the lighter nourished it with its own life-blood until the flame took on a life all its own.

Crowley stepped back, his grin widening as the fire began burning the cross and then the image of Christ himself. First his feet, then his legs until it was stretching upward and consuming the entirety of God's Son.

A drunken giggle escaped Crowley's mouth. Then another, until a rack of laughter consumed him, convulsing his small frame until he was doubled over and laughing so hard he could hardly catch his breath. He thought he might wretch from the pleasure.

A crash brought him back to his senses. Jesus had broken free of the crucifix and slid down the wall. There it was, a scene of damnation on full display: fire was eating away at the facade behind the pulpit at the front of the quaint country chapel. The boy's eyes grew wide with delight, then with fear as the giant hands of the beast he had unleashed began stretching over his head and wrapping around the interior of the sanctuary.

Crowley darted out of the sacred space, through the main doors, and down the stairs to his family's car, reaching the driver's side door—

Wait. The driver's side door. *Mother!*

He whipped around to face his deed, the fire growing to a

hellish blaze. He stood still, his lower lip trembling, hair matted to his forehead from the sweat dripping down his face. But then he leaned against the car door, folded his arms, and propped a foot behind him. His eyes narrowed, and one corner of his mouth began to curl upward with pleasure.

When asked later why he had started the fire and left his mother inside to burn to death, he had only one thing to say: "The Devil made me do it."

Nobody believed him. But it was true.

The Devil *had* made him do it. And he would do it again. Gladly.

A few years later, his father died in a car accident after a night binging in his favorite pub. He had taken to hard drinking when his wife of fifteen years passed, and even harder hitting of the twelve-year-old son who caused it to happen. It was all too much. Young Crowley had been plotting for a way to get rid of his father like he had his mother. It seemed like Fate or the Devil or Whatever had looked after him. Ironically, after becoming a ward of the state and bouncing around orphanages, he was taken in by a religious orphanage in Europe associated with the Catholic Church. And then he met Rudolf Borg, who put all the pieces together for him, giving him meaning and purpose—changing his life forever.

Crowley took another drag and blew, smiling as the smoke drifted out of the cracked window. Mayhem, destruction, fire. These were the tools of Crowley's trade that would forever remove the memory of that silly crucifix from his heart. The Devil made him do it once before, and he was making him do it again.

Gladly.

The truck jerked to a stop in a darkened warehouse. Crowley hadn't noticed the change in scenery until the driver's door slammed shut. He finished his cigarette, then flicked it out his door as he exited. The rear door was open when he circled around back, his prize awaiting inspection.

"Careful," he said to the men inside who were sliding the long encased Shroud out of the truck. "This isn't the final destination. It must remain intact for a very special ceremony in Germany."

"Germany," one of the men said. "You didn't say anything about Germany. How are we going to get this thing across the Rhine, let alone out across the Marne out of Paris?"

"You're not." Crowley aimed his gun and shot the man in the forehead. His head snapped suddenly backward, the body slumping against the inside wall of the truck.

"Anyone else have a problem?"

The five other men stepped backward in silence, arms raised.

"No problem, boss," the darker of the crew said. From Algiers, if he remembered. Muslim, a dedicated soldier to the cause.

"Good." He shoved the pistol in his pants at the small of his back. "Now, let's crack this open."

The men made quick work of removing the encased Shroud from the truck, carefully lowering it off the back and onto the solid concrete floor. Tools had already been brought into the rendezvous point to extract the holy relic.

The dark-skinned man picked up a crowbar to begin prying the Holy Image from its cocoon.

"No," Crowley said, putting out his hand. "Wait."

He lit another cigarette, took a long drag, and walked up to the relic that had caused him so much torment, kneeling in front of it. He stared into the eyes of the same image he had locked sight with thirty years ago in that country chapel, then blew out the smoke in its face. The haze mushroomed outward off the imprinted face of Christ behind the thick glass. Crowley smiled.

The Devil made me do it. Gladly.

He stood up and nodded to the Algerian. The man walked back over to the right side, looking for a place to wedge the bar. He scanned the side, then the top. He frowned. Nothing. He walked along the back, continuing to look for a way in. The man stopped, used his thumb to pick at what he thought was a weak point in the seal. Again, nothing. He looked at Crowley, who was taking another drag on his cigarette.

"What's the problem?" Crowley asked.

"I can't find an opening. It's sealed shut."

Crowley frowned and blew the smoke out of his nostrils in frustration. "Give it to me." He yanked the crowbar from the Algerian and smashed it against the corner of the frame.

No dent, no mark. Nothing.

He flicked his cigarette onto the floor, then hit it again, using both hands to come down on the frame.

Nada.

Not good.

He gave the Algerian a look, detecting a hint of vindication. He almost threw the bar at the man's head, but threw it to the side instead. He walked over to the set of tools lying on a metal table lighted by a halogen telescoping light. He picked up a sledgehammer, heavy and hard, with a well-balanced head.

Looked like the case was more sophisticated than he had anticipated. It wasn't going to give up the Holy Shroud without a fight. No matter. Crowley walked over to it and yelled as he swung the hammer with all of his might, connecting with the glass dead center.

The hammer bounced off the clear plane, sending it flying from Crowley's hands five feet away.

A giggle burst from one of his men standing near the back of the truck. Crowley reached behind his waist as he walked over to the man. He pulled out his gun and shot him in the chest, blood splattering across his jacket and face. The man gasped, making weak wheezing sounds, then slumped to the ground clutching the front of his shirt as blood seeped out of the wound.

Crowley wiped the blood off his face with the back of his hand.

182 | J. A. BOUMA

"Anyone else?"

The four remaining men were silent, eyes wide, mouths opened. They glanced at one another and shook their heads.

"Good." He put the gun at his back, then walked over to the Shroud's case. "Because it appears we've got some work to do."

CHAPTER 25

Total and complete disaster.

That was Radcliffe's response to Silas, Celeste, and Gapinski when they reported in at their new staging ground.

Once the French police had arrived to get their statements on the who-what-where-why following the firefight and explosion at Notre Dame, the three SEPIO operatives were directed by central command to a nondescript office several blocks north in the heart of Paris. The Order had several chapters throughout the world. Not only to conduct its educational initiatives and broadcast the memory of the historic Christian faith. But also to carry out its more kinetic endeavors. The office was spartan, but provided the three a hot shower, change of clothes, and secure equipment to debrief with Radcliffe back in DC. The hot shower and change of clothes could wait. The secure equipment to debrief with Radcliffe could not.

Celeste reached a frantic Radcliffe who demanded: "What the bloody hell happened?" She described in detail the attack, from the twelve or so operatives to the fleeing crowd to the controlled explosion and extraction of the Shroud through the floor.

He was gobsmacked.

Radcliffe said, "Nothing in all of my history as Master of the Order and Head Commander over SEPIO has happened on the scale as this terrorist assault on the Shroud at Notre Dame!"

The three sat silently as he unloaded, recognizing his exasperation wasn't with them, but the turn of events.

"The Vatican, nay the whole Christian community, had entrusted the Shroud to our care. And we failed them."

That stung, but they let him continue.

"The only saving grace for the operation is that the Shroud is set behind a sheet of impenetrable, transparent, multi-layer, laminated polycarbonate and sealed in a frame that's more secure than Fort Knox, as you Yanks would say, Dr. Grey."

Silas nodded as Radcliffe caught his breath.

"And thanks to the ingenuity of Zoe, here, we can track its location using the radio frequency device embedded in its backside."

The team knew about the security precautions developed by the Vatican a few years ago during their pre-mission debrief with Richter in the command center outside the cathedral. They hadn't planned on having to lean on them, however.

"Radcliffe, Silas here. How on earth did these operatives manage the heist?"

Radcliffe sighed. "Nous has grown far more sophisticated, I'm afraid. Which makes me doubly-worried for our future. They used demolition-grade detonation devices to create a controlled blast in order to remove the Shroud from below. Which you already knew. The other side of the story is the tunnel extended from underneath Notre Dame south under the Seine and connected to the old sewer system that runs under the city. Reminded investigators of a heist from a few years ago in Berlin. Thieves tunneled one hundred feet underground and through three feet of thick concrete walls to break into a bank's strong room, stealing money and valuables worth more than ten million euros. Appears to be the same crew."

"Good Lord," Celeste said. "So what's the plan?"

Silas said, "The plan is we go after the Shroud."

"Go after the Shroud?" Gapinski ask. "Are you nuts?"

Silas stood, "No, I'm not nuts! What else are we going to do? Let Nous steal the major proof I have to the validity of Christ's resurrection?" Silas stopped himself. "Steal the proof the *Church* has to the validity of Christ's resurrection and do God only knows what with it?"

"Well, yes."

Silas rolled his eyes. "What a joke."

Gapinski continued, "It's not that I don't care what happened to the Shroud, and all. But you saw how sophisticated they were, and what we're up against. I say we pause and regroup and wait for reinforcements. Besides, it's not like it's going anywhere. We're tracking it, and the thing is as big as a whale!"

"You seriously—"

"Alright, boys. Let's put away the swords." Sitting between Silas and Gapinski, Celeste put a hand on each of their knees. "Radcliffe, what say you?"

"Let me turn it over to Zoe. She can help fill you in on where we are at with tracking the Shroud."

There was a noise of movement, then static. "Are you there? Can you hear me?"

"Hear you, Zoe," Celeste said. "What's the status of the Shroud?"

"Shroud seems to be doing fine. We detected a few break-in attempts. Before the viewing, we lined the frame and glass with a number of sensors to monitor the condition of the Shroud's casing. It's definitely withstanding their attempts to break in, that's for sure. But it's not eternally impenetrable. They can get in eventually."

Celeste looked at Silas, detecting some relief on his face. She said, "And where is it?"

What sounded like a keyboard clacked away, then a few

mouse clicks. "A warehouse on the south side of the city, just outside the city limits."

"They've already made it that far?" Silas wondered.

"The good news is that the Shroud is still kicking, and so is the tracker. We should be able to locate and engage at will."

Silas stood. "Then that's what we'll do." He grabbed his Beretta off a table to the side, then slung his AR-15 around his shoulder.

"What, you're just going to go kick down some doors, Rambo?" Gapinski asked.

"Whatever it takes. Together or alone."

Celeste said, "Just hold on, Silas. Let's think this through."

"What's to think about? We've got the location of the Shroud. The longer we wait, the greater chance they have to move it or open it—or worse."

Celeste paused. "I've got another idea."

Silas sat back down and crossed his arms. "I'm listening."

"It's clear that Nous's plan all along has been more than merely discrediting the Shroud or preventing others from validating it. The amount of planning that went into extracting the Shroud at a rare public viewing was just too great."

Silas loosened his arms and nodded. "Clearly, destruction seems to be their objective."

"Right. So why don't we beat them at their game?"

"I don't follow."

"We're going to go after the Shroud. That's a given. But what if we did more? They want to prevent the Shroud from being scientifically and historically validated. Let's not give them the satisfaction." She looked straight into Silas's eyes. "Finish your work, finish what you started this week. Prove your original theory. That an event happened surrounding the Shroud, a radiological event. A resurrection event. Information is power, they say. Use it to shut Nous up and shut them down."

"But they've destroyed my work. I have nothing left. How could we possibly—"

It hit him.

Silas and Celeste said it at once. "The Church of the Holy Sepulcher."

"Yes, that's it!" He exclaimed, jumping out of his chair.

Celeste smiled. "Exactly."

"The Church of the Holy Whatchamacallit?" Gapinski asked.

"Holy Sepulcher," Silas said. "The burial tomb of Christ. Great idea!"

"Hold up. What? We know where Jesus was buried? Where have I been the last forty years? And why isn't that a thing?"

Silas smiled at the man's ignorance. "It is a thing. That's why there's a church there."

"Oh, yeah."

"It's a major pilgrimage site for Christians of all stripes. Originally, the second-century Roman emperor Hadrian built a temple dedicated to the goddess Venus to bury the cave where Jesus had been laid. After Emperor Constantine became a Christian two hundred years later, he demanded that the pagan temple be torn down and replaced by a church. And, according to Church historian Eusebius, it was during the building of the church that Constantine's mother, Helena, is believed to have rediscovered the tomb. According to tradition, Constantine arranged for the rock face to be removed from around the tomb, without harming it, in order to isolate the tomb. Now it's enclosed by an eighteenth-century shrine, the Edicule. The Eastern Orthodox, Roman Catholic, and Armenian Apostolic Churches all have rights to the interior of the tomb."

Gapinski leaned back and folded his arms. "Alright, prof, that's interesting history and all, but I don't understand. How's that going to help us?"

"For generations, priests and scholars and laypeople alike have believed that Jesus Christ was resurrected from the dead.

And many believe that what was left behind when that remarkable event occurred was his burial cloth, with the imprint of his pre-resurrected, crucified body left on it."

"The Shroud," Gapinski said.

"The Holy Shroud. Lots of people have tried to dismiss the image for a number of reasons, as medieval forgery or as some early church painting by Jesus' early followers who were trying to cobble together evidence to make Christianity respectable. All of that's been proven wrong. It's not a painting. It's a negative image of a man basically burned onto the fibers of the linen itself."

"So how does the Church of the…"

"Holy Sepulcher," Celeste offered.

"Right, Holy Sepulcher. How does that help us?"

Silas continued. "One of the outstanding issues sindonologists, or Shroud scholars, have sought to solve is whether a so-called neutron flux event occurred within the Shroud. Basically, they believe that only a cloth collapsing through a body giving off particle radiation consisting of a neutron flux can explain the Shroud's image. If the body of the Shroud dematerialized, a portion of the main particles of matter—protons, electrons, and neutrons—would have given off gamma radiation. While the penetrating neutrons, electrons, and gamma rays would have passed completely through the cloth as it fell through the body region, the protons and alpha particles would have absorbed into the cloth, resulting in the image. A flux of neutrons is one of the results of radiation naturally given off by the dematerializing of the body. So the only explanation is that the Shroud was irradiated with a flux of neutrons coming off from the resurrecting body of Jesus."

"Whoa, whoa, whoa! Radiation? Neutron flux? As in, a nuclear bomb went off in Jesus' tomb?"

"Something like that. That's what I was trying to prove with Avery, before—" Silas's breath caught in his throat. "Before everything went to hell. We had secured a sample of the cloth for testing, but since that sample was destroyed that option is off the table. The only remaining chance we have to prove the Shroud scientifically and historically authentic is the Church of the Holy Sepulcher. The same flux of neutrons that the dematerializing body of Jesus would have given off within the Shroud would have also been given off within the limestone walls of his tomb. If we could prove that such an event happened in the tomb, then we can prove, at least inferentially, that what the memory of the Holy Shroud itself preserves is real and true, as well."

Silas's brain started firing on all cylinders at the possibility of realizing his professional dream. Validating his work was within reach. It was totally possible!

"Can I just say," Gapinski said, "this sounds positively nuts? While I'm a sucker for the insane, how are we going to pull this off? Not to get all morbid or anything, but your guy, Avery, got blown up. His equipment died with him. How is it exactly you think you can prove your neutron whatchamacallit event happened in the slab of ancient rocks?"

Celeste grinned knowingly, then looked to Silas.

Silas returned the grin, then looked to Gapinski.

"I feel like I'm not in on the joke. Do you have a magic beanstalk hidden away in that knapsack of yours that I don't know about? Just gonna drop a doodad in your lap to test the tomb?"

Celeste nodded toward Silas. "Tell him."

"I've got all the doodad I need. His name is Sebastian. And he developed a rival neutron flux detector to Avery's. Was pretty angry when he learned I went to Avery instead of him about it."

Celeste asked, "Do you think he'll help you help us?"

"That's the thing. Well, two things."

"What two things?" Radcliffe pipped in from the phone.

"Not only does he hate the Church, he hates me."

"Always something," Gapinski huffed.

CHAPTER 26

WEWELSBURG, GERMANY.

I*t's been too long. Something must be wrong.*

Rudolf Borg stared out of the tall, narrow window at the bleak, overcast landscape below of leafless trees and barren fields and small, beige-brick houses. Another storm was gathering on the horizon, threatening the small town. The rain had been relentless the past week, offering only a few hours of relief scattered throughout the past few days. No matter. Borg preferred his days handed to him by the dark, hopeless feeling of foreboding and despair that accompanied relentless storms, anyhow, to the bright optimism and cheery delight of sunshiny days.

After all, that's how he preferred life itself.

Borg coughed as he continued peering from his perch, transfixed on the stone spire of an old parish church a short distance from the castle in the village's center. It was the one the Borg family had attended stretching back generations. They had even helped build the east wing. He remembered every Saturday the summer after the year he turned ten hopping in his father's truck and driving downtown to meet the men of the church to work on the expansion. Papa had even let him hammer some nails into the wood frame that held one of the walls in place.

It was also the summer his parents were taken from him,

leaving him orphaned, abandoned. And the summer he would meet the teenage Jacob Crowley who would become so crucial to his life, awakening something within himself, both primal and pagan.

As a child, he knew there was something different about him. The boys in his German working-class neighborhood were the rough-and-tumble type who battled dragons with stick-swords and played endless games of football and rugby. Not him. And he was teased mercilessly for it. It wasn't until he met Jacob Crowley in a French halfway house run by the Catholic Church that those feelings were honed, nurtured. The two had found in each other something they had never been able to find in anyone else: safety, understanding, companionship.

Love. Or at least the kind either of them could understand in their own ways.

Jacob also awakened within him an evil spark his parents had tried unsuccessfully to exorcise. Literally. After his mother had stumbled upon him stabbing a screwdriver into a large rodent in their backyard, she and Dad took him to see Father Grunwald the next morning. After they had found a cat with its throat slit, they sought the help of an exorcist the Father recommended.

Borg didn't remember much about the sacred ceremony, except something had happened that startled the exorcist so badly that he stopped the sacred practice and sent him and his parents on their way. Something that he himself had done while restrained by his parents beneath the priest's gold cross. Something his parents had refused to talk about, other than claiming it was sheer evil.

Whatever the exorcist had done had worked. The impulses to maim and torture and kill had subsided. Until he met Jacob. They had seen within Borg's soul a small, burning ember waiting to be fanned into a passionate flame. He would come to find out later that it was something within Jacob himself that had wanted to stoke those nascent interests in the pagan into something worthy of his entire life. Something that was appreciated even more when the two were claimed by the ancient Order of Nous as protégés. Over the decades he had risen within the ranks to trigger the moment that had been welling within Nous for countless generations, like magma silently flowing under the earth's crust waiting to burst forth in fantastic, finalizing destruction.

And that moment was now. One the two would share together.

Borg smiled at the thought of his name, Jacob Crowley. No one made his heart beat with both affection and frustration than that man.

He glanced back to his desk where his mobile phone sat, having expected him to phone in by now. Nothing. He looked back outside, tightening his hand into a fist.

He better not fail me again.

But then he relaxed his hand and hoped he was alright, that nothing had befallen him.

He fixed his gaze once again on his childhood church. *You have no idea,* he thought, a smile curling upward on one side of his mouth. He coughed again, then wiped his nose with the handkerchief in his pocket. Thankfully, the relentless, convulsive coughing and headache from the past few days had subsided. He had work to do, and he needed every ounce of energy for the coming days.

A knock at the door startled him. "Yes, come in."

"Sorry, sir." It was Felix, one of his trusted assistants.

"What is it?"

"Jacob Crowley, sir."

Finally.

"Why didn't he call my mobile? I've been waiting for his call for hours."

"He said he tried calling, but it went straight to voicemail."

Borg picked up the phone lying on his desk and tried to bring it to life. Dead.

"And apparently...there was a problem."

His head snapped up. "Problem? What problem?"

Felix shuffled over, head down. He handed the satellite phone to Borg. "Here. I better let him explain."

Borg snatched the unit from him. "Jacob? Is everything alright? Why haven't I heard from you?" He sent Felix away with the wave of his hand.

There was a burst of static, causing Borg to jerk the handset away from his ear before bringing it back. "Hello?"

"Rudolf? Are you there?"

He sighed. "Yes, I hear you. What's your status? I've seen the news reports, so I understand you met with success."

"Yes, we did. Successfully extracted the Shroud from Notre Dame, losing only a few men."

Borg cursed silently, not for losing the men to death; he understood such outcomes were inevitable, necessary for what they were trying to accomplish. He was concerned with the optics and questions and potential attention the men would bring to Nous when investigators set to work. No matter. They were well insulated.

"Good, Jacob. Good." He smiled as he stared back out at the cross affixed to the spire of his childhood church. Soon that would be torn down, as well as every other sacred symbol of the Christian menace.

Borg had realized silence had enveloped the line, as if his partner were hesitating on the other end. "Jacob...What aren't you telling me?"

More hesitation. Then Jacob said, "It's the encasement. The bloody thing is impenetrable. I'm worried we're not going to be able to extract the Shroud for the necessary ceremony."

Panic pinged his gut. He understood the Shroud was guarded by tight security measures, not the least of which was its casing. He hadn't expected it to be that secure.

"What have you done to extract it?"

"Everything. Crowbars, saws, drills, blow torches. Nothing is working. We did find a digital display concealed on the back panel that looks like some sort of unlocking mechanism. We might try hacking into it to open the casing, but I'm afraid we will meet with failure."

Borg could hear faint sniffles on the other end. "There, there," he said soothingly, trying to comfort his partner. "You did well. It'll be alright."

"But I failed you!" Borg could hear Jacob's throat catch with emotion. "I wanted to do this for you. For us and the cause. And it's an utter disaster!"

Rudolf had seen Jacob swing wildly from one emotional extreme to another ever since their days at the orphanage. One minute compassionate, tender, vulnerable. The next raging, rabid, cruel. It was one of the reasons he loved him so, and why he was the perfect partner for him, for his cause. But he needed to help him get a grip. And he needed to get a grip on the situation. He was losing control. Nous was closer than ever to unleashing their full, destructive forces upon the Church, completing the post-Christian project they had begun executing two centuries ago upon the West.

And he knew just the person to help them make the final lap.

"Listen to me. You did admirably well. What you accomplished will secure the interests of the cause in ways that Nous hasn't been able to for generations. Centuries, even. Now, listen to me. There is someone who can help, an ally in our effort who hasn't been called upon yet. But I think it's time we cash in this chip."

Again more sniffles and a deep, heavy sigh, as if Jacob were getting a grip on himself. "Alright. What would you have me to do?"

"Bring the Shroud to me."

More hesitation. "Don't you think it's too dangerous?

Roaming the Continent in an eighteen-foot truck carting Christianity's greatest relic?"

Rudolf sighed. He despised weakness. It was time to take control. "Jacob," he growled, adopting a tone he had honed over the years to make his partner fall in line. "Stop the whining, stop the sniffling, and load the Shroud back in the truck. Climb back inside. And drive your pathetic, weak little self back to Wewelsburg, so I can pick up the pieces to an operation you have barely managed to keep alive. Do you understand?"

He thought he heard Jacob beginning to break on the other end. Instead, Jacob replied softly, weakly, "I understand."

Borg's heart was thumping in his chest. He hated having to resort to this abuse, but the cause demanded it. They were standing on the knife's edge now, and there was no room for waffling. He would make up for the tongue lashing when Jacob came home.

"Good," he purred. "Now get going. I'll see you soon."

"Yes, Grand Master."

"And Jacob," Borg added before ending the call. "Sei vorsichtig, meine liebe."

Be careful, my dear.

CHAPTER 27

WASHINGTON, DC.

Sebastian Grey poured himself a generous glass of Cabernet Sauvignon, filling the red wine glass half full. The second that evening. He set the bottle down, then picked it back up and added another two-fingers worth of the deep, red liquid, draining the bottle. After all, it had been one of his marathon teaching days at George Washington University. He deserved it.

He set his glass down and loosened his bow tie with an exhausted sigh, then sat down in an overstuffed tan, leather chair in his well-appointed, two-bedroom row house in Adam's Morgan, a district in Washington, DC that had seen a revitalization in the past decade. Restaurants serving international fusion dishes from around the world had risen alongside flower shops and craft coffee houses, transforming the former sketchy neighborhood into one of the hottest on the DC market.

Luckily for Sebastian, he had bought in early.

He closed his eyes as the melodic siren song of the American saxophonist John Coltrane filtered around his spacious living room. Jazz and wine were the perfect evening combination after the kind of day he had.

As his Amazon Echo offered up another jazz tune from his

Coltrane playlist, he flipped on the TV to CNN to catch up on the day's news. Images of an apparent terrorist attack were streaming with a live correspondent onsite offering the gory details. This time Paris, at the famed Notre Dame Cathedral.

Sebastian took a generous sip from his glass. He asked Alexa to turn down the volume, and he turned up the TV to hear more. The French correspondent explained how the cathedral had been the site of a special viewing of the Shroud of Turin, the purported burial cloth of Jesus Christ.

Sebastian snorted. "Yeah, right."

The correspondent detailed how attackers had stormed the cathedral, killing several tourists and injuring several more in the panic. And then how a controlled demolition-like explosion had allowed the attackers to extract the Shroud from below the ancient building, stealing it out from underneath Vatican security.

Sebastian continued listening, sipping his wine, letting its boysenberry and oak notes sooth him as he considered the fairy tales people continued to believe in the modern age. Like a man rising from the dead to save the world from a vengeful Spaghetti Monster hovering in wait to cast unsuspecting men and women into an eternal, secret existence of darkness and fire deep in the belly of the earth.

He smiled, thinking about his brother, who himself believed in a man rising from the dead to save the world from a vengeful Spaghetti Monster hovering in wait to cast unsuspecting men and women into an eternal, secret existence of darkness and fire deep in the belly of the earth.

Speaking of which...

Sebastian's cellphone was dancing on the end table to his right, *Brother* glowing at the top of the LCD screen. He took another mouthful of his wine, then another, before picking up his phone and swiping it to life. The last thing he wanted was another lecture about his godless ways.

He swallowed hard. "Glad to see you're still part of the land of the living. How are—"

"Seba listen," Silas interrupted, "we don't have time for chitchat."

"Good to hear your voice, too. In fact, I'm doing just fine, thank you very much. Though my day was pretty frustrating."

"Turn on CNN."

Sebastian huffed. "I already did, why? Did you see the dreadful news coming out of Paris? Terrorist attack on Notre Dame and all?"

Silas said nothing. Then added, "I am the news out of Paris."

Sebastian set down his glass. "What are you talking about? What do you mean, *you're* the news?"

"I was asked by an organization," Silas stopped, then recovered, adding: "by Vatican security to help secure the Shroud of Turin on display at the cathedral."

Confusion swam through Sebastian's mind, mixed with too much drink. "Why were you at Notre Dame? And why did the Vatican want your help with security? Sy, what's going on?"

"I don't have time to explain. But listen, I need your help with something. You've got a reading and lab week scheduled for the semester at GW in the next few days, don't you?"

"Yes...Why?"

"You don't happen to have any plans, do you?"

"Gee, you know, I had been dithering about what to do with my week, given that I'm not at all busy at the moment with three or four conference papers and journal articles and experiments I'm running."

"So then no plans?"

Sebastian huffed. "What is this about, Sy?"

"I need some help."

"Clearly," he mumbled, draining his glass.

"I need you to come to Jerusalem with me. I need your help with a little...experiment."

"Jerusalem?" he exclaimed, standing up and walking over to his wine rack. "What for?"

There was silence on the other end.

Sebastian looked at his phone, then put it on speaker so he could open another bottle of wine. This time a Malbec. "Hello?"

"I need you to bring that portable neutron flux detector you've been working on, the one you told me about that rivaled Avery's."

"Oh, the one you should have asked to use in the first place for your silly, little experiment? Does this have to do with that blasted Medieval forgery that was just swiped from Notre Dame?"

"It's not a forgery!"

Sebastian knew that would get a rise out him. He pulled the cork out of his fresh bottle and poured himself another half-glass. He took it and his phone and walked back over to his leather chair.

"Whatever. But if you think I'm hopping on a plane to the Holy Land, you're more deranged than I ever thought possible."

"Seba," Silas started, his tone softer, gentler. "I need your help. For real. Just one day. There's a chartered flight waiting for you at Dulles, direct to Tel-Aviv. Get on it. Meet me for the few hours it will take to complete the test. Then get on the plane and go back to your life. It's that simple."

"It's never simple with you, Silas. And I'm sorry, but that's out of the question."

"Why?"

"Because I have zero interest in taking part in any sort of nonsense connected to the Church. And that's my final answer." He took a large swig of wine.

Silas said nothing.

Several more seconds of silence ticked by. Sebastian continued waiting for a comeback, sipping the Malbec and stewing over his brother's audacity.

Silas finally said, "I'm playing the brother card on this."

Sebastian's eyes narrowed, and he swallowed his mouthful of wine hard. *He's going there, is he?*

The one thing left of their relationship, the rule they had made when Dad passed.

Because their mother died giving birth to them, the Grey boys had no one but themselves after 9/11. So they made a pact: if either of them needed the other for help, for whatever reason, they could invoke The Rule. Neither of them could refuse, no matter what it was.

Including flying half-way around the world to help brother legitimize a religious unicorn.

Sebastian was about to speak when Silas added: "And besides, the amount of academic credit you'll reap from this gig...Believe me. You'll want in on this."

Now he's appealing to my ego? The man must be desperate. A small grin formed at the thought.

"Silas, I—"

A crash startled him. Outside, out back. He stood up suddenly, knocking his wine over, staining a taupe Persian rug. He cursed loudly.

"Sebastian. What's going on?"

There it was again. Only this time he heard grunting noises, from two separate voices. Then gunfire. Three shots. Silence. Then two more.

"Were those gunshots?" Silas yelled through the speaker.

"Yes," he said, his voice faltering. "At least it sounded like it. From out back."

"Lock your doors. Then hang up and call 911."

Sebastian hesitated, then set down the phone and hustled toward the front door. Before he could get past his baby grand piano, it burst open, the jamb splintering into pieces.

"On the ground, on the ground!"

Heavily armed men with face masks and dressed in black

rushed through the broken doorway, weapons drawn and pointed at Sebastian, illuminating his panicked face with white light.

"Alright, alright," Sebastian cried as he hit the hardwood floor, his hands outstretched high over his head.

"Sebastian," the phone yelled as he gripped it. "Sebastian!"

"SEBASTIAN," Silas yelled into his cell phone, jumping up from his chair. "Sebastian!"

Celeste jumped up as well in surprise. "What is it? What's happening?"

"I don't know! We were talking, and I heard a noise. A thudding sound. He heard it, too. Said it sounded like someone out back. Then there were gunshots, and I told him to lock the doors and call 911."

He stopped, his face a twisted mess of confusion and concern.

"And?" Gapinski asked, searching along with Celeste for details.

"And there were loud voices yelling at him to get on the ground..." Silas trailed off. "It sounded like he was taken!"

Celeste walked back over to the phone still on speaker. "Radcliffe, you still there?"

"Still here." They had conference-called him in on the conversation with Sebastian.

"Can you coordinate with local law enforcement to figure out what in God's name happened to—"

"No need, Celeste. Everything's alright."

Silas whipped around from the window, facing Celeste and Radcliffe's voice on the phone.

"What do you mean?" she asked for him. "What's going on?"

"SEPIO had been monitoring your brother, Silas, in case Nous tried to get to you through him. After what happened at Georgetown, we didn't want to take any chances. I'm glad we didn't. One Nous operative was shot dead behind his house. Another was killed using...other means, apparently."

"So he's alright, then?" Silas said, grabbing the phone.

"He's fine. A little shaken, but he should recover just fine."

Silas tilted his head back, relief washing over him. He breathed in deeply, then said a prayer of thanks. "Well, can I talk to him? Is he there?"

"Let me get the local force commander on the line."

Silas smiled at Celeste. Gapinski slapped Silas on the back, joining in the celebration.

"Uhh, hello? Sy?" His brother sounded shaken.

"Sebastian? I was briefed by Radcliffe, Rowan Radcliffe, the head of—it doesn't matter. Apparently, there was an attempt on your life or something. And they disrupted it."

"Who did? And why would anyone want to take me out?"

"I can't explain now. I just need you to come to Jerusalem, with your neutron flux detector. Can you do that for me?"

There was silence on the other end. Silas took the phone away from his ear and checked the display. Still connected. "Sebastian?"

"Oh, alright," he said. "I'll come. Which, given the circumstances, might be the best thing for me anyhow."

Silas sighed in relief, nodding at Celeste and Gapinski, mouthing: *It's a go.* "Thank you, baby bro. I owe you big time."

"Yes, you do."

After relaying instructions for his journey to Jerusalem, Silas hung up the phone. Before ending the call, Radcliffe said the local SEPIO team would take care of him, making sure he got to Dulles and the Order-chartered flight.

One way or another, Silas was going to get his results on the radiological event and the Gospels' story of Jesus' resurrection.

"Gapinski and I will rendezvous with you and Sebastian in Jerusalem after we secure the Shroud," Celeste said. "That is, if we secure the Shroud."

Silas smacked his forehead with his palm. "That's right, the Shroud! Wait, let me help. Two against however-many-there-are Nous operatives isn't very good odds."

"No, you go to Jerusalem and run those tests. Prove the Gospel accounts are right. Prove that Jesus arose from the dead." She nodded at Gapinski. "We've got this. Then we'll rendezvous with you there."

Gapinski released the magazine from his gun, then locked it back in. "We've got this."

Silas nodded. It had been a long time since he had trusted a team of comrades to execute on mission. But now, more than ever, he needed others to do what he couldn't do himself.

CHAPTER 28

"Zoe, how are we looking?" Celeste asked from the passenger's seat of their Order-issued gray Mercedes G-class SUV.

With Sebastian and Silas in the air on their respective flights, Celeste and Gapinski set off in pursuit of the Shroud. Zoe had been closely monitoring the tracking beacon embedded in its frame. So far it hadn't budged.

"Looking good, Celeste. Shroud is still in the abandoned warehouse off the A86, and its vitals are looking great."

Celeste was amazed by all the data points Zoe was able to track. Micro-sensors detected any change in the integrity of the frame, picking up all of the dings and hits and attempts to wrench it open. Thankfully, to no avail. The glass itself, with an array of sensors embedded around the perimeter, tracked light refraction and density, and if the glass had been compromised in any way. Accelerometers gauged whether it was sitting upright or lying flat. Humidity and temperature sensors tracked the internal environment inside the frame, which was vital, for the ancient linen had to be kept at precise levels to maintain its longevity. Finally, the GPS tracker could determine where the Shroud was located within 3 centimeters. It had barely moved since being driven outside Paris.

This gave Celeste some sense of relief as she and Gapinski sped through the still-slick streets of Paris in pursuit.

She asked, "Have we made any headway on the intel side of things? It sure would be nice to know who it is we're up against."

"We have," Radcliffe said, joining Zoe on the line. "Intel confirms Nous is absolutely behind the attack. The dead operatives all had their unmistakable marking. And after reviewing the footage from MIT, we saw the same marking on the hand of one of the figures holding Avery's laptop. I'm sending it to you now."

Celeste's phone alerted her to the incoming message. There it was, unmistakable:

She had encountered such a marking several years ago while on assignment in Austria. For years, SEPIO had unsuccessfully tried to locate Nous's center of operation. She was sent to make headway and had been attacked while tracking a lead. But her MI6 training intervened: she rendered one unconscious, one had escaped, and she had killed the other one. She wasn't proud of that one, and Radcliffe had addressed her serious breach of protocol afterward; SEPIO had a strict no-kill policy. But it was either him or her.

She chose her.

While she failed to dig up any meaningful trace on Nous's location, she was able to bring back the intel on the marking staring back at her.

Apparently, Nous took for themselves the emblem of the ancient phoenix, the mythic desert bird that cyclically regenerates itself from the ashes of its predecessors every five hundred years. Which was ironic, because the emblem had been a symbol of Christianity. Not only because of the cyclical nature of the Church—which had regenerated itself every five hundred years or so—but because for early Christianity, the phoenix represented the resurrection, the bringing of new life.

The phoenix symbol was a tangible icon to represent Nous's movement to shift the world into a new rung of spiritual enlightenment: a reimagined New World Spirituality rising from the ashes of the Church.

Celeste said, "Right, so we know this is Nous. Anything else you can tell us?"

Radcliffe answered, "Our source has confirmed that the man you are looking for is a one, Jacob Crowley. He has a long, sordid history of hostility toward the Church. He has surfaced on our radar off and on, and there are conflicting theories about why."

"Do we know anything about him?"

"Not really. It has been difficult to break into the various levels of personnel and personalities within Nous. We will keep working on our sources and coordinating the data-mining operation to paint a clearer picture of our antagonist. But in the meantime, it goes without saying: use whatever means necessary to retrieve the Shroud."

Celeste took a breath. "Understood."

"I'd sure feel a lot better if we had one more man with us," Gapinski complained.

Celeste shot him a look, eyes narrowing. Piercing and questioning.

"Wait, I didn't mean it like that. Like, I'd feel better if there was another human with us. Another version of the *homo sapiens* line of mammals, regardless of gender. I would definitely take an illustrious, very capable and smart and brawny female version of the *homo sapiens*—"

"Gapinski," she interrupted. "I get it. Keep digging, and our truck will fall into the sewers."

He smiled weakly, looking embarrassed.

At this stage in her career, Celeste had grown used to those kinds of comments from her male colleagues. Having clawed her way up through the Special Intelligence Service with Her Majesty's government, doing things her male counterparts would never be required to do, the second-guessing and looks and apprehension she endured was just par for the course. And then when she was recruited by Rowan Radcliffe, first as an agent for SEPIO and then as its director, it was simply part of life. Her Majesty's government was at least a safe place for women to serve. The Bride's Church, however, was not.

Not that Gapinski was being hostile. He was a jolly, good chap, had always respected her rank and taken orders without question. Same for Radcliffe; he had neither countermanded nor questioned her decisions, giving her complete operational control over SEPIO itself and its missions. It was everyone else within the Order and the Church that was the problem. MI6 and the rest of the secular world may operate as one giant Boy's Club, but the sacred was ruled by patriarchy. Luckily for her, such male dominance hadn't been modeled in her childhood home.

Celeste Bourne was the youngest of five children, four of which were boys. So she was used to fighting for her rights in the face of overwhelming testosterone. Her parents, Paul and Penny, were the ones who modeled for her how it could look for a woman to exist in a man's world, and how men and women could work together as different equals for God's glory and the world's good. For it was her father who mostly raised the children and took care of the house, while her mother worked as a high-powered executive. The match really was made in heaven: Daddy was a writer who worked on contract projects, as well as his own books; Mum was a publisher with a major UK publishing house in London.

Celeste had caught snippets of conversations between her mother and grandmother, how she was abdicating her motherly responsibilities to her husband; how her children were going to go "wayward" because of maternal neglect; how it just wasn't "bib-lical" for a woman to earn the bread while the man baked it. Her mother was unwavering. And every time she caught her daughter listening in, she would take her aside afterward to tell her that Granny meant well, but was wrong. Yes, God had designed men and women differently, but they were equals in his eyes and equally called to make his world a better place. Mum modeled that truth perfectly. Not that it was easy; the Serpent took care of that.

Celeste brought her mum's attitude to Oxford, where she graduated magna cum laude, and then to the intelligence service when she was hired as an agent. She would do the man's job a woman's way. And she succeeded marvelously, receiving commendations for her work in uncovering an al-Qaeda terror plot against Parliament and her work as a field agent in Palestine. It was through that experience that she met Radcliffe, and became part of SEPIO, leading to her current mission.

"How are we doing? Are we there yet?"

Gapinski's question snapped her mind back into focus. "Right. Looks like we're fifteen minutes out." Celeste continued glancing at the GPS tracker as they moved through the morning traffic, the blue orb pulsing as it remained stationary.

She set the tracker on the dashboard, then brought out her SIG Sauer. She released the magazine, inspected it, then slid it back in, locking it in place. She pulled back the release, sighted the barrel, then chambered a round in preparation.

"So what's the plan, chief? Surely, we're not waltzing in, guns blazing."

She retrieved the GPS unit. "We'll park a few blocks away...here." She pointed to an abandoned parking lot two blocks south of the warehouse complex. "That should give us enough distance to stage our pursuit, while also being close enough if things turn sour."

Between Celeste and Gapinski a radio crackled to life. "Celeste? Do you copy?"

It was Zoe. The two SEPIO agents looked at each other with equal amounts of concern and question. There was supposed to be a blackout on communication until the operation was complete and the Shroud had been secured.

Celeste picked up the comm unit. "Celeste here. What's going on, Zoe?"

"We've got a problem."

"Of course we do," Gapinski said, smacking the steering wheel.

Celeste shushed him. "Go ahead."

"How far out are you from the rendezvous point?"

"Just over ten minutes. Why?"

"Because it appears the Shroud is moving. Nous is on the road, and moving fast."

Gapinski cursed. "Always something."

CHAPTER 29

The morning traffic on Paris's A4 was a stop-and-go nightmare, ebbing and flowing in fits and starts. After leaving the warehouse, Jacob Crowley and his crew had jumped on the A86 and taken it north, the main artery leaving the City of Lights. And now they were crawling. Not the kind of forward movement he wanted for his seven-hour journey to Rudolf in Wewelsburg, Germany.

As one of his men drove, he sat in the passenger's seat tugging nervous drags on his cigarette, looking in his side mirrors for any sign of law enforcement. He had been surprised they had encountered zero resistance after their little heist. SEPIO was getting rusty. He hoped the afternoon drive would prove as eventless. Even so, he took comfort knowing an SUV of three of his men shadowed the truck just in case.

A siren caught his attention as he pulled in nicotine-laced smoke. Two of them were coming up behind them fast. One in the lane to their right, another in the lane to their left. As if they were making a play to box them in as they drove the center lane away from the city.

Crowley's man shifted in his seat, glancing out of both mirrors, clearly beginning to panic. "What do I do, boss?"

"Stay calm. Slow down, like the other cars are doing."

The blare grew louder, screaming at them to move over. As if it was listening to the authoritative command, the car in front of them applied its breaks, having the same idea as Crowley. The lane of cars straddling them on either side began veering off to the side to let the emergency vehicles pass.

Crowley glanced at his mirror as he retrieved his weapon from underneath his seat. The driver did the same, pulling out a semi-automatic.

"Keep that thing down in the well, you idiot! You're going to get us killed for sure."

The man shoved it back beneath his seat as the two police units cruised up to the sides of the truck, then sped past them as the sea of cars parted. Two other police units they hadn't seen followed closely behind in pursuit.

Apparently, some other terrorist was their target.

Crowley audibly sighed, settling back into his seat and putting his weapon back below. He rubbed his face and took out another cigarette, lit it, then pulled longingly at it. He closed his eyes and held the smoke, letting it settle his nerves back into place.

Seven hours couldn't come soon enough.

GAPINSKI USED the interruption by the four French police cars as an opportunity to make some headway through the packed Parisian highway, riding the wake the parted vehicles had left behind. They had made quick work of diverting their route toward the southeast side of the city when Zoe gave them word the Shroud was on the move, picking up the A86 after navigating some side streets, and then jumping on the A4 east out of Paris.

The GPS unit showed their target was up ahead, maybe a quarter mile. But they needed to close the gap fast until they were fully engaged again. From there, anything could happen.

"How close are we?" Gapinski asked.

Celeste said, "A quarter mile or so, but it looks like they are having the same idea. They're speeding up."

"I'm on it."

Gapinski hit the accelerator, pulling ahead beyond several cars before being forced to ease off as the traffic resumed its original pace and merged back into their lanes. He used his horn to signal his discontent. They used their fingers to signal theirs. A Renault compact cut him off, then sped away.

Gapinski cursed, then hit the horn again. "Damn French drivers."

"Don't draw attention to yourself. The last thing we need is Nous sniffing us out before we can pounce. Or the police. We got them locked in. It will all be over shortly."

"That's what I'm afraid of."

Twenty minutes later the traffic began to thin as they moved farther out of Paris's reach, giving them a window to make up the distance. It was clear the Nous operatives were playing it cautious, not wanting to draw attention to themselves by maintaining the speed limit. It didn't take long for Gapinski to catch up to them.

"There they are." Celeste pointed to a long, white van up ahead cruising in the center lane.

He let off the accelerator, changing to the leftmost lane to trail them and keep them in sight.

"Looks like we've got company."

Keeping pace with the white van was a black BMW X1. Inside were what looked like three other people. Sure enough, the white van changed lanes to their right a few cars up, so did the BMW. When it accelerated slightly, so did their shadow.

Celeste said, "Most definitely."

"At least these guys prioritize form over function. I'd put our Mercedes G-Class up against that Beemer crossover any day. If it comes to it, I can take them."

"Settle, tiger," Celeste said, eyeing the shadowing vehicle. "Let's hold back here for a while and see where they are heading. I prefer Ready-Aim-Fire. In that order."

"But that's no fun."

They continued following, holding a several-car pace behind the van, this time from the center lane in order keep a better eye on their target. Soon they were out of the orbit of the city and into the countryside headed toward Reims.

Gapinski finally said, "This is bananas. When are we going to do something? They are clearly road-tripping it. What about taking them now that the crowd has thinned?"

Celeste considered this. "I think it's time to check in with Radcliffe."

CROWLEY HAD NOTICED the gray Mercedes an hour back. It had come up suddenly in the sea of cars, then hung back in the left lane. He told himself not to panic; it was just another one of the thousands of Parisian commuters. But when they had changed lanes to settle in for the next five-hour ride toward their destination, it had shifted to the center lane. It was doing a good job of tailing them. Maybe it was a couple on holiday, heading out to explore and enjoy a countryside getaway.

Or, maybe not.

"Ai, come in," he said into his comm unit to the shadowing BMW. "Ai, respond. Do you copy?"

The unit crackled to life. "Sorry for the delay. Yes, we hear you. Everything alright?"

"Check out that gray Mercedes at your seven o'clock. What do you see?"

He waited for the report, fishing for another cigarette. He would feel better once they reached the Belgium border. But they were still a few hours out.

"Large, male driver. Female passenger. Both wearing dark clothes. Nothing seems suspicious."

"Did you run the plates?"

"No."

Crowley sighed, blowing smoke out his window. "Well, do that. Then report back." He tossed the comm unit in the center console, then took another drag, glancing back at the vehicle. They were tailing him. He just knew it.

Several minutes ticked by before AI reported back in. "The vehicle is registered to the gendarmerie of the Vatican."

Adrenaline sized him. The Order of Thaddeus.

All at once the Mercedes grew in stature as it accelerated hard toward the shadowing BMW, veering a hard right and smashing into its left corner, tearing into its fiberglass bumper and sending it swerving sideways into the center lane.

Crowley threw his cigarette out his window, then grabbed his weapon and cocked it into action.

Let's do this, SEPIO.

CHAPTER 30

"Let's do this, Nous," Gapinski growled, turning the wheel sharply to the right.

Celeste braced herself.

After updating Radcliffe on the developments, he had given them the green light to take any means necessary to secure the Shroud. It could withstand quite a beating, so don't hold back, he said.

They hadn't. They were actually doing this, right on the French highway.

Gapinski was right; he was able to take them with ease. The solid piping on the front end of the Mercedes easily tore through the back end of the BMW, sending it off course and into a minivan.

It wasn't a fatal blow, but it would do.

Gapinski straightened the wheel and stabilized their own course. She looked inside the car as they passed it and saw three male passengers, all shocked and shaken.

Had they made a horrible error in judgment, mistaking a car full of French businessmen for terrorists?

Nope. No judgment error at all.

"Watch it," she said.

The car quickly recovered, turning around and smashing into their Mercedes. It jerked to the left, but Gapinski's solid arms held the car firm.

Cars around them were beginning to scream and slow with alarm. The minivan the BMW had hit veered off the highway, its passengers fleeing into a field. This was a public gamble Celeste was hoping would pay off.

The Beemer swung around from behind, connecting solidly with the passenger door, startling Celeste. Gapinski cursed, but held steady, then cranked the wheel to the left to bring them to the leftmost lane. He clipped the bumper of a Mini Cooper in the center lane. It protested loudly.

"Sorry, dude, but I'm a little busy to care."

The two cars held steady, eyeing each other from across the highway. With the flick of his arms, Gapinski twisted the wheel to the right and floored it, so that the car was angling hard toward the Beemer. Celeste pushed deep into the seat to brace herself, just as the larger Mercedes connected broadside with the smaller SUV, sending it into steel guardrails along the side. He pulled left, then hit them again before accelerating hard and leaving them on the side.

"Did that do the trick?"

Celeste twisted backward. "Unfortunately, no."

The BMW was severely smashed along both sides but was still operational. And angry.

"Damn German engineering."

Time to end this before it gets even more out of control.

Gapinski swung the steering wheel to the left, crossing two lanes of traffic. Thankfully, everyone on the road had pulled back, giving him plenty of space for the maneuver. The BMW seemed startled by the move, holding course in the right-most lane. The cars continued running parallel next to each other, the white van taking point while the black car continued shadowing.

Celeste rolled down her window and aimed for the rear tire.

She fired, the shot went wide, and found nothing of interest. She lined up another, shot twice, then cursed. One buried in the rear bumper. The other went clear through the left rear paneling.

"Hold steady," Celeste shouted, "I can't get a clear shot with your erratic driving."

"I thought you were former MI6. Didn't they teach you how to shoot going eighty?"

Celeste was about to respond with a witty retort about how Gapinski almost flunked basic training when a succession of gunfire interrupted.

The Beemer had had enough. It was firing back.

Gapinski slammed on the breaks to sever their line of sight, bullets shattering the two passenger-side windows. Mercifully, the rest of the shots scattered into the air.

"Are you alright?" Gapinski asked.

Celeste brushed glass out of her hair and off her pants. "I think so."

Gapinski pulled back farther as the hostile Beemer tried to adjust its shot.

"We've got to end this. If I punch it, can you get the shot and take the tire?"

Celeste's heart was working overtime, the pressure rising in a way she hadn't felt since her days with MI6 in Palestine. It was up to her. No one else.

"Bourne, can you get the shot?"

Celeste snapped her head to Gapinski at the sound of her last name, hating it when men called her like one of the fellas from the team.

"Punch it."

He smiled, popping the clutch and flooring it.

She leaned out the window, SIG Sauer extended, sighting down the barrel. An arm inside the Beemer reached out bearing an assault rifle, readying its own aim. So she shot it. The weapon jerked up and shot wildly in the air, giving her enough of a diversion to send a bullet clear into the left rear tire.

It shredded instantly.

The car fishtailed, favoring its left hindquarters. It was clear the driver was no longer in control, so he put on the breaks in the middle of the highway. No reason soldiering on with a lame leg. They abandoned their vehicle and weaved through traffic, bailing off the highway and into a pasture before the authorities could arrive.

With the shadow disabled, Gapinski accelerated toward the white truck.

"That was easy," Celeste said, leaning back into her seat.

"Yeah, but what about that guy?" Gapinski pointed out the front windshield at the white truck ahead, which had pulled away, clearly spooked by its seemingly diminishing chances. "Nice shot, by the way."

Celeste blew the top of the barrel of her gun, making a bottle-blow sound. "Thanks. And punch it, I've got an idea."

Gapinski smiled. "I like the sound of this."

Within minutes he caught up to the white truck, running parallel to it in the leftmost lane with the center as a buffer.

"Now pull past it and bring the car right in front."

"I like the sound of this even better."

Knowing they were no match to ram nearly four tons of steel as they had the Beemer, Gapinski steamed past the truck, the driver's head turning in clear curiosity, if not panic.

Gapinski merged right so that they were now in the lead. Wasting no time, Celeste pulled herself out of her shattered window and twisted to face the white beast. Gun raised and outstretched.

As if the beast knew what was coming, it lurched forward, trying to make contact with its rear. Gapinski saw it coming too late. Celeste ducked back inside just as the front end smashed into the Mercedes, shattering the back window. As if to put an exclamation point on its rage, bullets flew into the back, though the angle of its height didn't seem to allow it to hit its primary target. The humans inside.

"Gapinski..."

"I've got it." He pushed the accelerator to the floor, the car pulling away quickly. The white truck tried to keep pace, but couldn't recover as quickly, giving Celeste another opportunity. She took it.

Positioning herself back out the window, she took aim. "Ease up on the accelerator," she said.

Just as the truck began pulling forward, Gapinski obliged.

There was a saying that stuck with Celeste in primary school from one of her world history classes when they covered the American Revolution. It came from a rebel Yank commander from across the pond during the Battle of Bunker Hill: "Don't fire until you see the whites of their eyes."

The sage advice had served her on more than one occasion.

And there they were.

Bingo.

The shot was singular, yet compassionate. A hot knife slicing through butter, the bullet burst through the tempered glass and out the back of the man's shoulder.

The government taught her vengeance; the Church taught her mercy. The Church won this time. Yes, she maimed the man, but at least he would live. He reacted with expected shock and agony.

The van careened violently off the highway, the incline causing it to topple over as it plowed through wire fencing and into a pasture, mowing over two grazing cows before it came to rest.

"What a shot!" Gapinski exclaimed.

Celeste looked back toward the toppled van as their car braked along the highway several yards past.

Gapinski put the Mercedes in Park, and they quickly exited

and ran toward the motionless white truck, weapons drawn for any hostility. Celeste led the charge, stopping short at the front of the upturned truck. She peered around toward the cabin, seeing no one.

Dammit.

They ran along the undercarriage to the rear of the truck to check its cargo. Celeste positioned herself to the right, while Gapinski readied himself to open the still-closed hatch. She nodded, and Gapinski slid the latch upward, twisted it, then flipped down one of the doors.

Celeste whipped around toward the opened door, weapon drawn for a fight. Finding none, she flipped the other door up and held it to let more light into the truck's bed.

There it was. The Shroud of Turin, jostled onto its face, but safe and secure.

She sighed audibly, then looked at Gapinski. "Stay here with the Shroud. I'll check the cabin."

She padded along what was the top of the truck, paused at the cabin roof, then peered around the windshield. The driver's side door was flipped open at the top. Still strapped into his seat was the driver, shoulder blown from Celeste's shot and blossoming with blood. He looked as though he had passed out. There was no one else.

Which meant that Jacob Crowley had escaped.

CHAPTER 31

The private charter courtesy of the Vatican that had transported Celeste, Gapinski, and Silas to Paris just fourteen hours ago was beginning to descend into Ben Gurian airport. Silas continued resting in the reclined seat, trying to recover from the few past days and gear up for the next day of activity in the Holy Land.

He held the Holy Image in his mind, praying that it would be recovered, that it was safe. For the world desperately needed its memory. After all, it is the "why" of the Christian faith.

For millennia, billions of people had believed something happened in history to a man named Jesus of Nazareth. That he was bloodied and butchered on those Roman boards of execution that held his limp, lifeless body. He died, for the sins of the world. The latter was more a matter of faith, but it was still rooted in events of history. Especially the historical fact that something happened to Jesus' body.

Sure, plenty of people had explained away its disappearance. Muslims claimed Jesus hadn't died at all, but merely swooned; he fell unconscious and then was revived by the special combination of coolness and humidity in the cave-like tomb. He was believed to have walked out and died in India spreading his message of hope and peace as a prophet of Allah. Not "the" prophet, mind you. Just another good-natured teacher of the Muslim God.

Silas knew this made no sense given the pornographic violence Jesus suffered. There would have been no way Jesus would have survived the artistic form of execution perfected by Empire Rome.

Then there were those of a more enlightened, Western sort who claimed the disciples stole the body of Jesus in order to shape Jesus' narrative into a legendary figure come to fulfill the messianic expectations of their people. Of course, this was similar to the excuse the Jewish leaders themselves offered to explain the body's disappearance. This made no sense, either. How could a band of scared, poor, and powerless twentysomethings and thirtysomethings fight a legion of battle-hardened, elite Roman soldiers guarding Jesus' tomb? The Empire wouldn't have let that body get away from them, given the political ramifications.

And yet something happened. At least the disciples believed something did. So much so that they willingly died for this belief. Yet if it didn't actually happen, if Jesus was still dead, why die for a lie? As Silas liked to tell his students, martyrs make bad liars.

No, something did happen two thousand years ago. Which the stack of papers incinerated at Georgetown and the data Avery collected that was on that blasted, stolen laptop proved.

He silently cursed how the events had unfolded since that fateful morning when he got word of Henry Gregory's death. By now he should have been being booked on every major news network in America. Strike that: booked on every news network in the world. To broadcast his glorious, seismic scientific and academic achievements.

But no. Instead, he was speeding through the stratosphere to Jerusalem when every fiber in his being told him it was a bad idea.

Yet the Shroud pushed him onward. The chance to prove

once and for all whether it had in fact been preserving the memory of Jesus' resurrection these two millennia compelled him to risk life and limb, again.

But it was more than that. More than the professional rewards from such a historical find. Even more than the metaphysical questions that would be put to rest.

Sebastian.

He hoped that involving his brother in the exercise would finally bring him back to the faith he had walked away from those many years ago. After all, how could it not? As a man of science, for years he had been demanding "proof" for the claims the Bible makes. Silas prayed that Jesus' tomb within the Holy Sepulcher chapel would hold all the science he needed to put his doubts to rest.

That was the hope, anyway

After landing, Silas caught a bite to eat in a food court near baggage claim as he waited for his brother to arrive. Two hours later, his blond-haired twin came bounding through the terminal, carrying a weekend bag and rolling a sizable, rectangular hardback suitcase behind him. The neutron flux detector, he presumed.

"Sebastian," Silas called. "Over here."

Sebastian caught sight of Silas, and he walked over to his table smiling flatly, but looking as sharp as always in a blue blazer and his trademark bow tie, a bright red one with pink polka dots.

"Nice bow tie," he said needling his brother.

Sebastian smirked. "Never leave home without one."

Silas stood and chuckled. "You'll probably want to ditch it and the blazer when we get to the hostel. How was your flight?"

"Dreadful. I had assumed the accommodations of a private charter would mitigate the stress of a long flight. Not. I swear we hit every possible air pocket and downward draft crossing the Atlantic. And they didn't even have a good Chardonnay. In fact, they didn't have any alcohol. Just bottles of water. And not Evian or Perrier, mind you, but flat airplane water."

Silas smiled as his brother continued complaining. That was the Sebastian he knew. "Thanks for coming. Appreciate the help."

Sebastian scoffed. "As if I had a choice. Here. Take this." He rolled the large case over to Silas.

He took it. "Wow, this is heavy."

"But it works. Unlike Avery's contraption. God rest his soul."

That was one trait the two brothers shared without to a fault: a competitive drive augmented by pride and a touch of arrogance. It was what allowed them to become some of the top experts in their respective fields at such an early age.

"How about we get going?" Silas said. "We've got an hour drive to Jerusalem, and I'm eager to get to the church and arrange a viewing of the tomb."

"First things first," Sebastian said standing up. "I need falafel, hummus, and a stiff drink."

Silas couldn't argue with that.

THE DRIVE from the airport to Jerusalem was mostly silent. Silas drove while his brother slept, which was fine. After years of not keeping up with each other, they didn't have much to talk about, anyway. He glanced at his brother, regretting the ways he had tried to compel him to accept his faith through what Sebastian termed his "Jesus talk," his attempts to slip in a comment or seven about the Bible or Christianity, leading to much of the distance.

Perhaps Christ's tomb would do what he himself could not.

They arrived at a city in mid-bustle, with a clear, cloudless late-afternoon sky encouraging the religious tourists to take full advantage of their Holy Land experience. Silas found a spot to park their rental a few blocks at the north end of the Old City near the Damascus Gate.

Small carts greeted them at the commanding entrance selling spiritual trinkets and bottles of water. Armed guards with serious guns resting against their shoulders guarded the entrance, a testament to the continued violence and division that had always seemed to plague this Holy City from before the fabled King David. A father and his two young sons, all wearing matching black suits with starch-white dress shirts and black yarmulkes passed them, probably on pilgrimage to the Jewish holy sites as much as the Christians that were lined up with matching lime-green T-shirts.

Walking through the ancient walls and into the Holy City was a sight to behold. In the distance to the left, the golden crown to the Dome of the Rock gleamed in the sunlight above the sand-colored buildings. More vendors greeted them from the Arab street market. Women with white head scarfs sold fresh vegetables from plastic cartons on the cobblestone street. Colorful shirts and dresses hung from entrances into other, smaller shops selling more wares for the spiritually hungry.

"Oh goodie," Sebastian moaned. "More Jesus junk. And Moses junk. Oh, look, Muhammad junk, too!"

Silas threw him a look, but sort of agreed. It was a travesty what the city so central to the three Abrahamic faiths had become. And at the hands of those who venerated the sites.

They continued on farther into the Old City, coming up to a cross street. The Via Dolorosa. Rising from the cobble street to the left was their destination, the Church of the Holy Sepulcher, a basilica dating to the fourth century marking the two holiest sites of Christianity: the place where Jesus of Nazareth was crucified, Golgotha, and the location where he was buried. Already that day a large contingent of Christian tourists had been through the religious pilgrimage site, and two busloads of more pilgrims had arrived as Silas and Sebastian walked up to the light brown structure. Over the centuries from when it was first constructed, several chapels and an enclosed colonnaded atrium were built, creating a massive structure in the heart of the Holy City encompassing several blocks.

Silas looked at his watch and the horizon. The sun had a few hours to go before it set and the Church was closed to visitors. Radcliffe had arranged a meeting with the Greek Orthodox Patriarch of Jerusalem. The two had been old friends back in their days as researchers at the Vatican Apostolic Library, and he was able to use that connection and Silas's credentials as a sindonologist to leverage thirty minutes of his time. The plan was to convince him to let them examine the tomb after hours under the guise of the restoration and examination project the Edicule tomb had been undergoing. If anyone could give them permission, it was him. And considering the circumstances, Silas hoped he would be sympathetic.

He helped his brother jostle the piece of luggage up a set of stairs to the court outside the three Greek Orthodox chapels in front of the church entrance. The group of tourists in lime-green shirts passed them as they approached the main entrance, seemingly eager to get inside and view the burial site of their Lord, their Savior.

Silas and Sebastian entered the church through heavy wooden doors, the sight inside giving them pause. Similar to Notre Dame, the sacred space was constructed using pale stone. But the flooring was an intricate pattern of black and white tiles. They walked farther in, toward the Catholicon, the center of the Church. The floor was paved with a brilliant pattern of rusty red and emerald circles and zigzags. Paintings of various icons and holy events hung on the gray stone walls. Up above was the real show.

Supported by majestic arches with columns depicting the four Evangelists—Matthew, Mark, Luke, and John—the dome of the Church's center was adorned with a golden Byzantine-style mosaic depicting Christ Pantocrator, the Ruler of All, wearing a bright blue sash holding the Scriptures peering down above.

Rays of light entered through the windows, cutting through the atmosphere and creating an effect of sacredness about the space.

"I must say," Sebastian whispered, "it is all very suggestive."

Silas smiled as he continued staring upward. "If you're not careful, Seba, the Holy Spirit may just convert you yet."

His brother smirked and walked away. "Let's get this over with."

The two walked back to the front entrance, where they saw an information booth. Silas approached a portly, dark-skinned man standing next to it who looked like he was in charge. "Excuse me, but are you on staff with the Church?"

The man dressed in black with a long, bushy, graying beard smiled broadly. "I am. How may I help you?"

"My brother and I, we're here to see the Patriarch, Theophilos III."

The man's smile fell slightly and brow furrowed at the revelation, clearly thrown off by a couple of tourists insisting on seeing his Holiness.

Silas continued, "You see, we have a meeting arranged. I'm a researcher with Princeton University in America, and he's a scientist with a prestigious university in Washington, DC. We've come as part of...part of a research project associated with Edicule restoration. If you give him a call, all should be in order. He's expecting us."

The man still eyed them with skepticism. He requested a moment to check on their arrangement and disappeared up a stairwell. Fifteen minutes later he returned, smiling.

"Right this way."

THEY WERE LED through a nondescript door and up a narrow stone stairway into a series of adjoining offices, then to the Patriarch himself.

"Welcome," the man said rising with an outstretched hand

from behind a large, intricately carved wooden desk, "in the name of the Father, Son, and Holy Spirit." He was a slight man, wearing the same pressed black garment as the other portly one downstairs, with a chest-length, wiry, silver beard and gray eyes that sparkled with invitation.

Silas took his hand, Sebastian did the same. "Thanks for seeing us."

"Anything to help my old friend Rowen Radcliffe, as well as a reputable sindonologist."

Silas smiled, his neck growing red. "Thank you, sir."

"I know your work well." The man smiled, then grew silent, clearly interested in moving the conversation along. Which was fine for Silas.

"Your Holiness, we need your help. I'm not sure if you are aware, but there has been a...a concerted effort in the last seventy-two hours to discredit and destroy the Shroud of Turin."

The man's eyes grew wide. "I had heard about the attack at Notre Dame during the Holy Image viewing, but what do you mean by...discredit and destroy?"

"It wasn't reported in the media, but during the attack at Notre Dame the Shroud was stolen."

He gasped, clasping both hands over his mouth. "No."

Silas put a hand up in reassurance. "It's alright. The Shroud is being recovered as we speak. But we believe the same organization responsible for the attack at Notre Dame and subsequent theft was also responsible for the attack on a conference on the Shroud in Washington, DC where the leading sindonologists had been gathered," Silas paused. "All of whom were killed in a terrorist attack. Except for me."

"My God..."

"I escaped with the help of the Order of Thaddeus. And Radcliffe recruited me to help me give validity to the Shroud and let its memory speak once again."

The man paid careful attention, but a look of confusion grew on his face. "This is indeed most tragic. But what can I do?"

Silas shifted in his seat and looked at Sebastian, then back to the Patriarch. "I'm aware that the Edicule and the interior of the tomb have been undergoing a renovation."

"Yes, we are restoring the sacred tomb of Christ."

"We need to examine the original limestone encased within the structure."

"For what reason do you need to do this thing?"

"We've come to verify the resurrection of Jesus of Nazareth."

The Patriarch frowned, his brow furrowing. "What do you mean, verify Christ's resurrection? The Gospels have already done this."

Silas smiled. "Yes, but you see, my brother has brought equipment to determine whether—" he stopped, glancing at Sebastian, who seemed content in letting him take the lead in this conversation. "To determine whether a radiological event occurred within the tomb itself, whether the limestone recorded any radiation particles."

Saying it out loud almost made Silas feel foolish. He understood the confused look across the desk.

"Look," he continued, "a friend of mine, Stephen Avery from MIT, had run some new tests on a piece of the Shroud to determine whether Jesus' resurrection could be scientifically proven. I'm confident he did prove it, but unfortunately, that data was lost in a terrorist attack, similar to what I endured in DC. We want to replicate his research by studying the closest thing, testing the limestone in the Edicule that your team of architects and scientists recently uncovered."

The Patriarch closed his eyes and held up a hand. "I understand what you are saying. I am sorry, but that is not going to be possible."

"Why not?"

"The original marble cladding has already been removed,

and we have already examined what was underneath. You'll be most pleased, professor, that the original limestone burial bed was revealed intact, and we have preserved it for another millennia."

"Yes, but we need—"

"I am sorry," interrupted the Patriarch, "but the matter is closed."

He stood up, ready to end the conversation. Silas and Sebastian joined him.

"Professor," his Holiness continued, "I realize that you have been through quite an ordeal the past few days, and I understand your role in care-taking and preserving the Holy Image. I thank you for that, and I appreciate your...academic interest in our work. But I hope you can understand that the sepulcher is not a thing to be prodded and poked like a baby pig."

"No, of course not," Silas whispered.

"It is a sacred thing, a holy thing. A thing to be revered and respected. Not researched. A thing to be believed, on faith." He made his way out from behind his desk, toward the two brothers. "Blessings upon you and your research, professor. It has been an honor to meet you."

Silas smiled. "Likewise, your Holiness."

The original man whom they sought for help materialized and led them back down the narrow stairwell to the entrance of the church.

"I trust your visit with his Holiness was meaningful and fruitful," the man said.

I don't know about fruitful. Silas smiled, saying, "Yes, it was meaningful."

"Won't you look around and pay a visit to the Holy Sepulcher?"

You can bet on it.

CHAPTER 32

REIMS, FRANCE.

J acob Crowley couldn't run anymore.

He collapsed against the gray, weathered walls of an old shed nestled against a line of trees along the outer border of a pasture.

Hold it together.

He gulped several breaths of the humid air to try to recover from the sprint from the disabled truck. After the driver had been shot, it had veered wildly from the highway and crash-landed in a cow pasture, taking out a few in the process.

God rest their souls.

He crossed himself out of habit, not thinking about it. Had it not been for his seatbelt, he would have flown through the windshield and ended up like one of those dead bovines. He had been lucid enough to understand what happened: SEPIO had won and would be coming for him shortly. The seatbelt buckle had jammed at some point, probably from the strain of the crash. Luckily, he had had his knife buried in his pocket. It took a bit of finesse sitting in his seat to fish it out, but he had succeeded in retrieving it and was able to cut through the thick nylon, burning through precious minutes.

Crowley had quickly stretched out of his nylon straitjacket

and carefully climbed over his companion, using him as a ledge to push against the door. The large hole in the man's shoulder was seeping blood, but he was unconscious. He struggled against the door, but it was wedged shut. He used the dashboard as leverage, then cranked the handle again and pushed with all of his might.

The door flew open suddenly, clanging against the side of the truck.

"Jacob," the driver moaned, startling him. The man's eyes flickered open. Crowley panicked and scrambled up the man and out the door.

He had stood on the truck and looked around, getting his bearings. They had slid several hundred feet off the highway's shoulder. Large tracks had been carved in the earth from the slide, and two cows laid dismembered in its wake. Cars had begun resuming their pace, whizzing past the overturned truck. Sirens were wailing in the distance, motivating him to climb down from the truck. As he reached the ground, two slamming car doors caught his attention. Up the shoulder off the highway, a car had pulled over.

A gray Mercedes.

SEPIO.

He had run to the front of the truck, then through a thicket of bushes to a large oak tree commanding the bank of a small stream.

Did they see me? Crowley wondered, panting from behind the covering. He had watched them slide down the embankment and run over to the overturned truck, creep around the vehicle, then look inside the cabin. One of them had sworn, both searched the immediate surroundings and farther beyond.

They must have known someone else was inside and escaped. Did they know it was me?

The jackhammer in his chest had grown stronger at the thought, motivating him to back away slowly, then shuffle amongst the small trees lining the stream, using them as cover as he escaped through the pasture.

Thunder rumbled in the distance. The day had turned from bad to rain. A light drizzle started tapping him on the head as he recovered against the old shed. He wiped his face with both hands, then buried his face in them as emotion began working itself outward. He slid down the shed's worn planks and sat on the damp grass. He rubbed his face, then buried it between his legs.

No. Stop it, you big baby.

Crowley snapped his head up.

What was that?

Movement behind him caught his attention. In the trees, behind the shed. The crack of a branch, and footsteps.

His heart galloped back to its previous pace. He pulled out his knife, cursing himself for forgetting his gun in his scramble out of the truck. He slowly rose from the ground, looking long across the pasture.

Nothing for miles.

More footfalls, in the woods behind the shed. He crept around the side, trying to discern whether it was man or beast that was coming up behind him.

"Boo!"

Crowley whipped around, blade ready to strike.

It was one of his men. Three, in fact. They were laughing.

"You should see your face, Crowley." The man laughed harder, doubling over.

He walked over to the man and punched him in the face. He stumbled backward, grabbing his left nose.

"You broke my nose mother—"

"Shut up. And get off the ground. We've got to move." He didn't wait for a response, starting off along a shallow stream running next to the shed.

The two other men looked at each other and followed Jacob.

"What's the plan?" one of them said, catching up to him.

"There's a safe house south of Reims."

"That's a few hours walk, at least," the other man protested.

Crowley kept walking, glaring at the man. He looked away, pulling back to walk with the other man whose nose Crowley had broken. The rain had mostly held off as they walked this way for several miles. They kept to the countryside and back roads knowing the authorities would be looking for them, the map on his phone keeping them on track.

An hour later it rang. The caller ID told him what he already knew.

Borg.

Jacob hesitated to answer, knowing what he would get.

"Hello?"

"Jacob. I had expected you by now. Is everything alright?"

Jacob started to answer but found no words.

"What's happened?"

Jacob said matter-of-factly, "We lost it."

Borg said nothing.

Jacob said softly, "Hello? Rudolf, are you there?"

Borg exploded in an expletive-laden tirade reminiscent of his father. Jacob should have hung up, but he was paralyzed with a mixture of fear and self-loathing.

"Do you realize what you've done? What you've failed to move forward?"

"I know I've failed you." Emotion caught in his throat.

"Me? Me?" Borg's voice rose louder. "I'm not the one you've failed! Nous has been biding its time for nearly eight hundred years, waiting for the opportune moment to strike. And now that the Order has a new hired gun in Professor Silas Grey, they are closer to dismantling our carefully laid plans entirely!"

Jacob stopped walking, the gravity of his failure setting in.

Borg continued. "Christendom has been slowly bending toward our will for the last two centuries. We have successfully challenged the dogmatic assumptions of the faith using all of the tools at our disposal, sowing doubt among the faithful as much as the faithless. Science. Spirituality. Even scandal within the ranks of their own hierarchy. Christianity is no longer a given. We nurtured teachers within their very own ranks to transform belief and trust into a mere feeling of religious affection. At our bidding, they transformed their Christ into a moral teacher, a Gandhi on steroids, making their precious cross unnecessary. And they cast doubt on the exclusivity of the faith in the face of the multiplicity of religious faiths in the world."

Borg paused, catching a breath.

"Doubt and skepticism reign. People want something they can sink their teeth into, something they can experience that has tangible benefits for their pathetic, little lives. Religion doesn't offer that anymore. Which is why the ancient Christian relics are so important now, why the Order of Thaddeus has stepped up its efforts at preserving the memory of the faith and exploiting these tangible, experiential reminders of the faith their people have forgotten and forsaken. And it's why the Shroud was so key to the new phase of our operation. If they are able to scientifically verify the historicity of the Shroud and the resurrection event, the cornerstone of the Christian faith, then the plans Nous has carefully laid for decades will be seriously set back. So that is what you have failed, Jacob. Not me. Nous."

Crowley's gut was twisting with a mixture of recognition and regret. Nous wouldn't tolerate this kind of failure. Rudolf might, but not the rest. What was he going to do?

"Which means you need to finish what you started. If you are going to have any chance of surviving this. Because there's one more chance for SEPIO to offer proof of the supposed resurrection of Jesus, and for Grey to salvage the work we stole from him."

Understanding flooded his mind. A smile curled upward as he realized where he was being redirected.

"You know what to do?"

Borg's words sparked hope within Jacob. He could still redeem himself, salvage the plans they had carefully laid for years.

"Yes, I know where to go."

"Do you have what you need?"

He looked behind him at the three men waiting for him off to the side. They seemed fine; they would do. "Yes. We're almost at the safe house outside of Reims. We'll resupply there, but we'll need a plane."

"Get across the German border to Flughafen Saarbruecken. A plane will be waiting for you at the international airport."

Another plan. This could work. The same energy that brought him to hold that lighter to the cross of Christ and let it burn was beginning to course through him again. The thought of recapitulating that moment in the chapel gave him a jolt of delight.

"Jacob. If you fail again—"

"I won't," he quickly said.

After all, burning things to the ground was his specialty.

CHAPTER 33

LYON, FRANCE.

"Forget Jerusalem for now. You're heading to Lyon."
Radcliffe had informed Celeste of the change after she debriefed with him after the car chase and losing Jacob Crowley. SEPIO command had received word from the same source that had led them to lend their support to the Vatican at the Notre Dame Shroud viewing. They had more intel on Jacob Crowley.

The source claimed that he had been the one behind both the MIT and Georgetown bombings, having attempted to take out both Stephen Avery and Silas, and then the Notre Dame attack and subsequent Shroud theft. He also seemed to be behind the theft of Avery's laptop and altercation, as the man matched the description of the one Silas was able to vaguely provide. It was also suspected that he had coordinated the assassinations of the three sindonologists and Henry Gregory, though that was unconfirmed.

There was a lot of blood on this man's hands.

While Celeste and Gapinski were tracking down the Shroud, Zoe had been coordinating a data trace on the mystery man, trying to discover anything that would motivate him to steal the Shroud, and also attack the people behind its authentication and research. She was able to piece together a timeline of his birth in Bath, England, and subsequent housing in a state orphanage, for reasons unknown. Then, mysteriously, he was transferred out of the country to a Catholic-affiliated orphanage in southern France.

From there the stream of information had run dry.

"There's nothing on the man after he left the orphanage in 1988," Radcliffe explained. "We need you to have a chat with the Head Master. See if you can get background on Crowley, the reason he was brought to the orphanage in the first place, what he was like while there. Anything that might play to motivation and offer clues to his whereabouts and next moves. He's expecting your visit, having been instructed by the Vatican to offer his cooperation."

An officer with the French police brought Celeste and Gapinski to a regional airport outside of Reims. From there they drove to a small town south west of Lyon, where the orphanage Crowley had spent his teenage years had sat since the early twentieth century.

It was a stately, sprawling building with stone masonry work and a modest chapel attached by a narrow-covered walkway. The grounds seemed well manicured, with flower and vegetable gardens. Boys were working them when they drove up the long, narrow driveway to a small parking lot in front of the entrance.

They announced themselves to a pinched-face woman at a front desk. Celeste explained they were with the Order of Thaddeus with an appointment to see the Head Master, Father Peter Matheus. The woman held a skeptical look, mostly directed at Gapinski who loomed large in a place filled with more slightly built men devoted to more mindful pursuits.

Within minutes after placing a phone call, Father Matheus bounded down the stairs. "Greetings, brother. Greetings, sister."

He was a tall, slim man who seemed more chipper than one would expect in such a seemingly dismal, depressing place. He sported black priestly garments, and a healthy shock of silver hair wrapped around his head, making up for a crown that had long grown barren.

Celeste held out her hand. "Thank you for seeing us on such short notice, Father." Gapinski did the same.

Father Matheus shook both at once, smiling. "Anything to help the Church. Please, let's go to my study."

Young, laughing boys scampered past the pair as they followed the man up a wooden, winding staircase two floors up. They passed hallways lined with doors that led to the dormitory rooms housing the orphans. The smell of baking bread and boiling stew filled their senses, giving them the impression the place was a homey refuge for what one would assume would have been a bleak existence for the group of forgotten and cast-aside children.

"We have nearly three hundred boys here," Father Matheus offered, "ranging in ages from eight to eighteen."

Celeste said, "We saw some of them out tending the grounds as we drove up."

He smiled. "Yes, we keep the boys to a regular routine of chores and work based on Benedict's Rule, as we are of the Benedictine Order."

She asked, "How long have you served here, Father?"

"Most of my adult life."

Celeste noted that would have placed him at the orphanage during the time Jacob Crowley had been housed.

He continued. "When I was certain I was going to be a priest, I joined the Benedictine Order, and then was later assigned to the orphanage. Which at the time I thought a funny form of divine punishment."

"How so?"

"As a teenager I hated rug-rats. And when I was called into the priesthood, I felt somewhat relieved knowing that part of the vows was celibacy. Which meant I didn't have to care for any of my own." He laughed. "So when I was assigned here, I thought it was God's divine discipline for some transgression. I really did."

He paused, deep in reflective thought.

"But then my heart softened, and I saw myself in them. And I realized the posting wasn't for my discipline, but for my delight."

"In what way?" Gapinski asked.

"We're all orphaned, my friend. And adoption by our Papa into divine Sonship and Daughtership is awaiting us all."

Gapinski smiled in recognition, his own story reflecting the truth of both realities.

Father Matheus led them into a nondescript study with a little window overlooking the drive that brought them to the orphanage. The interior was of average size, smaller than they would have expected for the Head Master. It was lined with simple bookshelves of pinewood boards and metal shelving hooks. At one end was a simple pinewood desk, more like a modest dinner table with no drawers and four post legs. At the other end, a frayed Persian rug, that had clearly seen many years of wear, covered the marred hardwood floors, playing host to a small couch and an armchair.

"Have a seat," Father Matheus said, motioning his two guests toward the couch. He sank into the armchair, folded his legs, and rested his hands upon his knee. "Now, how can I be of service to the Order of Thaddeus?"

Celeste began. "It concerns a former orphan who was here early-to-mid '80s. A boy named Jacob Crowley."

There was a flicker of recognition in his eyes, which blinked rapidly at the mention of Crowley's name. He held a smile and uncrossed his legs, then re-crossed them in the opposite way, but said nothing.

"Is there anything you can tell us about him?" Celeste asked. "I believe you were here during that time. Do you remember Crowley?"

"Yes, I was. But you have to understand hundreds of boys

come through here. Some of them stand out more than others, of course, but to remember a single lad from nearly forty years ago is a tall order."

Celeste smiled and wondered to herself why he hadn't answered her question.

"I understand, Father. But it is vital we get any information on Crowley, anything at all you could provide us. The reason he came to be at the home. What he was like as a boy. Anything on his whereabouts afterward."

"I'm sorry," he said interrupting. "I don't understand why the Order is interested in a single orphan from thirty years ago? What is this any concern of yours?"

Celeste looked at Gapinski. He nodded her onward. "We work for a project within the Order called SEPIO. We take active measures to guard and secure the memory of the historic Christian faith. And recently one of those memory pieces, a relic, has come under attack. We think Crowley might be involved."

"A relic, you say?"

"Yes. The Shroud of Turin."

This time his eyes visibly widened. He swallowed, then licked his lips and turned away, putting a hand over his mouth.

Celeste gave him a moment to consider this information. Then she continued. "You may have heard about an incident at Notre Dame Cathedral from a few days ago."

Father Matheus startled, his hand dropping to his lap. "That was him?"

She nodded. "Earlier in the week, there were two bombings in America, which we believe were orchestrated by him. And each of them was connected to the Shroud. We eventually recovered the relic, but not before chasing him and his crew through French highways. He is very dangerous, Father. All we want is to apprehend him and prevent him from hurting anyone else. Not to mention stop him from perpetuating any more destruction on the Church."

The priest looked away again out the window, as if considering her words. "Lord, forgive me," he whispered, then crossed himself. He looked at them both, face determined and urgent.

"He was here, during the time you say. He was...an unusual lad."

"How so?"

"For starters, he came to us from England. Was placed here after the orphanage he was staying in was shuttered."

"Is that unusual?"

"We do take some boys from other locations when they are closed or want for more space, but usually from our own country. Rarely from out of state, and certainly not from across the channel."

"Do you know why he was brought here, then?"

He shook his head. "I'm not sure. I just remember there being a to-do about it."

Celeste considered this. "Well, then why was he placed in orphan care to begin with, back in England?"

"Now, that's a story." He paused and looked out the window. "Young Jacob Crowley burnt down his childhood parish as a pre-teen. And with his mum dutifully cleaning down below."

"Sick," Gapinski said.

Father Matheus went on to tell them the remarkable details of the wicked deed, and how his father had abandoned him after the fact, first through abuse and then in a drunken accident. "Jacob had claimed the Devil made him do it. But here's the thing." He stopped, leaning in closer. "I believe it to be true."

Celeste and Gapinski looked at each other, understanding this revelation added a layer to the story.

"Do tell," Gapinski said.

"Shortly after young Jacob arrived, we began finding dead animals. Small things like frogs and mice. Then larger ones like a cat, even a dog. They were missing their heads. Their blood had been drained, and their bodies discarded afterward."

Gapinski showed visible disgust.

"One evening, on one of my rounds for our nighttime check, I heard chanting coming from Jacob's room. It was in a language I couldn't understand, a language that was unrecognizable. I opened the door to find him and another boy huddled around a candle, and they were dangling a dead mouse above it. To this day, I still remember the stench of burning flesh that hit me when I entered that room."

"It was some sort of ritual?" she asked. "Occult, maybe?"

"That's what we understood it to be. When we asked him what he was doing, he just kept repeating the same excuse: 'He made me do it, like before.' As you can imagine, we were all very concerned for him, as well as for the rest of our boys. We went so far as to ask for help from an exorcist assigned to our diocese."

"Exorcist?" Gapinski exclaimed. "Like pea soup and spinning heads?

Father Matheus grinned. "Not exactly, but close."

"What came of that?"

"Nothing. The diocese wouldn't allow it. We did the best we could to manage his care and minister to his soul...but I'm afraid we failed him."

"But why the Shroud?" Gapinski asked, interjecting into the conversation something that had worried him. "I understand if he was atheistic or possessed or combative when it came to all things Church. But why go after the Holy Image in this way? It seems so personal, the relentlessness and effort at discrediting and destroying it."

Father Matheus clenched his jaw, then swallowed and leaned back, tears welling at the corners of his eyes, as if a memory were rising to the surface too painful to recall.

"Come," he whispered, wiping his eyes. "Let me show you."

The priest stood and opened the door, then walked out of the room. Celeste and Gapinski followed. He led them down the hallway and around the corner to a more extended corridor. At the end was a set of double doors. He opened one side, then walked through. This room was far more significant than the previous one, with wooden bookshelf cabinetry and a solid walnut desk sitting before a bay of large windows overlooking the grounds. A small fireplace even commanded one end, with two plush leather chairs facing it. The room smelled musty, and a layer of dust was visible around the space, indicating it hadn't been used for some time.

Then they saw it, the two of them at once.

A replica of the Shroud of Turin. Not the entire linen, but the face.

The contrast of the image had been enhanced slightly so that the ghostly outlines of the man were more prominent. Its striking image and its placement in an orphanage in Lyon were confusing. And frightening.

Gapinski was the first to react. He didn't mince words: "What on earth is that about?"

Father Matheus had been staring at the floor since they had entered the room. "You mentioned the Shroud and Jacob and asked why it seemed so personal." He looked at the image. "That's why."

Gapinski and Celeste looked at it themselves.

"What's why?" Celeste asked.

He sighed. "Over the last decade, there have been a number of revelations concerning the Church. They began in America, the revelations that is. But the activity behind them has been a worldwide blemish that has marred Christ's precious Bride stretching back decades, touching every part of the Church." He added with a whisper, "Including orphanages."

She understood what he was talking about.

"The former Head Master was very good at what he did, caring for the boys with a love only a father could dispense. He loved every child that came through these doors with an undivided, indiscriminate love." He paused and visibly shuddered, reliving the dark memory. "But with such brilliant light, there is often a shadow side of darkness. Don't get me wrong," he quickly added. "By speaking of a shadow side, I don't mean to absolve him of any of the wickedness he perpetuated. What he did was pure evil. I only wish I had seen his zealous affection for what it was. Predation."

"You're speaking about abuse?" Gapinski said, voice thick with anger. "Sexual?"

Father Matheus nodded. "In this very room."

Gapinski looked around the room, reflexively balling one hand into a fist. Celeste stepped back slightly, as if the room repelled her. They were both sickened and ready to leave.

What went unsaid was that teenage Jacob Crowley was the victim of this wolf in priest's clothing. It began to make sense.

For years that poor child had associated that image with pure evil. It is no wonder he grew to hate it. To the point of wanting to destroy it, as well as anyone who sought to validate or defend it. Add to this hatred of the Shroud a seemingly already established hatred of the Church, and they were dealing with a much bigger problem than they had initially understood. One could only imagine what else he was capable of. Or planning.

"Thank you for your time, Father," Celeste said abruptly. "I think you've given us the fuller picture of Jacob Crowley we needed for our investigation."

"I hope so."

He opened the door to leave, then stopped short. "There is one more thing." He turned around to face them. "Jacob had a friend. Well, he was more than a friend. Apparently, they had a blood pact, some ceremony they performed binding them together as brothers. And...they were intimate."

"Intimate?" Gapinski asked.

The priest said nothing.

Recognition hit him. "I see. Like lovers."

He nodded.

"You wouldn't happen to have a name for us, would you?" Celeste asked.

"No, sorry I don't. I do know they were released at the same time when they turned eighteen. Their bond was pretty tight, the two of them having taken part in several of the...activities I discussed about Jacob earlier. I would bet that alongside or even behind Jacob's latest activity lie his blood brother."

That means this conspiracy to destroy the Shroud went far deeper than one man's personal, Freudian vendetta.

It also meant twice the trouble.

And twice the danger.

CHAPTER 34

JERUSALEM, ISRAEL.

The Church of the Holy Sepulcher was bathed in the full moonlight as Silas and Sebastian strolled up to the sacred Christian monument. After striking out with the Patriarch, the brothers had checked into a hostel just south of the Damascus gate, and a few blocks east of the Church. They were spartan accommodations, to be sure, but would serve as a place to rest and prepare for the night's mission.

Radcliffe had gotten him word an hour ago that the Shroud had been recovered. But the chief architect behind its theft, a Jacob Crowley, had escaped. It was thought that he was behind not only the Notre Dame attack, but the others at MIT and Georgetown, in addition to the subsequent laptop theft at MIT and previous murders of Henry Gregory and his colleges.

Those two details—Georgetown and Gregory—sent Silas's heart pulsing with a vengeance.

Celeste and Gapinski had abandoned the search, leaving that work to the police, and had been dispatched to follow up a lead in Lyon. Their trip began filling in some elusive details about the past few days. Not only had Crowley displayed demonic influence, having burned down his childhood church and killed his mother in the process, and had been caught engaging in seance and sacrificial ceremonies while at the orphanage. He had also been abused for years by a priest, and in his office with a replica of the Holy Image of Christ's face. It seemed the motive for this attack on the Shroud had been personal, as much as spiritual.

The two had also discovered someone else had been involved in Crowley's life. Apparently, they were inseparable, their friendship having been bonded in a blood pact, and one that was on the intimate side. There was the possibility they were dealing with two people. Though they had no leads on the second person, SEPIO sources believed him to be the Grand Master of Nous himself.

Celeste and Gapinski were already en route to Jerusalem to provide support, and would reconnect with Silas and Sebastian at the Church of the Holy Sepulcher for the limestone test. If they encountered any security or any other personnel, the plan was to pose as part of the reconstruction and research team doing late-night work on the Edicule.

That was the plan, anyway.

"Doesn't Jesus say something about going to hell for breaking into churches?" Sebastian said. He had been in a sour mood ever since they had left the Patriarch. He had little interest in the operation from the start. But executing it without the blessing of the head of the church, and then breaking into the place had turned him off completely.

Silas ignored him as they hustled through the deadening streets of the Old City. He looked back as they passed a group of tourists, all wearing the same lime-green T-shirts he had spotted earlier in the day. He wasn't a superstitious person, but wondered if it was a sign of some sorts, perhaps reassuring him that he was being watched over.

He hoped it was a good omen, given what they were about to do.

At the hostel, he had done some reconnaissance to prepare for their late-evening mission. Using Google Maps and other images of the church building he could find on the internet, he was able to scope out the perimeter and find some useful intel on getting inside the ancient structure. He discovered that on the east side was what looked like a small door, another entrance separate from the more public one they had entered through that afternoon. Probably a service access point for the staff and various ecclesial authorities who occupied the site. From maps and images he found, it looked like it would lead into the Chapel of Helen, then back into the Catholicon and through to the main entrance of the Chapel of the Angel and then to the Holy Sepulcher Chapel itself.

The brothers continued moving south on Beit HaBad Street toward the east entrance of the church. They passed a few penitential pilgrims lingering outside a pastry cafe before returning to the secular world they left for the afternoon. The scent of cinnamon and sugar made Silas's head swim with hunger. He realized they hadn't eaten since the airport, having been caught up in their mission. He was regretting the oversight. So was his stomach.

"This way," Silas said, directing them through a small garden a few blocks past the café nestled between two buildings. The full moon provided the perfect amount of visible light for their darkened path as they reached the concealed entrance, offering the perfect cover for their clandestine mission. They strolled through an alley beyond the trees and into a small courtyard bathed in yellow light.

"Act nonchalant," Silas whispered. "Like we're just two tourists who are taking an evening stroll."

"While lugging around a forty-inch black luggage case?"

He smirked at his brother. *Good point.* "Just stand over there, out of the light while I check things out."

Sebastian rolled his eyes but did as he was told, standing against a shadowed wall in the cover of the evening darkness.

A single outdoor light was positioned high on a wooden pole

near the church wall, making Silas feel exposed and nervous. Probably erected as a security measure to deter the kind of people he and his brother had become. He padded over to the small entrance, careful to pay attention to his surroundings as he went. He took the small set of stairs by twos, then tried the handle.

Locked.

That didn't surprise him. What did was that it appeared to be made of heavy, reinforced steel. The kind made to keep his kind out. A latch guard further protected the door handle, making getting in more difficult.

No matter. Silas knelt down to examine the lock itself. Your basic deadbolt. Not a problem. He reached in his back pocket for a set of lock picks he had brought along, then got to work. The minutes ticked by as he gently moved the picks inside the lock.

"You there."

Silas stiffened, then quickly stuffed the pick set back in his pocket.

He stood and turned around. A portly guard in beige military fatigues was moving slowly in his direction, his right hand resting securely on his hips. Probably on a weapon of some sort. He was short and stout. Not fat, but looked to be made of pure muscle and confrontational know-how.

Proceed with caution, Silas.

"Fantastic!" he exclaimed, smiling and slapping his hands together too enthusiastically. "I wondered when you were going to arrive."

"Excuse me?" The man had stopped several feet away, hand still resting on his hip, his face wearing a scowl of confusion.

"I'm part of the renovation and research crew from Princeton University. Here." Silas walked down the stairs, careful not to be overeager in his approach so that he scared the man into protective action.

On cue, the man backed up and put one hand up to stop

Silas. The other one gripped his hip more deliberately. He said commandingly, "Stop there, sir. Stay where you are."

Silas stopped short, hand reaching behind him. "Oh, sorry. I only meant to introduce myself properly." He slowly took out his passport and unfolded it for the man to see. There was nothing official about it, only proving that he was an American. But it gave the man something to look at, which is all Silas needed to continue the ruse.

"Doctor Silas Grey. Professor of religious studies and Church history at Princeton University." The man took a cautious step forward, eyeing the official document, the hand at his hips relaxing somewhat. "Flew in yesterday, and was told to show up at this door for the late-night excavation and examination project at the Holy Sepulcher Chapel."

The guard said, "I don't know anything about an excavation or examination."

Silas feigned surprise. "That's odd. The Patriarch himself told me to come to this very door. He said something about it being an entrance for personnel."

The guard relaxed his right hand from his hip, then dropped his arm to his side.

Good. Almost there.

"I'm not sure about this."

"Look, I can understand your confusion." Silas smiled and took a single, short step forward. "Someone you don't know is crouched outside a door, and you don't know anything about it. I'm as confused as you, frankly. I was told the door would be unlocked and to come in to begin my important work. I was merely trying to figure out what was wrong with the door when you walked up."

"I see," the man said. "But you have to understand I have no knowledge of this late-night work project. Forgive me, professor, but I'm going to have to call my supervisor. You understand. It'll only take a minute to verify."

Silas smiled and casually folded his hands in front of him. "Absolutely. Go ahead. I'm sure all will be in order."

The man pulled out a radio, keeping an eye on him as he pushed aside button to say something into his unit.

Silas was ready to rush forward to knock the guy out, when a thick arm reached around from behind the man, grabbing him in a chokehold. The man's eyes widened. His face grimaced in surprise and pain, and he tried grabbing hold of the arm as he was lifted from the ground.

The guard was twisted around as the mysterious person swung him around trying to subdue the guard.

Gapinski.

Celeste rushed forward as the two fought, syringe in hand. She quickly squeezed the liquid into the man's neck. Within seconds, the guard relaxed his grip, then went limp. Gapinski released the poor fellow's neck, then dragged him by the chest to a corner behind a large trash receptacle.

"Impeccable timing," Silas said.

Gapinski returned from handling the unconscious victim. "Figured you could use a helping hand. Or, in this case, an arm."

Sebastian came out into the open from his hiding place, eyes wide and nostrils flared. "What the bloody hell was that about?"

"Relax," Silas said. "He'll be alright."

"Rendering people unconscious and breaking into churches isn't what I signed up for! I don't care how binding our little pact is."

"I'm sorry, alright. It's not like I meant for this to happen. I had planned on the Patriarch understanding. This was plan B."

"Wait, you planned for this to happen? To lie and punch your way in?"

Silas shifted. "It's not like I plotted out a guard walking up on us in the dead of night. But I thought it might happen. We had to be prepared."

"And what if these two hadn't shown up? What then? Would you have gotten...physical?"

Silas said nothing.

"Alright," Celeste interrupted. "Let's put away the Cain and Able routine for now and get a move on, shall we?"

She walked between the two brothers, Gapinski followed.

Sebastian walked up to Silas and smirked. "Be careful, baby brother," he whispered. "You know where murderers and liars go."

Silas closed his eyes and sighed. He ignored the swipe, brushing past him to the entrance.

He made quick work picking the lock. The four quickly entered the ancient building and made their way farther into the sacred structure. It was dark and quiet, the ecclesial personnel having abandoned the church during the late hour for another day.

Celeste and Gapinski switched on flashlights, Silas followed with his. The LEDs cast white light over the walls.

"What the..." Sebastian said.

Hundreds of thousands of small crosses had been etched into the pale hallway walls, graffiti left over from holy warriors and pilgrims from the Crusades.

Silas walked up to a large swath of the markings, putting both hands against the cold stone wall. He traced one of the etchings with his finger, imagining the soul who traversed the thousands of miles to this very location to venerate and defend what he had come to authenticate.

And he himself was taking his place in that long lineage of defenders.

They kept walking, reaching the Chapel of Saint Helen, a twelfth-century Armenian church built by the Crusaders. Small orange flames still burned in their votives at the altar, representing the prayers of the faithful before God. As they walked past wooden benches through the small room, Silas said a prayer of his own.

For forgiveness for their deception, for protection for their mission, for success for their work, and for the evidence to convince his brother of the faith.

They passed more of the same Crusader crosses as they walked farther into the church, their footfalls echoing off the ancient walls. Even the columns and sections of the floor hadn't escaped the markings. There had to have been thousands of such markings throughout the church. He thought about adding his own cross to the collection, marking his personal crusade for the sake of the faith.

Maybe when this is all over.

The group passed the information desk where Silas and Sebastian had started this journey at earlier, then entered the rotunda.

Silas's breath caught in his chest as he sighted the Edicule, a tall, stout structure of gray stone and marble. The soaring eighteenth-century shrine contained two rooms, the first holding the Angel's Stone believed to be a fragment of the large stone that sealed the tomb. The second room beyond was the tomb itself, containing a small chapel housing the limestone where Jesus had laid buried. Scaffolding had been erected around the magnificent structure, as well as several plastic drapes for the efforts restoring it to its proper beauty.

He stood staring at the modest structure, imagining the countless souls who had come here to experience the memory of Christ's death and resurrection. The church was built starting in AD 325 and was consecrated a decade later. From pilgrim reports, it seems that the chapel housing the tomb of Jesus was free-standing at first and the rotunda was later erected around it in the 380s. For centuries, pilgrims would form a line seeking a tangible experience of the very place their Savior laid after he had died for them, seeking forgiveness for their sins and renewal for their faith.

Silas wanted to form a queue himself.

"Over here," Celeste called, redirecting Silas's attention to the task at hand.

He followed her and Gapinski over to the Edicule's entrance. The inside was bathed in an orange glow from two candles that continued burning down their wicks, providing light to the faithful and adding a feeling of holiness to the penitential space. Walls of white marble had been carved into ornate floral accents, and a floor of black and white marble revealed the craftsman's care that went into constructing this shrine. The middle was commanded by a square pedestal altar, and on it laid a small sarcophagus that held a piece of the stone that sealed the entrance to Jesus' tomb, the one that had been rolled away and had an angel sitting on top of it when the women came to care for Jesus' body—only to find it was missing.

Silas and Celeste walked inside, with Gapinski behind at the entrance.

Celeste paused at the stone, and said softly, "This stone is one of the reasons why I became a Christian."

"Really?"

"When I was at Oxford, I attended a religious rally put on by a local church. They brought in a speaker to share about why the Christian faith was believable and invited the students to ask questions. I hadn't grown up in the Church, but I was curious. I went with a friend, and one of the points the preacher made was on the women who found the stone rolled away. He mentioned in passing that the fact testimony of women are included in the Gospel accounts of Jesus' resurrection is remarkable. In those days, women weren't allowed to give testimony in legal proceedings. So the fact the Gospel writers included their eyewitness accounts in a story about the resurrection of a dead man is an important point of proof that makes the story believable. If the disciples made up the story, then why let women tell it? That was the quickest route to being discredited in those days, allowing women give evidence to validate a claim."

She paused and touched the vessel that held the stone, as if lost in the memory that brought her to faith.

"I don't know. The testimony of those women and the inclusion of that testimony in the Gospel accounts spoke to me. These women are the reason I believed. The reason I'm standing with you in this room now."

Silas smiled, then put a hand on her shoulder. Through the ornately appointed doorway, he could see the burial shelf. "Come on. Let's see what we've come after."

The Holy Sepulcher Chapel was a tiny, tight space made with the same pure, white marble as the Chapel of the Angel. To the right was the burial shelf, enough space for two or three pilgrims to kneel and pray and experience the memory of Jesus' burial.

"Wait a minute." Gapinski pushed forward into the space, leaving Sebastian out in the rotunda. He extended his light around the interior of the Chapel. "It looks like Christ's burial shelf is sealed shut with some kind of marble encasement."

Silas elbowed past him. "What are you talking about?" He used his own flashlight and saw what Gapinski had seen, then rushed over to the marble shelf. His mouth went dry as he ran his hands across the top of it, then around the sides and base.

Panic grabbed him.

"The Patriarch didn't say anything about it having been sealed!"

"Always something," Gapinski said, shaking his head.

CHAPTER 35

Silas found a hammer and flathead screwdriver among a chest of tools under a dropping of plastic against the rotunda wall.

He walked back over to the group who had been huddled inside Christ's tomb. "This will have to do."

"Really?" Gapinski said. "What, you're just going to chisel away, without any knowledge of what you're chiseling into? I mean, Jesus was laid right there, man!"

"What do you want me to?" Silas was louder than he intended. He took a breath. "We don't have any other option. And it's not like I haven't done this before. I've served on a few archaeological digs. I'll be careful."

Celeste said to Gapinski, "Do you have a better idea? Then give the man some space. I'm sure the good professor knows what he's doing."

Gapinski threw up his hands and stepped back outside the Edicule, crossing himself as he gave Silas space to work.

"How much longer?" Sebastian shouted from outside the chapel. "I've got work to do, and I'm not getting any younger. Neither is the night."

"We're working on it!" Silas shouted back.

Silas took a minute to examine the new marble slab that had been installed to cover the holy bench. It was roughly three-by-five feet and carved from creamy marble. He could see where fresh mortar had been applied to seal the limestone burial shelf underneath. He hoped it hadn't cured from when it had been applied.

Silas looked back at the watching group huddled outside the Edicule. "Wish me luck." He positioned the large screwdriver underneath the marble covering and lined up the hammer. He flexed his fingers, drew it back, then hit it again with force.

The sound was deafening.

"Jeez Louise that was loud."

Silas looked back at Gapinski, then readied another aim. He hit the screwdriver harder this time, finding success: a large piece of the fresh mortar chunked off. He smiled and hit it again, and again and again, pushing the makeshift chisel along the track of the seal, sending more pieces to the ground.

It took him an hour, but he was able to remove most of the freshly-laid mortar around the edges of the encasement. He set down his tools. "Here, help me."

Gapinski went into the small space to help Silas lift off the marble slab, each grabbing a side. In sync, they jostled the sides with a twisting motion to loosen the remaining seal.

"Are you sure you got it all? It seems stuck."

Silas frowned, then applied more pressure and strength to his twisting. The slab popped at his end, making it easier for Gapinski to heave his own end off. They gently removed the covering and placed it against the back part of the small chapel.

He took a deep breath, then peered over the remaining marble case to the limestone below. Emotion caught in his throat, his knees shook a bit.

"Wow," was all Silas could manage.

Below was a shelf of pale limestone with what looked like a depression carved into the stone.

The size and shape of a body.

"Remarkable," Celeste said joining in the viewing.

Gapinski crossed himself, then cupped his hands in front of him in reverence.

Silas whispered, "To think Jesus actually laid here. Right here, in this very spot after he had been crucified." He added, "What's interesting is that all of this is perfectly consistent with what we know about how wealthy Jews disposed of their dead during the time of Jesus. It's all very historical."

They continued taking in the sacred moment, letting silence linger for several minutes.

"Oh, come on already." Sebastian entered the chapel dragging his piece of luggage. "Let's get on with it. Time is not on our side."

Silas frowned at his brother's irreverence, but he understood the urgency. That guard wouldn't stay unconscious forever, and soon the night would give way to dawn.

He and Gapinski and Celeste moved out of the way for Sebastian, exiting the small space to allow him to work.

Sebastian opened his suitcase and brought out the neutron flux detector, a round, metal tube that seemed to take some heft. Accompanying the detector was a car battery and a stand in which to place the unit.

Celeste folded her arms as she watched Sebastian work to position the detector and connect the battery. "So tell me how this works."

"The neutron flux value is calculated as the neutron density," he explains, "measured as n, multiplied by neutron velocity, measured by v, where n is the number of neutrons per cubic centimeter, expressed as neutrons/cm3, and v is the distance the neutrons travel in 1 second, expressed in centimeters per second, or cm/sec. Consequently, neutron flux, or nv, is measured in—"

"Dude," Gapinski interrupted. "Layman's, man. Layman's."

Silas smirked. Sebastian huffed. "It measures whether or not a radiation event happened within the tomb."

Gapinski furrowed his brow. "Like a nuclear blast?"

"Like the resurrection," Silas interjected.

"Whoa..."

Silas smiled. "The theory is that an instantaneous burst of energy or radiation came from Jesus' body when it suddenly dematerialized. In fact, a retired nuclear physicist from Britain's Atomic Energy Research Establishment insisted with certainty that the image on the Shroud must have been caused by some sort of radiation. She called it nuclear disintegration, an event acting almost instantaneously, as with the flash of a nuclear explosion. The same thing happened in Hiroshima and Nagasaki. Permanent shadows were etched into sidewalks and the sides of buildings. Many of the scientists involved with analyzing the Holy Shroud concluded that the radiant energy coming from the body of Christ similarly caused the Shroud's image, describing it as a burst of energy as a sort of pulsed laser beam caused by dematerialization of the body into energy in a millisecond."

"That's remarkable," Celeste said, joining in on the awe-and-wonder.

Silas nodded. "That it is."

"And this doohickey will tell us whether or not that happened? Whether Jesus came back to life, back from the dead?"

"This...doohickey, as you call it," Sebastian chimed in as he continued setting up the device, "will only detect the neutrons and radiation particles from a radiological event. That's it."

Silas rolled his eyes. "That's true. Avery analyzed the Shroud itself. But as we know that data was lost. And I doubt the Vatican will give us another sample after what the Shroud just went through. This is another way of getting to the same conclusion: that Jesus of Nazareth was resurrected from the dead. History tells us that Jesus was laid here after he was taken down from the cross. And if science can show a neutron flux event occurred here in the limestone walls, then it would clearly have been an unprecedented event that suggests the resurrection did in fact happen. Right here in this tomb."

The room fell silent, as if contemplating the gravity of what they were about to do. A few minutes later Sebastian stood up. "Alright. We're good to go."

Silas shuffled over to Sebastian's side and crouched down next to the object. "How long will this take?"

"Patience, big brother. This isn't some plastic eBay-hobbyist buy. It'll take some time."

Silas checked his watch, then stood up and walked out of the chapel. He scanned around the rotunda, nervous about any intervention by the staff or otherwise that would expose their clandestine mission. He rejoined the group.

Then a noise caught their attention. Something dropping, like a pipe or a board.

They turned as one mass toward the opening of the Edicule.

"Maybe something from the renovations shifted," Silas said nervously, looking to Celeste.

Gapinski moved him aside, face set against the disturbance. "Wait here."

Celeste followed. She stopped just outside the Angel Chapel and folded her arms, her stance wide and ready as Gapinski kept moving farther into the rotunda, then beyond into the Catholicon. Silas joined Celeste outside the Edicule as his brother continued running his tests inside the chapel.

A few minutes ticked by with no more sounds and no sign of Gapinski.

Silas ducked back into the entrance, then called back to his brother "How much longer?" Sebastian shushed him, then went back to work. He frowned, then rejoined Celeste.

"It's probably nothing," Celeste said, leaning against a large column in front of the Edicule's entrance.

Silas said nothing, looking into the darkness for a sign of what might come, his heart hammering inside his ears.

Another sound jolted Celeste back to her wide, ready stance. It was more intentional, more deliberate than the half-measured sound they heard from inside the tomb.

Silas walked forward, hand reaching for his Beretta stored in his waistband at the small of his back.

Soft footfalls began echoing from far in the darkness. Two by two, from a single person. They seemed to be gathering steam, approaching with speed. They got louder, closer.

But then there were other sounds, like different footfalls farther back from where the first set began. In pairs, times three or four. Maybe five.

Gapinski materialized out of the darkness into the rotunda. He was running, and out of breath.

Silas withdrew his weapon. Celeste did the same.

Gapinski stopped short of the pair, out of breath.

"We've got company." He looked back from where he came, swinging his automatic around to the front. "Again."

CHAPTER 36

Silas hated guns. Hated violence even more. Not since Iraq had he even held one.

Until three days ago, that is.

He almost didn't bring it with him that evening. Surely there would be no need. What would anyone have against the Church of the Holy Sepulcher? Sure, there were the religious zealots on both sides of the aisle—well, all three sides of the aisle. But there had been a sort of truce between Judaism, Islam, and Christianity within Herod's walls, a truce against religious fanaticism.

Yet there he was, facing a cascade of footfalls growing closer and stronger in the dead of night outside the tomb of Christ.

And without one of his pills.

Silas's breathing was growing heavy, his head swimming with fight-or-flight adrenaline. His arms were taut, Beretta at the ready pointing outward, prepared for another round of hostiles to emerge. He flexed his fingers around the gun's grip and chuckled to himself. Because he wasn't even supposed to be there.

An inciting incident, they call it. A moment in time that changes the direction of life's choo-choo train from one track to another one veering off into an entirely new direction. Had

Henry Gregory not passed away, he wouldn't have given the keynote presentation at the annual sindonologist conference in DC. In fact, he wouldn't have even attended. Had it not been for that one incident inciting a new course for his life, he would be safely tucked into his king-size bed outside of Princeton, New Jersey, putting the polishing touches on a journal article unveiling the grandeur of his latest academic achievements.

But no. Inciting Incident had to go and rear its ugly head.

Like Joseph, from ancient Israel, being thrown into a well that just so happened to be sitting at the exact location where his brothers had been tending their sheep. Which led to him being sold into slavery by a caravan of slave traders who just happened to be passing by. Who then sold him to the wealthy man who then had him thrown into jail after his horny wife got too fresh with him for her own good, and then accused him of rape. Another incident which happened to have further implications for his life, eventually leading to him being made second in command of all Egypt. Which eventually led to his father Jacob moving his family to Egypt, and that family growing so numerous that they were enslaved and cried out to the Lord for deliverance. Which led to their exodus and the formation of the nation of Israel.

A string of incidents leading to more incidents incited by the one, but leading to more monumental and dangerous ones.

Like being planted at the foot of the Edicule of the Holy Sepulcher Chapel inside the Church of the Holy Sepulcher, ready to engage in battle.

Only now he wasn't just a soldier defending an army outpost against an insurgency. Now, he was protecting the burial of his Savior from those who would seek to destroy its memory.

Then a thought nagged him: before Jesus had been crucified, he was praying with his disciples in a garden just outside Jerusalem when a band of Jewish religious officials accompanied by armed Roman soldiers came to apprehend him. One of those disciples, Peter, tried to defend him by brandishing a sword, cutting off the ear of one of the high priest's servants. And Jesus had some choice words for him:

"Put your sword in its place, for all who take the sword will perish by the sword."

At times, the Church had determined that armed resistance was needed for the sake of the faith. Was this one of those instances?

He didn't know.

But he hoped Jesus would understand.

THIS WAS NOT GOING ACCORDING to Jacob Crowley's plan.

Then again, what had?

After coming upon an unconscious man lying in the shadows and finding the back door they intended to use to enter the Church of the Holy Sepulcher already unlocked, he and his team were on high alert. Then they heard sounds coming from deep inside the sacred building, a *tap-tap-tapping* that gave clear indication someone was there. It was supposed to have been abandoned, their contact at the church said so. No matter. It was just a matter of overwhelming whoever-it-was with force. Surely some construction worker or ecclesial researcher would be no match for four well-trained operatives.

Then one of his bloody fools ran into something in the darkened hallway, knocking it down with a clank. It took everything within him not to shoot the man on the spot. But they pressed onward.

Until they had spotted the large, looming shadow padding toward them with what looked like far too much firepower for a man of the cloth. He also looked suspiciously similar to one of the chaps from the Mercedes that disabled them on the French highway. They stopped their advance, but all at once the man quickly retreated.

They had been made.

No matter. Crowley was determined to finish what he had started. And determined to destroy the very thing that destroyed his soul.

WHITE LIGHT from the full moon filtered into the magnificent rotunda of the Church of the Holy Sepulcher from a central set of windows high above, the light bouncing off of dust as it made its way down to the sacred world below, illuminating the place Christians had venerated for generations and casting wide, ink-black shadows around the men and women dutifully recapitulating the efforts of those who had once stood the same ground to sing their *Te Deum* anthem after capturing Jerusalem in July of 1099 during the First Crusade.

In an instant, bullets shattered the ethereal air, punching holes through the plastic drapes around the Edicule and bouncing off of the thick stone columns supporting the rotunda.

The fight was on.

"Take your positions," Celeste instructed. "And remember: we aim to disable, not kill. A fine line of violence, I know, but the Order isn't in the business of destroying life."

"Don't tell that to our friends," Gapinski complained as he moved back into position.

They scattered in separate directions, having charted a loose plan in the minutes between Gapinski's return and the gunfire that had erupted. Before arriving, Silas had studied a map of the church he picked up at the information booth while waiting for word from the Patriarch.

He was glad he did.

It was clear the Nousati were heading toward the rotunda from the Catholicon, having traced the same route the four of them had taken earlier in the evening. Probably came in through the same side entrance. Which Silas just remembered he had left unlocked.

No time for self-cursing. Time to act.

Silas told Sebastian to remain in the Edicule, at the back in the Holy Sepulcher Chapel. No use him getting involved, and it was the safest spot. The three spread out in order to give broad return fire: Celeste to the right toward the main entrance, Silas to the left toward the Chapel of Mary Magdalene, and Gapinski dead-set in the middle. There was little cover in the wide-open space, but they made do with the debris scattered around the Edicule.

At once, Silas, Celeste, and Gapinski returned fire, aiming for the maw of blackness that was the Catholicon out of which the gunfire had originated.

What desecration, Silas thought as they unleashed a barrage of violence into a space that held the church's main altar on which the Holy Eucharist had been administered to countless pilgrims over the centuries.

He offered four more rounds of cover for Gapinski and Celeste, receiving nothing in reply.

The three held their positions, the nothingness of the moment growing worrisome.

What are they waiting for?

Then he realized their error.

Flanking.

The middle entrance from the Catholicon wasn't the only point of entry into the rotunda. Very quickly they would find themselves in a horrible position. Fish in a barrel, being picked from both left and right flanks.

Silas caught Celeste's attention as she waited across the room, motioning with his left arm that he was moving out into the chapel, then motioning with his right arm for her to move out into the Armenian Gallery where he expected part of the hostiles to come. She seemed to understand and started moving out.

He threw Gapinski a look. The man nodded, catching his cue to stay put.

Gapinski remained planted before the Edicule guarding the Chapel of the Holy Sepulcher, as much as Sebastian. Silas and Celeste moved out to confront the danger.

CHAPTER 37

Silas padded slowly through the North Transept, his Ranger training kicking into high gear. Every one of his senses was on high alert, having been honed during countless missions for such a time as this.

His eyes had adjusted to the suffocating darkness of the night-time church environment, but it was his ears he relied on most. He listened for anything that could be out of the ordinary as he continued making his way forward. A footfall, a sudden sniffle at the dust, even breathing.

Since the smattering of gunfire from the Catholicon earlier there had been nothing. An eerie silence flooded the sacred space.

Silas flexed his fingers around his Beretta as he reached an altar embedded in an alcove near the end of the Catholicon.

Again, nothing.

He exhaled, realizing he had been holding his breath for several paces. He slowly breathed back in and flexed his arms, then doubled around toward the Seven Arches of the Virgin.

That's when he saw him, crouched behind one of the massive stone pillars.

Silas padded forward, keeping his gun trained at the back of the figure as the rest of this body moved foot by foot by—

The toe of his boot caught the lip of a tile raised slightly at the corner, causing him to brace himself from falling with his other foot.

And alerting the Nousati agent to his presence.

The figure sprang to life, whipping around with his weapon outstretched, and sending four rounds Silas's way.

They sailed past him into the stone wall beyond as he ran forward, smashing into the man and sending him to the floor, as well as his gun skittering a few feet away.

He should have used his weapon, but shoved it into the back of his waist, opting to pounce on the man and render him unconscious. He pressed his forearm into the man's throat to restrict his air, but the man punched against the side of Silas's head, a large ring connecting with his temple.

A bouquet of stars and pain blossomed as Silas was hit, momentarily throwing him off balance, giving the assailant time to shove him off, recover his gun, and take aim.

But Silas leaned back on the floor and kicked the man in the gut. Then again.

The man got off a shot before doubling over, the round skipping dangerously close to Silas's left hip.

He stood and slammed the man's head into his knee, sending him backward with a geyser of blood running down the man's face from his nose. Before Silas could reach him, he sprang upright and advanced forward with speed, slicing a knife through the air.

This guy's like the T-1000!

Silas bent himself backward, but not in time. The knife sliced his upper arm.

That'll leave a mark.

He answered the insult by connecting his right leg with the man's arm, sending the knife skidding across the stone floor. He followed that up with a right hook across the man's jaw, then a left uppercut into his solar plexus.

The figure staggered backward, then twisted his body around to all fours in search of the knife. Silas caught him around the neck before he could reach for it, and squeezed until he fell unconscious.

"That was easy," he mumbled to himself as he released the man in a heap on the floor.

He felt his arm. It was painful to the touch, and his fingers came away slick with blood. He would live.

He backed up against the north wall, near a door that led into a small courtyard, then tore a piece of cloth from the bottom of his shirt. He tied it tightly around his arm.

That should do.

He crouched silently, leaning against the wall, breathing heavily and watching for any more movement.

Nothing.

He hoped Celeste and Gapinski were faring better than he was.

GAPINSKI LEANED against one of the tall pillars in front of the Edicule, holding his automatic rifle with one hand and running his free one through his thick, black hair. He trained his eyes forward for any sign of movement or assault, tuning his ears for any sounds that indicated movement in his direction.

Nothing at his end.

Several minutes had ticked by since Silas and Celeste had taken off in their respective directions. He hated holding his position, preferring action to babysitting. But he would do his duty like a good soldier.

"You alright in there?" he called over his shoulder into the chapel after Sebastian.

"Just peachy," came a muffled, distant response. "You?"

Gapinski smiled. The guy was a bit of a pain. But he liked him for it.

"I'm fine. Just stay back and stay down. This will all be over soon."

So far, there had been silence after the initial outburst of gunfire directed toward them from the center. Silas was probably right. They're flanking.

Gapinski heard several shots coming from the south side of the church, where Celeste had pursued the hostiles. They were angry and rapid and seemed like they were coming from multiple sources. He leaned off the pillar and walked forward toward the sound, craning his neck and holding his rifle out in front.

He thought he had heard some shots at Silas's end, but they seemed distant, and maybe something else. Either the hostiles had shifted toward the south and neglected the north, or Silas was faring better than Celeste.

He looked back into the Edicule. He saw Sebastian crouched in front of the burial shelf staring back at him.

Good boy. Stay there. You'll be fine.

More gunfire from Celeste's end. He looked back into the Edicule again, toward Silas's direction, then made a decision.

He ran toward Celeste, ready for action.

CELESTE HAD LEFT the rotunda and inched her way forward in the darkness past the Stone of Anointing, which tradition believed to be the spot where Jesus' body was prepared for burial by Joseph of Arimathea before being laid in the tomb. She had hugged the south wall of the Catholicon with her back while she kept her gun trained forward when she first heard it.

A loud clank, like hollow metal hitting the stone floor on the other side of the wall.

Then there was silence.

Right before the gunfire had erupted, catching her by surprise.

The only way out was a set of stairs leading somewhere above. She had laid down covering fire, then had taken the stairs by twos until she reached what was the Franciscan Chapel of the Crucifixion, a site commemorating the crucifixion.

And realized it was a dead end.

She was stuck.

Celeste tried to descend when she realized her mistake, but heard the sound of someone entering the stairwell, fast and large. So she moved farther into the enclosed space for protection, recessed lighting around the vaulted ceiling providing some relief from the darkness. The mosaics and decorations were beautiful, full of deep purples and blues, lively greens and reds. In the corner was an altar of white marble surrounded by golden statues underneath dozens of golden, red-trimmed incense urns. Encased in glass on either side and dimly lit were slabs of gray stone, the site where Jesus suffered and was crucified for the sins of the world.

She positioned herself behind a column facing the entrance, the altar at her back, training her SIG Sauer forward.

Bullets whistled passed her and ricocheted off the altar, making an unholy pinging sound.

That was close.

She sent three rounds into the stairwell, pushing the hostile back down the stairs with her gunfire.

There were two outcomes at this point in her choose-your-own-adventure. The man would come back for more, or wait her out. Either way, she cursed herself for her wrong choice.

Noise in the stairwell brought her out of her self-pity. She thought the man had chosen option A, but no one appeared.

When she trained her ears toward the noise, it sounded more like a scuffle than a return. Flesh-on-flesh blows, then grunts of pain and anger. A shot was fired. Then another. There was a muted scream, then a moan.

Then silence.

What the bloody hell is going on?

She would be prepared for whatever came next. Flexing her hand around its grip, she retrained her weapon at the entrance and waited.

"Don't shoot! It's me!"

Gapinski?

His six-foot-four frame appeared and crouched through the small door.

Celeste smiled, then stuffed her gun at the small of her back.

"Thanks. I owe you one."

"Buy me a round when this is over."

"Most definitely."

The two headed back down the stairwell, stepping over the Nousati agent Gapinski had incapacitated, and into the entrance area ready for anything.

But nothing came.

They moved forward along the west wall to the hallway where Celeste had been surprised before, then turned the corner to the right, weapon extended for a fight.

Nothing.

They pressed forward, Celeste, then Gapinski. Movement caught her attention to the left, but a second too late. The wall behind her exploded. Three shots in succession.

She and Gapinski fell back toward the entrance, but four more shots drove them down another stairwell. They kept going until they reached the bottom, a crypt of sorts. The Chapel of Adam, directly underneath the Chapel of the Crucifixion.

It was cool and damp and musty, with little light but a few flickering, orange flames from candles left over from earlier pilgrims.

It was also another dead end.

"My bad," Gapinski said as they paced the walls looking for an exit.

"Not again!" Celeste said, exasperated.

"At least there are two of us this time."

They moved to the south side of the chapel, just as three bullets bounced off the Nails of the Cross Altar.

Gapinski returned fire, but Celeste's gun clicked empty. She cursed.

"I'm out," she complained, several more rounds skipping off the walls.

When they stopped, Gapinski slid her another cartridge on the stone-tile floor.

"Make those count."

She nodded. *I plan on it.*

She slid the cartridge into her SIG Sauer, chambered a round, then knelt, and pulled the trigger, sending three shots toward the target. The first two went wide, shattering a vase near the stairs.

But the third hit its mark, catching the man near his shoulder.

"Must be my new, lucky shot," she mumbled to herself.

He cursed loudly, and she watched him stagger back onto the stairwell. He crawled back to escape, then used the wood railing to upright himself for support and hobbled upwards.

"Come on," she said.

Blood was smeared along the stone stairs and wall. Expecting to find him halfway up, they took the stairs slowly, guns trained forward. When they reached the top Celeste went first, then Gapinski.

But the man was nowhere.

The creaking of hinges to the left caught their attention.

The entrance door.

They pivoted toward the south entrance, but it was too late. Their target fled through the front door into the outside darkness.

She considered pursuing him, but decided against it. Disable, not kill, was the aim. And it worked. The door locked shut behind the man when he left.

"Another nice shot down there. You've gotta teach me your moves!"

"Maybe when this is over," she winked. "Why don't you go back to the Edicule and make sure Sebastian is alright and that no one has slipped into the chapel? I'll go find Silas."

"Sounds good."

Time to help him end this.

CHAPTER 38

After bringing his heart rate lower by regulating his breathing, Silas got up, pulled out his gun, and padded back through the Chapel of Mary Magdalene toward the rotunda to check on Gapinski and Sebastian.

He moved close to a column and edged along its circumference, trying to get a better view while remaining concealed.

The rotunda was empty, but for the full-moon light trickling into the sacred space.

Where was Gapinski?

Silas grew worried. He gripped his weapon tighter as he inched around the column toward the lit open space.

He strained his eyes in the barely lit room, the shadows and lighted dust playing tricks on him.

Wait. What was that?

He padded forward, holding his arms steady in front of him, clenching his gun tightly. There was something dark near the northwest corner of the Edicule. A chest of tools perhaps, or a barrel of debris from the renovations.

Then it moved, changing shape and shifting around the west face of the Edicule near the Holy Sepulcher Chapel.

He should take aim and take it out. But he couldn't bring

himself to shoot at the target, not with it crouched so tightly. He didn't want to risk killing him. And the thought of hitting the Edicule itself didn't thrill Silas, either.

The moonlight suddenly dimmed, a cloud having drifted into its view.

Perfect timing.

Silas used the window of darkness to pad forward around the perimeter of the rotunda, using the shadows as cover to approach the figure.

It appeared as though his back were turned to him, like he was hiding, lying in wait for something.

He crept closer, his legs tight with caution, taking deliberate steps forward, taking care that his shoes didn't catch any raised tiles this time.

At once the cloud outside that had obscured the moonlight had moved on. The stronger moonlight filtered back through the windows above, filling the sacred space with more light than before. The full shaft of light struck dangerously close to Silas's position so that he had to step backward under the shelter of the column.

Too late. He had been seen.

The figure raised his head suddenly and bolted upright. Then he sent three shots Silas's way.

Silas ducked into the Chapel of Saint Nicodemus and behind a pillar for cover.

The shots all went high and wide, pinging off the top and side of the rotunda, meant only for cover as the man ran along the north face of the Edicule and into the Catholicon.

Silas cursed, then ran after the figure, stopping short of the conventual church, hands gripping his Beretta, arms taut and ready. He padded forward, then slipped into the holy space, hugging the north wall as a clanging sound echoed his way.

Then there was nothing. Silence invaded the space, so did darkness as the clouds came back to conceal the moonlight.

There were no footfalls, no heavy breathing, no sounds. No nothing.

He continued moving through the center of the church. He crossed the threshold, and the high altar came into view.

Come out, come out, wherever you are.

A sound to his right caught his attention. He swung his gun in its direction, but there was no one there. He noticed the red, velvet guardrail in front of the altar had been knocked down. Must have been the clang he heard when he entered the Catholicon, and the figure must have run behind the high altar.

Silas crept over the downed, velvet barrier, then took the steps up the platform by twos, training his weapon forward at the entrance to the right that led behind the altar barrier. He cleared the space behind it visually, then moved into it, continuing to strain his senses for any indication that might give the hostile's location.

The moonlight came back, streaming through the windows above. And catching a darkened figure as he darted behind a column.

Instinctively, Silas popped off three rounds, the sound startling him as much as the sight that caused his reflexive action in the first place.

Hold steady, Grey.

He shuffled forward out of the moonlight and through two massive columns.

As he cleared the column, something came fast and hard down on Silas's arms, causing him to lose his weapon. It skittered across the marble flooring, down a flight of stairs and out of sight.

It felt as though his arms had been broken. But no time to focus on that now.

There was another swipe of the metal object swinging hard for him. He ducked in time so that it missed his head and connected with a column instead, sending a deafening clang through the enclosed space.

The miss gave him a chance to hit back. With his Beretta gone, Silas pulled a knife out from inside his boot. Crouching low, he jammed it into the leg of his assailant, connecting with thick flesh.

The man screamed and kicked outward, connecting with Silas's face.

The kick was reflexive, and the connection was accidental, but it sent Silas tumbling back down the stairs to the Chapel of Saint Helen below.

CROWLEY'S left leg blossomed in sync with his pulsing heart, pushing blood out of the open wound left by Silas's knife. The attack surprised him, so that he reflexively kicked his leg toward his assailant, apparently sending him off the edge of a set of stairs.

He always did have good reflexes.

He felt his upper thigh, assessing the wound. It was slick with blood, an inch wide and a few inches deep. He quickly removed his shirt and tied it tightly around the wound to staunch the blood flow. Adrenaline would take care of the rest.

He pulled out his Beretta and chambered a round.

Time to end this.

He approached the chapel below slowly, keeping his back against the stairwell wall as he carefully descended. A small amount of light filtered into the chapel through six small windows from up above. The sacred space was also lit by a single light hanging from an ornate chandelier and a grouping of candles left at the altar from the early evening Mass. This was going to be a challenge.

"Hello?" Crowley sang out as he stood at the chapel entrance. "I know you're down here mister. Where are you?"

He padded down the last stair and into the chapel. He swept the space quickly, not sensing the presence of anyone.

Where did he get off to?

He saw it coming from the corner of his eye. From behind a column commanding the center-left side of the chapel, it came at him quickly.

But he was quicker.

Crowley pivoted to the right before the fist connected with the left side of his face. He used the man's own force to knock him off his equilibrium, sending him onto the stone floor.

"Stay down!" Crowley yelled as he trained his Beretta at the man. "Don't even think about moving."

Crowley lumbered over to Silas, dragging his leg. The pain was searing now, the thrill of the chase having worn off. But the pleasure of knowing that all the moments of his life had brought him to this point in time overrode whatever agony his leg was causing him.

Before long, he would accomplish his life's mission. Everything he had worked for since that bloody orphanage would finally be complete: destroying a tangible object containing the memory of Jesus' resurrection, the central cornerstone of the Christian faith.

Silas raised his hands in defeat, sitting upright on both knees with arms outstretched in front of him. What was the use in trying? He had no gun. Blood was oozing down his arm through the strip of shirt he had wrapped around his wound.

It was hopeless.

"Hey, I know you," Crowley said, dragging his left leg and stopping a few feet in front of him. "You were the dog that came after Avery's bone a week ago."

Recognition seemed to register on the man's face. Boston. Then recognition transformed into remembrance.

"Dax," Silas whispered, eyes narrowing. "You killed one of our men."

"Did I now? What a pity."

Crowley still had his weapons trained on him. But the

memory of what happened to that twentysomething seemed to stoke a fiery rage inside the man, which he didn't like. He shifted his weight and gripped the weapon tighter.

Silas slowly raised a knee, keeping his eyes fixed on Crowley. In an instant, he lunched forward, plowing into his left leg.

Crowley discharged his gun with a deafening blow near Silas's head, firing into the stone floor. He toppled Crowley as he fell forward, catching his arm at an odd angle.

The gun went sliding, and both injured men moaned in pain.

Silas pivoted around as Crowley recovered, sending a right hook sailing past his face as the man leaned backward.

Crowley came in with a solid left hook of his own into Silas's right kidney. Silas dropped to the floor, but rolled away before he could land another blow. Crowley connected with stone instead, searing pain lancing through his wrist and up his arm.

Silas dove for the gun, but Crowley was on him before he reached it. He smashed his face into the floor and pulled himself forward over the man as he tried to recover.

Crowley grabbed the weapon and pulled himself up using the stairs as support.

He twisted around to face the man, weapon drawn. "This ends now!"

Silas was spent.

He had never fully recuperated from the bomb blast at Georgetown from earlier in the week. Add to that the chaos at MIT, Notre Dame, and now the Church of the Holy Sepulcher, and Silas wasn't surprised he had been defeated. Plus, life as a professor had softened the former Ranger.

He rolled over to his knees as Crowley twisted around to face him. "This ends now!" he growled.

Yes, it does.

"Just get it over with. I'm prepared to die."

"Are you now?" Crowley was breathing hard. "We'll see about that. But before you go, you should know you've lost. You may have recovered the Shroud, but I've got the next best thing."

What was he talking about?

Panic gripped Silas, his fight-or-flight impulse urging him to retaliate one more time.

Before he could, Crowley closed one eye and lined up his shot. He held it a beat before squeezing the trigger.

Silas gritted his teeth and held Crowley's stare, forcing the man to look him in the eyes.

This is it. Here we go.

Suddenly, the man lurched forward, the sound of three rounds echoing around the room.

Silas instinctively closed his eyes and jerked backward. He was breathing hard, his heart was pulsing at full speed. But he didn't feel any pain.

He opened his eyes and felt his chest. Nothing.

He sat up, checking himself over. No blood, no wounds, no nothing.

The sound of Crowley's body slumping down and folding to the side caught his attention, his face twisting to one side. Blood was seeping from his mouth, and he was gasping for final breaths.

"No matter," he managed to cough. "What's done is done."

Silas wondered what his cryptic final words could mean. Then noticed that behind him stood Celeste, gun still outstretched.

He stared at her wide-eyed. She saved his life.

Celeste stood still, feet spread apart and planted like trees in the floor, eyes staring forward. "I had to."

"I understand," he said, scrambling to get up to meet her.

"He was going to kill you." She lowered her gun and stood still, as if she didn't know what to do next.

"I know." He grabbed hold of her weapon, tugging it toward

him and pulling her along with it. They met in the middle. She met his eyes, he met hers, their mutual adrenaline magnetic.

He sighed, then smiled. "It's over."

She offered a weak smile and nodded, shoulders slumping as the tension of the moment dissipated.

"Uhh, guys?" Gapinski had appeared at the bottom of the chapel stairwell, breathing hard and eyes wide.

The two of them startled, then quickly pushed away.

"What happened here?" He asked.

Silas said, "Crowley's dead. It's over."

Gapinski looked down at the body slumped on the floor, then shook his head. "No, it's not."

What now?

As if reading his mind, Gapinski responded, "There's a bomb." He paused to catch his breath. "At the Sepulcher Chapel."

Silas clenched his jaw. Not another one.

"There's more." He paused, looking back toward the Rotunda.

Celeste said, "Gapinski, spit it out."

"It's your brother. He's been shot."

CHAPTER 39

Silas raced past Gapinski as they ran back into the rotunda, Celeste following close behind. He immediately made for the Edicule, cursing his decision to leave his brother's side.

"Sebastian?" he called, shuffling through the Angel Chapel and into the Holy Sepulcher Chapel.

Empty.

"Sebastian?" he called louder, making his way back outside into the rotunda, the shadows clawing at him like cruel, mocking demons as he left.

"Over here," Celeste called.

He ran toward the sound of her voice. Propped up against the north side of the Edicule was his brother. The sight stopped him short. He was moaning. Crouched over Sebastian's left leg was Gapinski. A belt had been wrapped around the wounded limb as a tourniquet.

The image of the darkened figure he had seen moments ago flashed into his mind.

Crowley.

The bomb.

His brother!

"What happened?" Silas said.

"I don't know," Gapinski replied. "I came back to the Edicule after finding Celeste, and I found him shot outside. I propped him up here, then used my belt to stem the flow of blood."

Silas smiled weakly to thank him.

"Is that you, Sy?" Sebastian moaned.

He ran over to his wounded brother and knelt. He could see some blood had pooled under him, ratcheting up his worry.

"It's going to be alright, Seba." He was breathless and couldn't concentrate. Couldn't form any more words. "You're going to be alright."

Jesus, he better be.

He turned to Gapinski and whispered, "Is he going to be alright?"

"He's lost some blood, but I think he'll live. It looks like I managed to stop the blood flow, but he needs a doctor, and soon."

Silas nodded. But then a dread of remembrance rose to the surface.

The bomb.

"You said there was a bomb?"

Gapinski nodded, then ushered Silas and Celeste over to the northwest side of the Edicule.

There it was.

A half bowling ball-size lump of combustible clay. Four pounds of that stuff could blow up a bus. There was at least double that stuck to the side of the ancient structure housing the tomb of Jesus Christ. And dead-center was a timer with red digits counting backward.

It read 6:23.

Then 6:22.

6:21.

Silas's mind was a vortex of panic, all training and expertise from the military draining down a hole of fight-flight-freeze hyperarousal.

He left the military because of years of stress dealing with this stuff. And now he was staring down the barrel of a red-digit timer threatening the life of his brother, his new friends, and the relic bearing the memory of Christ's resurrection.

"What do you make of it?" Celeste had crouched next to him as he stared at the bomb, frozen with indecision.

She waited a beat, then snapped her fingers. "Silas. Hello?"

He blinked, then looked at her blank-faced.

"Your file says you're the expert, here. You are the one to dismantle it. What do we do?"

He fixed his eyes on the device again. Given his training with the Army as an Explosive Ordnance Disposal technician, a unique specialty alongside his training as a Ranger, he knew that most action movies and books got it wrong.

Most firing circuits, that is, the circuit in an electrically initiated explosive device, like the one staring him in the face, can be interrupted in literally any fashion to render the device "safe." Remove or cut any wire, and you're good to go. None of this *which wire is the wrong wire*, nonsense. Firing circuits can be as complex or as simple as any other type of circuit.

Like the one counting down past 5:27.

Since the only other thing you need to complete the circuit is a power source, you can cut any wire in the circuit, thus breaking the circuit, and the device cannot work. There are still explosives present, and there are still measures that need to be taken for their safe removal, but the device will no longer function as designed. It's simple electronics, and the most common IED Silas encountered.

And yet...

He also knew that someone with a lot of electrical know-how could design a much better firing circuit. This is where the skill set of an EOD technician came into play.

Like Silas.

He sat staring at the device, diagnosing the circuit entirely before taking any action.

Was this just a standard simple circuit or a more complex collapsing circuit, the kind that cannot simply be interrupted at any point?

Someone could build a collapsing circuit in any number of ways, including using relays or semiconductors, and various other electrical engineering techniques. Back in the Middle East, he had seen all the possible ways to booby trap a circuit so that if a wire was cut, the device would still function.

Or worse.

The bottom line running through Silas's head as he continued assessing the device was this: usually, any wire can be cut; sometimes it can't.

Which kind was this?

Another minute ticked by. 4:03 was quickly leading to 0:00.

"Talk to me, Silas," Celeste said gently, as if trying to prod him onward. "What are you thinking?"

"I'm thinking this could go one of two ways." He looked at her. "Either we succeed and dismantle it. Or we don't."

"What comforting insight," Sebastian said.

Silas ignored him, working out the possible outcomes depending on which wire he snipped and which wires he left unsnipped.

Gapinski came up over his right shoulder, handing him a set of cutters he found in one of the tool chests. "Can we just move it?"

"We could. C-4 is a pretty stable explosive compound, comparatively. But I don't know how it's rigged. That timer could have some sort of accelerometer, triggering the bomb to go off. We need to disable it as-is. Which means cutting one of the wires."

Which means I need to disable it as-is by cutting one of the wires.

He brought his hand up to his chin and twisted his head from right to left to examine the device. Red, green, black, and gray. Those were his options. He flipped the cutters around in one hand as he recalled the rhyme all first level EOD techs learned that would guide him to make the right decision.

"You're crazy in the head," he mumbled "if you clip the red. Green means go, but not if there's gray. Don't play with gray no matter the day. Black means death; cut that one, you lose your breath. Live to see the light by cutting—"

He looked at Celeste, face blank with emotion.

"What is it?"

"There's no white wire," he said quickly.

Silas leaned over closer to the bomb, scanning from right to left, from top to bottom. Then he did it again.

Nothing.

"Live to see the light by cutting the white. That's the saying. Red, green, black, sometimes gray, and always white. There should be a white wire. But there's no white wire!" He cursed loudly, then stood up and raked his hand over his hair.

"What does that mean?" Celeste asked.

2:10.

2:09.

2:08.

Gapinski answered for him: "It means we're screwed. Sideways."

Silas knelt back down and shook his head, then wiped away a bead of sweat winding down his right temple.

Think, Silas.

He thought about who he was dealing with, Jacob Crowley. Then he reviewed some of the background Celeste had replayed from her conversation with Radcliffe and the intel she had gained from her and Gapinski's meeting at his former orphanage. He was a country boy from rural England, raised by a Catholic order after setting fire to his childhood church. He showed an interest in pyrotechnics, and certainly in violence. So a bomb matched his profile. But since he fell off the radar, he wasn't known to any governments or other civic organizations. So no military or police experience, formal training anyway.

And no white wire.

"Come on, buddy," Gapinski said, "Less than a minute to go."

"I know, alright!?"

0:56.

0:55.

At once he sat upright, resolve solidifying into decision.

It was a gamble. But like he said at the start: it would go one of two ways. Yes or no. Life or death. Correct wire—

Or not.

He held the clippers in his right hand, then reached for the gray wire.

He hesitated, the clippers sagging slightly.

0:40.

0:39.

"Silas," Celeste said.

He reached for the green wire and brought the clippers up to it, widening their mouth to sever the connection.

Then he stopped short, retracting them back to his lap.

0:26.

0:25.

0:24.

"Big brother, now would be the perfect time to show off, as you're so eager to do!"

Silas twisted sideways toward the voice of Sebastian, who was resting against the Edicule a few feet to his left.

He looked straight into Silas's eyes. "Just do it."

Silas nodded.

Raising the cutters up to the black wire, he held it steady, then chopped through it with one squeeze of the handles.

The countdown read 0:05.

Then 0:04.

Then stopped.

Silas had held the gaze of the digital counter. And his breath.

When he realized he was still alive and the Edicule and Sebastian were still in one piece, he sucked in a lungful of air, then slowly let it release.

"Yeah, buddy!" Gapinski said, slapping Silas on his back.

Celeste laughed with relief. "Cracking good job, Silas."

Silas eased himself to the floor, closing his eyes to center himself.

"Bravo, Sy. But I don't understand."

Silas turned toward his brother. "Understand what?"

"'Black means death, so cut that one you lose your breath.' That's what you said. Yet that's the one you cut. And nothing happened. We're still alive. Why? And how did you know that was the wire to cut when push came to shove?"

"Simple," he said. "Crowley was an idiot. These things aren't usually rigged like the movies. These kinds of detonators are usually just simple firing circuits. Sometimes not, but most are. Think of it as a lightbulb. The device initiator is a switch, like the timer. Turn it off, in this case by clipping a wire, and it simply stops."

Gapinski pressed him. "Yeah, but how'd you know that's what this was?"

Silas paused, then glanced back at the dead device. "I didn't. I guessed."

"You what?" Sebastian exclaimed.

"Nothing in his known background told me he had the expertise to wire a collapsing circuit. And since there wasn't a white wire, which there almost always is, I figured the guy didn't know what he was doing. So I figured it didn't matter which wire I clipped."

Sebastian huffed. "Well, thank the Universe you were right!"

CHAPTER 40

Within half an hour, the whole northwest side of Old City Jerusalem was consumed with military personnel and heavily armed police forces. The Ethiopian monks in the monastery above the Chapel of Saint Helena had called the police after they were awakened by gunfire —a most unusual and troubling sound for the men of peace, especially at that hour. The military made quick work of securing the church compound and setting up an impenetrable perimeter.

Medical personnel treated the bullet wound in Sebastian's leg on site. But given the severity of the injury and amount of blood loss, they transported him to Hadassah Medical Center in Jerusalem. They assured him the leg would be fine and assured Silas his brother would make a full recovery, but they wanted to observe him overnight out of an abundance of caution.

Silas saw him off, then promised he would visit him as soon as they let him leave.

"Bummer about your brother, dude," Gapinski said. "But he'll be alright. How's your arm?"

Silas had forgotten about his own wound. He looked at his right bicep, the strip of his shirt soaked a muddy crimson. He flexed the arm and winced.

Celeste said, "You might want to get that looked at."

"I'll be fine."

"That should leave a nice scar," Gapinski said. "Chicks dig scars."

Silas and Celeste both rolled their eyes.

The three of them stood awkwardly in silence, the moment begging them to say their goodbyes, but the weight of the last few days not letting them.

Finally, Celeste spoke. "Thanks for joining us on our little mission, Professor Grey. I mean it when I say that we couldn't have done this without you and your expertise."

"Yeah. You're a real badass. Join us anytime."

Silas grinned at Gapinski's compliment. "Thanks. But I think I'm hanging up my Ranger gear for good after all this."

Gapinski replied, "What, you're not in the mood for a good firefight anymore?"

"Not so much."

"Well, if you're ever itching to get back in on the action, you've got my vote."

"Thanks."

"Mine too," Celeste said. "Seriously, we could use you at SEPIO. And I don't mean just because you can handle a weapon. Although, we need to do something about your weapon of choice. The Beretta went out of fashion years ago."

Silas gave a chuckle.

She said, "What we did this week, racing through midnight streets, clandestine break-ins, firefights in cathedrals, and impro-vised-explosive-device disarmament is definitely not the SEPIO norm."

Gapinski said, "Makes for great barroom conversations, that's for sure."

Celeste smiled and nodded. "I'll give you that. But we're more about preserving the memory of the faith with words than fighting for it by force. Which seems to be what you are about too, professor. And we are launching a new archaeological initiative and have a state-of-the-art research library that I am certain you would fancy using, as well as shaping."

Silas considered this. "I hadn't realized all that the Order is involved with. I admit that sounds enticing, being on the front lines of guarding the memory of the Christian faith, and all. But the professor life suits me well. Plus, there are my students, and the opportunities I have with them."

"I understand," disappointment lacing Celeste's words. "Just do us a favor and think about it, would you?"

He nodded. "I can do that. I'll think about it."

But he knew he already had.

The three embraced before departing, the moment seeming to warrant it. Celeste and Gapinski walked off to give their statements to investigators with the Israel Defense Forces, then left for an Order safe house to connect with Radcliffe for a full debrief on the situation.

After giving his own statement to the authorities, Silas quietly slipped away from the cacophony of noise and activity.

He wandered back toward the rotunda, then into the Edicule. As he passed through the Chapel of the Angel, his hand brushed over the stone that was part of the seal to Jesus' tomb. Then he entered the Chapel of the Holy Sepulcher and knelt before the burial shelf.

Silas spent time meditating on Jesus' burial, and upon the death-by-crucifixion that led him to that vault of repose. He prayed for his brother's healing, and that the events would somehow leave an impression upon him spiritually. Then he prayed for himself, for his own healing. From the demons that continued to haunt him from his past. On instinct, he crossed himself.

He walked back out into the rotunda and passed the Stone of Unction toward the main entrance. Something caught his eye.

The Crusader graffiti that covered several of the large blocks that made up the church.

He approached the wall and found a small, blank spot amongst the thousands of tiny crosses memorializing the thousands of Christians who had similarly strived to secure the memory of the Christian faith and the integrity of Christ's church.

Just like him.

With his knife, he pressed hard against the wall, grinding two perpendicular tracts into the ancient, gray stone. Pieces flaked off as he worked the blade through the grooves, and he was left with a Roman cross. He blew the flakes away and rubbed the crucifix with a finger.

He leaned back and tilted his head, a smile curling up on one side of his mouth.

A fitting end to a journey that began by proving the one who hung upon those boards of execution defeated sin and defied death, paving the way to new life for all.

Including his own.

CHAPTER 41

R udolf Borg should have received a phone call by now.

What was it with that man Jacob Crowley? He loved him, and intensely so. But sometimes he wanted to wring his neck. He could be far too careless and seemed far too unconcerned about their important work. Where was the urgency, the passion to set ablaze what he himself had burned to the ground those many years ago? The time was ripe for dismantling the Church, the Spirit of the Age was auguring its eventual destruction.

Yet the man remained silent.

He squeezed the phone in his fist, staring out at the bleak landscape beneath his castle, the grounds below still dead from the harsh winter having yet to spring to renewed life. Soon enough he would usher in an age of spiritual renewal once the mushroom cloud of Christianity's nuclear winter dissipated. The Mind would take firm root in the heart of mankind, toppling God from his throne.

A divine man-god rising to take his place.

The first strike was supposed to have been the Holy Shroud. No, destroying it would not have destroyed the faith itself. Borg knew it was far too resilient than that. But in an age increasingly relying upon the experiential to convince the faithless and re-convince the once-faithful, Nous believed the Shroud would soon become increasingly important in the post-Christian world. And burning it would have destroyed that crucial memory-link.

He cursed Jacob at his failure. Yet destroying the Holy Sepul-cher would be a worthy consolation prize, severing yet another tangible reminder of the essential Christian belief that the tomb of Jesus is empty, as they claimed. He hoped he wouldn't have to explain to the Members why his lover failed a second time.

His hand vibrated, startling him and pinging his gut with excitement.

This better be it.

"You're late, Jacob," he growled. "Again."

His face immediately softened when he realized that the voice on the other end of the line was not whom he expected. His throat grew thick with emotion, his eyes began to moisten as he listened to one of his men recount what had transpired at the Church of the Holy Sepulcher.

Including the death of Jacob, at the hands of Professor Silas Grey.

"No! It can't be. My dear, my precious Jacob."

He collapsed into his chair, sobs wracking his body. The voice on the other end of the line waited in silence as the full range of sorrow turned to anger then transformed into rage. Borg was screaming and swearing, spewing hateful curses upon Silas Grey and his children.

Then all at once, he composed himself, as if every last drop of emotion had simply drained through a hole in his big toe. He sat up straight, took a deep breath, dabbed his eyes with his sleeve, then got back to work.

"This is a momentary setback," he intoned. "We move forward as planned. Make no mistake, this is a tragic reversal. Burning the Shroud and Sepulcher into ash would have gone a long way toward unfolding Purity. But time to dust off our feet and move forward. Have you been in touch with our friend from Chattanooga?"

The voice on the other end said he had.

"Good. Give him the final set of instructions. Make sure he understands the Council of Five has high expectations. By the way, what's that beeping, that noise in the background?" He waited for a response. "Hospital? You know the exposure that comes from using such facilities."

The voice understood, but he had no choice. He explained what had happened to him at the church, and afterward.

Borg rolled his eyes, wondering why he was surrounded by such imbeciles. "I see. Recover swiftly, then get back to work. It's only a matter of time before the Order of Thaddeus begins to catch up to what we have already begun to unfold. This was the proverbial shot across the bow. Rowan Radcliffe is no idiot. Neither is Celeste. Nor Silas Grey, as we both know. I'm afraid we've stirred the hornet's nest with that one."

The other voice agreed but assured him he would be dealt with.

"He better be. But I'm not worried. The Zeitgeist is on our side."

He hung up the phone then walked outside his study, the stone floor cold against his bare feet. He used the burnished bronze stairwell railing to descend to the floor below where the Thirteen and Council of Five were awaiting his news.

They will not be happy. They will be demanding, exacting.

Of me.

A flutter of fear passed through his gut, but he silenced it. He descended quickly, not letting the other members wait any longer. He passed the statue of Thoth, looking up into the mask peering down at him, regretting his failure to destroy the Shroud.

He came to the heavy golden doors behind which Himmler had performed his ceremonies steeped in the occult. Borg was supposed to have entered triumphantly to perform another glorious ceremony, something his Brothers had sought for centuries, yet were unable to secure. The destruction of the Shroud at the hand of fire and fury.

Yet, it was not to be. And now a ceremony of a different sort would take place where the Image was meant to be turned to soot and ash.

He pushed through the doors, the chilly, humid air causing goose pimples to spread across his skin. The sour smell of burning fuel and dried blood hung in the air, and the dim orange light of the burning light fixtures cast dancing demonic shadows behind the Thirteen and Council dressed in their ceremonial Bird-Men garb arrayed around the circular room, all reminders of the epochal events unfolding from within that would change the spiritual landscape of the world outside.

They stood as Borg entered, this time robed in a loose-fitting black silk robe, with nothing underneath. He strode into the chamber and down into its well, head held high and steady. The news he bore would have consequences for Nous's plans, yet he would remain vigilant, steadfast, resolutely in command. After all, he was their Grand Master, and they had other projects in the works to erase the memory of the Christian faith and destroy the Church.

But after he performed the necessary duty.

"Brothers," he began, "I bear unfortunate news. The Holy Sepulcher still stands."

A murmur of disbelief and disgust echoed throughout the chamber.

"I understand the gravity of this failure, the twin failures of losing the Shroud and now losing the Sepulcher. The Christians insist their god came back to life. The memory of that event is so central to their faith that removing that cornerstone would have begun a cascading collapse of it, leading to its eventual demise. Unfortunately, we failed." He cleared his throat, then added: "I failed."

"What of Jacob?" one of the beaked figures asked.

Emotion caught unexpectedly in Borg's throat. "He's dead."

There was no reaction to that news.

"Unfortunate," one of the Council of Five said. "But a necessary outcome in order to appease the Universe."

Borg couldn't disagree, yet fury sparked within against the suggestion. He suppressed it and continued. "We may have lost this battle with the Order of Thaddeus, but we will press onward. Several of our operatives are already in motion to undermine each of the central pillars of the Christian faith. The sufficiency of Christ's sacrifice on the cross. The necessity of faith alone. The authority of the Holy Scriptures. Even the origins of the Universe itself."

"Yet, you cannot deny this failure is a catastrophe," another Bird-Man said.

No, I cannot.

Borg said nothing, standing defiantly.

Bird-Man continued. "Destroying the Shroud and Sepulcher would have gone a long way toward completing the vision of our ancient Brotherhood."

"I don't deny the truth of your points." He paused, then said: "And I am prepared to pay the price through the letting of my blood."

Another wave of murmurs spread through the chamber at the mention of the ancient ritual. As Grand Master, he was able to make atonement for the sins of any of the other members. Unlike most acts of propitiation for the Council, his would not end in death. Close, but not final.

The second-ranking member of the Council of Five spoke. "Very well. Your sacrifice is accepted as payment."

A drum started a rhythmic beat behind him. It was low and steady. *Thump, thump, thump.* No variation, no departure. It would continue its tone throughout the ceremony, stretching into the early-morning hours.

Borg untied his silk robe, letting it fall to the ground in a soft pile behind him. He was naked, his pasty, white skin exposed for the Brothers. He knelt down before the Council in the well of the crypt, the same spot where Himmler had performed his pagan rituals. He would follow his lead.

A Bird-Man descended from one of five high-back, stone chairs at the front of the chamber. He bore a jewel-encrusted athame, the same ceremonial knife he had used to slit the throat of the goat just a few days ago.

The drum continued thumping in the background, its pace quickening as Bird-Man drew closer. Warm water began filling the basin, being pumped in from a hot spring that sat in a grotto underneath the castle. The temperature contrast was stark between the warm water and chilly air, causing Borg to shiver slightly.

Bird-Man now stood in front of him, the knife resting on both palms outstretched as an offering for Borg to take for his necessary act. He took it, the orange glint of fire bouncing off the polished iron blade.

The warm water had finished filling the basin, having risen to mid-calf. Borg sat down, the drum beat growing louder and more intense. In one motion, he reached across his left wrist with the blade and sliced. He did the same to his right one. Red liquid pulsed into the warm water.

Darkness would soon overcome him. But it would be only momentary.

For the man who stood in front of him would revive him back to life, to continue the plans he set in motion to end the Christian faith once and for all.

CHAPTER 42

Silas entered through the double doors of Hadassah Medical Center, the smell of disinfectant and disease overwhelming him. A kind woman at the front desk helped him locate his brother. He rode the elevator up to the fifteenth floor to check on his condition, nervously strumming his fingers on the satchel that rested on his hip, eager to get to what was inside.

When he stepped out of the elevator, he knew he was on the right floor. Orders were being given, and loudly.

"I need water. I need my bed adjusted. I need the curtains opened."

Silas smiled. *That's my Sebastian.*

He approached the ajar door, then slowly knocked.

"Can I help you?" a nurse questioned him.

"Sy! Just the person I need at a time like this. These people don't know how to properly treat a renowned physicist who almost lost his life to a raging madman."

"He's all yours," she said, smirking as she and another nurse left them alone.

Sebastian was in a hospital gown laying in a bed in a well-lit room with large windows facing barren hills, an IV stringing out of his left arm to a saline bag hanging behind him. A TV was playing CNN, volume muted, and international newspapers were scattered about the bed. Sebastian was an avid consumer of the news, and a bullet wound wasn't going to slow him down.

Silas walked to the side of Sebastian's bed. "Here, I brought you these." He held up a small vase of wildflowers he had purchased in the gift shop on the main floor. "Thought they would cheer the place up a bit as you..."

"Recover?"

Silas nodded, setting them on a small table in the corner.

"I'm so sorry I dragged you into this, baby brother. This is all my fault."

Sebastian waved his arms. "Nonsense. You know me. No one forces me to do anything."

"But I called it. I played the one card I knew you couldn't refuse."

Sebastian smiled. "Yes. And I agreed to it over fifteen years ago. Besides, this way I get an extended holiday. It's been years since I have taken a vacation. And I have always wanted to spend a couple of days traversing the inner recesses of an Israeli hospital."

Silas chuckled. At least he didn't lose his brother, in all of his demanding, sarcastic self. He pulled his satchel around and flopped it on Sebastian's lap.

"What's this?"

"A present."

A smile curled up on one side of Sebastian's face, eyes shining with greed. "Is this what I think it is?"

"Open it."

He threw open the flap and pulled out a laptop. On it was a file containing the contents he had extracted from the neutron flux detector. "I've been wondering if that contraption of mine actually worked."

Me too.

After the authorities had secured the church and medical personnel had taken Sebastian to the hospital, Silas had brought the neutron flux detector to the hostel he and his brother had arranged. Since the bullet wound had gone clear through Sebastian's leg, and he was plenty lucid when he left in the ambulance, he knew his brother would be fine. He felt a pang of guilt for not going with him directly to the hospital, but knew his brother would have wanted him to secure his device and the data inside. After all, he was as curious if their little experiment had worked as he was.

He knew there were reams of data stuck inside the device, but couldn't figure how to get it out. So he had called Zoe back at SEPIO command in DC. After connecting the unit to Sebastian's laptop, she was able to access the information inside and save it to a PDF so it could be analyzed. He had searched it for meaning, but the charts of numbers and graphs measuring this and that data point were indecipherable to him. There was a reason why he chose the humanities over the sciences.

Silas watched his brother consume the data, scrolling from page to page to page in search of concrete results. He carefully watched his face for any sign of good news, or bad. Sebastian kept a perfect poker face as he continued reading and searching, analyzing and deciphering the numbers and coded graphs.

Finally, after several minutes of silence, Silas said, "Well?"

His brother looked up. "Well, what?"

He sighed. "What does the data say? Was there a neutron flux event? Is it there? Did Jesus rise from the dead?"

Sebastian held up a hand. "Careful. Don't mix correlation with causation."

Silas took a step toward the bed. "So it happened? Inside that church, or rather in the tomb. A radiological event. The resurrection?"

Sebastian sighed. "Well, something happened."

"Stop being so coy! Tell me, what did your device find?"

His brother closed the laptop. "The device did detect the presence of particle radiation within the limestone walls. There was definitely a neutron flux within that immediate area."

"Yes!" Silas exclaimed, raising both hands high and clenching them in celebration. "I did it! I mean, *we* did it. You and I proved Jesus of Nazareth resurrected! You and me both, and Celeste and Gapinski. And if he was raised from the dead, then he is who he said he was. The Son of God. The Messiah, the Christ!" He walked to the window grinning, taking pleasure in his major academic achievement as he scanned the barren Judean countryside. The very hills Jesus himself had walked on, died on.

And resurrected on!

Sebastian leaned back and sighed, then mumbled, "I was afraid this would happen."

Silas turned around to face him. "Afraid what would happen?"

"You and this data. I admit I was skeptical when you played the family card and dragged me halfway across the world for your little fishing expedition. I played along, not at all believing we would find anything of consequence. But," he tapped the laptop, "I was proved wrong."

Silas crossed his arms with satisfaction and raised an eyebrow. "But?"

"But it doesn't prove a thing."

He let his arms drop and scoffed in exasperation. "Doesn't prove anything? Are you kidding me? If a body instantaneously dematerialized or disappeared, particle radiation would have been given off naturally, embedding itself not only within the limestone walls, but within the Shroud itself. From my conversations with Avery, I know enough about neutron fluxes and particle radiation to know that is simply unprecedented. It could only have otherwise been produced in a nuclear laboratory!"

Sebastian continued listening, not moving, not speaking.

Merely lying back with his hands folded on his lap, a thin smile playing across his face.

Silas continued. "For these particles to have radiated from the length, width, and depth of a dead body and neutrons to have been given off and settled within the limestone walls, which your device proves, I might add. This is solid evidence for the resurrection."

"Not necessarily," Sebastian finally said.

"It is, and you know it. Admit it!"

"There are a number of explanations for why there could be such particles within that tomb."

"Like what?"

"Atmospheric neutron flux from thunderstorms, for one."

"That's bull."

"No. No, it's not. And geothermal processes can produce such occurrences near the earth's crust, so perhaps there was a...a vent near the tomb that released gasses laced with such particles. So there's another."

Silas twisted his face in disbelief at the excuses his brother was giving for his continued disbelief. "Is there nothing that will convince you that you are wrong?"

Sebastian smirked. "Sy, why is it so easy for you to believe?"

"It's never been easy!" Silas roared. He closed his eyes, took a breath, and silently cursed himself for the outburst. He flopped down in a padded, wooden chair near the window and stared out at the barren countryside again, angry and frustrated. He may have succeeded professionally with his find, but he failed personally with his brother.

"I have doubts, too, you know," he started quietly. "Doubts that all of this...that this Christian faith business is just one gigantic, made-up hoax perpetuated by mentally unstable people given to flights of fantastical fancy, an opiate used by those in power to keep the masses in check, as Marx said, or something to keep the misery of life at bay and escape into an ecstatic state to avoid dealing with the reality that life began in chaos and will end in chaos, that the world will end not with the bang of trumpets announcing the return of Christ to make all things new, but with a whimper, the sigh of us all when the neurons in our brains stop firing on all cylinders, and we slip into the great beyond of blank nothingness."

Silas grew silent, wincing as he adjusted his arm to relieve some of the pain from his own wound. In the distance he saw a desert lynx trotting along the hilltop, the only thought consuming her was when she would get her next meal. No contemplation of life's deeper questions nor of the mysteries of faith.

Why can't my life be like that?

"Then what keeps you going?" Sebastian asked, breaking the silence.

Silas turned away from the window toward his brother. "What?"

"Your beliefs, your faith? Goodness, your very professional pursuits as an academic of theology and religion? What has kept you at it all these years, doggedly pursuing this white whale of spiritual affection?"

Silas stared back out the window. The cat was gone. He smiled. "The Shroud."

"How so?" Sebastian asked, sitting straighter in his bed.

He turned back toward his brother. "Something happened that Sunday morning in April AD 33. Jesus' body was gone. The Jewish authorities were freaking out. So were Jesus' very own disciples. And those freaked-out twentysomethings risked life and limb to declare to Rome that 'Jesus is Lord, Cesar is not.' And equally declare to Israel that God's promises had been fulfilled in Jesus, that he was the long-awaited Messiah. It's hard for me to imagine Christianity would have gotten off the ground had something monumental not happened in the tomb."

He paused, staring back out the window in search of his

desert-cat friend. "And besides, Saint Paul is right. If Jesus hasn't been raised, all of our preaching and singing and Christian work is useless. And so is our faith. The Shroud reminds me of that. It keeps me going, telling me that the tomb is empty. Jesus is alive. He is who he said he was. Who the Bible says he was. Which gives me hope for the future."

The two sat in silence, each contemplating the gravity of the Shroud's revelation in different ways.

Sebastian finally broke the silence. "Well, I wish I could join you in that hope."

Me too.

Silas got up from his seat. "I should let you rest. You've been through a helluva lot the past few days. Again, sorry about that. And thanks."

Sebastian smiled. "Just remember: you owe me. Big time."

Silas chuckled, then walked over to his brother's bedside. He leaned in and kissed him on the forehead, saying a short prayer.

Lord Jesus Christ, Son of God, have mercy on my brother.

He said goodbye, then walked out of the room. He prayed the same prayer for himself, and then thanked God for all that he had been given.

Especially the hope of a future resurrection from the dead and the gift of life eternal.

Amen.

CHAPTER 43

Silas arrived at the Turin Cathedral just before sunrise. He had arranged through the Order to spend time with his "faithful friend," as he and Henry Gregory had called it. He deserved it.

Cattedrale di San Giovanni Battista, the Cathedral of Saint John the Baptist as it was known, was located in the quiet, ancient town of Turin, in northern Italy. Directly behind it sat the Chapel of the Holy Shroud. Designed by the architect Guarino Guarini and built at the end of the seventeenth century, the Baroque-style Roman Catholic chapel was specifically constructed to house the Holy Image, where it has rested for centuries behind the high altar. It was nearly destroyed when a fire broke out, gutting the Royal Chapel, part of the cathedral, and the adjoining Royal Palace. Had it not been for the heroics of a fireman, Mario Trematore, who ignored risk to his own life by breaking into the Shroud's casing with his ax and dragging its container to safety, the ancient relic would surely have been destroyed.

Though the Vatican protested, Radcliffe had arranged for the predawn meeting. After all, Silas was one of the premiere sindonologists who had not only advanced the scholarship of the

Shroud and virtually authenticated it and the Gospel's resurrection accounts of Jesus of Nazareth. He had literally helped preserve it and its memory. They ultimately conceded it was the least they could do for the scholar to show their appreciation for his work. Afterward, they would usher it into safekeeping until they could ensure the threat against it had been eliminated and security measures enhanced.

For the morning, however, it was just Silas and the Shroud.

The taxi slowed to a stop before the Cathedral of Saint John the Baptist, the tall bell tower alight in the predawn light of the full moon. He paid the man, then got out. The cathedral hadn't changed one bit since the first time he had stood before it on his military-leave pilgrimage. He climbed the twelve stone stairs to the front entrance to the middle set of ornately-carved wooden doors. They were shut, so he pulled on one of them. The heaviness gave, and the musty smell of age and spicy scent of sacred ceremony filled his senses as he entered.

The chapel reminded him of Notre Dame: white stonework with thick columns and a high, white ceiling stretching toward heaven. Rows of wooden kneeling benches commanded the center, bearing testimony to millions of Christians who had made similar pilgrimages to get a glimpse of the object that bore witness to the memory of the anchor of their faith.

He walked slowly down the aisle, the air within the sacred space still and quiet. He caught a glimpse of his heart's affection at the front. He breathed deeply, then walked forward, drawn to the linen cloth by the same child-like wonder that had confirmed and reinforced his burgeoning faith those many years ago. As he continued forward, he passed shrines behind each of the arches along the side aisles. There were chapels dedicated to various guilds: bakers, blacksmiths, and goldsmiths. Chapels for the Virgin Mary, Saint Luke, and Michael the Archangel. Then there was the Chapel of the Resurrection, containing a panel painted by Giacomo Rossignolo in 1574 of Jesus' Resurrection.

Fitting.

The Shroud sat alone, flanked by two lighted candelabras, the orange glow making the ancient linen pulse, accentuating the Savior's image. A crucifix sat high behind it, looking down with recognition. Golden cherubim hung above the ornate Shroud altar, beckoning all who would come to join them in venerating the memory of Christ's resurrection.

Silas reached the Shroud, then stopped. He stood still, silent. He had stared at this ancient linen burial shroud more often than most, having memorized nearly every blood stain, burn mark, and imprint for his research. Yet the experience was always fresh, for it drew him back to the foundation of his faith, its "why."

A friend of his once quipped that Christ preserved for the world the fourteen-by-nine-foot piece of cloth for dumb jocks like himself, because without it they might never believe.

Yet he wondered if all the trouble had been worth it. Whether fighting for and preserving the fabled Shroud of Turin was even necessary. After all, Christ himself said to his doubting disciple Thomas, a man after his friend's own heart, that those who had not seen Jesus up close and personal, like with the Shroud, and yet believed would be blessed.

Isn't that the point of Christianity anyway, believing in faith that the Father raised his Son from the dead—providing salvation from sin and death and opening the way for eternal life?

Then he recalled an interesting passage from the apostle Luke's historical biography of Jesus and his movement in the book of Acts, from chapter one:

> *After his suffering he presented himself alive to them by many convincing proofs, appearing to them during forty days and speaking about the kingdom of God.*

Perhaps the Shroud was part of those convincing proofs that Jesus had given to his disciples—to us, even—proving he really was alive. And such memory-preserving objects were not only sometimes necessary for faith, but offered by Christ himself to provoke it, nurture it, and confirm such religious belief.

"Majestic, isn't it?"

Radcliffe had come up from behind Silas unnoticed.

He startled, glancing over at Radcliffe without moving. "Sure is."

"I never grow tired of beholding that face, tracing every blood-stain with my eyes and using the faint image to reconstruct the image of my Savior."

Silas smiled. "Nor do I."

The two stood side-by-side in silence. Then Radcliffe finally spoke. "How is your brother doing?"

"On the mend."

"And his faith?"

Silas paused, staring into those mystical, hope-filled eyes embedded within the Holy Shroud that invited faith and offered life. His own eyes moistened as he took in the image. He breathed deeply and shook his head.

Radcliffe sighed, and put a hand on Silas's shoulder. "After all that? After everything he experienced, the scientific results of your little experiment in the chapel?"

He shrugged. "What did Jesus say? 'Have you believed because you have seen me? Blessed are those who have not seen and yet have come to believe.' For some people, even if the resurrected Christ materialized before them, they would still have a hard time believing."

Radcliffe nodded. "Like Thomas."

Silas said, quoting from the Gospel of John chapter twenty, "'Unless I see the mark of the nails in his hands, and put my finger in the mark of the nails and my hand in his side, I will not believe.' And then Jesus called his bluff. He showed up, right then and there, materializing or whatever through a locked door, offering Thomas his hands and feet. 'Put your finger here and see my hands. Reach out your hand and put it in my side.'"

"But even Thomas exclaimed 'My Lord and my God!'" Radcliffe added. "He realized how foolish he had been and believed after he encountered him. Perhaps even after Christ exhorted him to not doubt but believe."

Silas considered this. "Yes, in that instance. But consider what Saint Luke wrote about in Acts, about giving his disciples many convincing proofs that he was alive. I remember reading that and thinking that was so odd. I mean, Jesus was alive, standing before them, asking for a meal, talking with them. And yet, they still needed even more convincing proof that he was actually, really, literally, bodily raised back from the dead to new life. Sure, Thomas gets the raw end of the sermon stick, but how many more unnamed disciples needed further convincing that Jesus was alive? After all that they had witnessed. After everything they had experienced with resurrected Jesus."

"He'll get there," Radcliffe reassured Silas. "I'll pray for him."

Silas smiled, then returned to the Shroud. A few minutes of silence passed. "So, Rowan, how did you find me?"

Radcliffe smiled and shrugged. "I know things. And what I don't know I can find out."

He smirked. He was just beginning to understand how true that was.

Radcliffe turned to face him. "We need you, Professor Grey. The Church needs you."

He closed his eyes and sighed, then faced the Master of the Order of Thaddeus.

"Why? Why me?"

"The circumstances of the last few days, this brazen attempt on the most sacred of Christian relics and the very memory of the central event of the faith has revealed a shift in Nous and its strategy regarding the Church. For generations, they had been content to remain in the shadows. Yes, there have been skirmishes here and there. But nothing like this." He turned to face the Shroud, leaning forward and resting against the railing. "Things have changed. There is chatter coming from every direction now around the globe. Plots here, plots there. Nothing concrete, all whispers of intrigue and possibility. But real, tangible threats developing against the Bride of Christ. Nay, Groom Christ himself!"

Silas startled at Radcliffe's intensity. He understood him to be a passionate man, wholly dedicated to the Order and SEPIO's cause. But there was an urgency to his voice that unsettled him.

"Forgive me for my passion," Radcliffe said. "And forgive me for seeming coy. What frightens me the most is that all of the impending threats and challenges brewing on the horizon are still so intangible. So undefined and, and poltergeist-like. We don't have enough manpower to decipher everything that is beginning to surface, let alone deal with the possibilities. And eventualities."

"Again, why me?"

"Why not you? You've got the academic chops, what with your extensive training in historical theology and Church relics, and having devoted your career to the study and preservation of the faith. Then there's your military training and expertise, an added bonus for sure."

Silas closed his eyes, then shook his head. "I don't think so. I put that life behind me years—"

"Yes," Radcliffe interrupted snorting, "trading it in for comfort and tenure."

"Nothing wrong with that."

"Of course not, when the world is right, and evil isn't knocking on the door. But bad men need nothing more to accomplish their ends, than that good men should look on and do nothing."

He faced Radcliffe, annoyed at the accusation. "Thank you, John Stuart Mills."

Radcliffe nodded. "Impressive. Most people say Edmund Burke."

"Well, I'm not most people."

Radcliffe smiled. "There's a real chance to do something, here. For not only the faith, but the faithful."

"I am doing something!" Silas said, anger flashing. He took a breath. "Look, I'm going back to Princeton to continue my research. I'm going to teach my students. I'm going to help them retrieve the memory of the vintage Christian faith in a way that, hopefully, gives them enough of a compelling experience of that faith to take an interest in it." He grabbed hold of the railing in front of the Shroud, gripping it hard. He said softly, "I'm not just looking on and doing nothing, basking in the warmth of comfort and tenure."

Radcliffe paused, letting the silence linger. "I'm sorry. I shouldn't have said that. I apologize."

"Thank you."

"But will you at least give it something thought? Pray about it?"

Silas gave a chuckle, then nodded and turned toward Radcliffe. "Alright. I'll pray about it. But I wouldn't hold my breath."

"Oh, I don't know. The Holy Spirit can be a powerful, convincing force when activated by prayer."

"So can free will."

Radcliffe smiled and nodded. "Touché."

"Goodbye, Rowan." Silas held out his hand.

Radcliffe ignored it, instead reaching in for an embrace. Silas leaned in and patted him on the back.

He smiled and turned toward the back of the chapel. He left Radcliffe, but then stopped mid-way, turning around for one final glance at his faithful friend. The One who bled on those Roman boards of execution, becoming nothing so Silas could become something, and opening the door to new, re-created life for all who believe in the One whose image is preserved within the Holy Shroud.

Then he walked down the ancient aisle and pushed through the heavy wooden double doors.

Back to the real world of faith, life, and everything in between.

AUTHOR'S NOTE

THE HISTORY BEHIND THE STORY...

This is the first story in a new series based on a fictional religious order that I conjured up in my writer's brain, called the Order of Thaddeus. The kernel of the idea came from my meditations on Jude 3: "I found it necessary to write to you exhorting you to contend earnestly for the faith which was once for all delivered to the saints." Jude is also known as Jude Thaddeus, or simply Thaddeus to some Christians.

As an avid reader of such authors as James Rollins and Steve Berry who themselves have created fictional organizations to thwart the plots and schemes of evil organizations bent on wreaking havoc on America or wherever else on the earth, I thought: why not create a similar world in which the Church is threatened by an ancient order hellbent on the destruction of the Christian faith? One that mirrors similar threats to "the faith which was once for all delivered to the saints," a faith that needs to be earnestly and intentionally contended for?

Thus was born this series, combining my personal love for action-adventure thrillers and the kinds of religious conspiracy stories that make Dan Brown giddy, along with my academic background and interest in Bible, theology, Church history, and the vintage Christian faith. I put the worldwide headquarters of the Order and SEPIO (another fictionally-crafted organization) underneath the Washington National Cathedral because I attended several services while living in the DC area and working on Capitol Hill. I thought it was a perfect location for the exploits of the Order. Of course, there isn't a secret special-ops group and religious order headquartered underground. That we know of...

My aim with these books isn't to preach. First and foremost I want to entertain like the best of thriller writers, spinning propulsive stories that take readers on an action-packed adventure, delighting and thrilling along the way. However, these stories are meant to offer a dose of inspiration and information for the journey of faith, leveraging research into Church history, biblical studies, and theology. They're definitely not sermons, but you'll gain a few insights on your adventure!

Now about this particular story of the Shroud of Turin, which centers on the theme of the importance of Jesus' resurrection, and how the Christian faith hinges on whether that core belief is true. And what happens when that belief is threatened—by powerful forces both inside and outside the church.

Ever since watching an episode of *Unsolved Mysteries* as a boy that chronicled the history and mystery of the Shroud, I have been fascinated with the fourteen-by-nine foot ancient Church relic. As a thoroughly Protestant Christian who later became a thoroughly Evangelical pastor, I probably shouldn't have held onto this fascination. After all, our kind tends not to put much stock in such things for grounding our faith. And yet a verse from the book of Acts has always needled away at my mind and faith:

He also presented Himself alive after His suffering by many infallible proofs, being seen by [the apostles] during forty days and speaking of things pertaining to the kingdom of God. (Acts 1:3)

Think about that: Jesus Christ, the Son of God, bodily raised from the dead to new life, offered his followers many more "infallible proofs" that he was in fact alive! Another version says that Jesus "gave many convincing proofs that he was alive" (NIV), as if the disciples needed *more* evidence that Jesus rose from the dead than the fact he was standing in front of them with nail-scarred hands and a gaping wound in his side.

So I've wondered, what if the Shroud was one of those convincing proofs?

Why not? Especially given the mountain of evidence that seems to point toward its authenticity. And that evidence is what this story is built upon, that the Shroud is real and that it preserves the memory of this vital aspect of the vintage Christian faith: the resurrection of Jesus Christ, which is proof positive that his sacrifice for the sins of the world worked and that his gift of new life is genuine.

Let's review some of that convincing evidence, which is based on my research using a few solid resources, including: *The Resurrection of the Shroud*, by Mark Antonacci; *The Truth About the Shroud of Turin*, by Robert Wilcox; and a scholarly journal article by Gary Habermas, titled "The Shroud of Turin and Its Significance for Biblical Studies."

One of the interesting pieces of the history of the Shroud is that before the image was widely known beginning in the sixth century, icons or images depicting the so-called Savior looked dramatically different. Pre-sixth century images of Jesus were missing the beard, his hair was short, and he looked baby-faced, almost angelic. After the sixth century when the image was more widely known the icons changed. Such religious images depict Jesus with a long beard, hair long and parted down the middle, and with a man's face looking oddly similar to the image on the Shroud. This gives anecdotal evidence to not only how the Shroud impacted the early stages of Christianity. But also the story itself, of its origins in Edessa as told by the venerable early Church historian Eusebius.

That story about the Image of Edessa or Mandylion recounted by Silas and Radcliffe is accurate. Eusebius recalled the account about the ancient King of Edessa who had sent a letter to Jesus inviting him to visit. There was a more personal motivation to the invitation, though: he was suffering greatly from an incurable disease. And he had heard about the many miracles Jesus had performed south of his kingdom in Judea and Galilee. So he wanted in on the action. Who could blame him? Unfortunately, as the story goes, Jesus declined, but he promised the king that he would send along one of his disciples to cure him after his mission on earth was complete. And he did. Jesus' disciples sent Jude Thaddeus, who had healed many while in Edessa. He also brought along with him something extraordinary: a linen cloth with a stunning likeness portrayed on its surface.

Again, Radcliffe's reciting of the tenth-century account of the Shroud is genuine:

And so, receiving the likeness from the apostle immediately he felt his leprosy cleansed and gone. Having been instructed then by the apostle more clearly of the doctrine of truth he asked about the likeness portrayed on the linen cloth. For when he had carefully inspected it, he saw that it did not consist of earthly colors, and he was astounded by its power.

Subsequently, the linen traveled around the world to various sites, including Constantinople where it is thought by many to have ended up in the care of another religious order: The Poor Fellow-Soldiers of Christ and of the Temple of Solomon, also known as the Order of Solomon's Temple. And better known as the Knights Templar or simply as the Templars. The opening prologue somewhat reflects this genuine historical account of the Templars possession of the Shroud, and their eventual demise.

But that's not all, because all of the physical properties of the Shroud described by Silas in his lecture and conference presentation are 100% real and scientifically validated. Here's a reminder of the fascinating list giving scientific and historical credence to the Shroud of Turin:

1. The faint imprint visible on the linen is that of a real corpse in rigor mortis. In fact, the image is of a crucified victim. This was the conclusion of multiple criminal pathologists during one of the most pivotal periods of dissecting and testing the Shroud in the 1970s.

2. One of the pathologists, a Dr. Vignon, said the anatomical realism of the image was so precise that separation of serum and cellular mass was evident in many of the blood stains. This is an important characteristic of dried blood. Which means there is real, actual dried human blood embedded in the cloth.

3. Those same pathologists detected swelling around the eyes, the natural reaction to bruising from a beating. The New Testament claims Jesus was severely beaten before his crucifixion. Rigor mortis is also evident with the enlarged chest and distended feet, classic marks of an actual crucifixion. Which means the man in that burial linen was mutilated in exactly the same manner that the New Testament says Jesus of Nazareth was beaten, whipped, and executed by means of crucifixion.

4. One of the more fascinating aspects of the Shroud is that it is a *negative* image, not a positive one. That

technology was not even understood until the nineteenth century with the invention of the camera when photography became a modern reality, which blows holes in the oft purported theory that the Shroud is merely a Medieval forgery that was stained or pained; it would be a thousand years until such ideas as negative images were understood, which no Medieval artist could have painted!

5. The positive image taken from the negative one left on the Shroud shows in detail many of the historic markers that connect to the Gospel accounts of Jesus' death. You have the scourging marks from a Roman flagrum on the arms, legs, and back. Lacerations around the head from the crown of thorns. His shoulder appears to be dislocated, probably from carrying his cross beam and falling. According to scientists who examined the Shroud, all of these wounds were inflicted while he was alive. Then, of course, there is the stab wound in the chest and the nail marks in the wrists and feet. All consistent with the eyewitness accounts recorded in the Gospels.

6. The image of the man, with all of his facial features and hair and wounds, is absolutely unique. Nothing like it in all the world. Totally inexplicable. And given there are no stains indicating decomposition on the linen itself, we know that whatever body was in the Shroud left before the decomposition process began. Just as the Gospel writers testify about Jesus' resurrection from the dead on the third day.

7. The man was interred according to Jewish burial customs at the time, being laid in a sail-like linen shroud in the manner they required. Yet, he did not receive the ritual washing, as the New Testament

indicates Jesus didn't, because of the Passover and Sabbath requirements for burying the dead.

8. Then there is the cloth itself, which is entirely unique. Nowhere has any other cloth been found to have depicted the image of a dead man on its surface. Again: in the history of archaeology and the study of historical artifacts, nowhere have we come across a burial linen with a body imprint.

9. The imprinted cloth is old. The linen itself has existed for over 600 years as the so-called Shroud of Turin, and nearly 2,000 years as the Image of Edessa, named after a small town outside of ancient Antioch in modern Syria. While carbon dating in the 80s placed the Shroud's age in the middle ages, around AD 1300, new evidence has roundly discredited both the results and method of that dating. Newer evidence places the date comfortably within the timeframe that Jesus was said to have been crucified and buried in AD 33.

10. The linen used of this cloth is a herringbone twill most likely manufactured and distributed throughout the Mediterranean world at least two thousand years ago. This is crucial, because it discredits the notion that the Shroud was a medieval forgery concocted by some confidence artist.

11. The odds against this image being someone other than Jesus are astronomical. 225...billion to 1, according to Paul de Gail, a French Jesuit priest and engineer. Which means it is not unreasonable to conclude that the man in the Shroud is indeed the historical person we know of as Jesus of Nazareth, around whom—his life, death, and resurrection—the Christian faith was launched and built.

12. That the man imprinted on the Shroud is that of Jesus of

Nazareth doesn't in and of itself prove or disprove that Jesus came back to life and rose from the dead. But there are strong indications that, at the very least, something extraordinary and very unusual occurred in the cloth.

This last point forms the basis of much of the plot, proving that an extraordinary event known as a so-called neutron flux event occurred in the Shroud of Turn. Mark Antoniacci believes this is one of the most pressing items to nail down in future research and testing. Much like my character Silas, he imagines that the resurrection would have created a radiological event within not only the Shroud, but the tomb—the other plot point. His description in his book is unequivocal and thrilling, highlighting a few more interesting features of the Christian relic:

---

only a cloth collapsing through a body giving off particle radiation consisting of neutron flux can explain the Shroud's faint coin and flower imaged, its cloth strengthening features, and the creation of additional C-14. If a neutron flux event irradiated the Shroud, this *alone* would have been an unprecedented event that could only be explained by the resurrection. Even today, to produce a neutron flux requires the facilities of a nuclear laboratory, yet the neutron flux cannot be made to come from a body let alone the length, width, and depth of a dead body. Similarly, if a neutron flux is shown to have occurred in the limestone walls of Jesus' tomb (which has been closed for centuries), it would clearly have been an unprecedented event that is consistent with and indicative of the resurrection having caused it. (235)

There are strong indications such an event occurred. Now all that's needed is a thorough testing. Perhaps Silas Grey could help! This, combined with the other mountain of evidence, not only indicates the Shroud is genuine, but that Jesus rose from the dead, which lends credit to the so-called Historically Consistent Method of Jesus' body disappearing or dematerializing. As Antoniacci explains, "With this dematerialization, particle radiation is given off naturally and the cloth falls through the radiant body, thereby encoding or causing every one of the Shroud's numerous image and non image features..." (235).

Alright, there's the information and research that sits at the heart of this entertaining story—something I strive to include in all my novels. What about the inspiration?

I'm reminded of something the late Nabeel Qureshi said, a Muslim who gave his life to Christ: the resurrection isn't the *what* of our belief, it's the *why* of the Christian faith. The idea that Jesus conquered death and rose to victorious new life isn't merely a doctrine or theological belief we mentally ascribe to; the resurrection isn't just *what* we believe. No! Christians believe in Jesus and put their faith in him *because* he rose from the dead; Jesus' resurrection is *why* we give our lives to Christ, just like Nabeel. Because if Jesus is still dead, we're all still screwed, the Christian faith is useless and futile, and Christians are of all people most to be pitied.

Now, whether or not the Shroud is genuine (I think it is) doesn't matter to the Bible's historical witness to the truth of Jesus' resurrection. If the Shroud was destroyed tomorrow, the truth of Jesus' resurrection would still stand. As the Evangelical scholar, Gary Habermas argues, "True, we do not have absolute proof for the identity of the man of the shroud. Neither do we need it to demonstrate the reality of the death and resurrection of Jesus (or for anything else in the Christian faith)." Yet he goes on: "But it appears to provide strong empirical corroboration for Jesus' resurrection, and when combined with the historical evidence for this event I would submit that we have a twofold apologetic from both science and history....It appears that it can provide continuing confirmation of the most treasured of our beliefs: the death and resurrection of Jesus Christ" (54).

Something monumental happened nearly two millennia ago. So much so that it compelled a bunch of scared twentysomething peasants and other followers of Jesus to give it all for the sake of the good news of Christ—to the point of death. There's no way these men and, eventually, women would have sacrificed themselves for a fairy tale. As Nabeel also says: why die for a lie? No, the reason why the disciples and others went on mission was because Jesus came back from the dead. Not as a zombie! As a real, live human being. And he gave many more convincing proofs he was alive. Perhaps the Shroud was one of those proofs.

That's why I hope you're not just entertained by this story, as well as not merely informed about the fascinating history and evidence of the Shroud of Turin and the doctrine of Christ's resurrection. I hope that in this novel you discover why the resurrection is so important and that it inspires you to trust Jesus with every ounce of your life. Because if he can conquer the grave, there's nothing he can't do! As the old Church hymn declares:

> *Because He lives, I can face tomorrow,*
> *Because He lives, all fear is gone;*
> *Because I know He holds the future,*
> *And life is worth the living,*
> *Just because He lives!*

Research is an important part of my process for creating compelling stories that entertain, inform, and inspire. Here are a few of the resources I used to research the Shroud of Turin:

- Antoniacci, Mark. *The Resurrection of the Shroud of Turin*. New York: M. Evans and Company, Inc., 2000. www.bouma.us/shroud1

- Wilcox, Robert. *The Truth About the Shroud of Turin.* Washington, DC: Regnery, 2010. www.bouma.us/shroud2
- Habermas, Gary. "The Shroud of Turin and Its Significance for Biblical Studies". *Journal of the Evangelical Theological Society* 24 (March, 1971), 47–54. www.bouma.us/shroud3

ABOUT THE AUTHOR

J. A. Bouma is an emerging author of vintage faith fiction. As a former congressional staffer and pastor and bestselling author of over thirty religious fiction and nonfiction books, he blends a love for ideas and adventure, exploration and discovery, thrill and thought. With graduate degrees in Bible and theology, he writes within the tension of faith and doubt, spirituality and theology, Church and culture, belief and practice, modern and vintage forms of Church, and the gritty drama that is our collective pilgrim story.

He also offers nonfiction resources on the Christian faith under Jeremy Bouma. His books and courses help people rediscover and retrieve the vintage Christian faith by connecting that faith in relevant ways to our 21st century world.

Jeremy lives in Grand Rapids, Michigan, with his wife, son, and daughter, and their rambunctious boxer-pug-terrier Zoe.

www.jabouma.com
jeremy@jabouma.com

f facebook.com/jaboumabooks

y twitter.com/bouma

a amazon.com/author/jabouma

THANK YOU!

A big thanks for joining Silas Grey and the rest of SEPIO on their adventure saving the world!

Enjoy the story? Here's what you can do next:

If you loved the book and have a moment to spare, **a short review is much appreciated.** Nothing fancy, just your honest take. Spreading the word is probably the #1 way you can help independent authors like me and help others enjoy the story.

If you're ready for another adventure you can get the next book in the series for free! All you have to do is join the insider's group to be notified of specials and new releases by going to this link: www.jabouma.com/free

GET YOUR FREE THRILLER

Building a relationship with my readers is one of my all-time favorite joys of writing! Once in a while I like to send out a newsletter with giveaways, free stories, pre-release content, updates on new books, and other bits on my stories.

Join my insider's group for updates, giveaways, and your free novel—a full-length action-adventure story in my *Order of Thaddeus* thriller series. Just tell me where to send it.

Follow this link to subscribe:
www.jabouma.com/free

ALSO BY J. A. BOUMA

J. A. Bouma is an emerging author of vintage faith fiction. You may also like these books that explore the tension of faith and doubt, spirituality and theology, Church and culture, belief and practice, modern and vintage forms of Church, and the gritty drama that is our collective pilgrim story.

Order of Thaddeus **Action-Adventure Thriller Series**

Holy Shroud • Book 1

The Thirteenth Apostle • Book 2

Hidden Covenant • Book 3

American God • Book 4

Grail of Power • Book 5

Made in the USA
San Bernardino, CA
12 March 2019